SPI
EGE
L&G
RAU

Also by Tash Aw

The Harmony Silk Factory

Map *of the* Invisible World

Map *of the* Invisible World

A Novel

• • •

Tash Aw

Spiegel & Grau
New York
2010

Map of the Invisible World is a work of fiction. Names, characters, places, and incidents are the products of the author's imagination or are used fictitiously. Any resemblance to actual events, locales, or persons, living or dead, is entirely coincidental.

Published in the United States by Spiegel & Grau,
an imprint of The Random House Publishing Group,
a division of Random House, Inc., New York.

Spiegel & Grau and Design is a registered trademark
of Random House, Inc.

Originally published in the United Kingdom by Fourth Estate,
an imprint of HarperCollins Publishers, London, in 2009.

LIBRARY OF CONGRESS CATALOGING-IN-PUBLICATION DATA
Aw, Tash.
Map of the invisible world : a novel / Tash Aw.
p.   cm.
ISBN 978-0-385-52796-5
eBook ISBN 978-1-588-36983-3
1. Orphans—Fiction.   2. Brothers—Fiction.   3. Indonesia—Politics
and government—1950–1966—Fiction.   I. Title.
PR6101.W2M37 2009
823'.92—dc22   2009012843

Printed in the United States of America on acid-free paper

www.spiegelandgrau.com

2   4   6   8   9   7   5   3   1

First U.S. Edition

Book design by Donna Sinisgalli

For my sisters, L L and S L

Did I not *once upon a time* have a lovable childhood, heroic and fabulous, to be written on leaves of gold, an excess of good fortune?

—ARTHUR RIMBAUD, *MATIN*

His voice lasted just a few moments. A fleeting tremor, never to be repeated.

—PRAMOEDYA ANANTA TOER, "YANG SUDAH HILANG"

My dreams are like other people's waking hours. . . . My memory, sir, is like a garbage heap.

—JORGE LUIS BORGES, "FUNES, HIS MEMORY"

Map *of the* Invisible World

*W*hen it finally happened, there was no violence, hardly any drama. It was over very quickly, and then Adam found himself alone once more. Hiding in the deep shade of the bushes, this is what he saw.

The soldiers jumped from the truck onto the sandy soil. They dusted themselves off, straightening their hitched-up trouser legs and tucking their shirts into their waistbands. Their long sleeves were rolled up thickly above their elbows and made their arms look skinny and frail, and the belts they wore were so wide they seemed to stretch their waists to their chests. They laughed and joked and aimed pretend-kicks at one another. Their boots were too big and when they ran they looked like clowns. They were just kids, Adam thought, just like me, only with guns.

They hesitated as they approached the steps going up to the veranda, talking among themselves. They were too far away; he couldn't hear what they were saying. Then two of them went up to the house and when they emerged they had Karl with them. He was not handcuffed; he followed them slowly, walking to the truck with his uneven gait before climbing up and disappearing under the tarpaulin canopy. From a distance he looked small, just like them, just like a child too, only with fair hair and pink skin.

Stop. Adam wanted to call out, to scream for Karl to come back. Don't leave, he wanted to shout. But he remained silent and unmoving, shrouded by the dense, thorny foliage. He could do this now: He held his breath and counted slowly from one to ten. A long time ago, he had learned this way of controlling his fear.

The truck reversed and then drew away sharply, kicking up a cloud of sand and dust; on its side there was a crude chalk drawing of a penis next to the words YOUR MOTHER _____. Overhead the skies were rich and low and black, pregnant with moisture. It had been like this for some days; it had not rained in a long time, but now there was a storm coming. Everyone wanted rain.

In truth it did not surprise Adam that the soldiers had come. All month there had been signs hinting at some impending disaster, but only he seemed to see them. For weeks beforehand the seas had been rough, the ground trembling with just the slightest suggestion of an earthquake. One night Adam was awakened from his sleep by such a tremor, and when he went to the door and looked outside the coconut trees were swaying sinuously even though there was no wind; the ground felt uncertain beneath his feet and for a while he could not be sure that it wasn't he who was swaying rather than the trees. The ginger and white cat that spent its days bounding across the grass roof in search of mice and lizards began to creep slowly along, as if suddenly it had become old and unsteady, until one morning Adam found it dead on the sand, its neck twisted awkwardly at an angle, its face looking up toward the sky.

Then there was the incident in town. An old man had cycled from his village in the hills, looking to buy some rice from the Chinese merchant. He'd just come back from the Hajj, he said; the pilgrimage is an honor but it isn't cheap. The crops had not been good all year; the dry season had been too long, and now there was no food left. He asked for credit, but the merchant refused point-blank. Last year there was a plague of rats, he said; this year there is a drought. Next year there will be an earthquake and the year after there will be floods. There is always something on this shit hole of an island. No one has any money, everyone in town will tell you the same thing. Prices are high, but it's no one's fault: If you don't have cash, there's nothing anyone can do for you. So the old man went to the pawnshop with his wife's ring, a small gemstone that might have been amber, set in a thin band of silver. The Chinese pawnbroker peered at it through an eyeglass for a few seconds before handing it back. A fake, he said, shrugging, a cheap fake. An argument ensued, a scuffle; insults of a personal, and no doubt racial, nature were exchanged. Later that evening, when the hot heavy night had descended, someone—it is not clear who—splashed kerosene on the doors of the pawnshop and took a match to it. The traditional wooden houses of this island (of which not many survive) burn easily, and within half an hour it was engulfed in flames. There were no survivors. The Chinese shops stayed closed for three days; no one could buy anything. Suddenly there were fistfights all over town. Communists were arriving from the mainland to capitalize on the unrest, everyone said. Gangs of youths roamed the streets armed with machetes and daubing graffiti on houses. *Commies DIE. Foreigners Chinese go to hel.*

It was like an article from the newspapers played out for real, the static images rising from the newsprint and coming to life before Adam's very eyes. The charred timber remains of burned-out buildings, the bloodred paint on walls. The empty streets. Adam knew that there were troubles elsewhere in Indonesia. He had heard there was a revolution of some sort—not like the ones in France or Russia or China, which he had read about, but something fuzzier and more indistinct, where no one was quite sure what needed to be overthrown, or what to be kept. But those were problems that belonged to Java and Sumatra—at the other end of this country of islands strung out across the sea like seaweed on the shore. That was what everyone thought. Only Adam knew that they were not safe.

Karl had refused to do anything. He did not once consider leaving.

"But . . ." Adam tried to protest. He read the newspapers and listened to the radio, and he knew that things were happening all across the archipelago.

"Why should we?"

"Because of your . . . because we are, I mean, you are *different*." Even as he spoke he knew what the response would be.

"I am as Indonesian as anyone else on this island. My passport says so. Skin color has nothing to do with it, I've always told you that. And if the police come for me, I'll tell them the same thing. I have committed no crime; I'm just like everyone else."

And so they had stayed. They had stayed, and the soldiers had come. Adam had been right all along; he knew the soldiers would come for them. He had imagined himself being in jail with Karl in Surabaya or somewhere else on the mainland, maybe even Jakarta, but now he was alone. It was the first time in his life he had been alone—the first time in *this* life at least.

He waited in the bushes long after the truck had gone. He didn't know what he was waiting for but he waited anyway, squatting with his backside nearly touching the ground, his knees pulled up to his chin. When it was nearly dark and the sea breeze started up again he walked back to the house and sat on the veranda. He sat and he waited until it was properly night, until he could see nothing but the silhouettes of the trees against the deep blankness of the sea beyond, and he felt calmer.

Night falls quickly in these islands, and once it arrives you can see nothing. If you light a lamp it will illuminate a small space around you quite perfectly, but beyond this pool of watery brilliance there is nothing. The hills, the scrubby forests, rocky shoreline, the beaches of black sand—they become indistinguishable, they cease to exist as independent forms. And so, sitting motionless in the dark, only his shallow breaths reveal that Adam is still there, still waiting.

2

*T*his is Adam. He came to live in this house when he was five years old. Now he is sixteen and he has no memory of his life before he came here.

Sometimes he wakes with a start—not from any nightmare, but from an uncomfortable sensation that he is staring into a huge empty space, something resembling a yawning bottomless well, and that he is engulfed by its vastness. It is at this point that he wakes up, for he cannot bear this great emptiness. Scenes of his childhood do not come back to him, not even when he closes his eyes and tries to re-create them in his mind's eye. In those moments between awakeness and sleep, when he has laid his head on his pillow, he tries to let his mind drift, hoping that on this night his past life will finally burst through the cracks and fill his dreams like warm, swirling floodwater, thick with memories. It never happens, though, and his nights are clear and completely dreamless.

Occasionally—very occasionally—he has glimpses of a single image, something that flickers dimly for a few seconds and then fades away again: black moss on a bare concrete wall, splinters of wood on the legs of a desk, the ceiling of a long, dark room, a piece of canvas, a tabletop riddled with the pinpricks of wormholes that seem to form the very surface of the table so that when he runs his fingers over them he feels only holes, nothing solid. There are some noises too. Rain clattering on a zinc roof like nails in a giant tin can. And a curious sort of murmuring, a monotonous hum of low voices half-whispering, half-talking. All he can discern are the sibilant *s*'s or sometimes *sh*'s, like a chorus of hushing. These sounds take place in a big room, something like a dormitory, which, needless to say, Adam cannot visualize. And once in a while, when he is doing something perfectly ordinary—

cycling into town or feeding the chickens or swimming over the reefs looking at the remains of the shipwrecks—a single word will light up brilliantly in his head, just for an instant, like a flashbulb. Shell. Easter. Snow. He will know, instantly, that this word has come from his past life in the orphanage.

But these fragments of words and images never mesh to form anything bigger or more intricate; they remain bits of broken mosaic that mean very little to Adam now. There are never any people or faces or bodies, or even animals in his memories, if you can call them memories.

There have been times in the past when this lack of recollection has been very frustrating for Adam. A few years ago, when his pubescent hormones made him angry and confused and a bit crazy, he wanted to find out about his birth family. He accused Karl of withholding information, of taking away his former life, of shielding him from the truth. Whenever visitors asked him what his name was he replied, "My name is Adam and I have no surname." At the time he enjoyed Karl's silence and inability to respond; the smile on Karl's face would set and he would not speak, and the guests would pretend to laugh, to find this funny. But Adam realizes that he was wrong to have done that, and it is he who is embarrassed whenever he remembers this awkward period in his life. There were no secrets to be found out, he knows that now. Life had to be lived in the present, Adam had learned.

And this is what he tells himself, sitting on the steps of the porch of this dark and newly lonely house. When he first came to this place he had to learn how to live in an alien environment. Now he must relearn how to do so. Looking into the house, the inside of which seems strange and distant once more, Adam tries to remember his first days here, how Past detached itself from Present and very quickly ceased to be relevant. Ten, eleven years—it was not so long ago. If he could remember how it happened, then maybe he could replicate it.

The whole of Adam's life began to take shape the day Karl brought him here from the orphanage. Images sharpened, smells became pungent, emotions articulated themselves, and the murky darkness of his past began to recede, slowly, into the distance.

Like a pet in a new home, Adam did not venture far from his room for the first few days (much later, Karl would indeed liken Adam's early appearance to that of a hatchling, or a newborn kitten, which Adam did not like, but only because he knew it was true). There was too much to take in, too much that was alien and unconnected with what he had known before. The continuous crackling of the wireless; the distant voices speaking in languages he did not understand. The colorful spines of enormous books. The bizarre gadgets scattered around the house (things that he would soon learn were entirely prosaic—a typewriter or a pair of binoculars—but which at that time seemed surreal, even threatening). And above all, this foreign man who walked with a slight limp and seemed as wary of Adam as Adam was of him. He did not dare come too close to Adam, and although he smiled in a gentle manner, Adam sensed an awkwardness in his regard, almost as if he was scared of Adam. Three times a day he left Adam's food for him on the table next to the bed. "Thank you, sir," Adam would say as the man retreated, leaving him alone to contemplate his new surroundings.

One day this man (who was called Karl, Adam learned) hesitated as he placed Adam's dinner on the little square table. The smell of peppery vegetable broth filled the room and made Adam feel hungry. Karl said, "Please don't call me sir. Call me *father.*" And he left the room, even more swiftly than usual, as if terrified of what he had just said.

Ridiculous, thought Adam. He could not think of this man as his father; he *would* not do so. He looked so strange, unlike anyone Adam had ever seen before—a character out of some far-fetched myth: fair hair that was almost the same color as his skin, eyes of an indistinct hue (sometimes green, sometimes gray, always translucent, like a mineral brought to life), a nose that seemed unreasonably and bizarrely triangular, and cheeks that had a pink blush to them. These were features born of a cold climate, Adam knew, even then. He dismissed the thought and began to eat. No, Karl was *not* his father.

For long stretches during those early days, Adam would sit cross-legged on his bed, his back resting against the wall, and listen to the unfamiliar noises of this new house: to Karl's footsteps padding gently on the floorboards; to the sound of music coming from the living room (he could not remember ever having listened to music before—certainly not music like this, so dense and foreign his ears could not process it). He lay in bed and listened to the insistent mewing of the cat, which sat ·watching him from the top of the cupboard; and he listened, above all, to the distant, hypnotic washing of the waves on the rocks that lulled him to sleep.

He understood why he was here. He understood too that he was one of the lucky ones. He had been taken away to start a better life here. But at this point in time he did not feel lucky, nor did he really know what *a better life* would entail.

As he drifted off to sleep he wondered if he missed the orphanage, and wondered if it was this that made him sad. But he experienced no nostalgia or longing; instead he found that his recollections of the or- phanage were already thick and hazy. Lying in bed listening to the con- stant wash of the waves he began to realize that the sadness he felt would not last forever; it was a different kind of sadness from anything he might have experienced previously. Somehow, he knew that in this new house, with this frightened, frightening man, he could overcome these sensations of sorrow. He had much to fear in this new life, but fear was no longer something huge and undefined and terrifying. It was something he could master. He knew that now. And so he would fall asleep. He slept a lot during those first days.

Eventually he began to explore the house, timidly at first, ventur- ing from his room only when he could hear that Karl had gone out. As his fear of the objects in the house subsided, he began to pull books from the shelves and look at the pictures. He could not read (that would come soon afterward) but he spent much time looking at pic- tures of lakes and forests that he knew were far away in cold countries, for the trees and hills did not look anything like the ones he saw around him. The fair-haired children in these pictures wore nice, thick clothes and looked strong-boned and happy, unlike the children Adam had known, who had not been very happy. They had been skinny, like Adam himself, and constantly tired, and some of the smaller ones had distended stomachs even though they had nothing to eat. Maybe it was easy to be happy if you had nice clothes and food and parents, Adam thought; maybe it would be easy for him to be happy from now on. He liked these pictures because they made him feel that he was like these children and not like the ones in the orphanage. These healthy Euro- pean children looked like immature versions of Karl, and as Adam watched Karl working in the yard outside, he could imagine Karl skating on frozen ponds or walking in pine forests; and Adam realized that Karl too was a long way from home.

Adam also found books with pictures of pictures—paintings of women who looked almost like local women, but not quite: They were fleshier and their eyes were brighter, not tinged with jaundice or cataracts. They wore flowers behind their ears and looked straight at Adam, as if questioning him: Where was he from? Was he one of them, or something else? He did not like these pictures so much.

Gradually he allowed Karl to read to him. They would sit on the narrow cane sofa in the last light of the afternoon, in the hour before dusk took hold of the island, and Karl would read magical stories from across the islands of Indonesia. Adam learned about brave little Biwar, who killed a terrifying dragon; about the ungrateful Si Tanggang, who left his fishing village and rose from humble roots (such as *ours,* Karl had said) to become rich and famous, and finally refused to acknowledge his poor mother; and about the beautiful Lara Djonggrang, turned to stone by the covetous Bandung after she had tricked her way out of marrying him. As Karl read these stories Adam would gaze out at the retreating tide; the waves were always flat at this hour, barely a ripple, and pools of calm water would begin to form in the recesses of the reef. He liked the stories—he can remember each one to this day—but most of all he wished that Karl would read him stories about those fair-skinned children who were full of laughter. In their world people were not turned into statues or animals, and night demons were not called upon to take sides in ancient feuds. It was safer over there, he thought.

But still, he was lucky to be where he was. He knew he should not ask for anything else.

Adam also discovered music, played on the record player which he soon learned to operate. The small box was made of chocolate brown wood on the outside, light-colored wood on the inside, and Adam would lift its lid and select (purely at random) six records, which he would stack carefully on the tiny mast that rose from the platter. Every piece of music made him realize how devoid of it his life had been before he came to this house. As he listened to a woman's lilting voice or a jolly melody played by a trumpet, he tried to remember if the children at the orphanage had ever sung the folk tunes that Karl often hummed, but he could recall nothing: A blanket of silence would fall over his memories, and suddenly the landscape of his past would become still and colorless, as if mist had drifted in from the sea on one of those cool days after rain when you can see nothing, just the faint outline of trees here and there.

Sometimes Karl would put his arm around Adam and squeeze his shoulders—a brief, warm hug to praise him for having chosen the records and starting up the player; he would see the edges of Karl's eyes pinched into fine wrinkles by a smile and he would feel better, as though he had done something good and new and surprising. He had never known that he was capable of causing happiness.

Adam cannot recall the precise moment when he began to think of Karl as his father and not as some alien with skin the color of dry sand and freckles on his face and arms. But he suspects that it took him a mere few weeks to ease into his new world, one in which this white man was no longer a foreigner but someone who was always present, who made Adam feel that this place was safe and unchanging and unconnected to the past.

My name is Adam de Willigen, he would say to himself during those first months, for it comforted him to do so. He would repeat the words aloud because he loved the sound and the rhythm they created; he loved contorting his lips into unfamiliar shapes in order to say them. It soothed him to hear his own voice too, and gradually he stopped thinking about what his surname might once have been. Nowadays whenever he hears his name he thinks, Adam de Willigen sounds just right.

Goedenavond, mijn naam is Adam de Willigen. You see? He can speak Dutch too. Only rudimentary expressions, however, because Karl is opposed to the speaking of Dutch in this house. He believes that it is the language of oppression and that Adam should not grow up absorbing the culture of the country that colonized his own. "We are independent now," he explained. "We need our own culture." English was their compromise—Karl deemed it "useful to know"—and Adam had daily lessons in it. On the rare occasions they had European visitors, English was the lingua franca, and on these occasions Adam surprised himself by feeling quite at ease speaking the language. His fascination for Dutch, however, continued for a very long time, his curiosity made stronger by the fact that Karl resolutely refused to speak it. Once, they received unexpected visitors, a Dutch couple who were fleeing their home in Flores and trying to make their way back to Holland. They had heard of Karl and his house when they arrived on the island and knew they would find a safe place to stay for a few nights while they arranged their passage back to Jakarta and beyond. They arrived with a single suitcase, looking sunburned and dusty. Karl welcomed them courteously and surrendered his own room to them, but for two whole days there was a strained silence, for the man spoke little Indonesian (he had learned only the unhelpful dialect of the Ngada of Flores) and his wife could speak none at all, save a few words of instruction to the cook before mealtimes. When they spoke Dutch it thrilled Adam to hear the sound of the rich, rasping words, but Karl responded briskly in English or else ignored them altogether. So that's what it sounds like, Adam thought, and all of a sudden the individual words and short phrases he had learned from looking at the Dutch books on the shelves began to make sense. He was upset by Karl's refusal to speak Dutch and by his refusal to be more hospitable. Adam did not understand why Karl could not be friends with these people, for they were just like Karl. In those days he did not yet understand that Home was not necessarily where you were born, or even where you grew up, but something else entirely, something fragile that could exist anywhere in the world. Back then Adam was merely angry with Karl because he did not understand this, or many other things.

The night before the couple left to take the ferry, Adam saw the woman sitting alone on her bed, folding clothes and arranging them into her open suitcase. She smiled when she saw Adam and said, "Come." Adam sat with her while she continued packing her belongings into the case. A pile of thin cotton shirts lay next to her, and Adam watched as she picked them up one by one and folded them carefully before rearranging them into the case. They were tiny, made for an infant, and decorated with pale pink and red flowers. She began to speak, very softly, in Dutch, even though Adam couldn't respond. As she spoke Adam thought of those healthy blond children in the picture books; somehow he knew that she was speaking of children. When she finished she touched his cheek very lightly and stroked his hair. She said something and shook her head; her smile was weak. "No understand?"

she said in Indonesian. She was right, Adam could not understand. He said, *"Welkomm aan mijn huis."* He had seen the words in a book and thought that he knew roughly what they meant. She broke into a deep, warm laugh. "Thank you, Adam de Willigen," she said, wiping her eyes. "Thank you."

These scenes from his Present Life are reenacted in his mind whenever he wishes. He is able to recall them with absolute clarity, the details as sharp and true as the day he witnessed them; he enjoys the power he wields over these memories, his ability to control them and carry them with him wherever he goes, whether walking in the rice fields or swimming in the sea. Even now, as he walks in the dark from the porch to the bedroom (he does not have to put on any lights—he knows this house so well), he finds that every episode in his life in this single-story cement-and-timber dwelling can be summoned at will.

From time to time he still attempts to conjure up something from his time at the orphanage, to piece together the fragments that float in his head; but nothing materializes and he feels immediately chastened—he should never have been so foolish. He knows that, however hard he tries, the first five years of his life will continue to elude him, that he should stop trying and simply let go. And yet, now and then, he cannot resist the temptation. It stays with him like a splinter embedded deep in his skin, which niggles him from time to time but is otherwise invisible, as if it does not exist at all. And when that tingle begins, he has to reach for it and scratch it, even though it will unearth nothing. In moments of quiet and solitude, such as this—stretched out on his bed, alone and frightened—he will sometimes delve into that store of emptiness.

Why does he do it?

Because amid the fogginess of his nonmemory there is one lonely certainty, one person who he knows did exist, and it is this that lures him back.

Adam had a brother. His name was Johan.

The only problem is that Adam cannot remember the slightest thing about him, not even his face.

3

This is just so depressing," Margaret said as she flicked aimlessly through the day's edition of *Harian Rakyat* before letting it fall limply on her desk. Even with the louvred windows open, the room was hot and still; the ceiling fan raised just enough wind to ruffle the pages of the newspaper. The headline read, STUDENTS REVOLTING IN CLASSROOMS.

"They're always revolting," she added. She had hardly bothered to read the paper. It was too hot and the news was always the same.

Din put a can of Coke on her desk. "I didn't know there were still any students in the classrooms." He picked up the newspaper and sat at his desk. "Have you read this? There was a fire in the Science block on Thursday. Arson, they think. Did you see anything? I didn't, and I was here all day. Look, they caught the culprit—he looks like one of your students, though it's difficult to tell. These mug shots all look the same to me. They're always nice, clean-looking boys from the provinces with glossy hair and pressed shirts."

"Either that or they're dead and lying facedown in a pool of their own blood surrounded by policemen, in which case they could be anyone. The police can kill anyone nowadays and we just say, 'Hey, there's a dead body,' without really knowing, or caring, who it was. It could have been one of mine. I'm surprised I haven't lost any yet. One of them told me the other day that they were making Molotov cocktails in the labs, for Chrissake. And you know what really got to me? Not that they were making bombs on campus, but that they thought I wouldn't care, that I would sympathize. What on earth are we doing in this place? It's just too depressing for words."

But in fact Margaret was not depressed. She had never been depressed in her life, a fact with which she consoled herself now and then, whenever life seemed particularly unbearable. "Tribes in New

Guinea do not suffer from depression, therefore *I* do not suffer from depression" was what she repeated to herself whenever she felt she was collapsing under the hopelessness of the world. True, she did not often feel like this, but just sometimes she would feel weighed down by a profound lassitude, something that seized her and drained her of all energy and hope and desire. This usually happened in those dead hours between coming home and going out again for the evening, and on the few times she felt it coming on she thought, "Uh-oh, I have to do something about this." And lately these dips in morale were accompanied by a funny tightening of the chest that made it difficult to breathe—just for a few minutes, but long enough for her to have to sit down and catch her breath. Maybe it was the humidity, maybe she was turning into yet another pudgy old white woman who couldn't take the heat; maybe it was age, god forbid. But eventually she would haul herself to the shower, and, feeling better, she would step out into the still-warm evening. No: What she felt now was not depression but something akin to boredom, though she was not bored either. She didn't really know how she felt.

"You're always saying that," Din replied, not looking up from his paper. "So why don't you get out of here? You at least have a choice."

"You mean, admit defeat? You know me better than that."

"I don't really know you very well at all. And I'm serious: Why don't you leave?" Din didn't look up from the newspaper but continued to hold it up in front of him so that it shielded his face. The back page bore a picture of a badminton player, his thick black hair slicked back in imitation of American movie stars, his smile reflected on the swell of a polished trophy. The headline trumpeted PRAISE GOD FOR THE THOMAS CUP. Margaret could not tell from his placid, monotonous voice what he truly meant. Only by watching for small signs like the faint narrowing at the very edges of his eyes (pleasure) or the slight indentation of his dimples (sarcasm or contempt) could she read what he meant.

"For the same reason as you," she said. "The job here's not finished. I can't just abandon these kids."

"So you do sympathize with them."

"If that's your way of asking if I'm a Communist, you know what my answer is."

"I'm sorry, I didn't intend any offense, and you know that I don't care about politics. I'm just interested to know why you stay here instead of going home."

"The States? Boy, you know how to annoy me. I was conceived on one continent, born on another, and raised on four—five if you count Australia. I lived in America for less than ten years, not even twenty-five percent of my life. Would you call that home? Why don't *you* go home? I've heard Medan isn't so bad. Or you could go to Holland—again. They educated you, after all."

Din lowered his newspaper and Margaret studied his face for clues. There was nothing for a while, and then a completely blank, unreadable smile. It was something she'd begun to notice only recently and it made her feel uncomfortable. Her ability to discern moods in other people was something else she was proud of. She had been doing it—and doing it well—ever since she could remember, before she could talk, even. She thought of the opening line of her (unfinished) doctoral thesis "Tchambuli: Kinship and Understanding in Northern Papua New Guinea," which lay in a locked drawer just below her left knee. That line read, "It is the nonverbal communication between human beings that forms the basis of all society." She had always believed that people (well, she) could read things that remained unsaid, just like tribes in the jungle who had little need for sophisticated language. She had never before come across someone like Din. Sometimes she found him completely Western, other times utterly Indonesian, sometimes primitive. She thought again of her thesis, locked away with her passport at the foot of her desk. She had not looked at either in such a long time.

"I have no family left in Sumatra and my Dutch was never very good," he said at last.

Margaret stood up and made a cursory attempt to tidy her desk. "Hey, I'm sorry. I shouldn't have said that. I don't know why I'm so crabby these days. It's just so frustrating."

"What is?"

Margaret lifted her arms to gesture out the windows, but then just shrugged, sighing. "Everything. You know what I mean."

Din nodded. "I think I do."

Margaret turned away from him and looked out the window across the low sprawl of gray buildings. Everything looked gray to her now in

Jakarta. The new, squat concrete shops, the flimsy wooden shanties, the six-lane highways, the dead water in the canals, the banners that were strung up everywhere across the city, whose whiteness dulled quickly from the dust and smoke and the exhaust fumes that choked the air. She did not know when she'd stopped noticing the colors and the details of Jakarta, or when this grayness had begun to form like cataracts that clouded her appreciation of the city. On the building across the concrete square hung painted banners that urged NO IMPERIALISM, CRUSH MALAYSIA or FRIENDSHIP TO AFRICA or EVER ONWARD NO RETREAT IN THE NAME OF ALLAH. She felt a sudden surge of irritation: Why was it that everything in this city was written in capital letters? Whenever she went to dinner at the Hotel Java the entire menu was in bold upper case, every item screaming its existence at her, insisting that she choose it and not something else, every dish jostling with its neighbor in a cacophony of advertisement. NORTH SUMATRAN FAVORITE FROM BANDUNG EVER POPULAR DISH OF TORAJA KINGS. As if this assault were not enough, the prices too were announced in oversize numbers, though it wasn't clear to Margaret if this was an advertisement of how low they were or yet another mild form of extortion, the like of which Margaret experienced every day. Maybe she could no longer deal with the noise and the crowds and the bullying and the corruption, and had, therefore, stopped wanting to see the city in detail; maybe this was why she had begun to see everything in terms of grayness. She mulled over the possibility of this sometimes when she picked unenthusiastically at a TYPICAL EAST JAVA DELICACY in the lavish black marble surroundings of the Hotel Java. Was Margaret Bates becoming soft? In the end she decided that it was the city that had changed. Margaret Bates had not softened with age. And that was the problem, she knew that. Adaptation is the key to human existence, she used to tell her students. The Ability to Adapt: That was another of her strengths, along with her Resistance to Emotional Instability and her Reading of Moods. Yet here she was, frozen in time, waiting for the city to change back into something she recognized. It would not happen. She had known a different country, a gentler country, she thought. She hated that word, *gentler*—it was maudlin and sentimental; it reminded her of the way old white fools would talk about their plantations and their brown servants. Suddenly she hated herself. "I have to do something about this," she said to herself, almost audibly, as she continued to look out the window at the dirty gray banners. I cannot go on like this. I must change, I must change.

"What did you say?" Din asked, folding his newspaper at last.

"Nothing," Margaret said, turning around. She looked at Din's clear, slightly watery eyes and felt guilty at having snapped at him earlier. She wished that she was able to think things through before saying them. "Let's get an early dinner. Then we can go to the Hotel Java or somewhere fancy, you know, have some drinks—something strong and colorful with a little umbrella in it. We can watch all those ridiculous rich people with their prostitutes."

Din pulled his chair closer to his desk and flipped open a notebook. "It's too early for dinner," he said, picking up a pen and removing its cap. He held the pen poised over the notepad but he did not write anything. "Besides, they won't let me into the Hotel Java. Not like this, anyway." He held the collar of his shirt between his thumb and forefinger for a second before letting it fall.

"I'm not taking no for an answer," Margaret said. She grabbed his hand and pulled him toward the door. "You're with me, no one will say anything. It's one of those disgusting privileges of being white in a place like this. Everyone says they hate Westerners, but as soon as an *orang putih* walks into the room they give them whatever they want. Every other *blanquito* I know breaks the rules and behaves badly, and tonight I intend to partake in this disgusting orgy."

They crossed the highway on the overhead walkway. Beneath them the never-ending traffic beeped and hooted and revved as usual, a river of bashed-up, rusting steel whose current flowed everywhere and nowhere. The sun had begun to calm slightly, hazy now behind the perpetual layer of cloud; the sky was a dirty yellow, a yellow overlaid with gray, and soon, when the sun was setting, it would turn mouse-colored and finally—swiftly—black. There was never any blue, nothing true or clear.

They walked along the road for a while trying to hail a taxi, but there seemed to be none today so they settled for a *becak,* ridden by an ancient Javanese whose face was so fleshless that they could see the outlines of his skull under the old-leather skin. He rode with surprising speed and agility, passing men and women pushing their cartloads of peanuts and scrap newspaper and fruit. Stallholders along the road cried out to them as the rickshaw went past; they offered watches, toys, magazines, bottles of Benzine. Often Margaret thought they would collide with something—a horse-drawn cart or a bare-framed jeep or a bicycle—but at the last moment their driver would casually veer past the obstacle. Every few minutes they went past an accident or a broken-down vehicle. There were few cars, few recognizable ones, anyway. Everything had been cannibalized, picked to pieces and reassembled to look like something else so that it was impossible to identify a car as a Datsun or a Fiat or a Skoda. Something could begin as a Mercedes, morph mid-chassis into a Cadillac, and end up as an open-sided truck.

She looked across at Din, whose serious expression never seemed to alter very much. A more or less permanent frown drew his close-set, almond-shaped eyes even closer together and lent his slim features an air of mild anxiety. She liked him. He was certainly a great improvement over the last few who had filled his position; they had been, by and large, American postgraduate students earnestly pursuing dull projects on the Economics of Oil or International Aid in Newly Independent Asia. Without exception, they had been spectacularly unsuited to life in Southeast Asia. The longest serving of them had stayed for two years, the shortest a mere three months. There were rumors that they might not have been bona fide students, that they were in fact working for the U.S. government, but Margaret could not substantiate these rumors. She did find it slightly odd that there was such a steady stream of American students wanting to be teaching assistants in Jakarta, but there was nothing to suggest that they were funded by anything more sinister than indulgent Ivy League scholarships. Once or twice she had casually slipped into conversation the presence of the CIA in Indonesia, which was an open secret in town, but she was met by blinking incomprehension, so she let the matter rest. In this city you could never be sure if anyone was who they said they were and, frankly, Margaret couldn't care less.

Din, however, seemed far removed from the sordid details of Jakarta life. He did not have a comfortable scholarship to fall back on, and Margaret felt guilty because there was no money to pay him properly. In fact neither of them had drawn any salary for this month and although he never complained she knew that even his small rented room would soon begin to weigh heavily on his finances. He said he had taken a room in Kebayoran, but she did not believe him; it would be far too expensive for him. She knew that he did not want her to think him destitute, just another semi-slum dweller. He wanted her to believe that he was an ordinary middle-class professional, and she was happy to go along with it. But she did not know how long he could continue like this. She did not want him to leave.

"Do you ever miss Leiden?" she asked. They were traveling alongside a canal filled with stagnant black water covered in a film of grease.

He shrugged. "Not really."

"But you said you liked it. You did really well there—academically, I mean."

"I didn't like the cold." He could be like this, uncommunicative to the point of sullenness. Margaret wondered if he suffered from that respect of hierarchy that (she had noticed) seems to plague all Asians, so that she, being his elder and superior, could never be a companion with whom he could converse freely. It troubled her somewhat to think of herself as a Mother Superior figure, wizened and stern.

"I can understand that," she said, deciding not to push too far. She wished he would relax in her company, and she began to imagine how the evening might proceed if she had her way. They would have something simple to eat at a street stall and then they would have drinks, lots of them, and at some point in the evening he would begin to confide in her, telling her all about his village sweetheart and the girls he had had in Holland; he would begin to trust her, think of her as his equal, his confidante, and the next morning, at work, they would be friends and colleagues and she would no longer feel awkward in his company.

She was not sexually attracted to him; she wanted to make that clear. She had worked out that he was twenty-four going on twenty-five; not quite twenty years her junior but certainly young enough to be her son in this country where girls of eighteen often had three children. Besides, she had long since shut out the possibility of romance. Once, in an age of endless possibilities, love had presented itself to her and it had seemed so simple, so attainable that all she had to do was reach out and claim it. Falling in love then had felt as easy as swimming in a warm, salty sea: All she had to do was wade into it and the water would bear her away. But she had not done so, and now the tide had retreated, leaving broken bottles and driftwood and tangled nets. It was a landscape she had learned to live with.

The lights had just come on in Pasar Baru. The air was filled with the steady hum of portable generators and strings of naked bulbs burst sharply into life, casting their harsh glare on to the faces of passersby. There were not many people there yet, and Margaret and Din were able to stroll around for a few minutes before settling on a place to eat.

"What do you feel like eating?" Margaret asked.

"Anything. It's up to you."

She'd known he would say that and had therefore already decided. "Why don't we just grab some *nasi Padang*? Since you're Sumatran. It'll make you think of home."

They chose a place at random, sitting down at a folding table that wobbled when Margaret put her elbows on it. Din sat facing her, though he did not look at her face but stared into the space beyond her left shoulder. He looked clean and neat, as he always did, his plain, white short-sleeved shirt uncreased even at the end of the day. He never seemed to perspire. This evening he was not wearing the thick, black-rimmed glasses that he wore at work, and Margaret was glad because she had a clearer view of his eyes. "Isn't this nice?" she said. "The first time we have been out together." Even as she said so she was aware of the inappropriateness of it: she, a white woman, he a young Javanese man, together in public. They didn't like this kind of behavior, the Indonesians, she knew that. Perhaps this was why he was being so stiff. She looked around quickly but could see no other foreigners. A young woman came and took their order; she looked sexless in her baggy male clothing—oversized shirt, buttoned at the collar, and dirty, pleated trousers—and disapproving. Margaret felt her own décolletage, modest though it was, suddenly too revealing.

"Tell me about the research you started in Holland," Margaret said once they had ordered. They were on surer ground if they stuck to work matters; he liked talking about his work. "Pre-Islamic religion, wasn't it?"

"More or less," he said, his gaze shifting gently but noticeably so that he met her eye and held it. It caught her off guard, this sudden switching of moods, and she blinked and smiled to hide her unease. She didn't like being taken aback this way. "Actually it was a bit wider than that," he continued. "I was looking into writing a secret history of the Indonesian Islands in the Southeast, everything from Bali eastward. To me those islands were like a lost world where everything remained true and authentic, away from the gaze of foreigners—a kind of invisible world, almost. Such a stupid idea."

"Why stupid?"

"Oh." He smiled, suddenly bashful again. "Such a big subject—too big for a little guy like me."

"I think it's a wonderful idea. You shouldn't give up."

"No, there's no hope for someone like me. I was stupid to think I could do something like that, as if I were a Westerner." He spoke with no bitterness but a despair so deep that it felt almost calm. He won't be shaken from it, thought Margaret; it was so frustrating.

"What a thing to say," she said, trying not to sound didactic. "You can do anything you put your mind to. I'm not saying it's easy, but if you want something, you'll get it. Don't be so defeatist."

The food arrived, dishes of watery curries of meat and vegetables. Margaret peered at the rice and noticed that it had been mixed with maize. "I think we have a civic-conscious vendor on our hands," she said. Since the previous year's drought every meal was a lottery. Sometimes your rice would be rice, other times it would be a gritty bowl of ground meal, in accordance with government recommendations.

"Maybe you're right," Din said with a shrug. He spoke as if trying to convince himself of something. "My idea was that we needed a history of our country written by an Indonesian, something that explored nonstandard sources that Westerners could not easily reach. Like folk stories, local mythology, or ancient manuscripts written on palm leaves—"

"*Lontar,* you mean."

"Yes. When you think about the standard approach to history, all the historical texts, you're really talking about Western sources. It's as if the history of Southeast Asia started with the discovery of the sea routes from Europe to Asia. Everything begins at this point in time, but in fact so much had already happened. The empires of Majapahit and Mataram had been established; Islam, Hinduism, Buddhism . . . I wanted to retell the story of these islands because I have a theory that their history is beyond the comprehension of foreigners—sorry, you'll forgive me for saying that, I know—"

"Forgiven—"

"—and that history has to be told by a voice that is non-Western . . ."

Din continued talking, but Margaret had become distracted by a boy who had sat down three tables away. He was an Asian of indeterminate age—anywhere from fourteen to twenty-one—not malnourished like most of them were, but still somehow ragged. His dirty white T-shirt bore a logo of an animal on the front (a bear?) under blue and gold letters that said BERKELEY. He appeared at once lost and deeply focused. Was he looking at them? She glanced at him once or twice and each time he ducked away just as she turned her head in his direction. Establishing eye contact too freely was a mistake many foreigners she knew made, misjudging Asian regard. What their smiling faces suggested was not always accurate, and what your own smiling face transmitted was not always what you intended. There was nothing on his table; he had not ordered food or drink.

". . . and of course the unknown story of Muslim seafarers."

"Well," Margaret said, "why don't you just go ahead and do it?"

Instantly Din fell pensive and silent, as he played with the pool of curry in which he had drowned his rice. "No one will fund me. I asked everyone in Holland and they all said no. They think it's about politics. And here, well, the president talks about grand projects, but we all know there's never going to be any money. Not for people like me."

Margaret did not answer. She looked at his slim, sloping shoulders as he toyed aimlessly with his food. He had a way of making the morsels on his plate seem meager and almost inedible. There was nothing she could do for him, she thought; perhaps she ought to give up. Perhaps she ought to have given up on this country a long time ago. It was still early in the evening, but she was already tired.

"Let's go for a drink," she said. She would shake off this lethargy; she knew she could.

Din's face twisted into a half frown. "Um, no thanks, actually. I'm quite tired today. Maybe I'll just go home."

Margaret stacked the empty dishes on top of each other, to signify the end of the meal. "Just come for one quick drink. You'll enjoy it from an anthropological point of view if nothing else. Come on." She waved a few bills at the vendor.

"Really, it's very kind of you, but I don't think I'd be comfortable at the Hotel Java."

"Rubbish. You'll have a ball. I told you, I never take no for an answer." She smiled sweetly and knew that he would come: When she decided she wanted something, she was never refused.

As they got up to leave Margaret turned back to look one last time at the boy with the Berkeley T-shirt, but he was no longer at the table. She looked around at the stalls, expecting to see him half-hidden behind a pillar or milling in the crowds, but she could see nothing. He had been there at the table half a minute ago and now he was gone.

"Well, what fun this is going to be," Margaret said brightly.

BUILT IN 1962 to celebrate the Asian Games, the Hotel Java sits on the edge of a sweeping roundabout in an area that might be called downtown if this city had an uptown. Like so many of the brutalist concrete buildings springing up around Jakarta, the hotel's angular lines and slightly industrial appearance were meant to remind the beholder of both Le Corbusier and the Bauhaus aesthetic: international yet functional. The roundabout in front of it is in fact a shallow, perfectly circular pool from which jets of water spurt majestically at a young peasant couple standing on a tall narrow plinth. The hotel and the fountain are just two of the many projects designed to impress visitors to Jakarta with the city's dynamism, and were commissioned by Sukarno himself (the president's majestic erections, Margaret called them). Not more than two years had passed and already the toilets in the hotel were unpleasant; some of the bulbs in the grand chandelier in the lobby had burned out and hadn't been replaced; the carpets were scarred by cigarette burns and the table linen dyed with old wine stains.

"Looks as if the president's erections are faltering," Margaret said as she looked at the chipped edge of the bar. She had had two martinis already. The first had gone straight to her head and the second had slipped down all too easily. She was trying to make the third one last, but it was difficult; she felt a flush in her cheeks and she wanted to drink quickly. She was already quite light-headed, she knew, but she felt strong again.

Din stood with his elbows on the bar, facing away from the room. He stared at the rows of bottles arranged on the mirrored wall facing him, as if examining every single label. He would take only a Coke, no matter how hard Margaret tried to persuade him otherwise. He wouldn't even drink a Bintang. She was usually sensitive enough not to transgress cultural boundaries—but Din was different. Yes, he was Muslim, but he had lived for three years in Europe and was not just another unsophisticated small-town Indonesian. If they both had a drink, she thought, the alcohol might help break down the boundaries that remained between them and they would be friends.

There was music, a band and a pretty Filipina in a tight white dress singing *"Solamente Una Vez"* in bright, clear notes, rolling her *r*'s impeccably while shaking a pair of brightly colored maracas to accompany the Cuban drums. The bar was not full but it was already very noisy, the air smoky and filled with men's voices. There were a lot of men here and not many women; not many locals either. The only Indonesians present seemed to be women, and nearly all were prostitutes.

"Here you have the Occident's finest at play," Margaret said. "See those two guys? Pulitzer winners a few years back. They're supposed to be reporting on one of the most urgent political situations in the world and what do they do? Chase after girls they can't get at home. And that idiot over there, yes, that one canoodling with the Batak girl, he's meant to be administering aid for the World Bank, but it doesn't look as if he's capable of administering anything but a strawberry daiquiri."

"Do you know everyone here?" Din asked.

"I recognize a few faces."

A big pink-faced man with sandy hair and freckles came through the doors and headed straight for Margaret. He had a young local girl with him, tall for a Javanese and quite fair. "Margaret, how are you? Haven't seen you in ages—not since last year's Fourth of July party at the Lazarskys'. Who's the boyfriend?"

"He's not my *boyfriend,* he's my colleague at the university." She was about to introduce Din when she noticed he had slipped away, heading for the bathroom. "How's the *girl*friend, Bill?"

"Fine," he said, putting a fleshy arm across his companion's shoulders, "just fine. Her name's Susanti, but I just call her Sue."

"Been together long?"

"Guess so. Longest since I got here, at any rate." He laughed, patting his pockets in search of his cigarettes.

"Wow. Two weeks? Congratulations."

He smiled for a moment then broke into an overhearty laugh. "You just kill me. You're still just so . . . Margaret."

"See you around, Bill."

A table and two chairs became free at the back of the room, in a shadowy corner where the lightbulbs had gone out. Margaret went over and sat down, making a cursory attempt to fiddle with the bulbs. She preferred everything to be bathed in light, preferably sunlight. It was not that she was afraid of the dark: She just did not like it, for it frustrated her not to be able to make things out clearly. The windows looked out onto narrow streets away from the noise and great rush of traffic of the grand roundabout. There were not so many people here, just a few of the embassy drivers waiting for their bosses to finish dinner. They milled about in small groups, smoking and exchanging gossip. Most of them were smartly dressed in creased trousers and khaki shirts, but there were a number of other locals who were more difficult to place: bodyguards trying to look casual, perhaps, or local journalists bribing the drivers for information. Margaret tried to discern the differences between them. She was good at this, good at spotting what lay behind this Asian mask of inscrutability. She had learned to do this in the jungle, with tribes who wore real masks and whose body language was indecipherable to outsiders, and she applied it with great success everywhere in Indonesia, even in this city of three million people. In America and Europe she had not been quite so successful; her antennae did not pick up the right signals with other Occidentals. She had not really even been able to understand her parents.

"So who was your friend earlier?" Din said, joining her at the table.

"What friend?"

"That American man."

"Bill Schneider, you mean? He's not a friend. He works at the embassy. Not exactly sure what he does—something to do with finance.

Well, okay, I think he arranges all the bribes from our wonderful country to your wonderful country to build all your wonderful projects."

"Like this hotel?"

"Probably. Although I think this hotel might have been funded with Japanese bakshccsh—not that it makes any difference. Bill and his lot certainly have their fingers in the pie now. I tell you, that man is *every*where."

They watched him drinking a tall glass of beer with a group of friends. He stubbed out his cigarette with clumsy little jabs and punched people on the shoulder to emphasize his jokes. He laughed a lot, always loudly. From across the room they could only catch snippets of what he was saying. ". . . last year the Yankees got unlucky, this year they're gonna step up. . . . I'm tellin' ya, you can't lose with a name like Yogi Berra. . . ."

"He can at least speak Indonesian," Margaret said, "and Russian too, which is a big help in this town."

Din nodded. "His girlfriend is very pretty."

"He's got bags of that *je ne sais quoi* that girls find so irresistible: U.S. dollars. Do you want another Coke?"

Din shook his head. "Thank you, but I have to go. It's a long way home for me."

"I think I'll head home too. I'm sorry the evening was a bit dull."

They walked through the grand lobby where smart-looking men in bush jackets and expensive women in shimmering dresses turned to look at them. They stood at the entrance for a moment or two, unsure of how to bid each other good-bye. A kiss? Out of the question. A hug? Still too intimate. Handshake? Too formal.

"See you tomorrow, I guess," Margaret said, holding up her hand in a stilted wave.

"Yes," he said, and a smile flashed across his face, not the infuriating unreadable one, but something thinner and tired. He looked curiously frail as he walked briskly down the curving driveway, past the long row of shiny black limousines, before disappearing into the stream of traffic. The lights in this part of the city made the sky look pale and hazy, even at night.

"Margaret," someone called out. It was Bill Schneider again. He did not have his girl with him this time. "I saw you leave and I thought, She can't be leaving us so quickly!"

"Well, I am leaving, Bill."

"Wait." When he smiled he showed off the top row of his perfect teeth. "You remember what we talked about last time we met . . ."

Margaret looked him in the eye then looked away. "Yes."

"And . . . ?"

"And what?"

"Well," he paused. "We need to know what you . . . think."

She did not answer. A steady stream of limousines drew up before them; the revving of the engines and the exhaust fumes made her feel sick, and the whistling of the doormen rang sharply in her ears and made her incipient headache grow worse. She wanted to go home.

He stood watching her, not saying anything. Margaret felt he was prepared to stay there all night, waiting for her to answer, but in the end he said, "I'm sorry. This is not a good place to speak. You sure you won't come back inside for one more beer? No, you're tired, of course. Look, come by and see me in my office. Soon." He handed her a folded-up newspaper. She saw the same smiling badminton player she had noticed earlier in the day, one half of his face disappearing into a crease. Bill leaned over to kiss her on the cheek. "Come soon, Margaret."

"Taxi, madam?" asked the doorman.

"No thanks, I'll walk for a while." She went down to the road and stood watching the swirling traffic before her, assailed by the pleading cries of the child beggars and the shrill calls of the boys and girls lined up on the other side of the road. It hurt Margaret to look at them, so she turned away, trying to pretend that the noise was something mechanical and inhuman. The city had never seemed so enormous, so overwhelming, so chaotic, and its enormous overwhelming chaos was growing worse every day. Not wishing to walk any longer, she hailed a taxi that stank of clove smoke. She unfolded the newspaper and looked at the front page. Bill's handwriting—a surprisingly elegant cursive— read: *Page 5: PS Great to see you again. B*

She flicked through the pages. More protests in Europe against the imprisonment of Mandela. Sukarno condemns Gulf of Tonkin resolution. Abebe Bikila promises gold for Africa. Brezhnev to provide more aid for Indonesia. Drug use in Malaysia reaching epidemic proportions; Britain offers no help. Communists arrested in outlying islands. It all looked familiar to her—surely she had read it all this morning?

She looked again at page 5. Below the article on Communist arrests was a small picture. In the dim light at the back of the taxi it was difficult to make out the already blurred photograph of twenty or so men in a police cell. But there was one face, paler than the others: a European.

· 4 ·

$\mathcal{I}$n 1841 the *Nan Sing,* a Chinese vessel sailing under the Dutch flag, set sail from Canton bound for Batavia laden with a cargo of porcelain, silk, and tea. Caught in unseasonably bad weather just south of Cape Varella, it began to move southeastward, drifting for many days until, lured by powerful currents, it crashed on the notorious reefs off the rocky shores of Nusa Perdo. Exercising his ancient right of looting shipwrecks, the sultan immediately ordered his fleet of little boats to recover the precious flotsam from the wreck of the *Nan Sing.* Enraged by this transgression, the Dutch authorities in Batavia demanded the return of the cargo and ordered the sultan to submit to Dutch rule. When this was predictably refused, several skirmishes took place, escalating into a standoff that lasted two days. There followed a further fifty years of shipwrecks, looting, and halfhearted attempts by the Dutch army to bring the island under its control. No great energy was expended in the subjugation of Perdo because the island had neither spices nor sandalwood. Covered in scrubby bushes and dominated by a dead volcano, this unobtrusive island virtually disappeared in the constellation of more attractive islands around it, until, late in the century, the discovery of kayu putih trees and rumors of rich gold deposits brought the white man back to these shores, and this time they did not leave. The sultan died by his own hand and the island came under Dutch rule.

No one really knows how the island got its curious name, which does not seem consistent with the rhythms of the (now virtually dead) local dialect. Writing about Muslim sects in the eastern archipelago in the prewar *Revue des Études Islamiques,* a French scholar named Gaston Bosquet suggests that the name of this island is a bastardization of *pieds d'or,* a reference to the fascination held by early Western visitors for the shoes of gold cloth worn by the princes of the royal household in the seventeenth century, and to the idea that these explorers might have been walking on fields of gold. Given the relative poverty of this island, however, such explanations seem highly implausible (rumors of gold reserves turned out to be a myth). No more likely—though a touch more romantic—is the idea that members of a Portuguese reconnaissance expedition in the early sixteenth century foundered on the rocky coastline of the island, as so many were to do in the centuries that followed. Marooned hundreds of miles from the shipping channels between Malacca and China, they called this place the Lost Island, Nusa Perdo—a name that continues today. This might also explain why, in town, there are three local merchants whose surnames are Texeira, De Souza, and Menezes, even though they look thoroughly Indonesian.

These were the stories that Adam loved above all others—the unofficial history of Perdo; he clung to them dearly, afraid they would desert him. He knew exactly why he found them so comforting—they gave him a reason to be different: maybe he too had foreign blood in him. And this was why he did not look like the other children on the island, why they hated him.

He often wished that he had the coarse curly hair of the local boys, as well as their sturdy square faces that made them look, well, *rudimentary,* more suited to the sharp changes of weather on the island. Sometimes, if he stayed out in the sun for too long, the skin on his forearms and knees would begin to smart, as if rubbed with fine sand, and by the end of the day it would feel hot and taut, properly burned by the sun, just like Karl's—a *foreigner's* skin. On those occasions he wished that he had the other children's darker, thicker skin that turned to leather by the time they were teenagers, shielding them from the elements. He wished he did not have his straight hair and brittle jawline and fragile cheekbones; he wished he did not stand out quite so much.

For one bucolic year after he moved into his new home, he did not have to worry about other children—or, indeed, about anything else. Much later in his life he would remember that first year with a mixture of nostalgia and regret, and he would experience that odd sensation of sorrow and yearning said to be a trait peculiar to people of the southeast, even though he himself was not *genetically* native to the region. But the truth was that life during this time was simple, blissful, and untroubled, in a way that can only happen when two people are desperate to achieve happiness.

Their days were idyllic and filled with all the things that fathers and sons dream of sharing. They made kites in the shape of birds that sometimes swept effortlessly into the sky but more often crash-landed after the briefest of flights, much to Adam's and Karl's amusement; they played *takraw* in the yard, Adam's plump legs proving surprisingly adept at juggling the hard rattan ball, Karl less so because of his one weak leg; they hollowed out lengths of driftwood and collected lengkeng seeds to play *congkak,* a game which Karl explained had been brought to these islands by Arab sea traders many hundreds of years ago; they found an old biscuit tin among Karl's things that contained chess pieces, and drew a chalk chessboard on the floor of the veranda that had to be resketched every time the rains swept in and washed it away.

It was a Spartan happiness, it is true. Sometimes, Karl often told him, it is better not to own things, especially precious things, because they will be lost or taken away; *things* cannot last beyond your lifetime. Karl did not spend any money on toys, for example, or anything he deemed to be ephemeral or trivial. Once or twice, Adam had paused in front of the glass cabinets at the Chinese store in town, admiring the brightly colored toy cars and plastic squirt guns. "No one here can afford these toys," Karl had said, gesturing in the vague direction of the villages on the coast, "and yet they're quite happy. We don't need these things either—we're just like everyone else."

And so they pursued simpler pleasures. Adam learned to wade into the shallows and, when the sea was calm, he'd paddle out over the reefs with Karl. He would float along quite calmly for a while but then he would be panicked by the enormity of the ocean, the endlessness of its possibilities, and he would start to flail around, desperate to regain the sureness of the shore, until Karl came over and held his hand. His previous world now seemed empty and colorless, but in this world there were kaleidoscopic fish, purple sea urchins, and pulsating starfish; and beyond the coral there was the promise of shipwrecks, their silent corpses filled with treasure from a lost time. Later, Karl would tell him about each of the wrecks: One of them had been shipping opium to China, another had been decommissioned from the British navy; the biggest one contained hundreds of bottles of precious wine from

Oporto and Madeira, still drinkable. In this way Adam learned the history of Perdo; about the opium wars, Catholicism, and the destructive power of religion and the unjust conquering of Asia by Europe.

This is how Adam believed his new world would begin and end—in this place where he was safe from danger but connected to the possibilities of the world. It was then, however, that Karl began to talk about school.

"Can't I just stay at home and learn things from you, *Pak*?" cried Adam, trying to stem his growing unease. "What else do I need to learn?"

"What you need to learn isn't contained in textbooks. You need to learn how to live with other people your age—how to be like everyone else. You mustn't become too privileged."

But Adam already knew that he was not like everyone else. That was why he was here in the first place, living on this island that was not his real home, with a father who did not look at all like him.

Other children. The very sound of the words made him feel sick. For nearly a year he had had little contact with other children. He had seen them in town whenever he and Karl went in for supplies, but he avoided their cold hard stares and clung to Karl's side, never looking directly at them. He saw them crouching by the roadside, blinking the dust from their eyes as he swept by in the car. And farther along the beach he sometimes saw them splashing in the shallows in the late afternoon when the sea was flat, the shadows of the trees reaching across the sand toward the water's edge. Their faraway cries were shrill and threatening.

DON'T WORRY, YOU'RE just like the other boys," Karl said as he took Adam to school that first day. He spoke in a calm voice, yet Adam knew that Karl himself was not convinced by what he was saying. "You'll enjoy being with compatriots your age. If ever you feel scared, tell yourself, 'I'm just like everyone else here.' "

The school was a one-room shack on the edge of town, a squat, concrete block with a roof of corrugated iron. Adam loathed it from the beginning; its very appearance made him feel sick, and spots of color appeared in his vision, as if he was going to faint. *(I'm just like everyone else here.)* There were about eighteen or twenty children crammed into the small classroom, all boys, save for one girl whose roughly cropped hair made her look like a boy. One side of her face was obscured by a birthmark, a purple red cloud that stretched from her temple to her jawbone. Adam had to stare closely before deciding that she was indeed a girl; she stuck out her tongue and threw a scrunched-up piece of paper at him. The other boys gathered around him and examined the contents of his new canvas satchel: an exercise book with a buff-colored cover, a pocket atlas, and a new box of colored pencils. His classmates tore the pages from his books and folded them into paper airplanes that they launched into the air with sharp spearing motions. Adam watched as bits of the atlas glided past him: The pink and green of the United States floated dreamily in circles until it stubbed its nose on the blackboard and fell abruptly to the ground; the whiteness of the Canadian tundra swept out of the window in an arc, into the dusty sunlight; and the silent mass of the Pacific Ocean that Adam loved so much, dotted with islands (Fiji? Tahiti?) lay on the cracked cement floor, waiting to be trampled.

At the end of that first day he did not have the strength to cycle the entire distance home; he pushed his bicycle along the final sandy stretch, too tired even to cry. When he reached the house he let his bicycle fall to the ground; he sat on the steps to the house watching the pedal spin lazily to a stop. There were sea eagles hovering against the powder blue sky, barely trembling in the wind. Karl sat with him and put his arm around his shoulders. He shook his head and said, "It's a privilege, you know."

"What is?"

"Education. You saw those kids at school? What kind of families do you think they come from?"

Horrible ones, Adam wanted to say. Filthy, mean, horrible ones.

"Poor ones. Farmers or fishermen who can't read or write, and yet everyone has had to pay to get into that school. They take a little money or a carton of cigarettes to the education officer and beg him to put their child's name on the school list, and if they don't have cash they take a goat or some chickens or sacks of rice. There isn't space for everyone, so the kids whose parents pay the most get in. I had to do the same—I paid the most because I'm ... well, they look at me and their minds are made up."

"Because you're foreign?"

"Because I'm rich. Or at least that's what they think."

Adam watched as Karl lifted the bicycle and set it upright; its handlebar and pedal were covered thickly with sand that fell to the ground in clumps. "The point is," Karl continued, "none of those people can afford to send their children to school. They'd rather have their kids with them, working in the fields or out at sea with them. Then they have to pay for uniforms, shoes, books. Why? Because they want their children to read and write, to have nice jobs in offices and drive cars in Jakarta. They might not realize it, but they believe in the future of this country."

The next day he sent Adam back to school again.

The teacher taught them simple grammar and rudimentary arithmetic. She made them practice the letters of the alphabet and introduced them to new words, writing them out on the blackboard in short sentences that no one but Adam could make sense of. It did not seem to matter to her that almost everyone in the class was asleep or staring red-eyed out the window at the grassy plains pockmarked with blackened heaps of half-burned rubbish, where skinny goats picked through the piles of waste, dragging plastic bags out of the cinders. CITIZEN. REPUBLIC. PRESIDENT. REVOLUTION. WESTERN IMPERIALISTS. *I am a citizen of the Republic of Indonesia. The president of the Republic of Indonesia is President Sukarno. President Sukarno led the revolution against the Western Imperialists who destroyed . . .*

"It's hot," someone whispered, "I have to go home." Adam turned around and saw the girl with the birthmark slumped on her desk, twirling a dry strip of coconut leaf in her fingers. She brushed the leaf lazily against Adam's back. "Are your parents expecting you home too?"

Adam nodded. Close up, he could see that the discolored patch of skin on her face was not a birthmark but a scar, an inky mass of tissue that looked almost smooth, like a pebble on the riverbank, crisscrossed by long-dead veins. She was a few years older than Adam but no taller; her fingernails were dirty and worn.

"Actually, I only have a mother at the moment," she said.

"At the moment?"

"Yeah, my father's in jail. Don't know when he'll be out. I'm an orphan! That's what my mother says when she gets in a mood and starts crying. 'I am a widow! I am nothing! My daughter is an orphan! Oh, my daughter is an orphan!' "

Adam giggled. She was much darker than he was, yet she did not seem entirely like the other kids; she spoke with a different accent too.

"My name's Neng. What's yours?" She tickled his neck with the leaf.

"Adam."

"I have to go and collect this month's rice from the district office later. Want to come with me? It's not a long walk. Besides, you have a bicycle. . . ." Her smile showed off two gaps in her teeth.

"Umm, I don't know. My father will be worried if I don't come home."

"Come on, it won't take long." She reached out and brushed the leaf softly across his cheek, giggling as she did so. "I know a shortcut back to where you live."

By the time they left school the sky had dulled slightly with patches of silver blue cloud, and it was no longer oppressively hot; the sea breeze had picked up, signaling the possibility of the sudden sharp showers for which Perdo is famous. Adam and Neng had just reached the end of the path that led to the main road when they saw a group of boys from school waiting for them, squatting at the edge of the broken tarmac in the shade of a sea almond sapling.

"Hi, friend," one of them said, standing up. He had taken his shirt off and tied its arms around his forehead so that it fell down his back like the headdresses of Arab sheikhs that Adam had seen in books. This boy was bigger than the others, and when he spoke his voice cracked, alternating between a child's high-pitched squeak and a manly croak. "This is the little orphan who lives with that European man. You're his servant, yeah?"

"No," Adam said, "he's my father."

The older boy threw back his head and laughed. There was a circle of dried-up spittle around his lips. Behind him Adam noticed that one of the other boys was playing with a dead bird, stretching its red and black wings across the sand as if willing it to fly. "Yeah, yeah. You lick the shit from his toilet." He pushed his fingers into Adam's collarbone with a rough, jabbing motion, making Adam lose his balance; his bicycle fell from his grip and dropped to the ground. The other boys laughed. "What a weakling," the gang leader said.

Adam tried to pick himself up but found that his legs had turned to jelly; his face felt hot and he could not speak. Pressure filled his head, and he felt like vomiting. His ears filled with a great rushing noise, the kind you might hear if you are standing on the seashore before a violent storm, when the froth of the waves blanks out all other noise and makes you lose all notion of where you are. He lay on the ground, kicking feebly at the coppery leaves of the sea almond that lay scattered on the ground. The people standing over him seemed blurred, wobbling as though shaken by gusts of wind. He began to shiver.

I am just like everyone else I am just like please I am just

"Anyway," he could hear the man-boy's croaky voice, "whatever the white man is to you, he's rich. He can buy you another bicycle. This one's nice." Adam saw feet moving around him and heard the chain of his bicycle ticking. Someone tugged the strap of his satchel, which came away from his body as if it no longer wanted to belong to him.

"Stop!" Neng shouted. She put her hands under Adam's armpits and hauled him into a sitting position. "This is not fair. Leave the bike or I'll kick your balls."

"Oh-oh, look who's talking," the croaky voice said. "What you going to do, help this weakling? Look how tiny he is! Look at those little fat legs. He's not worth getting beaten up over. Right, boys?" The voice was steadier now, threatening.

"At least he can read and write. You're nearly an adult and you still can't read." Neng was trying to yank Adam into a standing position but Adam's legs were still weak.

"You just want the bike for yourself, that right?" The man-boy took a step toward Neng; he looked nearly twice as big as she was.

"Just leave him alone."

The boy raised his hand and hesitated a second before slapping Neng hard. "You're just a dirty foreigner too," he said. "Look at you, a dirty monster." Neng stood blinking at him, as if she had not been struck.

"Careful, Yon," a smaller boy said in a quiet voice. "She's Madurese. You know what they're like."

"I don't care," the boy croaked. "These bloody foreigners, they come here and all they do is cause trouble, taking our land. They're going to chase us off our own island soon, there'll be nothing left for us. There'll be more of them than us! That's what my dad says. He's fed up with them. Need to teach them a lesson from time to time, he says."

"Yon, c'mon, let's take the bike and go. Don't get mixed up with the Madurese. They're big-time trouble."

"But this one's only a girl. My dad says all Madurese women are prostitutes anyway. The sooner we teach her who's boss around here, the better."

Adam had managed to get up to a half-kneeling position, one leg still trailing on the ground, when he saw Neng raise her knee, swiftly, in one firm, neat motion; it thudded into the boy's crotch with a loud squashy noise and he crumpled silently to the ground. He put his hand between his legs to protect himself but it was no use. Neng stood over him and continued to kick him in that same spot, sometimes hopping up and down to stamp on his crotch as if putting out a cigarette. His cries cut through the ringing in Adam's ears and made him feel less sick; it was as if someone had doused Adam with cold water, and he was able to rise slowly to his feet. The other boys had backed off; Neng was straddling the bicycle and ringing its bell. "Come on," she said gaily to Adam, as if nothing had happened. She patted the horizontal bar in front of her. "You sit here, I'll cycle. Okay? Great. Off we go!"

Along the coast road the wind was fresh and tinged with the softness of impending rain. The clouds strained the sunlight that fell on the waves, and this made the sea look calm in places but dark and mysterious in others. It was often like this on Perdo, where the slightest shift in the weather could change the very nature of the island. On those days when the sun was high and unflinching the possibility of rain would seem ridiculous, and on rainy days, when water soaked through everything, you might believe that even if the sun were to reappear, it would never be able to dry the moisture from the earth. But there were other days too—days such as today, when you could feel both the dry dustiness and the heavy moisture that made up the very air on this island.

Neng produced a banana from her pocket. It was blackened and squashed, the pulp beginning to ooze from its tip where it had been torn from its comb. "You look tired," she said, handing it to Adam. "Eat this. It'll make you feel better."

It was very ripe and mushy and sweet. Adam ate it quickly and wiped the stickiness from his fingers on his shorts. Maybe it was the fresh breeze, maybe it was his imagination, but the trembling in his chest began to subside, his heartbeat calming. He blinked; there was dust in his eyes and he turned his head from the wind. His face was very close to Neng's now, and he could see the tiny imperfections, the fragile creases of skin on the scar on her face. She was smiling and stuck out her tongue at him, just as she had done on the first day of school. It was beginning to rain. The first heavy drops of a shower fell through the leaves above them.

"Hey, it's getting late," said Neng. "You look tired. I think you should just go home. We're not far from where you live."

"But I want to go with you—you know, to help you collect your rice."

The bicycle slowed to a halt and Adam had to hop off. "Don't worry, I'll go on my own. Your father will be worried. Besides, you look really tired. I don't want to get the blame—I've been blamed for enough things already!" She handed him the bike and began to walk off into the distance, heading away from the coast into the hills. The rain was falling heavily now, an earnest downpour that would not ease up for at least an hour, maybe two. Adam felt a sudden panic at being left behind and started to follow her. She turned around and said, "If you follow me I'll kick your balls too."

He watched her splash through the puddles that were forming on the road; the rain fell like a thick curtain of mist, and within a few seconds she was out of sight.

As he cycled home, Adam felt the rain running in thin rivulets down his face and neck until his entire body was wet. Occasionally a gust of wind would sweep raindrops into his eyes and he would have to slow down and blink hard just to see where he was going; his sneakers were soaked through and his toes felt clammy and gritty. But the rain and wind were not cold, and he was no longer tired. Funny, he thought: At this moment, he didn't even fear what tomorrow might bring.

"Where have you been, Son?" Karl said, rushing to meet him with an enormous towel that he held between outstretched arms, the way the fishermen hold their nets before flinging them out to sea.

"Nowhere," said Adam, letting Karl towel his hair vigorously. "I just took my time. It was . . . it was raining."

With his head wrapped in the darkness of the towel, Adam knew how unconvincing this sounded. For a moment, he considered telling Karl all that had happened. He was doing something wrong, he knew that. He knew he ought to share everything with Karl because Karl did the same for him; Karl had taken him in and shared his whole life with Adam, so why couldn't Adam do this tiny thing for him? He also knew that if he was going to tell Karl he must do it immediately, otherwise the opportunity would be lost. Two, three, four, five seconds. The moment was gone.

Adam did not feel bad at all. Now that the moment was over it did not seem as if he had done anything wrong. Karl lifted the towel from his head and draped it across his shoulders, letting it fall around him like a cape. He looked at Adam unblinkingly, waiting for an explanation, but Adam merely stared out at the murky sea.

Karl said, "You should go and change out of those wet clothes."

The next day, Neng was waiting for him in the shade of some trees, not far from where the main road curved toward the town; the dirt track that led to school ran like a tangent away from the road, disappearing into the bushes beyond. "Let's skip school, maybe go for a walk. It isn't going to rain today," Neng announced, squinting at the sun.

They left the coast behind and began to cycle along the gravel paths that led into the hills, and when the path became too steep they hid the bike behind some bushes and began to walk. The coarse earth crunched underfoot, the black volcanic sand sticking to Neng's bare toes and covering them like tar. She talked endlessly, pointing things out to Adam: a flock of brilliant green parakeets fluttering like giant locusts in the distance; a boulder the shape of a hand with its fingers cut off; the coral reefs, which, from up in the hills, resembled a map, a huge, watery atlas.

She told him about herself too. Her father was in jail because he'd killed someone, she said cheerily. Well, not exactly killed him, but the man he'd had a fight with had died, purely by accident. All Neng's father had done was hit him; okay, he hit him quite hard, even her mother said so, but still, he wasn't the only one. There had been lots of men fighting, it was just a street brawl outside the rice merchant's, you know, just by the clock tower. But her father was the only one who was still in jail. Just because he's Madurese. It was so unfair. He didn't even want to be on this island anyway.

"Then why did you come here?" Adam couldn't remember where Madura was, but it sounded far away. He tried to remember his lessons at home with Karl, when Karl had shown him where all the big cities and islands of Indonesia were.

She frowned, looking closely at him with squinted eyes as if she had spotted something nasty on his face. "God, you're dumb. *Transmigration*. We were forced to, just like everyone else."

They had had nothing in Madura; it was an overcrowded island where there were a few cows and too many people who had no food and no work. They had been promised work, she said, in a place where there were few people and much land. The government was building a new pumice mine and there were lots of jobs, and maybe the workers would be given some land of their own. Her parents didn't even know what pumice was. Don't worry, the official had told them; we will give you rice to eat every month and your kids will go to school. But the mine was never built. There was no land for them, and often no rice. They'd been in Perdo for three years, but there was no work at all.

"What about you?" Neng asked. "Where did you come from?"

Adam shrugged. He looked around, hoping to see those parakeets again, but there was nothing.

"Sorry," she said, reaching out and touching him on the elbow. Her scar obscured her cheek and made her look as if she was only smiling with half her face. "I forgot you're an orphan."

"That's okay." He smiled. But he thought to himself: It was not okay. Why did he not know which part of Indonesia he was from? What dialect had his parents spoken? Even orphans had to come from somewhere. It was not that he had never dared ask Karl, but rather that it had never occurred to him to ask. He had known little of his past and cared even less, and he had liked it that way. So why was he now troubled by this lack of knowledge? Suddenly he felt guilty at having missed school without telling Karl.

"Come on," Neng said, breaking into a run, "there's something I want to show you." Beyond the trees the grassland gave way to a rocky plain covered with cacti and scrubby bushes; in the distance the land rose toward the point of the dead volcano that dominated the island. Neng disappeared behind some rocks, and when Adam caught up he saw that she had crawled into a natural depression sheltered from the sun and the rain, a scooped-out hollow so perfectly formed that it seemed man-made.

"Here, look," Neng said, showing him a stash of objects. She picked up a small comb made from pink plastic and ran it through her spiky hair. "I found it on the road, just lying there waiting for me to pick it up."

"But that's stealing," Adam said, repeating what Karl had once told him.

"Don't be stupid. If something is thrown away, it means its owner doesn't want it anymore—in that case anyone has a right to take it. Idiot." She showed him other things she had found: a small motorbike made of tin, rusting where the paint had worn off; a cracked mirror; a book with a frayed paper cover showing a large sea fish about to be attacked by a diver wielding a knife (there were some words in German too, but Adam was not able to read them); and a doll with blue eyes and dark curly lashes. Its painted blond hair looked like a scar on its head, an imperfection. Neng picked it up and cuddled it as if it were a real baby, holding its head to her cheek and swaying from side to side; she sat down with her legs crossed and looked out of the miniature cave. They could see over the low trees to the tawny flatlands and the sea in the distance. "No one can see me in here," she said. "It's my secret place." She leaned over and kissed him on his cheek and he could smell the musty unwashed odor of her clothes and skin. He blushed, and withdrew slightly; her lips felt funny—dry and hot; he wasn't sure he liked it. She giggled and continued to cuddle her doll.

From then on, they skipped school every day, cycling as far as they could or taking long walks into the interior. In the coves of the south coast they stood atop the steep fern-covered cliffs and saw the shipwrecks poking out of the surf; in a rainstorm in the hilly forests they were chased by wild goats; in a dried-up riverbed they found the giant stones for which Perdo is famous, those ancient boulders inscribed with fragments of scrolling words in a foreign language that Adam copied in a notebook and later found out were Spanish (and also nonsensical: *dream* and *madman*). They met a team of scientists who were taking rock samples not far from where Adam lived; they wanted to build a mine, but they did not say what kind. One of them, an American, gave Neng and Adam three dollars each and an old T-shirt that said BERKELEY. Neng said Adam should have the T-shirt. She didn't want it; she was happy enough as it was, not because of the money, but because her father would finally, FINALLY! have a job in this mine. That was what she kept repeating to Adam as they cycled home. She turned around and made funny faces at him, the bike zigzagging along the road. Above them, a flock of birds winged their way slowly southward, small, black flapping triangles against the blue white sky. Maybe they were migrating to cooler climates, Adam said, to Australia, and Neng replied that he couldn't possibly know such a thing. He did not know what kind of birds they were; and he did not know either that this would be the last thing he would say to Neng.

The next day she was not waiting for him at the bend in the road, and when he got to school she was not there. He asked around and everyone said, Oh, yeah, that Madurese girl, her parents went back to Java or somewhere else, dunno, happens all the time with migrants, they weren't born here so why should they stay?

Adam continued at school; his days were not the same without Neng. His nights, which had for some time been calm and heavy with sleep, became unreliable once more. The sensation of emptiness that punctuated his slumber returned, more frequently and powerfully than before. In his sleep he felt suspended in a void, and he would wake with a start, his legs jerking madly. When he awoke in the dark, he felt as if he had dreamed about his brother, but no image of Johan ever stayed with him, and he realized that his sleep had been as dreamless as ever. He had merely imagined dreaming of Johan—a dream of a dream. He thought he had banished fear from his life, but it was clear that he had not. He would go to the window and stare out at the inky blackness, at the shapes of the trees silhouetted against the night sky, and it would calm him a little to know that he was not in his Old Life with its unknown terrors but in his New Life with its known terrors, which were far less terrible.

One morning he awoke to find a large box on his bedroom floor wrapped in colorful paper printed with a pattern of butterflies and bow ties. There were creases on the paper as if it had been left folded for a very long time.

"Happy birthday," Karl said, appearing in his doorway. Adam suddenly realized he did not know when his birthday was. At the orphanage there had been no celebrations—at least none that he could remember. "I didn't know when your birthday was so I decided that, from now on, we shall celebrate it on the anniversary of your arrival in this house." Adam had not realized that he had spent an entire year there; it seemed only minutes since he'd arrived.

"Why are you doing that?" Adam asked as Karl closed the shutters and door. It was a dull, drizzly morning, the sea mists remaining longer into the morning than usual.

"You'll see," Karl said, placing the box on Adam's bed. "Go on, open it."

Adam picked nervously at the wrapping paper until he saw a flimsy cardboard box, frayed and torn at the edges. It bore a picture of a curly-haired woman gaily spraying her underarms with deodorant. She wore bright red lipstick to go with her bright red dress and she showed off a bright red flower in her hair.

"That's just the box," Karl said, taking it from Adam. "Here, I'll show you." He reached inside and produced a glasslike object, not quite a globe. "It's a magic lantern. Let me show you how it works." He switched on the table lamp and placed the lantern on top of it. All at once the walls of Adam's bedroom faded away and suddenly he was in a forest in Europe. A thicket of pointy trees engulfed his cupboard and from the trees a handsome blond boy emerged, riding a horse that glided over yellow moors. The sunlit sky swirled over this scene, golden and streaked with fantastic clouds. There was a castle too, honey-colored, but it was sheared off by a wide arc and faded into pearly blankness.

"Sorry, that's where the disc fits into the lamp," Karl said, reaching for the lantern and fiddling with it. For a moment the hollow gloom of Adam's room returned once more but then, once Karl had adjusted the lantern, the dream resumed. A princess with pale blond hair and a blue gown stood atop the half castle, pleading with the youth to come to her.

"His name is Golo," Karl said. He was reclining on the floor, his arms folded behind his head as he stared at the magic sky. "And the lovely maiden is called Genevieve. Isn't she pretty?"

Adam nodded. He too lay down on his bed and looked at the sky. The rain drummed lightly on the roof and in the distance there was the faint rush of rough seas.

"It used to be mine," Karl said. "I was about your age, I suppose, maybe younger. We had already left Indonesia and were living in The Hague. I had trouble sleeping. Every night there was a scene. My nanny—my Dutch nanny—would come into my bedroom and put the magic lantern on for me. I loved Golo; I wanted to be him. I would lie in bed hoping my mother would come and kiss me good night. I'd imagine her saying, 'All right, my child, I'll kiss you one last time, like Genevieve, but then you must go to sleep.' She never came, but at least I had my magic lantern to make me feel better."

That night Adam ate his birthday dinner of meat loaf and fried potatoes as quickly as he could. He got into bed and turned the lights off, his room transformed once more into an enchanted forest. He thought about Neng, about the time she had tried to kiss him; he knew that she would never come back. He felt a bitter numbness that seemed familiar, as if left over from his Past Life in the orphanage, and he knew he had to blank it out before it took hold. He took a deep breath and counted slowly from one to ten. He had to eliminate this feeling from his New Life.

"Good night, my son," Karl said, opening the door and breaking up the forest. "I know you've been having a difficult time, but just remember, we're very lucky people. I hope you've had a nice birthday."

Adam nodded as Karl turned the light out. "Wait," Adam said quietly in the darkness. "What day is it today? What's my birthday?"

Karl paused at the door. "It's August seventeenth."

Later Adam would learn that August seventeenth was also Independence Day. On his birthday there would always be rousing songs on the radio as well as the president's speech, the whole of which Karl would insist they listen to. There would be red and white flags hanging from the eaves of houses, and in the evening there would be festivities in the villages—food and dancing—that continued late into the night. Before

he went to bed Adam would put on his magic lantern and stare at the
swirling scenes that he knew so well, and he would listen to the far-off
sounds of laughter and smell the faint sweetness of grilled meat and
charcoal smoke that carried on the sea breeze.

No, Adam thought: He was not *just* like the other boys.

Slow down, Johan, slow down.

They sped through the silent city, neon lights staining the night with electric temptations. *pussy cat $$$ shanghai dream copacabana fantasy girls girls girls.*

Please, Johan, slow down, Farah said. You'll kill yourself one day if you keep driving like this.

At darkened intersections he ran the lights without even looking. He never looked out for other cars, he never looked out for anything. Don't worry, he said. It's okay. It's late, there are no cars. He drove with his head held back as if blown by the wind, but there was never any wind in this city.

Shit, Bob said in the backseat, this is great. He cowered as they careered around the roundabout, the new tires of the Mercedes squeaking. Farah gripped the door tightly and said again, Please, Johan, for god's sake, but she knew that there was no use talking to him when he was in one of these moods.

Hey, Johan, hey, guys, Bob said. Let's go down to the river and see what's happening with the girls. Friday night, all the Mak Nyahs will be out. Come on, let's go.

No, Farah said. I don't want to go. Johan, please.

Come on, Sis, be a sport. Let's have some fun. What do you say, Johan? Everyone knows that those Pondans have the best tits in town. I want to see their little dresses with their asses sticking out, oh, yes sir.

Johan smiled and shrugged. Okay, why not.

They slowed to a crawl as they left the lights of the broad tarred road and turned into a narrow lane, then into another alley, then onto a long thin road that ran along the shallow muddy river that hardly seemed a river at all, just a trail of sludge between two huge mudbanks.

Kill the lights, Johan, kill the lights quick.

The Merc crept along silently, hardly a rumble from its engine. Shadows stirred in the deep canopy under the old rain trees. There were a few cars parked along the road but it was difficult to tell if anyone was in them.

Get an eyeful of that baby, Bob said, sticking his head out of the window. The girls emerged from the darkness, singly or in pairs, linking their arms as they sashayed toward the car. There were all kinds of girls—Chinese girls, Malay girls, Indian girls, and especially girls who were boys—but in the eternal nocturne of this street they were just girls.

Which ones are real, which are fake? Farah said. I can never tell.

A duh, you're really stupid, aren't you? Bob giggled. What do you mean?

I mean, which ones are really girls? Don't tell me you know which ones are, you know—

Transvestites? Johan said.

Yes, boys pretending to be girls.

Is it important? Johan laughed. He had a cold, hard laugh tonight. Farah did not like it when he got this way. Why do you need to know? Don't tell me you want some action?

You're disgusting.

Johan said, They aren't boys pretending to be girls, they're boys who *are* girls. Some of them aren't even boys anymore, they're real girls . . . just like you.

Ceh. Farah shook her head. Don't say that, they're not like me.

Wow-ee, Bob cried. Hey, girl, show us your *tetek.*

The prettiest ones are farther up, Johan said, by that Austin under the big tree.

They stopped the car. There were about a dozen girls on the street. They felt safe now, they knew this car was not a police car. A couple of them walked in front of the Merc, swinging their hips and flicking their long, glossy hair. Their calf muscles were taut and sinewy in their high heels and they swung small beaded handbags over their shoulders. Hey, boys, they cried, love your big car. Come here, boys, come and see what Mummy has for you.

Come on, Johan said and stepped out of the car.

Shit, no way—Sis, stop him! That boy is crazy!

Johan come back, come back, Farah pleaded, it's dangerous. But he was already some distance away, walking like he always did in his bright springy way with his hands in his pockets.

Johan, Farah's voice was an urgent whisper. Her footsteps in the dark: She was running. He did not look back. Ahead of him he knew there was a crumbling brick wall, just the right height to hide a couple crouching down behind it. And by this wall there would be a girl, always the same girl.

Hello, this girl said. Hello, handsome. She was not tall and not short, the same height as Johan. She had slim shoulders and sturdy hips and she never concealed her face under a thick layer of powder, not like the other girls. I haven't seen you in a while, she said, lighting a Winston. Where you been?

I've been around.

Is that your new girl?

No, that's my sis.

Pretty.

Actually, she's my adopted sister. Farah, Regina, Regina, Farah.

Hello.

Hello, Princess. Regina took a long drag of her cigarette. It glowed like a jewel for a second or two before fading again. Listen, children, nice to see you, but I have stuff to do. You know. The cops have been down here already tonight touching the girls up and taking our money, so . . .

Yeah, sure, see you around.

Who's that? Farah whispered. Oh my god, Johan. *Please* don't tell me you've been seeing prostitutes.

In the dark he made a slight movement with his shoulders, like a shrug but not quite. As they went past the Austin a girl got out of it, smoothing her hair away from her face. The bangles she wore on her wrist filled the air with a lovely metallic symphony, but the car suddenly started up and its lights filled the road with a sharp glare and suddenly there were people running for cover, dashing across the pool of light that swept along the lane before leaving it in darkness once more.

Shit, a baritone voice called out, I thought it was the cops again, now my hair's all ruined.

Hair? Call that *topi keledar hair*? Darling, it's a crash helmet, just take it off next time.

Where did you guys go? said Bob. Let's get out of here. He was quieter now, sitting with his arms folded and his hands tucked tightly under his armpits as if it were cold. I want to go home. I'm tired.

No, Johan said. Not yet. The Merc emerged from the alley and burst into life once more.

Sometime afterward, when they were still driving, they reached that moment in the night when there were no more lights on the streets and the air that came in through the windows no longer felt hot and sticky.

Johan said: Do you ever get this feeling, Farah?

What feeling?

That your life is not your own. That you can't control it.

No, what do you mean?

I mean, do you ever feel that your real life is somewhere else, that someone has stolen it and taken it to another place far away from here?

Farah looked at him and shook her head. No, Johan, Mummy says we're not allowed to talk about that. Let's go home.

No, said Johan. Anywhere but home.

In this fast young city he did not want to sleep, he did not want to stop. This was a place that had no past, only the present. What happened yesterday was just a dream; last week was forgotten, last month never existed at all. Every night was the same. Your life started afresh at six thirty, repeating itself like a clock. There was no escape. It was always like that in this city.

5

*T*he telephone stopped ringing just as Margaret opened her eyes. It had been ringing for a very long time. Her head hurt terribly. She squinted at the clock: 9:40. She could not remember the last time she had woken up so late. She was turning into a grand old white housewife, she thought to herself as she padded her way slowly to the bathroom; she wished there was a bell she could ring so that some dusky, half-dressed youth would appear bearing two aspirins on a silver tray. She had fallen asleep in the rattan armchair in the sitting room and had remained there for some time before being woken by a stiff neck. She had summoned just enough energy to stumble into her bedroom and had fallen into bed without showering, and now she felt suffocated by her own cold sweat, as if someone had coated her skin with a thin layer of wet paint.

The phone rang again as she dressed. Now that she was awake and fully conscious, the phone seemed curiously dangerous. She picked it up slowly and put it to her ear but did not say anything; she barely even breathed. There was silence, as if the person on the other end was holding their breath too, and the air in her bedroom began to feel stifling. The line clicked and went dead. "Probably just the exchange acting up again," she said aloud. The sound of her own voice reassured her, and she began humming to herself, a vacuous tune that she soon realized was the song she'd heard at the Hotel Java the night before. Somehow she knew the phone would ring again, and this time she would not be so cowardly. Dressed now, the pain in her head dull rather than stabbing, she reached for the phone as soon as its harsh drilling started up.

"*Hell*-o," she said loudly, challenging the mystery caller.

There was a half-second's pause. "Margaret?" Din's voice sounded timid, almost scared.

"Yes, hi, Din, it's Margaret here. Did you try calling me earlier? Just a second ago?"

"Um, no," he said. "Are you okay?"

"Sure," she said, sliding her feet into her shoes. She was sure it was he who had rung, it must have been. "You recovered from the horror of last night?"

"It was interesting, actually, I was thinking about it on the way home. I'm glad you took me along. Maybe we'll do it again sometime."

"Sure. Maybe."

"Are you sure everything's all right?"

"Why shouldn't it be all right?"

"Well, it's just, you're always on time, that's all. You're usually here before me, so I thought I'd ring you to see if you were okay."

"What did you think might have happened? That I fell prey to a wanton taxi driver? I just overslept, that's all."

Din did not answer for a while. Margaret imagined his inscrutable smile. "Okay, then," he said calmly. "Maybe I'll see you later."

"Yeah, maybe." She let the phone fall into its cradle with a crash and walked into the sitting room. The swirling, green faux-marble Formica tabletop was half-covered in bits of paper and photographs. Margaret had not bothered to put them back into the box that lay at the foot of the armchair. Last night, her head heavy with drink, she had wanted to look at all those dead images. She had not seen them for a very long time, and it had taken her a while even to remember where the box was. She had recovered it from the small storeroom into which she threw everything that she did not use on a daily basis, things that accumulated in layers as the years went by. And so, working her way through the archaeological dig of her life, she had found it preserved like a rare fossil in the preadult period, buried under old college textbooks but lying (more or less) on top of a box labeled CHILDHOOD IN NEW GUINEA. Once consigned to this storeroom, things rarely resurfaced; geckos laid their eggs on the spines of books and mice crawled into boxes to die. Margaret had no idea why she had spent a good hour and a half on her hands and knees, struggling with the flashlight wedged between her chin and shoulder, to free this box from its tomb of memories. She had looked at the pictures until it was very late, until she was alone in the night, when even the scooters and dogs and radios had fallen silent. She had been surprised to see how little she had changed, and had felt an unexpected surge of happiness when she recognized herself in the pictures. She had grown older, of course, but the similarities between the fifteen-year-old Margaret and the forty-something Margaret were obvious: the slight, adolescent build, the firm unfleshy arms, the hair pulled back neatly from the face, the chin raised in a perpetual challenge, the pouting smile. It was definitely Margaret.

She wondered if she would recognize the other people in the photos if she met them today. She certainly had not recognized her father when he lay on his deathbed. She had flown back to New York and driven upstate through an incipient snowstorm to be with him, kept warm only by the vestiges of the Jakarta heat. She had found him in a room that stank of disinfectant in a nursing home on the outskirts of Ithaca, his face pale and mottled, bleached of color. The few wisps of hair on his head had grown too long and fell like threads of fine white silk across the scabs on his scalp. He looked like just another old man, like the ones playing cards in the hall. He was barely sixty but the cancer had taken hold.

When he smiled he felt a terrible pain in her chest; she had never believed that sadness could be a physical sensation. During that brief weak smile, she had recognized her father, the one whose image she had always kept in her mind's eye. And she was glad when he closed his eyes again, for he became an old man once more, someone foreign whose pain too was foreign to her.

Here, in the photos, he was just as Margaret remembered him: lean and deeply tanned, barefoot and wearing a sarong, often staying in the background, ceding the spotlight to his wife. Margaret had not seen her mother for ten years and wondered if she would recognize her now.

Margaret put all the photos except one back in the box and tidied the table. She picked up the newspaper article that Bill Schneider had given her, looking at it once more under the magnifying glass. It didn't help. The picture only became fuzzier, its indistinct dots revealing no further clues. There was one white man in the crowd of twenty Indonesian ones, that was for sure. They were in a cell, or the back of a dark room. The flash of the camera had surprised a few of them; their faces were raised open-mouthed and dazed, looking straight at the viewer. The others just sat cross-legged, their heads bowed to their chests. Right at the back, the solitary white figure sat calmly with his back propped up against the wall, his head turned at an angle as if examining something on his leg. A small part of his neck was revealed, like a fragment of a precious mosaic. Margaret studied it at length; the slight curve of it was unmistakable—or was she just imagining the similarity? She had spent most of the night comparing the photo in the newspapers to her old photos but could not reach a conclusion.

The streets were already teeming by the time she stepped out into the dusty sunlight. Along the shady lanes near her house the drains were no longer overflowing but filled with shallow puddles of oily water, blocked by dams of rubbish rotting slowly in the heat. Two mangy dogs picked listlessly through the tangle of tin cans and empty sacks and vegetation as Margaret walked past a row of shops, their bamboo blinds lowered against the sun. A hundred and fifty years ago, when Dutch Batavia was at its zenith, these shops contained bags of spices and tea and fragrant wood bound for Europe, where there was no limit to their prices; this was the port from which European fantasies were stoked to frenzied extremes, but you could sense none of the past glory in the streets of Old Jakarta. The voices of prosperous merchants did not echo in the narrow lanes, the clink of gold coins had disappeared a century ago. Even in the south of the city, in the place that some people called "New" Jakarta, Margaret could see only decay. She had witnessed its growth, the simple, functional houses built seemingly overnight, stretching in rows like crops, punctuated by enclaves of big houses, where the roads suddenly widened and high cement walls hid immense Western-style mansions, the bright terra-cotta tiles on their faux-Tuscan roofs just visible above the walls. But everything aged so quickly here, Margaret thought; Jakarta had a way of dragging everything into its slimy mess, of making new things look old. Moss grew on surfaces of smooth cement; the sun and the rain wore down metal and stone and made them look dirty. In Jakarta she could never really escape the feeling of being in a slum.

She wandered into the square ringed by the last of the great buildings of old Batavia, stumbling slightly on the remnants of the cobblestones. She flagged down a jeep taxi in front of the porticoes of the once-handsome, almost-derelict old city hall, watched by a group of soldiers who huddled in the shade of a wooden lean-to, sharing a *kretek* between them. "Hey, lady, got a cigarette?" one of them shouted out without much enthusiasm, as if anticipating Margaret's cursory shake of the head. She knew he wanted Marlboros or Camels, proper cigarettes, not the cheap *kretek* he and his friends were smoking. Not long ago she'd always carried a pack of Lucky Strikes with her. You could bribe anyone with American cigarettes. That was the curious thing about the human animal, she thought: Even in times of famine they would sooner reach for luxuries than a sack of rice. A stick of tobacco laced with noxious chemicals was worth more than a meal for a child, that was why she'd always had cigarettes with her, but they had become so difficult to buy, so expensive, even for a foreigner.

The jeep jerked its way through the traffic, heading slowly south to the heart of modern Jakarta. The weather was on the turn now: The damp air of the monsoon season was beginning to blow into the city, the risk of heavy thunderstorms growing with each week. For the past few months the winds had been dry and dusty, the moisture bleached from the city, every object like tinder, ready to catch fire. Sometimes the air was so dry it was hard to believe that this city lay on the coast of a tropical island. The flimsy houses in the slums they now passed reminded Margaret of dead leaves on a bonfire, heaped up on top of one another, waiting for a single match or smoldering cigarette butt. There were always fires in the slums in the dry season, and every week for the last three months she had passed the blackened remains of houses, charred fragments of timber and corrugated iron, that just lay there, day after day, becoming part of the cityscape. And yet in a few weeks' time they would be damp and slimy from the blocked drains and the pools of stagnant gray water that collected after the rains, and Margaret would forget the desiccating heat of August. How quickly we forget, she said to herself, how quickly we forget.

"Stop here, please," she called out. The taxi shuddered to an abrupt halt outside one of the smart, modern buildings on the fringes of the newly laid out Merdeka Square. The giant rectangular box made from smooth gray concrete had shiny glass in the windows and a facade of fashionable honeycomb shapes. Air conditioners hummed faintly behind closed doors as she crossed the immense foyer, her sneakers squeaking on the shiny terrazzo floor. Behind a semicircular desk a security guard dozed in his chair, his head hanging limply to one side, his hands clutching a thin exercise book to his belly. There was no one else around; a solitary swallow fluttered aimlessly against the vaulted ceiling, desperately trying to find its way back out of the building. Margaret continued until she reached the back door, reemerging into the heat. In the shadow of the big, new building stood an older, smaller one, its timber upper floor giving it the air of a village house. There was hardly any space between the two structures—no lawn or yard, just a narrow drain. Typewriters clacked without enthusiasm in the stillness of the afternoon as Margaret went up the creaky wooden stairs. The radio was on, broadcasting one of the president's speeches—a repeat, Margaret noticed—his voice urgent, persuasive, utterly convincing. There were a few men in the room at the top of the stairs, two of them hunched over typewriters, the others napping in flimsy reclining chairs or on canvas cots. The shutters were open but here in the shadow of their enormous neighbor there was never much light, just a perpetual gloom.

"Hello, Sailor," she said.

"My dear god," one of the men said, leaning back in his chair, "it's Jakarta Jane, sweetheart of the forces. To what do we owe this most splendid honor?"

"Nothing, just thought I'd pop by to say hello," Margaret said, easing herself into a chair.

"I've never known Margaret Bates to 'pop by' to say hello. What do you want?" He had an open smile, his youthful face surprisingly creased with lines. He was a stocky man with broad, hairy forearms and thick farmer's fingers that looked thoroughly unsuited to writing or typing.

"Do I detect a note of cynicism there, Mick?"

"Not a note, a whole goddamn symphony. Rudy—get Margaret a beer, will you? And one for yourself too. In fact, one for everyone. We need no further excuse for a beer now that Margaret Bates is here."

The other man, a stout young Indonesian, retrieved three bottles of Krusovice from a fridge that stood against a bare wall like a piece of modern art. He brought one over to Margaret, bowing slightly as he did so.

"Hey, Rudy, did you know that Sukarno himself tried to get her into bed? He had such a hard-on for her."

"Do shut up, Mick." Margaret smiled and accepted the cold bottle of beer. Her headache had faded to a dull throb and she was feeling hot and dehydrated. "That was so long ago."

"Ah-ha! You admit it!"

She turned to Rudy. "Just ignore him. It's all rumors. You know what you boys are like, forever looking for scandal. Journalists will be journalists—especially if they're Australian."

Rudy shrugged his shoulders indifferently but continued looking at Margaret.

"I had another job back then, it was different. I met the president a few times at official functions," Margaret began to explain, without knowing why she felt the need to. "He seemed to like me, and he remembered me. You know what powers of memory he has. I was friendly with his staff, so journalists used to ask me to arrange appointments at the palace. All these dirty boys—"

Mick put the bottle to his lips with comic lasciviousness, his tongue curling outward.

"—started a rumor. You know the president's reputation with women. Well, just for the record, he was always very correct with me."

"Um-hmm," grunted Mick as he drank his beer.

"Very pleased to make your acquaintance anyway," Rudy said before returning to his typing.

"So what *do* you need from me this time, darling?" Mick asked.

Margaret picked up a slim, loosely bound book from Mick's desk and began flicking through it—a collection of Chairil Anwar's translations of Rilke. "Do you find him faithful to the original?"

"He's better with Gide. With Rilke it's like he's trying too hard, like he *wants* to be in tune with Rilke. There's no such clunkiness with Gide, it's like they know each other. Anwar would have been great with Rimbaud. They've so much in common—that unfettered lifestyle, don't-give-a-damn hair. . . . Shame he never discovered him. They'd have been the perfect couple."

"Bill Schneider accosted me at the Hotel Java last night."

Mick leaned back in his chair. "Damn, I thought you'd come to talk about Rilke. What the hell were you doing with that man? Bill Schneider—even the name makes me want to retch."

"He gave me this." She handed over the page she had torn from the newspaper. "Have you heard anything?"

He looked at the page briefly. "What's so special? There's a civil war brewing, darling. Commies are being arrested and killed all the time—even in godforsaken little islands. Where is Perdo? Never even heard of it."

"Look at the picture carefully. There's a European in there. Right there," she said, stabbing at a spot on the page with her finger. "That's not usual. There aren't that many foreigners hanging around in Indonesia, Mick. One of your sources must know something about this."

Mick picked up the paper and looked at it again, holding it up at an angle to catch the dim light. "Why did Bill Schneider give you this?"

Margaret shrugged. "Beats me."

"It's someone you know, isn't it?"

"Uh-uh." Margaret shook her head. "No idea who it is." She did not know why she lied.

Mick smiled as he put the bottle of beer to his mouth. "Hmmm."

"Honest," Margaret said, trying to sound bright (she was good at sounding bright, she told herself; she was even better at being flippant). She retrieved the piece of paper and refolded it neatly. "I just thought, well, this poor guy's out there, stranded, his embassy probably doesn't even know. He's about to be flung in jail or even worse, a shallow grave along with lots of Communists. I guess Schneider just thought that with the contacts I have—well, used to have—I might be able to do something. But I can't. It's not the same anymore."

Mick did not reply; a moment of silence passed between them, the staccato tapping of Rudy's typewriter the only noise in the airless morning. Margaret looked down at the folded piece of paper in her lap. The newsprint was blurring and the paper itself was becoming oily and limp from the humidity and the moisture on her fingertips. She wanted to reach for her bottle of beer, but suddenly the simple act of stretching out for it seemed impossibly difficult. Her head began to hurt again, the heavy numbness giving way once more to waves of stabbing pain in her temples. "I mean," she said at last, quietly, "I just don't get mixed up in that kind of thing anymore."

Mick smiled and said, "Your beer's getting warm."

"Please, Mick, can you help me? I need to find this man. I feel I need to do something."

"Dear old Margaret, always the do-gooder." He frowned and ran both hands through his dark wavy hair, rubbing his scalp as if he had an itch. "I don't know, it's getting difficult for our guys to gather information. Even our local fixers get in trouble with the army. There are soldiers everywhere, looking for trouble. Worst thing is that we don't have enough cash to bribe everyone. We haven't got enough money coming through from the U.S. channels. CBS doesn't use me anymore; the BBC's gone silent. ARTC are the only ones coming up with the goods for me right now. I just don't know, Margaret."

"Please."

Mick sighed.

"For old times?"

"We never had any old times, you heartbreaker."

She stood up and tried hard to smile. "Oh, we would have gotten married and had twelve kids, if only you didn't"—she mouthed—"like *boys.*"

"Oh, you wound me. I die, I faint, I fail."

"Truth hurts. Call me."

She made her way slowly back through the adjacent building. There were more people around now, neatly dressed office workers carrying piles of papers as they walked unhurriedly across the lobby of the building. They glanced at Margaret with sleepy, bloodshot eyes. Some of the women were wearing the *jilbab,* their heads covered in scarves that came down to their waists, shrouding their slight torsos and revealing only their calm, powdered faces. Margaret became aware that the squeaking of her sneakers was the only noise she could hear echoing in the cool emptiness of the space. She could hear no one else's footsteps, and even the distant drone of the air-conditioning had fallen silent.

Outside, the city was white and dusty with heat. She put on her sunglasses and began to walk. "Hey, lady," men called out, ringing the bells of their *becaks* to get her attention. She moved away, ignoring them. She wanted to walk; she wanted to move her body and clear her mind and not succumb to this immovable pain in her head. She continued past the dirty white facade of the Catholic cathedral, its spires rising forlornly into the sky. There was a thin patch of fresh whitewash on the walls next to the entrance, but she could still read the messy red graffiti underneath: CRUSH CHRISTIAN IMPERIALISTS.

"Hey, lady, *hey,*" the *becak* drivers called. "Hey, pretty lady. *Oy!*" A group of three or four of them followed her in their shaded rickshaws, shouting incessantly. Suddenly their cries were all she could hear. The sound of the cars and the buses and scooters faded into a vague, distant roar, like the sound of the sea as you approach the coast but cannot yet see the water. She had to get away from these men, she thought, and crossed the road, wading calmly into the traffic, picking her way westward to the barren expanse of Merdeka Square. She headed toward the construction site of the soon-to-be National Monument. The gigantic column was pushing slowly into the sky, its thick base shrouded in scaffolding. Monstrous pieces of machinery lay scattered around it, silent and unused like ruins of a lost civilization. The earth in the square was bare and easily turned to mud by the heavy rains of the monsoon, but now, after a few months without rain, it was crumbling to dust, and she kicked up little red clouds as she walked briskly along in the heavy heat. It felt like a desert here, Margaret thought, uninhabitable by man.

She continued briskly, feeling the heat on her head. Stupid to come out without a hat, but she was not a delicate white flower that wilted under the sun. She marched on through this deserted island in the middle of the swirling city, trying to ignore her headache. A mangy dog trotted alongside her for a few moments and then sloped off to find shelter. In the distance, in the meager shade of a spindly acacia, she noticed two boys, shirtless, their backs propped up against the tree trunk. She was not in the mood for a hassle, but a quick glance confirmed that there was nowhere to go: All around her there was just a great emptiness with no pathways to divert her trajectory, no cover, no excuse to change direction. Besides, she thought, if she changed tack now they would spot her and know that she was avoiding them, and then they would come after her. She knew this for certain; she had lived here so long and knew these people so well that she could predict what would happen. The best thing to do was to carry on as if they were not there. They might be too lazy or tired to harass her. They were just kids: What could they do? In any case she must show that she was not afraid.

"Hey, cutey," they shouted as she went past. She noticed at once that they did not call her Auntie or Mother or any other respectful term by which she was often addressed by young men. She should have been flattered but wasn't; she carried on briskly. Instantly, they were at her side, flanking her as she lengthened her stride. Their frames were slight, even fragile at first glance, yet Margaret saw that they had the expressions and wiry musculature of older boys. Quickly she determined their age: fourteen or fifteen, old enough to be dangerous.

"Hey—Dutch? British? American? Give us money, U.S. dollars." They spoke with the rough accents of the Bimanese or Sasaks; these boys were from the outer islands, not Jakarta.

She continued looking straight ahead. "I don't have any money with me. If I did I would give you some, but I don't. Now go away, leave me alone."

Thrown by her fluency in Indonesian, they were quiet for a moment. "One dollar," one of them said, holding up his index finger. "Just one dollar."

"No."

"Okay, *rupiah*. You have *rupiah*."

"I told you, I have no money." They were still a long way from the edge of the square, a long way from the sea of traffic in the distance.

The first boy stepped in front of her and stopped dead. "You're lying."

He stood very close to her, looking straight into her face. He had a scar running across his forehead, a purple white streak against the almost iridescent bronze of his skin. The pungent odor of his sweat filled Margaret's nostrils and she could almost feel the sticky heat from his body. She looked him straight in the eye and was glad for the extra protection of her sunglasses. "I am telling you to leave me alone."

His face broke into an ugly sneer, his lips parting to reveal surprisingly strong white teeth. "Why?"

"Because I say so."

"So what? Give me *rupiah*."

"No."

Out of the corner of her eye she saw another three or four youths jogging toward them, street kids, just like these two, shirtless and barefoot. She moved to one side and resumed walking, faster now: She had to get to the edge of the square.

There were bodies around her, but she kept striving for the road, for the noise of the traffic. Someone reached out and touched her, a hot clammy hand on her bare forearm. Don't run, she told herself, don't run. There was a tug at her shirt, then a pinch on the side of her stomach. She broke into a run, kicking up a cloud of dust. The low roar of the traffic grew louder and she heard someone shout out behind her, a single sharp adolescent's cry, but she did not turn back until she had reached the side of the great wide road with the comforting cacophony before her. She was breathing hard: She could not remember the last time she had had to run. She hurried across the road, enjoying the angry beeping of the scooters, and when she reached the other side she looked across at the square. Suddenly it seemed far away and unthreatening, shrouded in a veil of dust.

She blinked. The sun had begun to fall from its midday peak, the light becoming silvery and blurred through the thick haze of exhaust fumes and dust. The shapes of the boys in the distance shimmered in the heat, floating, it seemed, on a watery surface. "Margaret Bates," she said aloud, wanting to hear her voice: It sounded hoarse and slightly shaky. "Pull yourself together. Right now." It was nothing serious, she told herself. You let your guard down for a second and when you do that in a city like Jakarta you'll get into scrapes, Margaret Bates, you know that full well. It's no big deal.

They were just boys, just boys.

She continued walking for a few hundred yards until she reached an unkempt lawn that lay like a haphazardly placed rug in front of a large, handsome villa. The white paint of the house had faded to a dirty gray; the columns that divided its facade into neat squares were carved with graffiti, and swiftlets nested in the eaves. Shaded by rain trees, the building felt ancient and damp, and the cool darkness of its deep verandas instantly made Margaret feel better.

"Good afternoon," the woman at the reception desk said to her, standing up quickly as if she recognized Margaret, as if she had been expecting her.

"I was wondering if I could look through the old issues of whatever newspapers you have—not that old, in fact, quite recent."

"Of course," the woman said. She wore a neat beige knee-length skirt and a white blouse. Pinned on her shirt was a plastic brooch of a bumblebee with a smiley face, and in her perfectly straight hair there was a headband of the same yellow as the bumblebee's cheerful cheeks. "This way, please."

Margaret followed her into a large somber room that smelled of camphor and damp wood. No one else was in the reading room, and most of the bookshelves were empty, or else stacked with nondescript cardboard boxes. There were no windows on the ground floor; above them was a narrow gallery decorated with cheap modern oil paintings of cockfights and buffaloes and paddy fields. The arched windows of the gallery were dirty and stained and panels of glass were missing here and there.

"It is all ready for you, over there," the woman said, pointing at a recess at the far end of the room.

"But I need something quite specific," Margaret said.

The woman smiled a broad toothy smile that looked unnervingly like the bumblebee's. "You will find it all there."

The alcove was in fact larger than she had thought, and dominated by a table on top of which various newspapers had been arranged in neat piles: the *Harian Rakyat, Indonesia Raya, Sinar Harapan.* It looked as if they had been specially laid out in the hope that she would come along and consult them. She settled down to a pile of *Harian Rakyat* from the midfifties. Ten years did not seem like such a long time and yet the font and indeed the writing style seemed archaic to her, so innocent and free. The pages were brittle and yellowed and foxed by the humidity, and the few pictures that appeared in them were as blurred as Impressionist paintings. She squinted in the dim light: Maybe she needed glasses. Every time she came upon an article on the repatriation of Dutch citizens she paused, searching for names or faces. She had no idea which names or faces she was looking for, but she knew that sooner or later she would come across something that would help her.

"Here you are, madam." Margaret looked up and saw the bumblebee smiling at her. The woman put a glass of almost fluorescent iced syrup on the table next to Margaret and went away again. Margaret hesitated, but she was suddenly very thirsty. She sipped it cautiously at first, and, finding it not as sweet as it looked, finished it in a few gulps. She let a piece of ice slip into her mouth and sucked on it as she continued looking through the newspapers, her tongue feeling pleasantly numb. She worked her way briskly through each pile, pausing occasionally.

REPATRIATION CONTINUES

JAKARTA, 6 December 1950—The repatriation of Dutch families from Indonesia is continuing in earnest. Numbers of Dutch nationals leaving Indonesia are estimated to be on the increase. Today a special KLM flight left from Halim Perdana Kusumah airport filled with the latest families departing for the Netherlands. Most of them are happy to be leaving Indonesia, just as we are that they are leaving. Photo: Mother and child wait to board plane. Isn't that a cute Teddy Bear! Don't cry, Teddy Bear!

REVOLT IN AMBON

AMBON, 16 January 1951—Following the disbanding of the colonial army in July last year, a small number of former soldiers have refused to join the new armed forces of Indonesia. It is estimated that no more than 40 of these traitors have turned down the chance to participate in President Sukarno's building of the great Republic of Indonesia and arrangements have been made to ship them away to the Netherlands. "I have to leave my family behind and I will be very lonely in the Netherlands, but I have no future in Indonesia," says one of these traitors whom we will only call Tomy. To Tomy and his friends we say, Good Riddance!

DEATH IN THE PLANTATIONS

Special Report by Affandi Suprianto

NUSA PERDO, 2 December 1953—In this little-known corner of Indonesia a war is being fought to rid the country of the last vestiges of Dutch colonialism. On a 200-hectare Kayuputih plantation . . . a battle that symbolizes the hardship of ordinary Indonesians . . . neoslavery and oppression . . . Following the death of his daughter Santi, aged 4, plantation worker Adrus Utina . . . concession-owner Joos van Eerde . . . funeral costs . . . pleas unanswered . . . misunderstanding . . . subsequent dismissal . . . fellow workers protested . . . all rewarded with dismissal . . . burning of warehouses . . . accidental shooting . . . ultimatum . . . following morning the van Eerde family fled the compound . . . plantation under the control of the workers' co-operative . . . revolution beginning even in outlying islands . . .

MY WONDERFUL LIFE:
Renowned Artist Jos Smit Talks About Heartache and Happiness

BALI, 19 January 1957—He has had successful exhibitions in Sumatra and his beloved Bandung, and his reputation is now sky-high. Collectors of his work are said to include the president himself, but acclaimed artist Jos Smit's career would never have begun if he had not come to Indonesia. Now settled in Bali, he is convinced that he has found his spiritual home. "I suppose for me it is what Tahiti was to Gauguin—beautiful colors and light, not like the gray gray gray of Holland. . . . Tradition of painting . . . many famous Westerners, Spies and Bonnet, whom everyone knows but other minor figures like Karl de Willigen too." As for his nationality, he is utterly sure that he made the right choice, even though he sometimes feels sad for the loss of friends. "I took an Indonesian passport as soon as I could, in 1950. All other Dutch Indonesians should have done the same but they didn't have the courage. I had no hesitation. For nearly ten years I have only spoken Bahasa Indonesia. I can't even speak Dutch anymore! The only regret I have is that sometimes I speak to people and I can see in their eyes that they think I'm Dutch, not Indonesian." When asked about other former Dutch contacts who might still be in Indonesia, such as de Willigen, he says, "I have had no contact with them for years. They are probably all back in Holland, or else dead."

UNITED STATES PEACE PROGRAMME—
Aid Package for Indonesian Army

JAKARTA, 6 September 1958—Photo: President Sukarno attends reception at U.S. Embassy in Jakarta (L–R, the president, Ambassador Howard P. Jones, General Nasution).

Margaret examined the hazy image. In the background there hovered a number of people, including the unmistakable figure of Bill Schneider, his already thinning hair neatly combed, eyes alert, watching every detail. He looked exactly the same as he did today; clearly life in the tropics suited him.

She rubbed her eyes. It was getting late, the room darkening quickly in the blue twilight. She rearranged the newspapers haphazardly and went to find the librarian. The reception desk was empty, cleared completely of papers and books. "Hello," Margaret called, but no one answered. The swiftlets that nested in the eaves of the roof were coming alive in the gathering dusk, fluttering from their nests in search of insects. Margaret left the building and began the long walk home. Her head no longer hurt and she felt ready to face the city.

She walked through the narrow alleys of Glodok, the air filled with the aroma of incense and cooking and blocked drains: a powerful, even heady combination. Never go there at night, foreigners cautioned, but Margaret always found it pleasant, especially in the evenings. The ceaseless sounds of human industry—the clatter of pans and dishes, the dull thud of sacks unloading from lorries, the indistinct clinking of hardware—comforted her, for in the half darkness it was easy to imagine that here, in this warren of streets, the city had not changed in two hundred years. Trapped in the maze of dead ends and unnamed streets, she could not see tower blocks or concrete monuments or glass statues; and under the cover of night the decay of the buildings around her became less noticeable, making the city seem gentler, more human.

Farther north the old square was quiet and empty now, the colonnades of the great buildings filled with a deep gloom. The soldiers she had seen earlier were gone, replaced by people trying to find a place to sleep. Suddenly she was eager to get home and glad she was not far. She longed for a cold shower, a modern American one with powerful jets of water that would strip the dust and grime from her hair and face and make her skin tingle when she stepped into it, but instead she knew that she would have to stand under the dribble of her makeshift shower that consisted of a hose and a watering can. The water would be tepid, heated in its thin pipe by the sun, but still, it would be good enough. And then she would have a whiskey, a strong one, and then she would fall asleep and forget about today, about everything.

She hurried along the final stretch until she reached the low wooden gate in front of her house. She could hear the distant ringing of her telephone as she fumbled in the dark for her keys, running across the yard. It was not until she was almost at the front door that she realized there was someone there, a body slumped on the steps. It was a boy, a teenager, crouched over in an almost fetal position. Margaret got closer and saw that he was asleep. Disturbed by the insistent ring of the telephone, he began to stir. He shifted uncomfortably; across his white T-shirt the word BERKELEY was emblazoned in large letters. Though closed, his eyelids trembled lightly, rapidly, as if troubled by dreams.

6

*O*ne day, not long after he turned thirteen, Adam ran away from home. He woke up that morning and decided he would look for his mother.

For some weeks before this he had been feeling strange, not at all himself. He would be agitated by the smallest thing: the mewing of the fat white cat outside his window, or the squeaking of his bed frame every time he turned over on the too-thin mattress, or his closet door that never closed properly—things he would not normally have noticed. He was irritated by Karl too—by his uneven club-footed gait, by the pinky whiteness of his skin, which seemed obtrusive against the dull green landscape, and, above all, by the way Karl sometimes mumbled to himself: indistinct words in an indistinct language under his breath without even realizing he was doing it. "Was I talking to myself again?" Karl would say, clearing his throat and attempting to laugh whenever he noticed Adam glaring at him. "Just a silly poem I remember from a long time ago." But it did not matter what he said, for Adam would try to ignore him, but as soon as the dreadful half whisper started, Adam felt a curious sensation in his head, a pinprick that welled up quickly into a hot, almost burning feeling that filled his skull, pressing especially insistently behind his eye sockets. He would no longer be able to read or concentrate on what he was doing and would be so overcome by this pressure in his head that he would have to retreat to his bedroom. There, on his bed with his pillow over his face, he would still hear Karl's voice.

As if guilty by association, Karl's music soon began to annoy Adam too. It made no difference what it was: The moment Karl moved toward the record player, Adam's back would stiffen. Violins that had previously thrilled him now sounded harsh and screeching; operatic voices, amusing before, were suddenly ridiculous. Adam took to leaving the house altogether. Heading for the sea, he would clamber over the rocks and make his way as far up the shoreline as possible until even the faintest strains of Karl's dying heroines were drowned out by the hush of the waves. One or two outrigger canoes would be floating on the steel blue sea, their sails trembling gently in the breeze; small nets would be flung from the boats, the fishermen hauling in meager catches of mackerel and skipjack and anchovies. Adam would sit watching until his head felt clear and calm once more, the anger draining from his body.

"What's wrong with you? Why are you so angry?" Karl called out after him the first time he got up and left the room, mid-aria, and ran down to the sea. Until this moment, facing this thing that filled his head—anger beginning his New Life with Karl—Adam had never truly known what it was to feel angry. He wondered whether this anger meant that he was somehow changing, and if so, how. He would lie awake in bed thinking, Why am I angry? and, finding no answer, would become angrier still.

At school he suddenly became conscious of what he was: an orphan. He had never been aware of this status, for many of his classmates seemed to be orphans too. Every so often someone would drop out of school to work in the rice fields or help with the nets, and Adam would learn that their father had drowned at sea or their mother had died in childbirth; now they were an orphan. On this island it seemed entirely normal to have lost at least one parent. But one day they had a new teacher, a young Sasak who had studied at the Universiteit van Indonesië. He taught them the difference between orphans who had lost one parent and those who had lost both. There was a word that distinguished the two: *piatu*. It was important to be precise with our Indonesian language, the teacher said; we have to use it carefully and with pride. This revelation troubled Adam greatly. Had he been orphaned once or twice? Was he a *true* orphan, more pitiful than the others? He went home and consulted Karl's dictionary, kept on the highest, dustiest shelves like some forgotten, forbidden relic. Perhaps he would be less of an orphan in Dutch. He would discover that in every language but his own he would be an ordinary, unremarkable orphan. He remembered the Dutch word for *orphan* and found it quickly, but the definition was full of words he did not understand and left him more frustrated than ever.

One evening, just before dinner, Karl put on some music—a *Keroncong* song's repetitive stringy notes. They sat down to their meal: overcooked mutton curry and rice.

"Not hungry, Son?"

Adam did not answer; he did not even bother to shake his head. With his spoon he built mounds of rice on his plate and then mashed them into the shallow pool of curry before rebuilding and remashing them. The edge of his plate was decorated with faded purple flowers whose stems disappeared into the brown swamp that Adam had created.

"Adam," Karl said, "please don't play with your food. A lot of people on this island are surviving on one meal every three days, and I mean one meal of rice mixed with tapioca."

Adam dabbed at the curry. He found a morsel of meat and tried to cut it using the side of his spoon, but the mutton was tough, full of tendons.

"Use a knife, Adam, you're making a mess."

Adam went to the kitchen and returned with a blunt butter knife. He began to saw at the piece of mutton listlessly, as if he had already given up.

"Please," Karl said, "don't hold your knife like that. Put it between your thumb and forefinger—you're not holding a pencil."

Adam looked straight ahead, avoiding Karl's gaze and glaring instead at the piano. Then he smacked the knife down on the table, catching the side of his plate and upending a thick glob of curry onto the tablecloth. He felt his eyes well up with hot tears, his head prickling with that burning sensation that he now knew to be anger; and this time the anger seeped downward too, filling his chest and belly.

"Don't you leave the table, Adam," Karl said, his voice still calm. "You're going to stay here and finish the meal that you are lucky to have. If there is something you are not happy about, say it—but don't you dare leave food on the table."

Adam had already risen, his chair pushed back, his hands clutching the side of the table. He remained in this state of limbo for some time, making no attempt to wipe away the thick streams of tears flowing down his cheeks.

"I want to know," he said at last. "I want to know about my family."

Karl sighed. He placed his fork gently on the edge of his plate and then leaned forward, resting his elbows on the table. He held up his hands and looked at his palms, intently, as if trying to decipher the secrets of his own life. He lowered his face into his hands and sighed again. "I found you at the orphanage, that's all. You know the whole story. There's nothing more to tell."

Adam looked away from Karl. "Everyone has a history, you told me that yourself. I want to know about my life—my *real* life."

"But this," Karl said, gesturing weakly with both hands at the space around him, "*this* is your life. Isn't this enough?"

There was no breeze that evening. The rose-colored lace curtains over the always-open windows did not stir. Adam stared at their pattern of chrysanthemums and palm leaves. The room suddenly felt airless and utterly still.

"Your mother was not local." Karl spoke in a measured monotone, as if he had rehearsed saying these words a thousand times before. "Some people said they had seen a fair-skinned woman in the village the day before you were found. She had the complexion of a Sumatran or a Malay and she spoke differently, with a big-city accent—Jakarta, some people thought, but no one was sure; it was difficult to understand what she was saying. Someone asked her where she had come from and she said, 'From a place far away.' She asked directions to the orphanage. She had a baby. It was so silent and still that some people thought it was dead. There was a toddler too, a little boy with glassy eyes that never blinked. The villagers saw the woman walking along the paths leading out to the hills, along the rice fields that were very green that year. The next day she was gone and there were two new children at the orphanage. This is all I know."

Adam noticed that he had, quite suddenly, become curiously clear-headed and calm. His breathing had slowed considerably. He wondered why he could not react more powerfully to what he had just heard—it did not seem like a revelation but a mere affirmation of something he already knew; it confused him that he should feel soothed, not agitated, by this news.

"So she went back to Jakarta," he said eventually.

"I haven't a clue. She could just as well have been from Surabaya or Medan or even Singapore. This is what they told me when I went to the orphanage. They mentioned nothing else—no father, nothing." Karl reached across and laid his hand on Adam's arm; Adam felt it on his skin, cold and clammy and heavy. "Son, please believe me, that is all I know."

"What about," Adam said, hesitating, "what about my brother?"

"They say he was taken somewhere far away—Kuala Lumpur, they thought. The people who adopted him did not want to say where they were taking him."

Adam looked at Karl's furrowed brow and tired, red eyes. He moved from the table and felt Karl's grip on his arm loosen and fall away limply. Karl remained at the table staring blankly at the remnants of their dinner, which lay on the chipped china plates, illuminated by the stark light of the single bulb hanging low over the table. It was as if they both knew that by the next morning Adam would be gone, and there was nothing Karl could do to stop him.

The idea of Jakarta or any other big city held no terror for Adam. For several weeks now he had been reconstructing his own metropolis, rebuilding it in his mind as he went about his daily chores. While sweeping the yard he summoned a vast flat plain circled by distant hills; while feeding the chickens he painted an aquamarine sky, troubled by rich rain clouds. After dinner he would hurry to bed, longing for that intense, magical hour when he could return to the focal point of his Jerusalem: a neat modern bungalow with whitewashed brick walls, a roof of red clay tiles and a compound filled with plants in pots. This was the house where his mother lived. There were a few cats—sleek blue gray ones—which his mother would pick up now and then and caress. There was a child too—his brother, Johan—but it was more difficult for Adam to picture this boy, who resisted Adam's attempts to bring him to life and so remained consigned to the shadows. Adam concentrated instead on constructing the streets around his mother's house. They were clean and modest, busy with scooters and *becaks* and bicycles, lined with houses like his mother's, simple and unadorned, lived in by decent people; but beyond this unsullied heart the city grew darker, murky with unseen danger. There were wide avenues that stretched into the distance, running into nothingness; there were great silvery buildings full of people doing things that Adam could not comprehend; there were areas of brilliant colorful light and slums where there was no light at all. Sometimes the streets were full of urchins and millionaires, sometimes there would be no one.

He imagined this city into existence, and now it seemed more tangible than the barren place where he lived. He knew he had to leave. He knew he had to find this faraway city.

The ferry was not as big as he had expected and there were many people waiting to board. The bus journey from the other side of the island had not been so bad, and he had a pocketful of dollars that he could feel pressing on his thigh. Setting off from home that morning he was so light-headed with excitement that he almost felt sick. It had been one of those rare, cool mornings when the sun kept low behind a thin veil of cloud, and there was no dust in the air, just a hint of rain. But now, standing alone at the docks, the sun high, he was hot and tired. The boat that lay just beyond the jetty seemed too flimsy to withstand the crossing to Java. It must once have been painted gaily in greens and yellows, but only a few curled flakes of paint still clung to the dark, slimy timber. Its single deck was already full of people, but the crowd nonetheless insisted its way forward, bottlenecking at the gangway. There was no shouting, no agitation, just an eerie hum of voices as people tried to force their way onto the boat. Adam could not understand. There were men reaching across from the edge of the boat to take children whose mothers held them out pleadingly, and occasionally a bag would be tossed from the crowd onto the boat, from invisible owner to unidentifiable recipient.

Adam noticed a boy standing next to him. He was older than Adam and wore a clean T-shirt with a bright orange globe on it; he did not look like the other boys hanging around the docks. "You'll want to hurry or you'll miss your chance to go across," he said.

Adam squinted, shielding his eyes from the sun.

"Everyone's leaving because of the drought. They think it's better over there, over in the big cities where there are foreigners, but it isn't.

I've come from there, I should know." He laughed as if he had told a joke and Adam could not tell if he was serious. "Oy! It's one big turd, this whole country!" he shouted in the general direction of the ferry, then giggled. "There's no escape!"

Adam began to move away.

"Hey, do you want to get on board?"

"No thanks," Adam said. "I'll come back tomorrow." He did not know how he would achieve this; he had no idea where he would sleep or eat or hide from the crowds: Tomorrow seemed an eternity away.

"It will be the same story tomorrow, my friend," the boy said, catching up with Adam, "and the day after and the day after and the day after. But listen, I can get you on board."

Adam stopped and looked at the boy. He looked normal, just like Adam. "How?"

"I know people here. People who can get you on board."

"Really?"

"Sure. All it takes is a bit of money. You have money, don't you? We don't need much—enough for a pack of cigarettes, plus something for me. Hey, fair's fair, isn't it? I'm only asking for some coffee money, nothing more."

Adam hesitated but found himself nodding.

"Don't worry, I like you. You're my newest friend! Don't give me anything now. When you get on the boat, a friend of mine will come and find you. I'll tell him you're my buddy—just give him enough cash to buy some *kretek.* How about that? My god, you're so helpless, look at you. Okay, don't worry, don't give him anything. We'll do it for free. This is your lucky day—we'll do you a favor. Just remember, if you ever get to Jakarta and make it big, remember me: Sunny." He pointed at the logo on his T-shirt. "That's me, unmissable, unforgettable, just like the sun."

"Thank you," Adam said. "But how do I get on the boat?"

"Okay," Sunny said, putting his hand around Adam's shoulders, guiding him back toward the overcrowded jetty. His voice dropped and he sounded very serious. "This is the hard part. Stand with me in the crowd, pretend we're just going to go forward. That's good, just like that. Slow down, just ease up a bit. I'm going to leave in a few seconds, but don't panic, I'll be back—that's it, just there, steady now, not too fast. Wait until I come back for you. Don't shout or draw attention to yourself, just wait here for me. Good luck."

Adam felt the hot crush of bodies around him, the sour smell of perspiration making him feel ill. The crowd did not seem to be moving forward, and Sunny had vanished. Ahead of him there was a little girl holding a painted cage with a songbird in it. She stared at Adam with limpid eyes.

"They've closed the gangway," someone said.

"Shit, it's the third day I've missed that boat."

"Can you afford to bribe someone? I can't."

"Come on, let's go. No chance today."

When the crowd had dispersed Adam remained on the docks with the nursing mothers and listless infants and old men and women who did not dare to venture too far from the jetty. Tomorrow there would be another boat, they said, as they watched the boat draw away, carving a smooth *V* in the steel blue water behind it. It seemed to move so slowly that Adam felt he could have swum after it. He waited for Sunny for a very long time before giving up.

His throat began to feel numb from thirst and he could not swallow. He walked back toward the village, beyond the coconut groves where some families had begun to build makeshift shelters from lengths of tarpaulin and driftwood they had found on the shore. He would buy some food in the village, he thought, and he would find somewhere to sleep. Someone would give him a bed. They would not refuse him, for he had money, American dollars.

He stopped at a shop that sold drinks. There were men playing cards and drinking coffee, and Adam suddenly felt very hungry. He wanted a bun, one of those sticky sweet rolls that Karl bought him whenever they went into town. Across the shop there was a brown box sitting on a counter, stained with grease that seeped through the cardboard in patches: imaginary countries on a fantastic map of the world.

"Leave those cakes alone, you little thief," someone called out.

Adam turned to face his accuser, a plump woman with a mole at the edge of her mouth that made her look as if she was smiling cheekily. "But I have money . . ." As he heard his own words, Adam realized that he sounded as if he was lying. He put his hand in his pocket: nothing. The other pocket: nothing.

"You kids are getting worse every day," the woman said, smiling her lopsided smile that was not really a smile. "You're like mangy dogs, you lot. Get lost."

Adam went back to the docks. It was turning dark and a baby was crying. It was thirsty, Adam thought, so thirsty it could not even cry properly. Its thin dry cough drifted over the sound of the water licking at the quay and the distant chugging of a tugboat. He sat against a low wall, next to an old blind woman, and pulled his knees up to his chin.

Later, in his half sleep, his imaginary city came to him once more, unbidden. He regretted having created it and wished it would go away; he wanted it to leave him tonight and every night for the rest of his life. But still those images filled his head, at once glittering and hazy. Yesterday they had made his sleep rich with excitement, today they made him feel foolish. He knew he would never find his mother. He was no longer sure he wanted to.

It was very late when Karl found him asleep at the base of the wall, his head resting sideways on the small bony pillow of his hands. He looked as if he was listening for a heartbeat deep in the ground.

"Let's go home, Son," Karl said softly.

The car had never felt so comfortable. It smelled of beeswax and Karl's clean clothes and its engine rattled in a patient monotone. Karl gave him a bottle of water and some biscuits wrapped in newspaper. They drove along darkened roads, the broad sweep of their headlights illuminating thin clouds of insects. Karl put his hand on the back of Adam's neck; it felt broad and very cool. The fresh evening air eddied through the open windows and Adam realized he was weeping.

7

*J*esus, you certainly don't eat like an Indonesian," Margaret said as she watched the boy finish his second ham sandwich. In the last hour he had consumed half a pack of processed cheese slices, plus the last of her Cracker Barrel cheddar (much-prized, carefully transported from Australia, like treasured contraband, by Mick whenever he went on home leave: It was the closest thing to real cheese they could get); a jar of peanut butter, spooned directly into his mouth like soup; a few slices of old dry ham, curling and brown at the edges; six slices of bread; a handful of raisins; and two bottles of Pepsi. She had expected him to turn his nose up at the meager contents of her refrigerator, or else pick cautiously at the curious assortment of unspicy food, but he had not hesitated. He clearly had not eaten in some time.

"Now tell me again how you got here, how you found me . . . Adam." Margaret hesitated over the name. She pronounced it in the Indonesian way, because he looked Indonesian, but she was not entirely certain which language she should be speaking, or indeed how she should be communicating with this boy. He had started by speaking to her in English, with more than a hint of a Dutch accent, which disconcerted her; but when he switched to Indonesian, which he did quite frequently and randomly, she found his accent impossible to place—a real problem, given that she usually adjusted her accent to that of the other person (that was another of her strengths: Mimicry and the Creation of Rapport; her Balinese accent was especially quick and fluent). "Just take your time—I want to know everything."

He began to speak, his mouth still full of ham sandwich.

"Please slow down," Margaret said. "You'll be sick if you continue eating like that; in fact, it's making me feel ill just watching you."

Watching him was, in fact, an unsettling but not wholly unpleasant experience. He was an interesting case study: neutral Indo-Malay features with a suggestion of Minangkabau-Malay ancestry, an essentially clear complexion darkened by the Spartan life of the southeastern islands, which made him look at once refined and rudimentary, thus proving Margaret's long-standing belief that the way we look—our basic features, stripped of clothing and mannerism—is affected by the conditions in which we live. It was as if a Sumatran nobleman had copulated with a tribeswoman from Irian, and this was the result. His hair was thick and slightly wavy, still damp from the shower she had insisted he take. It was shorn at the back and sides and combed over purposefully at the top with a side parting that looked like a fold in a great black sea, so precise she wanted to trace her finger along it.

"Please forgive me," he began and coughed—a stifled half cough, almost like punctuation, an expression of politeness. "I am very rude. I have many things to tell you. Or, more precisely, to ask you."

"Well, I'm all yours." Margaret tried to remain calm. She wanted to appear interested but not intrigued, to hide the sudden flush in her cheeks and the rapid tick-ticking in her chest that made her breathing quicken. His intonation, his choice of words (*or, more precisely*), that somewhat mannered old-world formality, the slight abruptness, the nervous cough—she had heard these words before, many years ago. She had known these unmistakable speech patterns so well and had kept their echoes somewhere in the archives of her consciousness, like old record albums she thought she had lost. But here they were, clear and true, with only the slightest distortion, as if the vinyl had warped with age—or maybe it was just her; maybe *she* had warped with age.

He began to relate to her, starkly and without any fuss, exactly what he had seen. "It has been nearly ten days since he was taken away. I do not know what they have done with him. This is him, I mean, he . . ." He put his finger on the photograph that was on the table. "This one, here."

The photo sat squarely in the middle of the smooth green Formica surface. Adam had put it there as soon as he had entered the house, and it had remained there untouched throughout his shower and his meal. Margaret had left it alone; it lay there like an unknown, perhaps dangerous object that warranted caution, even though she knew perfectly well what it was.

"Here," Adam said, sliding the photo toward her, his index finger still fixed to the same point. "This is my father."

"This one?" Margaret wondered if she sounded disingenuous to him.

"Yes. He's actually my foster father, which is why we, well, don't look alike."

"Yes, I had deduced that. What's his name again?"

"Karl de Willigen." Adam looked at her with a slight frown; he seemed anxious, a touch confused. "And this is you, isn't it?" His index finger landed on another grainy figure, standing next to Karl. They were both dressed in sarongs; she wore a floral lace tunic, he a stiff, boxy white shirt and Balinese headdress. There were others too, Europeans, all in local costume. Margaret had never seen the photo before. It looked like a terrible fancy-dress party, she thought, embarrassing and offensive; she wished it *had* been a party, which would have made it less awful. A part of her wished that she had no recollection of these people or of this time of her life, but there was no escape: Her perfect memory retained everything.

"Um-hmm, I suppose it is. The evidence is pretty unequivocal, isn't it?" Hearing Karl's name pronounced in exactly the same way he would have pronounced it—with the soft *v* and soft, breathy *g* made her head spin. She couldn't handle *that* voice coming from *this* body. She looked at Adam and smiled. "It's from a long time ago. I've changed so much; we all have. I'm sure Karl doesn't look like he does here." She laughed a breezy laugh.

"Actually, my father still resembles his image in this photo. Very much so. It's as if the years have come and gone and not changed anything."

"Really?"

"I found this picture among his things."

"He keeps a photo of us—I mean, old photos—on his desk?"

"No, it was in his boxes."

"Oh."

"In hunting for clues I violated his privacy, I know, but I was desperate. I found this picture and then also this one—" He produced another photo, this time of Margaret on her own. Her hair was short, much as it was today, only curlier and messier, neatened only slightly by a single clip that pulled the curls off her forehead. She was sitting cross-legged, all gamine elbows and knees; her cheeks were freckled from the sun, her eyes squinting as she pulled a face. She looked impossibly young and happy.

"God, I look like Anne Frank," she said.

Adam turned the picture over and showed her Karl's elegant hand-writing: *Margaret, Ubud, December 1938.* "So I searched some more, looked in his address books and old notebooks and diaries from his time in Bali. He mentions you quite frequently—"

"Really?"

"Yes, so I knew who you were: Margaret Bates."

"What does he say about me—in the diaries, I mean?"

"I didn't really read them—I wasn't prying, you understand, I was just looking for clues. I need to find my father. Well, anyway, I digress. I memorized your name and address at the university. It has taken me nearly a week to reach Jakarta. Luckily I had some money, U.S. dollars. My father had a secret hiding place in case of emergencies. He showed me where it was as soon as I got to the house. No secrets between us, he used to say. So I paid people to drive me. I bought cigarettes and liquor for truck drivers. It was hard. I did not know if you were still alive, if you even existed. Sometimes . . ." He paused and rubbed his eyes. He looked very tired all of a sudden. "Sometimes, when I was falling asleep on a bus or truck, I wondered if I had just dreamed you up." He was playing with some breadcrumbs, rolling them between his fingertips until they became tiny sticky balls. "I remembered quite clearly my father speaking of you. Over the years he mentioned this person, 'Margaret,' and even though I was small I remember thinking that I would like to meet this American woman who had been my father's friend."

Margaret reached across and patted him on his forearm, a somewhat tentative tapping rather than a soothing squeeze. The thin bones on the back of his hand twitched and for an instant Margaret thought he was going to cry. His shoulders were hunched over, making him seem rounded, even fat.

He continued staring at the table and shook his head. "I can't explain why I have just come to you, and more particularly why I have told you all this."

Margaret cleared her throat; she felt an odd sensation, something she did not immediately recognize. This boy looked so lost and forlorn and alone that she wanted to reach out to him and cradle him like an infant until he fell asleep. This is crazy, she thought: Surely it couldn't be a parental urge she was experiencing. He was an adolescent Indonesian male whom she did not know. Earlier she had noticed his eyes; shiny black beads for irises, the whites unnervingly white, not tinged with jaundice like so many other local kids. Her Ability to Analyze had deserted her and she did not know what to do with him.

"It's very late," she said at last. "You must get some sleep. We can talk some more tomorrow morning."

He nodded and then looked at her with his perfect eyes. "Will you help me get my father back?"

Margaret looked down at the rolled-up bits of breadcrumb on the table and nodded. "I want him back too."

$\mathcal{M}$argaret first fell in love with Karl roughly twelve minutes after she set eyes on him. She was fifteen, he twenty-seven. She would fall in love with him several more times over the many years that followed that initial meeting, but those occasions were less precisely recalled, blurred as they were by the various instances of falling out of love with him.

She remembers that first falling in love without any hint of sentimentality or nostalgia. It took her more than ten minutes but less than fifteen to decide that she was in love. She knew this because she checked her watch, which she had been given for her birthday that year and which she loathed, a stupid Mickey Mouse watch, his yellow gloved hands pointing the time (why on earth had her parents chosen such a thing? Didn't they know her at all?). She also knew that it was not a theatrical *coup de foudre* (the like of which she would perhaps experience later) nor indeed a surge of primitive lust, but something far more conscious and deliberate. Margaret had simply decided to fall in love. She did not tumble helplessly into schoolgirl hysterics; she experienced no shortness of breath or palpitations or any of the more vulgar symptoms often associated with falling in love. At fifteen, she was already capable of making such decisions.

They met at the local Barong dance, catching each other's eye for a brief moment, Karl acknowledging her presence with a quick, shy nod, as if deferring to a more established member of an invisible hierarchy. Margaret responded by waving from across the bare dirt clearing where the dance was to take place. She continued to observe him for the duration of the event, noticing at once that he had the look of someone who had just arrived in Bali, someone struck by all the misty-eyed beauty of this fabled Eden. The symptoms were clear: the sudden serenity of expression; the inability to speak, to express oneself adequately because one did not have the vocabulary to capture what one saw or felt; the slowed-down walk that imitated the Balinese, conscious of the lack of grace in the Western posture.

His sand-colored hair fell across his forehead and made him look adolescent, timid, and slightly lost. He sat cross-legged in the dirt, like the locals, his sarong (yes, he already had one) tucked neatly into his lap. He watched intently as the music started, piercing, discordant, eerie: notes and rhythms that could not be understood by the Western ear. There were cymbals, gongs, bells, and, most of all, the heavy drumming that surged and ebbed without pause. Fantastic figures appeared, shrieking horribly, their faces shrouded by masks inhuman and terrifying. Karl did not blink, not even once. He looked helpless, as if he had stumbled into an unknown world where nothing made sense, where he was a child once more. Margaret felt a sudden surge of something she had never felt before. Analyzing this feeling afterward, she would conclude that it was a combination of many things: feelings of superiority, of experience, of wanting to be a guide, a teacher; wanting to gather something vulnerable in her arms and nurse it to health; the urge to be physically close to something warm and clear and soft. She looked at her watch: It had been ten minutes since she had first spotted him.

The dancers, all male, clad in traditional white sarongs, began to stab at themselves with their *kiris,* some of them falling on the ground, writhing in pain; others bent over double, shivering, the wavy blades pressed firmly against their chests. Their muscles were strained, sinewy, their skin slick with sweat. Their eyes were wide and hollow and some of them were crying; as ritual dictated, they had slipped into a trance. The air was filled with tortured groans, an immense demonic anguish. Margaret giggled. Karl was perspiring intensely, his expression beginning to match that of the dancers, at once empty and furious, like a child recently woken from sleep. She wanted to hold him and stroke his hair and assure him that it was all a dream, a bad, cheap, silly dream that didn't mean anything.

At last the temple custodians began to calm the men, reviving them from their entranced battle with evil by throwing holy water over them. Bunches of smoking coconut leaves were brought and stamped on to hasten this recuperation, and after a long time the crowd began to disperse. Bodies lay on the dirt, inert as corpses, their heads cradled in the loving arms of priests or friends. Margaret made her way over to Karl. He had managed to stand up but had not moved away. He looked dazed, surveying the carnage before him.

"Was that your first time?" she said.

"What? Sorry?"

"Was that the first Barong dance you've witnessed?"

Karl looked at her uncomprehendingly. "I think I fell into a trance too."

"Oh my *god*." Margaret could not stifle a giggle. "That wasn't a real trance. They know there are foreigners here. It's never the same when there are lots of *tourists*."

"Right, sure. But . . . are there lots of Westerners here? I didn't think so. I'm not a tourist though. I was born here."

"In Bali?"

"No. Buru. I'm sure you don't even *know* where that is." His eyes were no longer glazed over, and he was smiling.

"Of course I do. It's part of the Moluccas. Just a stone's throw from New Guinea, the last island in the world, where *I* was born—on the floor of a mud hut, if you must know. I spent most of my childhood there, with the briefest of forays back to the wilderness of America, then Fiji, with a stopover in Australia, then here. You're not going to beat me when it comes to exotic origins, so just drop it."

"Oh. I see."

They started walking up the hill to the village. He had an easy, loose-limbed gait. "I left Buru when I was four. My parents went back to Holland. So I don't really know it at all."

"Can't you remember anything?"

"Just fragments here and there."

"I can remember everything—and I mean *everything*. Okay, not coming out of my mother's womb—I can't remember that—but I can remember things that happened to me when I was two or three."

He looked at her with the clearest gray green eyes she had ever seen. He was not a tall man, she remembers thinking, almost as short as she was. *"Mon Dieu,"* he said. "That's impressive."

She giggled. "Why did you say that? In French, I mean. Couldn't you have said, 'My god'?"

He shrugged and smiled, blushing a little (she thought). "I'm sorry. I lived in Paris for a number of years and things just stick in your head, I suppose. I've just come from there, so every time I open my mouth I'm still half-speaking French."

"Speech patterns do have a way of sticking to you rather quickly. What were you doing in Paris?"

"Studying. I was at L'Ecole des Beaux Arts. I'm an artist, a painter."

"Oh god, not another one."

"What do you mean?" He stopped walking, the smile vanishing from his face.

"I didn't mean anything in particular. There just seem to be an awful lot of painters here at the moment. Every other person who steps off the boat from Java seems to be an artist. They keep going on about the wonderful tropical light here, the lush vegetation, but it isn't any different in northern Australia, so why don't they go there? Because they want to paint bare-breasted women with doe-eyed expressions. Either that or they're homosexual. Lots of strong, willing boys to paint here. We're very welcoming in Bali, as I'm sure you've heard. Which camp do you belong to?"

He looked away and blushed (definitely, this time).

"Oh hell, I was just joking. Don't take me too seriously, will you?"

He struggled with the fold of his sarong, trying to tighten it around his waist. His shirt tails became caught up in the ugly knot he had made, which he now clutched in one fist. "Are there too many artists here, do you think?"

"No no no, I was just joking. Well, half-joking. There's Walter, of course, and Rudolf, and several others whom you will meet in due course. Really not that many. Here, let me help—"

"I'm fine—" He began to protest, but Margaret reached toward him with both hands and firmly took control of the errant piece of cloth, working deftly and quickly.

"Anyway," she said, "I'm sure you're better than they are. Being born in Indonesia must help. The first four years of one's life are terribly formative—with the accent on terribly. You didn't have an unhappy first four years, I hope. I did. But that's another story." Looking down, Margaret noticed his shoes. They were slim and smooth, and she realized she had never seen an expensive pair of shoes before. She imagined them in a grand shop window on a grand avenue in Paris waiting for a delicate pair of feet to slip into them. "There you are, all done."

They stopped in front of a compound of houses. "Thank you," Karl said. "This is my place. I found a room here last week." Two old women sat in the yard, waving at them, smiling toothless smiles. Karl did not make any effort to invite Margaret to inspect and approve his lodgings, which she had expected, given that she knew about these things and he didn't.

"Good. Is it nice?"

"Yes, I think so."

"You think so? Great." Margaret felt momentarily irked by his smugness. How would he, having just come from Paris of all places, know if a village house in Bali was "nice"?

"Good-bye, then."

"As I said earlier, if you want to see real trances you should come up to where we live. What you saw today was just . . . entertainment."

"Certainly," he said, sounding uncertain, and began to retreat into the safety of his compound. "I'm very much looking forward to discovering this country" (another little hesitation), "or, more precisely, to seeing you again." As he crossed the yard in his beautiful shoes he looked impossibly dainty and small. When he was halfway across he turned to wave at Margaret, his fine hand waving tentatively, once, twice, as if he had only just learned to bid good-bye to another person. He looked like a child, Margaret thought, just like a child.

· 9 ·

*P*lease say yes, Mick, I really do need your help this time."

There was a deep sigh on the other end of the phone, followed by a pause that lasted just half a second too long, and which Margaret knew instantly signaled the end of his resistance.

"Come on, Mick, it's for me. You once said I'm the only person you'd ever trust completely, and I said the same—well, almost the same. Of course that was back when you were still in love with me, before you discovered—"

"—I was never *in love* with you."

"You know I wouldn't ask unless it was something important, something big. Besides, I don't have anyone else I can turn to."

"I suppose I can't resist a *cri de coeur* like that."

"I knew you couldn't. Come as soon as you can."

Margaret put the phone down and went back to the sitting room where Adam remained asleep on the cane sofa, one arm dangling limply, its curled fingertips almost touching the floor. With the other arm he had gathered a cushion to his face to smother it from the late-morning light filtering through the too-thin curtains. Margaret noted with mild dismay the fading colors on the cheap nylon. The printed peonies had been bleached from deep red to a watercolor pink and there were ugly gray lines of dirt marking the folds. Adam had un-packed the contents of his cloth bag and laid them out in a small pyra-mid on a chair: a pile of clothes, neatly folded; a map; a book called *Diving to Adventure*; a frayed old notebook, held together by a single rubber band; a few biscuits in a plastic bag, most of which had been crushed to crumbs. His BERKELEY T-shirt hung separately on the arm of the chair, as if waiting for her to take it. She looked at it for a while and then reached out for it. Maybe this was what mothers were meant to do, Margaret thought, as she felt a funny twinge in her chest. She certainly could not recall her own mother doing any washing—unless she counted rinsing a sarong in a jungle stream as washing. Life with her parents had been resolutely Primitive, an existence that called for the lowest levels of hygiene and the most basic sanitary conditions, even if more modern amenities existed ("the point of studying such cultures," Margaret's mother would say, "is to experience their lives *completely*"). Occasionally, during sojourns in Asian cities, they would bemoan the lack of Western infrastructure—tarmac on roads, running water, electricity, stoves that didn't burn the house down—but it was more a reaction against being taken out of the jungle and thrust into contact with civilization. When, finally, they did move back to the States, they did not know what to do with these bizarre contraptions. There was a Bendix in their house in Ithaca, a hulking machine with a power-wringer, but Margaret's mother chose never to touch it; instead she employed a neighbor's son to take their dirty clothes to the Chinese laundry and their clothes would return some days later, immaculately pressed and folded. It reminded them of their Primitive Existence, Margaret reasoned: They may have lost the jungle but at least they still had Asians to carry out the most basic chores for them.

"Um, Adam," she said, reaching out and touching his shoulder, "I've got to go out soon."

When he opened his eyes he stared at her as if he had been waiting for her to wake him, but his eyes were still curiously blank, as if the world had not yet filled his consciousness.

He blinked. "I'll come with you."

"No, you can't."

"Why not?" He rose and ran his fingers briskly through his hair to smooth it down. He looked around for his T-shirt before reaching for the pile of clothes, all the time holding the thin sheet to his chest.

It made her strangely happy to see him rested; a pleasant smile had settled on his face, making him look younger than he was; it was as though he felt safe in her house, she thought, as though he trusted her. "I'm sorry, you can't come with me because I'm going to the U.S. Embassy to try and get some information on your father. They're quite touchy at the moment about random Indonesians breezing through their gates. And this T-shirt is going to be washed." She held it hanging from one finger like a rag. "I won't be long. There should be some food in the kitchen—help yourself to anything. Just promise me you won't leave the house."

A CROWD OF PROTESTORS had gathered outside the embassy, about two hundred students spread out on the edge of the square, spilling into the road. They squatted beside sagging banners—CRUSH MALAYSIA, DOWN WITH WESTERN IMPERIALISTS—smoking cigarettes and chatting placidly. They wore pieces of cloth tied in bands around their heads and some of the boys were bare-chested. A few of them began to chant something, standing up and waving long, thin sticks, attempting to rouse the others; but it was too hot and they were too tired, and the incipient revolt quickly died down.

"Very tedious, this anti-Malaysian nonsense," Margaret said as they drove through the gates. "Surely they can't keep it up much longer."

"You underestimate Sukarno," Mick said. He had developed a new way of speaking that Margaret had only recently noticed, his lips pressed tightly together, never opening very much, as if he was gripping a cigarette between them. He had quit smoking a year ago, he said, but it was as if his lips still retained their shape. "This *Konfrontasi* thing's become an obsession, something absolutely essential to his existence. The choice of the word is telling, I think: He wants to *confront* the whole world, particularly Malaysia. He really hates all that it represents—I think he actually dislikes the idea of a small neighboring country slipping relatively painlessly into independence and becoming rich while his own country is in a mess."

"So you don't think it's all part of his game, then? I thought it was just silliness, you know, this Asian loss of face. He's pissed off that the Malaysians don't want to join him in whatever he's doing, and now he's just using them to further his—well, whatever he does."

"Oh, everything's a game with him, but it's beginning to feel a bit out of control. Things are accelerating, and I'm not sure he's got a firm grip on all the bits that are whizzing around him. This Malaysia thing is pushing him further and further toward communism, and that pisses the Americans off even more. What began as just a flirtation with the

Soviets and the PKI quickly became a hand job in the backseat of the car, and now it's threatening to become a full-blown marriage, which I'm not sure he wants."

"I hope your award-winning reports aren't quite so imaginatively illustrated."

"You know what I mean." He smiled. "It's as if Sukarno's been driving a big fat fast car, but now it's careering out of control."

Bill Schneider was waiting for them in his office. There was a photo of two children on his desk, a boy and a girl of about eight and six respectively, the boy wearing a baseball glove. Behind them was a lawn and a short section of white garden hose snaking its way toward the girl's shoe; there was a suggestion of a clapboard house in the background.

"My kids," he said, noticing Margaret looking at the photo. "They're back in the States. Great, aren't they?"

"Yes, they look very healthy. How's your wife?"

"My ex-wife is fine. We communicate infrequently, mainly through our lawyers."

"Shame. I think I remember her at Cornell—nice girl. From Vermont, isn't she?"

Bill nodded. "Good memory. That was a long time ago . . . I'm glad you decided to come, Margaret. It's nice to have you back."

"Back where?"

He shrugged and reached for the photo of his children, adjusting it minutely as if it were a valuable painting in a museum. "Back in the fold."

"Listen, I haven't come here because I've suddenly decided that you're my best friend. You know precisely why I came. A friend of ours has gone missing, and I need your help in finding him."

"I see," he said, smiling. He picked up an ashtray and moved it to another part of the desk, regarding it with the air of someone who had just rearranged the furniture in their living room. "A friend."

"Bill, we've had our differences over the years, but we've always worked something out. I'm not the easiest of people—I'm the first to admit that—and I know I often say things that maybe I shouldn't, but I know that you're essentially a good guy trying to do good things."

"Am I?"

"Yes, I believe so. Despite that repugnant facade."

Bill Schneider smiled and shifted his ashtray again, testing it in a new position. "This friend of yours, he isn't American, is he?"

"No, Dutch. Dutch-Indonesian, to be precise. I think you already know that."

"That's a problem, Margaret, because I can only look after the interests of U.S. citizens. Anyone else is beyond our jurisdiction. Our policy is not to get mixed up with everyone else's affairs."

Margaret let out a half snort, half laugh. "Please don't speak to me as if I'm an idiot. Your job is based entirely on getting mixed up in other people's affairs."

Mick reached over and touched her arm lightly. "Calm down," he said softly.

"Drink, anyone?" Bill got up and went to a cupboard. He opened it with a key to reveal a small icebox.

"Great, I'll have a beer, thanks," Mick said breezily.

"Hemlock, please," Margaret said.

Bill set three bottles of Budweiser on the desk, placing them neatly on rattan coasters. "Would you like to hear a story?" he said.

Margaret rolled her eyes. "Not really, but you're going to tell us anyway."

"Just indulge me." He smiled and took a sip of his beer. The air conditioner began to rattle, a rhythmic click-click-clack that grew louder every few seconds and then faded away to a hum before becoming louder again. The ceiling fan was on too, its blades edged with dirt, spinning lazily, barely stirring the air. "Some years ago a U.S. scientist came upon an ancient burial site on one of the islands on the fringes of the Moluccas. I can't remember which island it was, but it doesn't really matter. It was just one of the twenty thousand that make up the modern Republic of Indonesia: Its real name is irrelevant for the purposes of this story. Let's call it Nusa Laut, Sea Island, Island of the Sea, whatever—"

"Imaginative."

"Just let me get to the end. On this island—Nusa Laut—the indigenous population was made up largely of animists. There were also Christians and Muslims who moved there over the last few centuries, though neither group practiced their religion in the pure sense—theirs was a religion mixed with a hefty dose of local beliefs: spirits in the jungle, in the rocks and the streams and the sea, things that affect the everyday lives of the people who live on Nusa Laut—shall we call them the Lautese? Or the Lautians? Yes, that sounds better, doesn't it? This curious mixture of peoples managed to find a happy way to live, and over the centuries, constructed ancient worship sites—temples and grottoes and shrines—and burial grounds that got swallowed up by the jungle. The locals were aware of these places, but they never thought twice about them—they were just there, part of the landscape. Then one day a geologist, an academic, comes along. Professional etiquette forbids him from taking anything from the island but he sees a fragment of a stone carving, a piece of a deity's face—a nose, part of some lips, cheekbones—enough to convey a sense of complete peace in him. He looks around and slips it into his backpack. His local guide says nothing because it doesn't matter to him—hey, it's just a piece of stone, right?— and besides, he's afraid of the white guy. The geologist takes it back to the States. He loves this rock. He doesn't take it into the lab, he just keeps it in his study, locked away in a drawer. He takes it out and admires it from time to time. It's beautiful, just so goddamn beautiful. That's all it is to him: a thing of beauty. In fact, it's the only good thing in his life. His career is going downhill, his wife left him some years back and he's hit the bottle. One day he has a heart attack. The paramedics find him with an empty bottle of Jack Daniel's in one hand and this piece of stone in the other. They look at it and figure, it's old, it looks, well, archaeological, and this guy was a scientist, right? So they decide to return it to the university. It then passes through one hand to another until it ends up in an exhibition on tribal artifacts on campus. Nothing fancy, just a display of things collected over the years by the anthropology department. Africa, South America, Southeast Asia—it's all the same to them. People come and they look without seeing, if you get what I mean—it's all just old *stuff.* But one of the people who turns up is an Indonesian, okay, some kid from Jakarta on a Ford Foundation scholarship. He wanders in because he's got nothing to do between classes and it's cold outside, and he looks at the piece of stone and thinks, hey, that's Lautian. Unmistakable. Where did they get that from? It's a rare Indonesian artifact that was looted and needs to be returned to its home country. He makes a complaint to the school, they raise it with a senator they know, he raises it with the State Department. The Indonesian guy speaks to his buddies back here about it and the next thing you know, we've got the Soviets making speeches to us about stealing the ancient heritage of the Lautians. And on this little island itself, there are riots because of it, they're rounding up every Westerner they can find and shooting them for being Imperialists who take advantage of Indonesia. Of course there are many Lautians who say, 'This is crazy, stop this nonsense, this is none of our business, we're being jerked around.' Guess what happens to them? They get shot by the PKI. Sukarno sends in troops to quell the Communists, but no one's sure how hard he's trying, because he wants to be friends with the Communists too, and suddenly there's all this shit around us. Twenty years ago a stone was a thing of beauty, now it's a political tool. So ends the tragic story of Nusa Laut."

"That's a very touching parable, but how does it help us at this particular point in time?"

"That *parable,* as you call it, really happened. And when that fat, angry file comes through from Washington demanding answers, where do you think it ends up? Right here." He tapped his fingers on his desk. "I have to deal with so much crap, you wouldn't believe it. Why do you think I'm going to bust my balls to find one white guy who's probably on his way back to a cozy house in The Hague with a log fire and furry slippers and a nice, big-assed wife?"

"Because you know that I can do something for you in return. That's why you gave me the newspaper clipping." Bill Schneider leaned back in his chair. The rattling of the air conditioner had stopped. Out of the corner of her eye Margaret noticed that Mick was picking the label off his beer bottle, peeling the wet paper off in bits. "That's very," Bill began, "very mercenary of you." The sides of his mouth (Margaret thought) grew taut, as if he was trying to stifle a smile of satisfaction.

"Cut the bull, it's what you want."

"What ever happened to old-fashioned patriotism? Shouldn't Americans help each other out in times of distress?"

"If you help us find our friend, I'll do whatever I can to help you in your sordid machinations. That's the deal, isn't it, Bill? It always is with you."

"Your idea of sordid isn't the same as the rest of the world's, Margaret. You're like a dinosaur, trapped in a lost world."

"It's quite nice in my world, thank you very much."

"Don't worry—I'm not going to ask you to do anything you're not comfortable with this time."

Margaret stood up. "I'm sure you'll be in touch. Our friend's name is Karl de Willigen."

Bill Schneider said, "I know."

They drove through the gates, honking to disperse the mob. The mood had changed: The students were closer to the barricades in front of the entrance and were chanting and shouting more loudly. There were more soldiers too, standing close together with their rifles cradled against their chests. Something landed with a hollow thud on the roof of the car: a dirty canvas shoe. It rolled down the windshield before settling on the hood in front of Margaret. Mick revved the engine as they inched through the crowd; people were hitting the car, slapping the windows with their bare palms, and every so often the door handles would snap noisily as someone tried to open the doors. Mick accelerated now and then, just a bit; the staccato jerking of the car would clear a space in front of them before the bodies closed in once more. Margaret looked straight ahead, avoiding the gazes of the faces pressed against the windows.

"Traffic's bad today, isn't it?" Mick said. He sounded cheery, but Margaret easily discerned the note of anxiety in his voice. He reached for the radio and flicked it on. *"If you're fond of sand dunes and salty air . . ."* the voice crooned, *"you're sure to fall in love with old Cape Cod."*

"These guys look as if they're high on drugs," she said.

"The only thing they're high on is Sukarno's revolution. They know they want change, but they haven't got a clue how they want to achieve it. Don't worry, they're just students—you've probably taught most of them."

". . . if you like the taste of lobster stew served by a window with an ocean view . . ."

They broke free from the last of the demonstrators and slipped away like a boat freeing itself from a shallow shore, escaping into deep water.

"What did Bill Schneider mean by 'this time'?" Mick asked as they joined the sea of cars and *becaks* and trucks.

"*. . . you're sure to fall in love with old Cape Cod . . .*"

"What did he mean by *what*?"

"*This time*. He said he wouldn't ask you to do anything you didn't want to—*this time*."

"Did he? I wasn't paying attention."

"What happened last time?"

"I don't have a clue."

" 'It's the nonverbal communication that forms the basis of society.' What do you think you're communicating now?" They had come to a halt in the traffic. A young boy, shirtless and barefoot, wearing a dirty pair of maroon shorts, pressed a newspaper against the window and held out one hand for money.

"Nothing—especially since I don't know what you're getting at."

"You're twirling your hair and fiddling with your nose, and only just resisting the urge to bite your fingernails because you know I'll notice it. And you're frowning as if you're confused. I'd say you were communicating the fact that you're lying. Doesn't take a fucking anthropologist to work that one out."

"Bill Schneider said a lot of things—I can't recall every single detail. Besides, he's not exactly Chekhov when it comes to choosing his words, in case you hadn't noticed." She was feeling very hot; the windows were still closed and she began to think that even the choking Jakarta air would be better than the stifling heat of the car. "Can we turn this godforsaken music off?" She reached for the dashboard and fiddled with the knobs, but nothing worked.

"Whatever he is, he isn't a fool. So, you worked for the CIA? How fantastic! You never told me."

"Even you know how ridiculous that sounds."

"Not as ridiculous as your denials. It's obvious you were thick as thieves with Bill Schneider. Come on, what did he have you do? Was it . . . sexual?"

"One day when you're in a less immature mood I will tell you all about my very limited involvement with Bill."

"That had better be soon, otherwise you can ask him and not me to drive you around town."

The Jakarta sky was a murky ocher color, a blank canvas of yellow brown haze. If you stared at it long enough it glowed, faintly but definitely, becoming phosphorescent like a neon bulb. From behind this curtain of smog the sun cast a light that did not seem real; everything in this city looked uncertain, imprecise *". . . if you spend an evening you'll want to stay watching the moonlight on Cape Cod Bay. . . ."* Margaret continued to gaze at the sky. She rolled down the window and felt the rush of hot air against her face, and, before long, the dust and grit on her lips and tongue. She could not make out where roads merged or stopped, or where the buildings began and ended. There was only the iridescent sky above her.

Go on, take this.

There were no lights where they were. The city glowed faintly in the distance but they were beyond its grasp now. The car lay on the muddy road flanked by rows of bushes leading deeper into the palm oil estate. Johan reached for Bob's outstretched hand. He could just about make out a dark square on the paler background of Bob's palm. It was a piece of paper, but he could not tell what color it was. He lifted it with his fingertips and put it in his mouth and then took a sip of whiskey from the hip flask he had with him.

Thanks, Bob.

Anytime, Brother.

The shapes of the darkened bushes around them seemed to swell like rain clouds on a December afternoon. Now and then a car would drive by on the main road and its headlights would sweep past, filtering through the foliage in a burst of white light before leaving them alone in the dark once more.

Not again, for god's sake, Farah said. You said we were going to the movies tonight, you said we were just going to have a nice, quiet evening.

We are, Johan said. Everything's . . . quiet. Okay, we're going home. Enough of this. Hey, Sis, Bob said. Just take some of this and you'll feel better. Where the hell do you two get this stuff? Johan shrugged. All over. Anywhere. Don't lie to me. I don't see it when I'm walking down the street. Who gives it to you?

No one gives you anything in this town, Johan said. He held up his hand and made a twiddling motion with his thumb and forefinger. Everything has a price.

Johan has friends everywhere, Bob said. Especially in Bangkok, don't you, Johan?

The brotherhood of Asian nations, that's what it is, Johan said. There's a new world order. Freedom to trade, it's our right. But this, this excellent product, this comes all the way from the U. S. of A. He laughed and made that twiddling motion with his fingers again. Farah's face was lit by the moon but somehow blurred. Johan blinked but could not make out the details of her features. Her skin looked powdery, almost white, clearer, brighter than ever. This light, he said, it looks like frost. He reached out to touch her chin. He needed to make sure he was not imagining it.

Get lost, she said, and swatted his hand away. You wouldn't know what frost looks like, you've never seen it.

There was frost in England when we went last year.

Not where we were there wasn't. Oh god, look at you. Your eyes. I hate it when this happens to your eyes. I feel as if I'm staring into a big, black, empty well.

I'm okay. I'm okay.

Leave him alone, Sis. Bob lay sprawled out on the backseat. He's fine. Everything's just fine.

Johan, you're in no shape to drive. What the hell is Daddy going to say if he finds out? Give me the keys.

What are you going to do? You don't know how to drive. Johan started up the car as he spoke and reversed slowly until they were on the main road. Don't worry, your daddy isn't going to find out.

He's your father too. And you know Mummy always wakes up early. She'll kill you if she sees you like this. Please drive slowly, Johan. Let's go home.

No. We're going to the movies. I promised you.

They sped toward the city, streaming along the smooth roads that led sinuously into the heart of this bright new town. They glided past construction sites for the new housing estates on the outskirts, fields of mud and concrete ringed by chain-link fences. In the purple moonlight they looked like an ocean, an ocean troubled by small jagged waves carrying all manner of flotsam. Quickly, then, they were in the city. The buildings flowed past them, blurred and glittering, casting their lights upward into the sky. Sometimes, Johan thought, sometimes it doesn't feel as if I am in the city, *the city is in me*.

Outside the Rialto a throng of people was basking in the golden glare of the ten thousand bulbs that lit the theater and the neon billboards spread across the theater's facade of angular pigeonholes. Next to a sign saying NO PARKING there was a thick rope strung across two iron posts. There were some boys and girls laughing cold, hard laughs. They watched the Mercedes as it crawled to a halt.

Don't look back at them, Johan, Farah said. Just don't provoke anyone.

Johan honked, pressing long and hard until the crowd dispersed. An old Chinese man emerged, bent over, hurrying, and uncoiled the rope from the posts. It hung from his hands like a dead python. He waved the car into a space just outside the steps to the theater.

Hello, Tuan, hello, Miss Farah, he said as they walked up the stairs. Coming for the midnight show?

Hello, Seng, Farah replied. How's your grandson? Must be big now. (Johan, Bob, she whispered, for god's sake try and behave normally, *walk faster.*)

Miss Farah, if you want, tonight midnight show is *The Love Eterne,* otherwise just started there is *Story of the Sword and the Sabre,* part one, or *Three Dolls of Hong Kong.*

Oh, I thought *From Russia with Love* was still showing.

James Bond finished yesterday. So sorry, Miss Farah.

Johan said, It's Imperialist Western nonsense anyway.

Next month we are going to have *Contempt*. Don't know what it's about, but sounds good. That French woman on the poster looks so beautiful.

That's fine, Seng, three tickets for the midnight show then, please. What was it again?

The Love Eterne. This way please, for you—no need to pay.

Of course must pay.

Please don't mention it anymore, Miss Farah.

Johan settled in his chair in the musty darkness of the theater. Over the wild symphony of the music there was the steady crack-cracking of people eating pumpkin seeds, splitting the shells between their teeth before dropping them onto the floor. It sounded to him like drops of rain falling heavily on sand, the start of a storm at the seaside. He remembered his first holiday with his new family in Port Dickson. He had wanted to see the sea, to find out if he was still frightened by it. So he had gone into the water late in the afternoon, when it was raining, when he was not supposed to go swimming. The raindrops were heavy and cold on his head, the sea warm, so warm, and when he put his head under water the sound of the rain falling on the surface of the sea was just like the sound of the rain on the zinc roof at the orphanage, only softer. He had closed his eyes. Brilliant colored cloudbursts filled his head. He could feel the pulse in his temples, quick and insistent. His cheeks were hot but he felt a thin chill at the back of his neck.

It's so bloody hot in here, Bob said. I'm sweating like a dog. Is there even air-conditioning in here? This place is rubbish, you wouldn't get this in Singapore.

Shh.

The Technicolor screen swirled with vivid hues. Johan tried to follow the story, but he could not make sense of it. All he could see was the wash of color. Blue hills. Streams of gold cloth. Fluorescent green fields. Rivers of pure cobalt. A violet sky. There was a girl pretending to be a boy, falling in love with a boy. She loved him, but he did not love her. Or maybe he loved him, but he did not love him.

Johan, stop laughing. Are you okay?

Fine. Everything's perfect.

He loves him but he goes away from him. She goes away, far away. He realizes that he loves him and she loves him and he loves her. He feels sad. She feels sad. They both feel sad.

Why?

Why what? Johan, please stop mumbling.

There is plenty of wind. It is cold in here. They both die. There is a storm. White powder fills the world. Rainstorm on sand.

Johan. Farah put her hand on his arm. Her fingers are not cold, not warm, just perfect and unmoving and strong. I'm worried about you. Johan, look at me. She touched his face gently. *Look at me.*

The white shower was over and the light was dim on her face, dancing faintly across her small nose and wide-open eyes. Don't worry, I'm happy now, Farah.

She gripped his arm tightly. No you're not.

I am. I can't remember anything.

Breathe deeply, slowly.

I wish it could be like this all the time. I wish I could forget everything. I don't want to remember anything, Farah. Nothing at all.

Will you two *shut up* over there? Bob said.

Farah? I'm here.

Later, when they were back in the car and the world seemed less brilliant, Johan looked again at Farah. Her hair was messed up by the wind blowing hard through the windows as they sliced along the darkened streets. He said, What kind of dreams do you have?

Don't know. Mostly nice ones. Sometimes scary. I guess just normal ones. You?

I can't sleep at night.

I know. I can hear you fidgeting and coughing. Sometimes you sigh and cry out. Are your dreams so bad?

If I fall asleep it all comes back to me and I wake up again.

Farah turned around to check that Bob was asleep. What comes back to you?

The orphanage. The boys. The rain dripping through the roof, the sound it made, like a ticking of a huge clock that would never stop. The dorm was long and thin and there were rows of cots, just sheets of canvas between pieces of wood, not even real beds, and the rows were so close together there was barely any space to walk between them. You could hear the breathing of the other boys when they were asleep and every night there would be someone crying in his sleep. And my brother—

—Oh no, Johan, you know we're not supposed to talk about that. She put her hand on his.

That's such a stupid rule. Why? I do—

Shhh, she said.

He liked the sound her lips made. You're the only one I can talk to, Farah, the only who has ever—

No, Mummy cares. She loves you.

No, he said. She needs me.

They did not stop. They drove through the silent city.

10

*A*fter Margaret left the house Adam found himself alone, again.

Being alone was not something he was good at. He had realized this over the past week, during his long voyage through the islands and along the never-ending sweep of the Great Post Road through Java. There had rarely been a moment when he had been physically on his own. Whether on the boat from Perdo or the bus coming into Surabaya, he had been surrounded by people, by bodies that jostled against him and voices that shouted obscenities at him. Waiting for the bus in a village near Yogya he had endured a whole evening of an old Madurese woman reminiscing about the island she had left behind; he sat under purple neon lights, listening to her tales of knife fights and ghosts. On the ferry three nights before, he had listened to a young couple sing songs of love while he was throwing up violently into the dark blue water. The words had spun wildly in his head— *"across the wide wide sea I will wait wait for you you"*—making the rocking of the boat seem even worse. And yet, in spite of the endless cacophony and the crush of people, he had begun to realize just how alone he felt. He had also begun to realize how little he liked it. Loneliness, this curious state of being alone, was not something he had ever experienced in his life with Karl. It had not even crossed his mind that he should ever feel alone. In fact he had, if anything, only known the opposite sensation, of wanting to be rid of Karl, to *be alone* in that house by the sea.

During the seemingly endless bus ride on the Great Post Road, punctuated by nighttime stops at nameless villages, he had tried to think about whether he had ever been lonely at the orphanage. He was never left on his own, of that he was certain. There were always other boys around him, and though their faces eluded him, their presence remained: a shifting mass of bodies swirling around him, even in his sleep. But in this shadowy crowd he had never felt alone, or even lonely, as he did now, because there had always been someone more constant with him, someone who remained by his side and was not part of the amorphous mass—Johan, whose face he could not, sadly, recall. He closed his eyes. The bus jolted as it rumbled over the potholes; his bottom felt sore and he could feel the metal bars through the thin vinyl-covered seat. He knew that Johan's face would not miraculously appear to him after all these years, but he could not resist reconstructing his brother, as he so often did, in these drowsy presleep moments, using the few fragments he had retained: Johan's perfectly straight bearing (he had been the tallest of all the boys in the orphanage); his shaven head (that one was easy: They had all had shaved heads); his curiously long fingers, with the middle three on each hand exactly the same length, so that when he held them together they seemed squared-off, cut neatly at the end; his earlobes (or at least one of them) shaped like a tiny, fleshy flower that you could reach out and pinch, time and time again, but never crush; and finally this: the smell of soap mixed with something harsher, like turpentine, or kerosene—he could not be sure of this last detail. Adam was no longer even frustrated by the fact that Johan's face remained elusive. He re-created Johan's entire being, as he always did, imagining how he might look today; and yet he resisted giving his brother the final defining features: no eyes, no lips, no nose. He knew that whatever details he supplied would be wrong.

He went to the back of the house, where Margaret had indicated he would find a shower. There was a bathroom, not dissimilar to the one he and Karl had at home, but much smaller and dimmer, its zinc roof covering only half the space, leaving the rest exposed to the sunless sky. One half of the floor was damp and smooth, the other pockmarked with star-shaped bird droppings and bits of dead leaves that had not yet been cleaned up. There was a hose attached at one end to a tap; the other end disappeared into a bucket that had holes drilled into its base. Adam turned on the taps and watched the water begin to fall, rainlike, onto the smooth stone floor. At home they had a large earthenware pot from which they scooped water with a pail, sluicing themselves generously; he wasn't certain what these tentative streams of water would do. He stood under this miniature rain shower; it felt odd to be standing naked in the rain, and Adam could not decide if it was pleasant or not. He let the droplets wash over him for a few minutes, slowly becoming more at ease, though when he turned the tap off he was still unconvinced by this new method of washing.

At least he was clean again. He had hated wearing the same clothes for a week, hated the way people looked at him as if he were just another street urchin. There had been that Chinese shopkeeper in Magelang who had chased him out of the shop when he had gone in to look for something to eat. Adam had barely touched the bag of dried squid before the man had come after him, waving a stick at him as if he had been a dog, and he had run away, his face hot with shame, even though he had done nothing wrong. In the hour before rejoining his bus, everyone had looked at him in that suspicious, wary way as he wandered the streets in the fading afternoon, in that town between two great mountains. He had never felt so dirty in all his life.

He made his way to the kitchen and began opening the cupboards tentatively, but found only an almost-empty jar of peanut butter and a few cans of something called ravioli, which seemed utterly mysterious to him. He searched for a can opener but could not find one. Meals were never this complicated at home. Adam just turned up at the dinner table and the food was there, prepared either by Ibu Som, who came every other day to help with the housework, or by Karl himself. These meals were always simple, especially when Karl cooked. Often they ate only plain steamed rice (which Karl had never managed to master, and consequently, emerged from the pot in stodgy wet lumps) with some *sambal* or pickles. During these meals they would eat quickly and in silence, and Adam would know not to ask why they could not have the type of food Ibu Som cooked; he understood that Karl was making some sort of point by eating as simply as possible. He knew that it was to do with "empathy for our fellow citizens" and "not profiting from the misfortune of others, just because we have more money." At one of these Spartan dinners, even though he had not uttered a word, Karl had caught his eye and said, "It's just a reminder." Adam was not sure what this was a reminder of, but he had chosen not to ask.

He opened the refrigerator and found a hard, putrid lump. Its label read ROMANO WHEEL. It did not smell at all appealing, but memories of dinners at home had sharpened his hunger and he cut a wedge of cheese and ate it. He cut the rest of the lump into pieces and put them on a plate, wanting to arrange them like spokes of a wheel but finding instead that they created a miniature atoll, like the haphazard clumps of coral on the seabed as he drifted over them. As he ate, he opened his notebook and wrote:

> *Things to Tell Margaret*
> *my father was wearing a blue shirt when they took him away*
> *it was definitely soldiers and not the PKI.*
> *(Communists always kill their captives, soldiers don't always)*
> *(And i can also recognize Communists—they dress very badly because*
>   *they are poor)*
> *my father's only crime is to have been born a foreigner*
> *i searched the house for clues but found only pictures of you and my*
>   *father you looked very happy*

He recalled scrabbling around nervously among Karl's papers, afraid he was transgressing some undefined boundary. The memory of Karl's room—his small desk, his curling handwriting on sheets of paper, the smell of mothballs and old books—was clear and unwavering.

He looked up from his piece of paper. The radio crackled in and out of tune: "Indonesian paratroopers . . . landings in Malaysia . . . skirmishes with British forces . . . deaths . . . prelude to invasion. He thought he heard the front gate creak open but there had not been a car. He went to the window and looked out; there was no one in the yard, just a black-and-white cat with a broken tail licking itself in the shade of the potted plants. There was a scattering of dead leaves across the yard, and Adam noticed that most of the plants were parched, their foliage turning crinkled and crispy at the edges. It was never like this at home (one of Adam's more important daily chores was to ensure that the plants were well watered). He returned to his list. There was a song on the radio, a *keroncong* tune with its frilly strings and sweetly sung melody. It was important that he concentrate, he told himself; he needed to provide Margaret with all the information he could so that she would help him. He was seized by a sharp sense of anxiety, one that he had experienced several times over the last few days, always accompanied by visions of Karl in a squalid prison cell that he shared with badly dressed Communists who would try and steal his shoes. There would be no food and very little water, and the water would be dirty and make Karl sick. Adam closed his eyes and rubbed his temples, which had begun to ache. He made a quick mental calculation: Karl had been missing for eleven days—not quite enough time to die from starvation, but certainly enough time to die from dehydration. A noise startled him, and when he opened his eyes there was a man in the room.

"Hello," the man said, though it sounded more like a statement than a greeting. He was half-frowning but smiled, as if trying to hide displeasure. "Who are you?"

Adam did not move in his chair. He rested his hands lightly on his knees, wondering what he would do if the man lunged at him. He had managed to go a whole week without being accosted on his travels, and now, when he thought he was safe, he had let down his guard and allowed a stranger into Margaret's house.

"Who are *you*?" Adam managed to say.

The man did not answer immediately but instead placed a package on the table. It was wrapped in newspaper and cinched with a rubber band. "I've brought something—it was for Margaret, but I guess she's not at home."

Adam stood up and backed away slightly.

"Don't be afraid. My name is Din," the man said, unwrapping the package to reveal a bunch of bananas, perfectly ripe. "I'm one of Margaret's colleagues—well, I'm technically her student, but she doesn't really supervise me. Here, have one. They're very hard to find nowadays." He tore off a single plump banana and held it out to Adam.

"I was just passing by—I tried the telephone but the lines are down. Happens a lot these days. The exchange is always a mess, what with the troubles on the streets." He looked out the window as if expecting someone. "I hope Margaret is okay. There weren't any classes today, everything's been canceled, it's a mess. Margaret normally comes in to the campus anyway, and when she didn't, I got worried. She still cares about her students, even though they don't actually do any studying anymore. She's probably the only person in the world who still cares."

"She seems very nice. I like her."

"Are you a student too?"

"No," Adam said, taking the banana. "Well, not a university student, if that's what you mean. I'm too young. I'm not sure if I'll go to university—my father hasn't decided yet."

"That's a shame," said Din, settling into an armchair facing Adam, "because education is the future of our country. So, who are you?"

Adam paused to consider his questioner, a small slight man dressed neatly in a short-sleeved shirt and cotton trousers with a crease running sharply down each leg. He would not be stronger than Adam if they got into a fight, Adam thought—not unless he was armed, which he did not appear to be. "My name is Adam de Willigen," he said. "I am a friend of Margaret's too." As he said that he blushed and felt as if he had just told a lie.

"What kind of name is that? You're making it up."

"No, I'm not," Adam said. There was something in Din's face that irritated him: the nondescript features that took on an air of self-righteousness, the gently furrowed brow, the slim Sumatran nose—all these things suddenly became pronounced and dislikable.

"Did you give *yourself* that name? Why do you want to be *Dutch,* of all things? We should be breaking free from all that. Don't you know anything? That is why we've been fighting for the last twenty years."

"They were not all bad. And anyway my name is also that of my father, and he is as Indonesian as you are."

Din smacked his forehead with his palm, just once, hard, and squeezed his eyes shut. Adam hoped that he had hurt himself. "Not another one of these self-deluding white people. I hope you don't believe any nonsense he might have told you. It makes me so angry."

Adam did not reply. If it had been his house he would have asked Din to leave.

"Okay, so you're too young to be a university student," Din continued, his voice dropping to adopt a more conciliatory tone, "but you must have some idea of the revolution that is going on. You don't look like a stupid, uneducated boy. Listen, we Indonesians—I mean, *real* Indonesians—need to determine what is best for us. We have to forge a path to our destiny."

"That is what my father tells me. Indonesia will decide what is best for itself."

Din lifted his chin and half-laughed, half-sneered. "Listen to that. You don't even believe it yourself. It means nothing—you're just repeating what someone told you. 'Decide what is best'? It seems your whole life has been determined by someone else. Some foreigner decides what you should do—go to university or not, eat or not, pray or not. We *know* what is best. What is best is to live in a world that is not controlled by the West for their unjust intentions. What is best is to have a future where Asian and African countries control their own destinies. For three hundred years, someone else has written our history books for us, but now we have to rewrite them."

"I suppose so."

Din pinched his own forearm. "Look—we have the same skin. Same color. I would not lie to you."

Adam nodded. He realized that he had never heard another native Indonesian speak at length about anything other than the tide or the waves or the drought or the rice harvest. It felt odd to hear someone who looked like him talk in the same kind of language that Karl used, only with more urgency.

"Your father—okay, well, he's not your father, but I can see why you call him that—I'm sure he's a good person. But he cannot decide your future for you. He can no longer even decide what to do for himself— all the Dutch people are being sent back to Holland. What are you going to do? Go back to Holland with him?"

The music seemed louder, more shrill now, but Adam could not make out the words. He shrugged. "Yes, I suppose so."

"And once you're there? What will you do then? Do you think you'll blend in, with skin this color?" Din reached across and pinched Adam's arm lightly. "You won't. Believe me, I've been there. You'll be treated worse than a dog. Your so-called father will start to become ashamed of you, and people will say things about him, about you. You'll have no work, and you'll become a burden to him. You'll be completely dispirited and you will realize that you only have one place left to go: Indonesia."

Adam shook his head. He knew this was not true. He tried to remember the Dutch phrases he knew, the expressions he had gleaned from visitors or that Karl had breathed secretly, all those words in that forbidden, magical language. *Mijn naam is Adam de Willigen. De zee is leeg. De schapen zijn verbrand. Zo was het nu eenmaal!*

"Let me share my experience with you. I lived in Holland for three whole years. I went there full of hope. I was young and bright and I was selected for a Dutch education—can you imagine how I felt? My father was so proud of me. He was completely illiterate. So was my mother—she died when I was a baby and her only wish was that I escape our village. My parents wanted a better life for me and so they sent me to school in Palembang and then to university in Jakarta. They were so happy when I won my scholarship to Leiden. They told everyone I was going to be a professor, even though they didn't know what that meant—they just liked the sound of the word. It sounded important to them. Professor, president—these words have power over poor, uneducated people. I arrived in Holland thinking I was special, that I could change things. It was raining when I arrived. I took this as a good sign—an omen of great things to come. Not even a week later, I realized that Dutch rain is not like Indonesian rain. One brings a chill to everything it touches, the other brings life. It did not stop raining in all the time I was there. Someday, if we become friends, I will tell you about the thousand injustices I suffered over there, but for now, all I will say is that they were the longest, darkest, coldest three years of my life."

Adam paused. He wanted to ask a hundred questions about Holland, to ask all the questions that Karl had refused point-blank to answer—whether there were windmills and placid canals of cold, clear water and plump black-and-white cows and quiet cobbled streets—but he knew that he would not get the answers from Din.

"Was it really terrible?" he asked.

"I'll tell you the whole story sometime. Let's just say that I realized one thing: that the only place I could call home was this"—he gestured around him. "Indonesia might be a shit hole but it's *our* shit hole. We will never be happy anywhere else. What's happened to your so-called father anyway? If he's so wonderful, why isn't he here to look after you?"

"He's missing. They took him away—the army took him."

Din said nothing for quite some time, but stared straight at Adam, his eyes moving almost imperceptibly. On either side of Din's mouth, Adam could discern tiny muscles twitching, just briefly, as if Din was going to smile. But he did not smile. He said, calmly but very firmly, "He's abandoned you. I thought as much."

"No, he hasn't. Margaret is getting in touch with him. He's coming back very soon." Adam tried to sound casual but he knew he was not convincing. He tried to tell himself that Karl's return was indeed imminent, but it was too much to hope for.

"Tell me," Din said, his face adopting a more serious, less confrontational expression, "you're an orphan, aren't you? Why are you expending all your energy looking for your foster father when you could look for your *real* family?"

Adam shrugged. "I don't know anything about my parents. They're probably dead. They wouldn't want me anyway—that's why they left me in the orphanage in the first place."

"Rubbish! Of course they loved you. They were just too poor to care for you." He leaned forward, his elbows resting on his knees. "Tell me everything you know about your family."

"Honestly, I don't know anything. I don't want to know anything about my past. Please stop asking me."

"No, I won't stop because it's important. You need to know about your past. It's who you are." Din's voice softened and he smiled. "Look, surely you have some clue about your background? I mean, look at you. You're clearly Sumatran, for a start—just like me! I can recognize a fellow Sumatran when I see one."

"Really?" Adam was caught off guard by this revelation; not even Karl had been able to tell him where he was from. He stared at Din's face and was disconcerted to find more than a passing resemblance: the skin tone, the way the eyes sat evenly on a fine-boned face. He recognized these things, and was disturbed by them.

"Yes, it's clear you're Sumatran. There's been so much movement across the islands over the years, what with this stupid transmigration policy. Good principle, bad result. Javanese should live in Java, not in Nusa Tenggara, Sumatra should remain Sumatran, and so on. So we know your ethnic background. What else? Brothers and sisters?"

Adam hesitated. He did not see why he should say anything to this person, but at the same time there was something about this invasive, almost repugnant man that made Adam think that he would under-stand everything about Johan. It was crazy, he thought, but he might know things about Johan, just as he had known things about Adam. "I think . . ."

"Go on," Din said, his voice calm and soft. "I'm listening."

"I think I have a brother."

"That's great," Din encouraged. "You're sure of this?"

Adam could hear his own breathing—perfectly regular and even. He nodded. "Yes. I have a brother." This time the words did not seem so awkward; they sounded firm, comforting.

"You were separated when you were very young, weren't you? That's tragic."

"Yes." Adam nodded. He began to feel slightly light-headed and dizzy and wondered why.

"It must be difficult for you." Din continued speaking softly, paus-ing carefully as though appreciating the enormity of what Adam had just shared with him. "All these years without your brother, alone."

Alone. Yes, thought Adam, alone.

"I don't know if it helps," Din went on, "but you are not on your own in this respect. Many many young children—tens of thousands, maybe hundreds of thousands, possibly millions—have been orphaned in the last few decades, just like you. Poverty and disease and this stupid transmigration policy have created generations of orphans. If a poor family has to move to another part of the country they often leave their children behind because they don't know what awaits them in their new home. They think they'll come back for their kids or send for them later, but they never do."

As Din spoke Adam realized why he felt giddy—it was relief, of course, relief at being able to speak about Johan without feeling baffled or guilty or lost. It bothered him that Din, whom he had met only five minutes ago, should have so many insights into his life; Adam had not yet even decided if he liked Din.

"So what do you know about your brother?" Din was patient and coaxing, no longer insistent as he had been earlier.

Adam shook his head, half-expecting to be reproached.

"Nothing?"

"I get so angry that I can't remember anything. I hate it."

"Hey, hey, don't beat yourself up. It's not your fault."

A car drew up outside, its engine rattling to a halt.

"We'll talk about this some more," said Din, "but only if you want to."

The metal gate creaked open, the mailbox clanging loudly. Adam stood up and saw Margaret approaching the house with a European man.

"I think," Din lowered his voice until it was barely more than a whisper, "we'd better keep what we've been discussing a secret for the time being, don't you?"

Adam nodded, though he was not quite sure why he should hide their exchange from Margaret. All he understood was that he was already complicit with Din in some way.

Margaret paused briefly as she stepped into the house. She looked slightly perplexed to find Din there, thought Adam.

"I didn't know you knew where I lived," she said by way of greeting. "What brings you here?"

"I got your address from the registrar's office. I rang a few times but there was no answer, so I thought I'd come over and check to see if you were all right. You didn't come to the campus yesterday so I thought—"

"Thank you for your concern, but I'm perfectly capable of looking after myself. I see you've met Adam."

"Yes. Well, um, I'm glad you're okay."

On seeing Margaret, Adam experienced the feeling of relief and security he had felt upon meeting her for the first time the previous night. The image of the young Margaret and Karl standing together in the photograph came back to him and made him remember why he had come to this city in the first place: to regain his father. "Any news?" he asked.

She frowned and shook her head; she came toward him and put her arms around him, surprising him with a long, firm hug. It did not feel foreign or bizarre to him that she should do this; he was glad that she did. "No news yet, I'm afraid, but we have our contacts working on a way to find him. We *will* find him."

Din said, "I'd better go now. I just wanted to check that you weren't in trouble. Nice to meet you, Adam." He slipped on his black canvas

shoes without bothering to undo the laces. As he closed the gate behind him he gave Adam a brief nod and smiled. Adam turned away; he
did not want Margaret to see that something had passed between him
and Din, something that amounted to a betrayal of her trust and hos-
pitality. He was glad that Din had gone.

But it disturbed him to find that he could not forget all the things
that Din had told him.

11

*A*s Margaret stood in the kitchen waiting for the kettle to boil, she tried to figure out why she had so readily embraced Adam. She could not explain what had made her feel so happy upon seeing him again, why she had been overwhelmed by a sense of relief bordering on joy at finding him safe and eagerly awaiting her return. When he stood up to greet her, the expression on his face was one of such hope and anticipation and vulnerability that she had to respond. And so she had gone up to him and put her arms around him, circling his chest tightly, as if she needed to reassure herself that he was still there. She had done so without thinking, and for all the time their hug lasted—three, four, five seconds? More?—it ceased to matter that Din and Mick had been in the room, watching.

The kettle began to whistle. Margaret poured the boiling water into the teapot and watched the darkening water swirl with tea leaves. She remembered her mother's words to her when she was a teenager. "You're not a tactile child, are you? I have no idea why," her mother would say, sighing. "I suppose it's my fault—didn't cuddle you enough when you were a baby, or stopped breastfeeding too early. Oh dear, it seems all that Freudian nonsense is true after all. Do try to be more physical, Margaret, more *expressive*." It used to rile her intensely whenever her mother said this, largely because she knew it was true, but also because she wished she found it easier to reach out and touch other people. It was not that she did not like touching or being touched—she liked both. She had no idea why it did not come naturally to her. And yet she had hugged Adam without a moment's hesitation or embarrassment, the self-consciousness returning only later, once they had detached themselves from each other. "*I've* never got that from you," Mick had whispered as she brushed past him on her way to the kitchen.

She opened a can of condensed milk and poured it into three mugs, stirring in the tea. She had made Mick stop on the way home so that she could buy some food for Adam—two loaves of bread, an assortment of canned meat and sardines, and a bag of hard candy. She had never been a good cook, or even particularly interested in food (that, at least, was something she had shared with her mother), but in recent months her lackadaisical approach to feeding herself had worsened, and she rarely planned meals. She would last most of the day without eating anything, and at some point in the evening she might think, I'm hungry; and then she would stop at the closest place for a bite to eat. Sometimes it was an expensive restaurant in a luxurious hotel, sometimes it was a satay or *mee bandung* stall by the roadside, sometimes it was a bag of peanuts at home—it made little difference to her: It was all just food.

So why was she now seized by the urge to make sure her kitchen cupboards were full? She stood before the array of canned goods, wondering how she could prepare a wholesome, tasty meal for Adam. It troubled her to think that he had not had a healthy meal for days; the remnants of his breakfast of hard, almost-moldy cheese lay on a plate in the sink, the dried-up bits of rind looking like old bread crumbs. Margaret felt ashamed; she had to change her ways, quickly, or she would not be able to help this boy.

She sliced a loaf of bread and emptied the contents of a can into a saucepan (Great Wall of China Fried Dace in Black Bean Sauce—she did not even know what *Dace* was); she tried to light a burner but the pilot light was out. She dipped her finger into the sauce and found it cold and slightly slimy—perfectly acceptable to her, but not for Adam. She opened a tin of Spam—the picture on the can showed what looked like a leg of ham cut into slices on a platter decorated with festive ribbons and balloons, but when she opened the can she found only an opaque layer of fat. She had no idea what lay underneath. Okay, don't panic, Margaret Bates, she told herself, don't lose control, you can do this.

"Mick," she called in a half whisper, half cry, "I need help."

"You said you were going to make dinner," he said as he came into the kitchen.

"Yes, but . . ." she gestured at the growing mess around her. "I just don't know how. I'm not even hungry, but I need to feed the boy."

"All right." He sighed, dropping his shoulders theatrically. "Let me see what I can do."

"Oh, thank you, Mick. I was really really hoping you'd say that." She went up to him and thought about giving him a hug but ended up patting him on the shoulder instead.

In the living room Adam was idly winding the red enamel alarm clock that usually sat halfway up a bookshelf. Margaret was not sure it even worked anymore. A couple of banana skins lay flaccidly on the table; fruit flies rose from them in a spiral as Margaret sat down facing Adam.

"Sorry, I ate some bananas," he said.

"Are you okay now?" Margaret said, looking anxiously in the direction of the kitchen, hoping that Mick would hurry up.

He nodded. "I'm fine." In his hands the clock revolved slowly, the words *golden cock made in china* spinning around and around again.

"My father has a limp," he said, concentrating on the clock. "He walks in a funny way. Did you know that?"

Margaret nodded.

"One day, I don't know why, he came to meet me at school. He bicycled, but he was not used to it and it was far. With his weak leg he couldn't go very fast and the bike wobbled and looked very stupid. All the other children were laughing at him, and I remember feeling ashamed and wishing that I had a different father, one with two strong legs."

"He thought it would go away, but I guess it didn't."

"You don't think he would ever abandon me, do you?" he asked without looking up at her.

"Of course not. It's been many years since I've known him, but from what I remember of him, he isn't the type who would just get up and leave when the going gets tough. Believe me, I should know."

"Mm." He did not sound convinced. All his childlike hope and energy had drained away, and now he seemed tiny and weak. She wanted to reach out to him, but this time she hesitated.

"I often wondered," Adam continued, "why my father never married. I asked him once if he had ever loved anyone. He nodded and said, 'But it was difficult. The world was a different place when I was a young man. There were other things to think about.' I didn't know what he meant, but I remembered it clearly because he seemed so sad when he said it. I knew not to ask him again."

"That sounds awful."

"I used to imagine that you were his wife and that we would one day settle down together, as a family." He looked up at her and smiled, and suddenly he did not look so fragile. "Crazy idea, isn't it?"

She laughed with him. "Very."

"Did you love each other?"

The question was delivered calmly but swiftly, and Margaret had not anticipated it. Caught off guard, she could only smile vacantly at him. It was, in fact, a question she had asked herself hundreds of times over the course of her life. She was still not sure of the answer.

"Wait, don't starve, weary travelers—salvation is at hand!" Mick appeared from the kitchen bearing a tray of food. Margaret watched as Adam ate and it made her feel unaccountably happy to see him being nourished. His last question still echoed loudly in her head, bringing back the memories of a hundred minor incidents that might have determined the answer: Yes, they had loved each other; or, no, only one of them had loved the other; or, it was never so easy. Karl had been right: There had been more pressing things to think of in the world than love.

Evening brought with it a languid rain shower, drumming a monotone on the roof. Adam looked more at ease now that he had eaten; he was smiling again and asking Margaret questions about the United States and Europe.

"I think you should go to bed now," she said when it was very late. She insisted that he take her bedroom and wouldn't take no for an answer. She would sit and chat with Mick for a while. She didn't mind the sofa. She checked on him after half an hour, and again after an hour, anxious that he should sleep as soundly as possible. She pulled the curtains shut to keep out the droplets of rain that were blowing in through the windows; Adam had kicked the thin sheet away from his body, and she drew it back up to his chest, moving it as gently as possible so as not to wake him up.

"It's weird, seeing you like this." Mick chuckled gently.

"Like what?"

"I don't know—nervous, as if you're not quite sure what you're doing. I've never known you to be anything but in control. I've never seen you—hmm, how shall I put this?—so tender."

"You mean I'm a cruel, heartless witch?"

"No, no, just . . . I don't know, it's funny."

"I *am* nervous. We still haven't heard any news from Bill Schneider. I don't know if we can trust him—and besides, I'm not sure just how much he can do."

"You Americans still have plenty of connections in this country, despite official relations. Let's wait and see."

"We can't afford to wait, Mick. This boy's future is at stake. I can't bear the thought of him homeless, without the only family he's ever known." She stood at the window and watched the rain wash thin rivulets of mud across the narrow street. The dead leaves in the front yard made a crackling noise as the raindrops hit, but otherwise all the usual noises of the neighborhood had ceased: the barking of dogs, the howling of copulating cats, the scooters, the radios, the angry shouting of young men, the crying of babies. All that stopped when the rains came. It was late now; the immense city was settling down to its brief sleep.

But Margaret was not sleepy. She could not stop thinking about the question that Adam had put to her, the one she could not answer: Had she loved and been loved in return?

12

*T*onight something strange is happening to Adam—or more precisely, something strange is happening to his dreams.

As he felt the first warm waves of drowsiness wash through his head, he had become aware of something out of the ordinary, something that did not usually accompany his sleep. It was a smell—sweet, complex, and faintly milky: Margaret's room. Turning his head so that his nose rested against the pillow—her pillow—he'd inhaled deeply. This perfume was not very strong; it seemed to hover over the bedclothes, evaporating if he breathed in too much of it too quickly. If he tried to fix it in his senses it would disappear, but, sooner or later, it would return to him. It was a smell that seemed to have existed long before him, that was everything and everywhere, cocooning and protecting, at once a lullaby and a stimulant.

And on this night, because of this perfume, or because of some other unfathomable reason, his dreams are clearer and sharper; and in fact they do not even seem like dreams.

These are memories. Adam knows this even though he is asleep. These are memories of his Past Life.

Tonight, images come to him as they sometimes do, but they do not dissolve into that terrible emptiness or flicker faintly on the edge of his sleep. They seem instead to drift like bits of flotsam that cling together to form a raft of recollections.

He is in a room, a small, square room with a concrete floor that looks smooth, almost shiny, yet he cannot feel this smoothness; his feet feel leaden and clumpy. This is why: He is wearing shoes. He does not normally wear shoes. He looks down at his feet and sees a pair of canvas sneakers, frayed at the toes where they have been scrubbed clean with a coarse brush. The rubber soles squeak as he swings his legs. This is a sustained image, but will it lead to anything else?

Yes. There are other people in the room—three, to be exact. One of them is a man who is wearing a white shirt with long sleeves rolled up to his elbows. There are fine golden hairs on his forearms, glinting in the light. His hair is the color of sand, and his voice is not like that of the others. This is Karl. Karl is talking to another man, or, more precisely, he is listening while the other man speaks. This other man's voice is calm and lilting, like the first tentative notes of a song. He is trying to persuade Karl of something. Adam understands that there is a problem. Something is not right. He understands that Karl is to take him away, but the man is saying something that Adam can't understand. He can only hear the voice, cajoling, urging, and suddenly he begins to feel afraid.

Through the open window he can see the silvery green leaves of a lone coconut tree, spindly and tall, jutting out from the scrubby bush. It is the only thing of color in a landscape bleached by the drought. Yes, there is a drought. It is hot. Adam begins to feel tired, as if he is fainting, fainting into a deep sleep.

     •   •   •

Johan. Wake up, darling. Are you okay? You sleep too much, baby. You've been in bed all day—look, it's nearly dark. Daddy will be angry if he sees you asleep again. You know what a temper he has. Look what Mummy's bought you, some of your favorite *kuih lapis. Adoi,* why so sleepy all the time? Poor darling boy, look at you. Come on, *sayang,* don't spend your life in bed. Such a waste. Hmm? Don't mumble. Here, drink your Milo. Mummy put extra milk in for you so your skin will be even nicer. When I first saw you I said to myself, *aiyoh,* this boy's skin is so smooth. You were so beautiful even as a small child. All the others were very ugly, all dark and skinny. What? Why *jeling mata* like that? Why don't we go out to dinner tonight, just you and me? Farah and Bob can stay and do their homework. Come on, let Mummy take you out for a treat. I want to. Daddy's at the club with his friends this evening. We'll go somewhere really nice, okay?

There was a song playing in the elevator as they went up to the restaurant, an American song that was always on the radio. Johan did not know what it was called, or who the singer was, he just recognized bits of the chorus. It was something like *can't get used to lovin' you*, or *losin' you*, he was not sure which. There was a young Chinese couple in the elevator with them. The woman knew all the words but the man only knew the last part. He sang it out of tune, in a voice like a child's, and she giggled. *You-oo. You-oo.* Her hair was thick and glossy and set in an arc that came down one side of her face, ending in a curled tip. Her lashes were heavy and her eyes outlined in black. Johan thought, She wants to look like Chan Po-Chu or some other Hong Kong singer. She was laughing gaily and looking up at the ceiling of the elevator as if she was looking at the sky, as if there was no roof above them and she could see the moon, or perhaps flocks of birds flying across the night sky.

There was a table already set for them right by the glass walls that offered a panorama of the lights in this darkening city. Not long ago, on a holiday by the sea, Johan had gone swimming on his own, late at night when everyone else was asleep. He had crept out of their beachside chalet and walked into the warm, clear water and swum over the fields of coral, which, in the moonlight, looked like a shadowy map of an unknown world where the boundaries were uncertain and the countries kept changing shape. And when he went deeper still, beyond the shallows where the water was black, he had seen clusters of fluorescent light, and he had thought maybe these were pearls or sea creatures, or maybe it was light from the sky, refracted in funny ways. When he came back, Farah was waiting for him, sitting on the sand with her legs crossed. She said, It's dangerous to go out there on your own, but she said it gently, as if she didn't mean it, and then she asked what he had seen, and Johan told her about the brilliant lights in the dark, fathomless sea. Come and see them, he said, but she didn't dare, even though she wanted to. He could not stop thinking about those lights. Even now.

Hello, Mister, can you stop staring at the lights for a second? I know it's a nice view but you can at least look at your mummy once in a while. Anyone would think you've never been out in town at night. What on earth do you do every night, anyway? I ask Farah and she says, Oh, Mummy, don't *worrylah,* we just go to the movies, relax at the hawker stalls with our friends. Relax, my foot. I know you don't just drink *teh-tarik* when you go out. Every time I see my friends I'm worried they're going to say something about you, especially that Mrs. Teo, she loves saying things like, Wah, I hear your boy Johan is very popular with the girls, huh? I can't stand that. Oh, Johan, what am I going to do? You were always such a good boy.

Beneath them the city seemed to be moving, slowly, the lights blinking, the shadows shifting. Johan felt tired and slightly ill. He needed to move. He needed to be in a car, going fast, not sitting here at this table.

And besides, Johan, kids are getting into trouble every night, good children from good families, not just naughty boys from Selayang. The FRU are beating people up left, right, and center just because they feel like it. After dark they treat everyone the same, whether you're a gangster or a normal teenager. Can you imagine the shame if . . . if something happened to you? Daddy's position would be . . . oh I don't even want to think about it.

I won't get into trouble. I promise. Don't worry, Mummy.

Oh, baby, Mummy's not saying you do anything naughty, I'm just saying *be careful,* that's all. Now, what looks good? This place is brand-new, just opened. For two weeks I've been saying to your daddy, Please can you take me to that new place? But he says no, too expensive. Ridiculous! Look how he spends on other things. Just order anything you want. We're going to have a nice time. Australian steak for you? Shall I have lobster thermidor?

Anything. Please order for me.

Look, look! Can you see? The restaurant really is revolving!

Yes, Mummy, I can feel it. It was a lie. He could not feel it moving.

Wow, look at the view, Johan. When Daddy and I moved here just after the war there was nothing here—nothing! Now look at it. Just in the last ten years, my god what a change. When you were a little boy this was just a big *kampung*, can you remember?

The food arrived and he ate it even though he was not hungry. He cut into the meat carefully and watched the knife slicing slowly through the bloodless flesh. He dabbed at his mouth with the corners of his napkin now and then and poured some ice water into his mother's glass.

It's so nice to be out to dinner with you. Sometimes Mummy just needs to show you how much she loves you. You've always been my special one. My perfect son.

You've got Bob too.

Yes, Bob, of course. But Bob came after you. You were my baby, just mine. Anyway, I don't know why Daddy started calling him Bob when he was a baby. Darling, I said, we call Johan Johan and Farah Farah, why do we call Hisham Bob? But he just, well, you know what he's like. Sometimes you know when not to argue.

He loves Bob. Bob's his real son—he looks just like him.

Don't say that, darling. Daddy loves you too.

You know he doesn't. Don't pretend he does. He hates me. He hates even looking at me.

It hurts me to hear you talk like that. I wish you weren't so angry with your daddy and me all the time. Take it back.

Why did you adopt me?

Oh, darling, we promised we would never talk about that again. Why do we always have to go over the past? All that history, it's another world, baby, it doesn't exist anymore. Why do you keep bringing it up?

I like hearing about it. Don't know why. I keep thinking, maybe one day you'll tell me something different. Sorry, Mummy, I'm not angry with you. Please tell me, it makes me feel better.

You know I couldn't have babies for a long time. We tried so hard, and all Daddy's family were saying, When is Salmah going to have a baby? When is Salmah going to have a baby? as if it was my fault. That's when we went to Indonesia. We have to go somewhere far far away, Daddy said. I don't know why. Daddy didn't speak to me for the whole journey there. There, I never told you that before. But when I saw you, I knew. I knew I found my baby, my very own son.

Okay, I'm sorry I asked. Don't cry, Mummy. I don't want you to be unhappy.

The restaurant did not seem to be revolving at all. Johan looked out the window and saw that nothing had changed. The patches of light were no longer moving. Johan looked at the silhouette of the hills in the distance, the rise and fall of the slopes, and thought maybe if he stared long and hard he would see them move sinuously, like the dragon-shaped lanterns the Chinese kids would hang during the Autumn Festival; they would light candles and place them in the hollowed-out dragon bellies so that they flickered and shifted and cast funny, silken shadows on the walls. But he knew the hills and the city would not move, no matter how hard he tried.

Mummy, he said in a softer voice, will you tell me again about my brother?

No, please, Johan, I can't stand talking about that. Oh my god. She wiped her eyes with a thin handkerchief. It makes me feel sick remembering how— oh—how he . . . It makes me sick . . . lucky you didn't see. Anyway, Bob is your brother, your only brother. Don't you forget that, darling.

Okay. I'm sorry, Mummy.

I don't think I can finish my food now. It's too much for me.

Are you sure, Mummy? It looks very good. Mine is delicious.

No. Anyway I have to watch my figure.

I'm sorry, Mummy. I won't ask you about all that stuff again. Promise.

Across the room the Chinese couple who had been in the elevator were reaching out to each other, fingertips brushing against fingertips, barely touching, just seeking reassurance that the other person was there, wanting to know that they could grab hold of each other and never let go if the restaurant started to spin out of control. Johan wished that the room would revolve faster and faster. He wanted to see what the couple would do, because he knew that they would not remain together.

I'm just going to the ladies' room to freshen up, then we should go, darling. I'm tired all of a sudden, I don't know why. I feel so hot, oh, I think it's age. My son is nearly a man now, what do I expect? I must be an old woman! Give me five minutes, then home.

Alone at the table Johan looked at the Chinese girl. She was wearing a slim-fitting flowery blouse with a mandarin collar and very short sleeves that showed off her arm, her still-extended arm that lay flat on the table from elbow to fingertips. They were getting ready to leave, heading back out into the night, and Johan felt calm because he knew that soon he too would be driving through the city.

The elevator doors opened and a man and a woman stepped out. Their faces were obscured by a bouquet of orchids on the bar, but Johan could see that their arms were linked, elbow locked comfortably into elbow, and he could hear the waiters' voices, servile and nervous and twittering, and he could discern the color and tone of a young woman's taut calf, the slenderness of her hips contrasting with the stoutness of her middle-aged partner as they were shown to a table at the far end of the restaurant, hidden in a niche perfectly made for secret lovers.

Johan got up and went to the shiny marble desk at the front of the restaurant. Please take my bill to my father, he said. He's over at that table there. Yes, Dato' Zainuddin. Just tell him it's from his son. Johan, yes. He'll settle the bill for me.

In this new, rich city, Johan thought, people's lives were like currents out in the open sea, pulling them to places they could not resist. It was no use swimming, you just had to surrender to the waves and see where they took you. A long time ago, when he was small, he'd imagined himself borne away by the sea. He wanted to be dragged away by the waves, which would leave no trace of him. If he had done so, his brother would be in this expensive restaurant, the perfect happy son for Mummy and Daddy. But Johan had not dared, and so he was still here.

Come on, Mummy, let's go. I've taken care of everything. Please don't say that, it's nothing, really, it's nothing. You give me so much pocket money anyway. Take my arm. Careful, the doors are closing. Look at the time. It's late. Don't worry, I'll drive carefully.

13

*W*hen the telephone rang, Margaret knew it would be Bill Schneider. He said, "I've got news."

She listened for a few minutes without speaking. Bill was always quite precise about what he knew, and what he wanted. For a very brief moment she remembered all the things he had said to her when she first met him, many years ago. He had been very direct, and she very gullible. It was a time she did not care to remember, but she could not stop remembering. She said "yes" and "mm" several times, then she hung up. All in all, it was not a very long conversation.

"You were trying to keep your voice down," Mick said. He had not moved from his reclining position; his eyes were still closed. His body was too wide for the modest Asian sofa and he had to lean slightly on his side, pushed up against the cushions in what looked like an extremely uncomfortable position. "You sounded very shifty indeed."

"Not at all," Margaret said, sitting down. "I was just trying not to wake anyone up." She realized that she, too, had fallen into a too-deep sleep in the armchair, waking up with the crick in her neck that brought with it nagging aches and pains. She thought of some of the places she had slept: on the bare boards of a Dayak longhouse, listening to the snuffling of pigs under the house; on the mud floor of a Sepik dwelling; on the back of a truck traveling toward Bromo, propped up against sacks of rice, surrounded by cages of defecating chickens. She had managed to sleep quite happily then, and she had never woken up with a bad back or a stiff neck or a cramped arm as she did so often these days. She could not remember ever waking up from a night in a jungle lean-to feeling out of sorts, plagued by a mild sense of dread, wondering how she would fill the day ahead of her. The days seemed to take care of themselves back then; the hours went by and there was never enough time to do all she wanted. Now there was only time, and time created space—and nothing could occupy the space that it created.

"Do you ever wake up afraid of what the day has in store for you, Mick?" she asked.

"Usually I have a bad hangover and all I want to do is find an aspirin. Or another drink. So, no, I'm not afraid, just desperate to clear my head. But don't try and change the subject. What did Schneider say?"

"Shh." Margaret lifted a finger to her lips. "You'll wake Adam." Night was turning quickly into dawn but in those twilight moments there was still a heavy calm, troubled only by the bored halfhearted yap of a dog in the distance. "Bill thinks Karl is being repatriated. It seems he got picked up in an army raid on Communists. They weren't expecting to find a Dutch guy, he just got trawled up in the net—you know, like some prehistoric fish that everyone thought was extinct but gets hauled up with a big catch of sardines. Sheer accident that they got ahold of him—he was so far off the radar that he would have got away, but it seems nowhere is out of reach these days, Mick. The army has its tentacles everywhere."

More dogs were barking now, calling idly to one another across the rubbish heaps that littered the streets. The air smelled fresh and moist, but in a few hours it would be hot and dusty again, and the memory of last night's rain would evaporate into the ocher sky. "It seems that Karl is still here, in Indonesia. At first they kept him with the farmer-fishermen Communists from the islands. You know what they're like, they're rednecks. They panic at the sight of a white guy—either they try and marry their daughter off to him or they lock him up. Then he got moved to Surabaya, then the trail begins to get fuzzy. There have been one or two repatriation flights from East Java, but Bill can't find any trace of him on those lists. He thinks Karl is here in Jakarta, waiting to be flown back to Holland. Bill's contacts are trying to find out more, but it's not easy. U.S. dollars can't buy everything nowadays, and besides, no one's really interested. There are bigger things on the horizon. Even Bill says so. He was honest about our chances of finding Karl. There's big trouble not far away, he says. You were right, Mick. Something terrible is about to happen."

"It's the Communists, isn't it? They're falling out of favor and Sukarno doesn't know if he should get in bed with them or chop their balls off."

"That's what Bill says. The Soviets and the Chinese are pumping money into Indonesia and no one knows where it's going, or what they're doing. The army's getting very nervous about the whole thing—they don't know what's going to happen."

"No one knows anything anymore."

Margaret watched Mick reach for his long-empty bottle of beer and scratch at the last remnants of the label with his fingernail. "I just *cannot* accept that there is a white guy wandering around Java and we can't find him," she said. "No, I *will* not accept it."

"You're on a losing wicket, darling. This is a country of more than a hundred million people. Why should any Indonesian care about some solitary white guy who's gone AWOL when they're dying of hunger and on the brink of a civil war? The Dutch are ancient history in this country, can't you see? Even if your guy *is* in Jakarta—and there's no guarantee he is—we still need to find him in the biggest, dirtiest, most wretched and corrupt city in the world. There is *no* chance."

"That's always been your problem," Margaret said, raising her voice. She felt curiously energetic; the stiffness in her neck had ceased to bother her and she was no longer feeling lethargic. "You've always just accepted the way things are, you just go with the flow. Ever since I've known you, that's been the way you are. It's so damn frustrating. What is it you used to say to me when we first met? '*L'action c'est pas la vie,* so why bother?'—or some bullshit like that."

"Actually it was '*L'action n'est pas la vie, mais une façon de gâcher quelque chose, un énervement.*' It's from Rimbaud."

"Whatever. That's why you're still a third-rate hack, stringing for the mediocre newspapers of the world. You have a brilliant mind and you're in one of the hottest political climates in the world—and still you refuse to get your act together. We can find Karl. It can't be that difficult. Come on. You've got scores of contacts in Jakarta. Call your journalist friends. I'll speak to people I know, I'll sniff around—I have a nose for these things. We'll find him. Don't be so defeatist. And will you stop picking at that bottle, please?"

"You haven't told me why this Karl de Willigen is so important to you. I presume he's the long-lost love you never confessed to having had."

Margaret looked him squarely in the eye and contemplated telling him the whole truth: how she sometimes woke up in the night and remembered exactly the way Karl looked in the half-light of a Balinese dusk; how she remembered being sixteen and in love, knowing that she would be clinging to her memories a quarter of a century later. She said, "It's complicated, Mick. We were very close friends. He must have represented something to me, though I've never figured out what, exactly. But do you really think I'm the sort of woman who pines after a man? Get a grip on yourself, Mick Matsoukis. I'm doing it for the boy. I want him to get his father back. Don't you?"

"Speaking of which, what are we going to do with the boy?"

Margaret paused before replying. Her initial instinct was to keep Adam by her side every moment of the day. She had not felt at ease leaving him on his own at home. He was too vulnerable, too helpless. But the thought of losing him was even more frightening. "He stays here," she said, dropping her voice. "It's too dangerous having him with us. Maybe I'll call Din and ask him to look after the kid. Let's just get through today and see how we make out."

Daybreak over Jakarta was swift and uneventful, the darkness of the night sky replaced decisively by its murky daytime haze; noncolor substituted noncolor in a quick, perfunctory sweep. There was no ceremony, no lingering moment of aching beauty during which one might reflect on life and love, or yearn for things lost, or things as yet unrealized. The change was ruthless and efficient and unsentimental—typically Asian, thought Margaret. She liked it that way. She was no longer a prisoner of the night and all its limitations. In the intense days of this city she could accomplish anything she set out to do.

"I'll check in with you later this afternoon," she said, starting to make herself a cup of coffee. "And remember, Mick: This is your big chance too. The mother of all stories is just around the corner, and it's got your name written all over it."

THE WHOLE CITY seemed to be clad in the *Merah Putih*. The stark scarlet and white of the young republic hung from every window and lined the streets on hastily erected flagpoles. It adorned the city in every conceivable manner: Giant banners hung veil-like over entire facades of buildings; streams of tiny flags were strung up high over the roads, fluttering in the wind like starlings on a wire; municipal workers painted huge, stylized murals—one featured a waterfall that swirled and cascaded its river of red white water on to the beholder; trucks were painted half-red, half-white; little girls wore red and white ribbons in their hair and ate red and white bonbons; young men riding three to a single motorbike wore bandannas of red or white that trailed behind them and made them look like warriors as they weaved through the red white traffic on the red white roads. And the president's face was everywhere, proudly regarding his red white city, at once virile and benign—and a good few years younger than he was, perfectly preserved at that moment of independence in '45. At least it brought relief to the grayness, Margaret thought, but it was already beginning to seem dull to her. She had seen thirteen Independence Day celebrations, each one grander and more lavish than its predecessor, marked by the construction of a grandiose "gift" to the nation, some useless futuristic monument or stadium or theme park. She had become inured to it all, familiar with the grotesque. She remembered—with no sense of regret, just a tinge of sorrow—how those first Independence Days had seemed so exciting, so full of promise. She was newly arrived from Europe and her whole life was waiting to be rebuilt, much like this new country with its young president. She had been ready for change, ready for the task ahead of her, and so had they. She looked around this city now: They had lost their way, but she would not allow herself to be dragged away with it.

She tried to remember how she'd felt back then—not just how she or the city had looked, but the optimism she had felt. The physical scenes were easy enough to recall. The streets were muddy and barely covered with tarmac; even the center of the city seemed to be filled with *kampungs* that ran indistinctly into one another, clustered on the edge of the black canal where people washed and lived their entire lives. There was the smell of drains and sewage (*that* hadn't changed) but also the odor of camphor, she remembered, a woody, heady smell that made her feel good, even healthy, like some mysterious fortifying medicine that was everywhere in the air; all she had to do was breathe.

What was more difficult to recapture now was that well of strength, that sensation that no hurt or sadness or damage of any kind could not be put right. Nothing was beyond repair, everything was achievable. It wasn't that long ago, goddamn it, so why didn't it just instantly come back to her? Everything she looked at had seemed full of promise, even Bill Schneider.

She stopped the taxi at Pasar Baru and stepped into the labyrinth of stalls on the fringes of the great bazaar, passing quickly from bright sunlight to deep gloom. The alleyways between the shops were narrow and slightly damp and lit by kerosene lamps, even in the daytime; the dim yellow gaslight only added to the gloom. She went past stalls that sold stacks of cloth that smelled of old mothballs and others that sold cheap silvery handicrafts that glowed under the lamps; there were dried-meat stalls, dried-fruit stalls, raffia-string stalls, rubber band stalls, shoelace stalls. She knew her way to the coffee stall where Bill was waiting for her.

"Hello, sweetheart," he said.

"It makes me shudder when you say that."

"There was a time when it didn't. I remember it very well, you know." He smoothed his thinning hair across his head, even though not a wisp of it was out of place. He had not lost any hair in the years that Margaret had known him; he had always looked like this—an overgrown schoolboy forced into a man's body, someone who had learned the gestures of adulthood long before his time without truly understanding what those gestures meant. And now that he was an adult, it was too late to recapture the innocence of his youth. It seemed that only Margaret had ever seen this part of him. She had latched on to that tiny bit of goodness, she thought, and had wanted to make it her own. She had spotted him talking to a group of friends in the Arts Quad early that fall semester—his first and her last. He was wearing a blue blazer and gray flannels and was smoothing his hair down in long, languid movements—just as he was doing now. At first she had thought that it was a reflex action triggered by nervousness, but once she had spoken to him a few times she knew that he was a boy who had never been nervous. Maybe it was about control, she thought, though she wasn't sure. He'd asked her out. They'd driven along the banks of

Seneca Lake and shared an ice-cream sundae in Geneva. What do you think Geneva in Switzerland looks like? they wondered. And when he put his hand on hers it felt light, as if it belonged to a child; it was freckled and pale and hovered nervously without settling. And then, years later, when he turned up in Jakarta, she had taken him to Sunda Kelapa to look at the old fishing boats and he had said, Wow, I've never seen anything so beautiful, as if he really meant it, as if he had stumbled upon a whole new world, and it had been Margaret who had helped him discover it. And at that moment of wonder at Bill's innocence she had fallen resolutely out of love with Karl (or, to be more precise, with the memory of Karl). She remembered that clearly. She had told him about how she had fallen in love with a Dutch artist in Bali when she was in her teens, yes, a crush, that was it, a silly schoolgirl crush; Bill had laughed and said, "That's hilarious." And now he was using it against her.

"I'm sorry, Bill, I don't know if I can give you what you want."

"Of course you can, sweetheart, I'm not asking for much. You've done it before." He leaned across the table and touched her forearm. She expected his hand to be clammy but it was dry and smooth, as it had been twenty years ago.

"It's different now," she said. "The students don't trust me anymore. They don't respect me."

"That's not the Margaret I know. I hope you're not being deliberately unhelpful."

"Honestly, Bill. I just—I just don't have my finger on the pulse anymore."

"Look, Margaret," he said, sweeping his hand across his forehead again. His voice changed suddenly, becoming calmer, less cajoling. His fingers began to feel curiously heavy on her arm. "I need names. Commies. That university is a hotbed of activism. I just need to know who the ringleaders are, what they're planning. You have an ear to the ground. We have these kids just out of grad school sitting in offices analyzing political trends, trying to tell us how the next few months are going to turn out, but it doesn't count for anything. I have one guy, fluent in standard Indonesian *and* old-fashioned Javanese, PhD in linguistics, picking apart all of Sukarno's speeches from the last ten years, looking for clues as to how this guy is thinking, what he's going to do next—and you know what? We still don't have a clue. You remember that outburst six months ago, when Dean Rusk announced there was to be no more aid to Indonesia? In every newspaper in the world Sukarno screamed, *'To hell with your aid.'* This kid wrote a twenty-page report on that one line. Conclusion? Sukarno doesn't want U.S. aid. Jesus. But *you* know, Margaret. You hear things. You're one of us, but it's like you're one of them too. How about your colleagues? I hear your research assistant has an interesting background."

"Din? You're crazy."

"I have information, Margaret—*intelligence.* Something is being planned on that campus, something big. I need to know what it is, and whether it'll harm our interests."

"Our interests? What does that mean? For years I reported on the students to you because I thought you wanted to help, because you were new here and you needed information to help this country to help itself. That's what you said. God, I was stupid. If we hadn't been . . . oh, forget it. This is crazy. What sort of intelligence do you have on Din? I just cannot believe he is a danger to anyone."

"I can't tell you that, Margaret, but you have to trust me. Please. Just give me whatever you can find out. You might think I'm exaggerating, but your country needs your help. Your people need you. The world's gone crazy and America needs all the help it can get so that it can help others. And don't forget that I'm doing all I can to find your *friend.*"

Margaret did not say anything. A number of witty, cutting responses began to form in her head but faded away quickly. There was really nothing left for her to say.

Bill's hand was still on her arm. "Call me tomorrow," he said suddenly, as if some bright memory had reentered his thoughts after a long absence; his fingers tightened slightly around her wrist, pleading rather than threatening. "It's Sukarno's big twirl before the cameras of the world. This year's Independence Day speech is going to be something else. The temperature's going to be raised quite a few degrees. Let's listen to it together. I think I can get access to the presidential palace—a friend will fix it for us. Please say yes—it'll remind me of my first days here, running around town with you. You'll see all your old contacts, and you never know who might help you."

Just say no, Margaret thought. She paused. The breathless excitement in Bill's voice was not genuine, she told herself; he doesn't care about you, or about the past, or even about himself. This man is an actor, a fake; it's part of his job.

"Okay," she said. "I'll come."

14

*T*he poet known as Hanawi, who celebrated the lives of the fishermen and subsistence farmers of Perdo and its neighboring islands, remained unknown during his tragically short lifetime, despite a prodigious literary output over a career that lasted a mere decade before he drowned at age thirty-two. He had taken his little outrigger far out to sea, its gaily painted hull braving the swell of the powerful waves that morning, according to the fragments of hearsay and eyewitness accounts that have since crystallized and become quasi history. He knew these waters well (which schoolboy can forget the immortal lines "And thus the sea is my country/It is my land, my sky/Indeed, it is my blood"?), but that day the skies were exceptionally dark with clouds and everyone knew a bad storm was about to break over Perdo. Most of the other fishing boats came back early, but Hanawi's did not. The storm lasted two days, and when the waters had calmed the fishermen found his boat washed up on the rocks that circled the western end of the coral reef. Its frail mast had been broken but the sail was curiously intact, floating in the clear, green water. After the storm, the sea was glasslike and flat once more; it was hard to imagine that there had been a storm. It is like this in Perdo: The changes are so absolute, so extreme, that you can never believe anything else exists before or after the very moment in which you find yourself.

The manner of his death no doubt contributed to the image of the romantic poet who lived the authentic life of the masses. In language of extraordinary simplicity, he captured the harshness and beauty of rural life. His verse was free from the conventions of court poetry with its formality and associations with nobility: His voice embodied a sense of freedom and pride that echoed the lives of poor villagers, a sense of liberation and identity that has taken on greater importance in recent times, even (or perhaps particularly) in the cities. Take these lines from his celebrated poem "Hartini," for example:

When seas are dark, anxious, the quick swell of each wave
lifts the boat quite some way, as light as an arrow.
When you fly, all your tears—yes, tears—are for now, save
the few which may, just may, be shed for tomorrow.
When the catch is bounteous, on those rare fine bright days,
the mackerel seem to play, spinning a small rainbow.
You notice her eyes: fierce, yet lost, too, in a haze.
Come back, you want to say. Come back from your sorrow.

Can you hear that it is a double pantun? Hanawi uses this traditional everyday form in new and playful ways, tweaking it, making it seem casual and more modern—but none of this is really relevant. What is important is that even illiterate villagers can relate to the rhythms of this style. We grew up with it, our ears are tuned to it. And so, in a funny way, it means something to us all. We feel what it is to be one people, free in our own country.

Does it matter, then, to find out that Hanawi was not, in fact, born on one of these remote islands but into a prosperous family of Chinese immigrants in Malang? He did not grow up speaking the coarse dialect of Perdo with its dull vowels and overemphasized consonants, but Javanese of a very stately variety, in addition to what was to become standard Indonesian and, of course, Dutch, educated as he was at the Hoogere Inland School. At home his family spoke Teochew, the language of his forefathers who had emigrated from southern China midway through the nineteenth century. It is true that he shunned the trappings of sophisticated Javanese life in favor of a simple existence in the islands, but he was able to do so because of the wealth and generosity of his family. He wrote ode after ode to the lives of fishermen but did not himself work as one; in fact, he never worked at all. Do you think this affects the authenticity of his voice? Does this change the way we read his work? When political leaders quote lines of his to show how in touch they are with the lives of ordinary folk, should we be moved, or simply howl with derision?

"Um, I'm not sure," Adam said at last. It was hot; not the brilliant heat of the islands, tinged with the smell of sea winds under swirling skies, but a kind of dead, lumpen mass of stickiness that clung to every bit of his skin; he could even feel it on his eyelids. The scant shade of the *becak* offered little protection against this assault and there was not a breath of wind. Adam felt he was being slowly suffocated. He blinked several times. His eyes felt ill-equipped to deal with the city; it was very different from the one he had imagined. A dog trotted past, and Adam saw that it had something embedded in its hindquarters, a bit of shrapnel; the flesh and skin had grown back over it, covering it with a lump of tissue so that only the tip of it poked out.

On top of all this, Din talked endlessly, his arms flailing to emphasize words, becoming more and more agitated, his voice growing hoarse as it competed with the noise of the traffic. He had been in an irritable mood ever since he'd turned up at Margaret's house earlier that morning and announced that she had asked him to look after Adam. He seemed glad to find Adam alone.

"But aren't we better off staying here?" Adam protested. He felt uneasy at the thought of leaving the snug safety of the house. He had quickly developed quite an attachment to it—its contents seemed oddly familiar to him, and he did not want to leave. "Margaret left a note saying not to leave."

"You can't stay in all day, can you? Don't you want to see a bit of Jakarta? Come on, let's go and discover things. I'll be your tour guide. Don't you trust a fellow Sumatran?"

Adam remembered how Din had been generous in his advice the previous day; he meant well, thought Adam, feeling childish and immature at being afraid to venture out with his new guardian. They would simply go out for the day and Margaret would not even have to know about it.

Din's monologue had begun placidly enough—something about the difference in culture between Perdo and Jakarta, about uniting everyone in Indonesia because it was such a big country. By the time they flagged down a *becak* he was in full flow. Nothing escaped his wrath; he had a lecture prepared for everything: why the streets were so dirty (low self-esteem, bad education); why we had low self-esteem and bad education (the Dutch, corrupt politics); why we had corrupt politics (poverty, America, the Dutch, ignorance of history); why we ignored our own history (poverty, America, the Dutch, corrupt politics).

"You are a classic example of a badly educated orphan," Din said. "It's not your fault. You were abandoned and left to fend for yourself without any understanding of the world around you."

"That's not true," Adam said. "I *am* educated. My father taught me everything—literature, music, even politics."

Din curled his hand into a fist and punched his own forehead, hard enough to make a dull, thudding noise. He closed his eyes, and Adam thought maybe he had hurt himself. "A self-deluding orphan, I see. Right, tell me all about the conference that took place in 'fifty-five, right here in Indonesia. Don't know? I'll give you a clue. It happened in Bandung. No? I'll tell you: the Conference of Newly Independent Asian and African Countries, hosted by the president. The start of the new world order, which we control. What about the Nonaligned Movement. No? Do you see what I mean?"

Adam did not quite see what Din meant, and it frustrated him that he could not fully grasp what Din was talking about. It also disturbed him that Din had all this knowledge that he himself lacked. Part of him did not believe that it was all true. He thought he knew about Bandung. It was an elegant city in the hills where the air was cool, a place people fled to, hoping to escape the heat of Jakarta and stroll along elegant boulevards lined with noble, old buildings. He decided he would not say any of this to Din. Compared to what Din knew, all his learning suddenly felt insubstantial and flimsy—a child's view of the world. The years of learning from and listening to Karl had not amounted to anything. He felt like an infant in the glare of Din's brilliance.

"You see the world through a European's eyes," Din continued before Adam had a chance to respond. "Your own eyes do not work. You can't see how the world is changing around you. That little country just to the north of here, our neighbor—what's that called?"

Adam knew the answer. He had come across it in the papers and on the radio. "Malaysia," he said, trying to sound casual, not too pleased with himself.

"You see? How predictable."

"But it's there," Adam said, pointing ahead of him, as if Kuala Lumpur lay just beyond the horizon. "It exists, doesn't it?"

"No! That is the point—Malaysia does not exist!" Din shouted suddenly, his head jerking. "Malaysia"—he pronounced it as if speaking a foreign language, his voice squeaky, like a child's, and Adam remembered the children's voices at school, mocking his surname: De Willigen? De Willigen? and he remembered the hurt and the shame he'd felt, the shame for something that was not his fault—"Ma-*lay*-sia is a British construct! It is a work of pure fiction, created by the old Imperialist countries to destabilize Indonesia and all the newly independent countries of the world. It was created so that Britain and America and their cronies can continue to have a presence in this region, but I tell you, their time is finished, *finished*! We will invade them and crush them, all those Malaysian puppets. They look like us and even speak our language—but they do not know they are being used. This is why we beat them in the Thomas Cup: They are not masters of their own destiny. *We* are."

Din fell silent for a moment, his chest heaving with an exhausted satisfaction. In that instant the roar of the Jakarta traffic took over, seizing the initiative from Din's monologue to fill Adam's ears with its own rhythms. And yet Adam knew that Din would not, indeed could not, stay silent for long. "My brother," he said, "is in Malaysia."

"What?" Din said, turning to look at him. "I thought you didn't know where he was."

Adam shrugged. "I don't know anything for certain."

"Oh god, this gets worse. Not only do you think like a white person, you have a brother who lives in a neo-Imperialist country. This *becak* driver must be lame. Why is he so damn slow? The speech will be starting soon. We're going to listen to it with some of my friends. You'll learn things. It will be good for you."

There were about a dozen people in the wood-and-tin shack that stood at the far end of the collection of flimsy structures that formed a courtyard. They were on the edge of a sprawling shantytown bordering Kebon Jeruk, where the houses still seemed solid and at least semi-permanent, built more from timber than pieces of rusty corrugated iron: They would at least weather this rainy season, and maybe also the next one. Deeper in this labyrinth, away from tarmac roads and running water, the houses were a patchwork of salvaged scrap: flattened oil drums, biscuit tins, fragments of tarpaulin, splintered lengths of wood, torn mosquito nets—anything that would bring momentary respite from the rain and the sun. But even here, on the fringes of the *kampung,* Adam had seen a tiny house with walls made from pieces of advertising boards. In front of this house a young woman was fanning a wood fire that refused to light properly. Next to her was a child, a girl, no more than three or four years old, naked except for a dirty ribbon in her hair; she looked up at Adam as he walked past and retreated shyly into the shade of the house. There was no front door, just a gap in the walls that read . . . kes you ten times stron . . . mous all over the world, now avai . . .

"Of course these houses will not last very long," Din shrugged, "but they can be quickly rebuilt. We are strong, practical people, remember," he said.

They came upon a circle of men and women not much older than Adam; Din had explained that they were all students at UI. "This is the orphan I told you about," Din announced casually to his friends, as if he had simply said "Sundanese" or "Torajan." Adam felt angry with himself because he did not have the courage to explain and modify this description to a group of strangers (he *did* have a father, after all). But then again, maybe Karl was dead, and now he was an orphan twice over.

"Your orphan doesn't look very happy," one girl said. She was about Adam's age, perhaps slightly older, and spoke in a voice similar to Din's—steeped in a confidence that suggested formal education, with proper articulation tempered by a casual Jakarta accent. Their sharp, clever voices were a code, thought Adam, a method of conspiracy; he did not belong with these people. And yet this girl was not exactly like Din. She had a relaxed quality, a self-assuredness that ran deeper than mere education. It came from something else, something that Adam thought he could recognize: privilege, that sense of being special. He didn't know if he could even call her a *girl.* She looked his age, but everything about her—her poise, her stylish hair (short and falling in soft curves on either side of her face, like a movie star's, unlike the severe and functional hairdos of the other girls present), her easy vowels, the way she sat, legs crossed, one elbow propped on the table—made her seem like a mature woman.

"Orphans never are," someone else added, and suddenly everyone was speaking.

"How can they be?"

"It's impossible to find true happiness if you're an orphan."

"That's not true. Orphans are the only ones who are free to find their own happiness; they don't have their own history so they create it for themselves."

"But, Z, that's just an illusion. Their lives are determined for them by people who have no relation to them whatsoever—total strangers dictate their future. They have no attachment to anything, they stumble around in the dark until one day something happens to set them on a different, random path. I don't call that freedom."

"But that's just what it's like for all of us!"

There was laughter, either cold and scoffing or shrill and juvenile.

"We run a revolutionary magazine called *Z,*" said the girl with the stylish hair. Her name was Zubaidah, she explained, but she was known only as Zu, or even just Z. "I hate my full name. It's too ... pretty. When we started the magazine it needed a name, something that was not crass and obvious like the other dull, dogmatic pamphlets you see—*Revolusi, Time for Change, The People's Voice,* and so on. It's not easy to come up with a name for an underground literary newspaper, you know, so we just named it after me, just to give us something to get started."

"But then I had a brainstorm," a youth of perfect complexion said. He had long hair that hung in fine strands almost to his shoulders; he was trying to grow a beard, but he'd managed only a meager mustache and a straggly goatee. " 'Z!' I said—the last letter of the alphabet, ignored, mysterious, underutilized. Perfect!"

"Awie is the poet among us, you see," said Z.

"In fact, *Z* stands alone at the end of the alphabet, lonely, without any prospects in life, abandoned by all the others. It is the orphan of the alphabet—it should appeal to you."

He slid a flimsy, shoddily bound magazine across the table toward Adam. "Our latest issue."

Adam flicked through it, pausing occasionally, pretending to read; he nodded, feigning comprehension and appreciation. The dense text was punctuated by several cartoon drawings. There was one of the president in bed with a busty European woman, their huge feet protruding from the tangle of sheets, toothy grins etched across their faces.

It was set next to another drawing of the president gnawing on a gar-
gantuan chicken drumstick in a field of wilting rice; in the background
a farmer surveyed the cracked mud, his shoulders hunched. The caption
under both drawings read: OUR HERO.

"Shh, quiet—the speech is about to start," said Din. He had not lost
his frown, which seemed, if anything, to have deepened, creating little
crevasses across his forehead. He glared at Adam and jabbed his index
finger in the direction of the radio that sat on a chair, all on its own in
the middle of the group. They all shuffled their chairs toward it, leaning forward, elbows resting on knees, chins cradled in palms, ready to
fall deep into concentration. Adam copied their movements. He remembered the tales of ancient philosophers that Karl had told him
about and felt as if he were a pupil or scribe at the feet of some elec-
tronic preacher. There was a moment of near-complete silence; they
could not hear even the faintest crackle of static from the radio. In the
distance there was a baby's cry, a thin wail that started and then stopped;
there was no other noise from the slums around them. Adam wondered
if the radio had failed at the crucial moment. He held his breath, listening. No one moved. And then the voice began speaking in a tone at
once urgent and measured. He had never heard a voice like this before:
rich with calm strength and intonations that seemed both foreign and
familiar. He felt a hot surge running through his body, filling his head
with a sudden, giddy excitement he could not explain. He remembered
wading into the sea for the first time, into the warm gentle surf, with
Karl standing in the shallows; he remembered the brilliant reflection of
the sun on the water, the wild feeling of danger when he uncurled his
toes and surrendered his body to the waves, his arms and legs moving
with a freedom he had never known, as if he had only just discovered
his body; he remembered too dipping his head under water and finding an entire watery world whose depth and enormity he had never
discerned from land, a place in which he was powerless and small. He
was gasping when he resurfaced, afraid of being dragged away; but part
of him had wished, secretly, to be taken by the sea. ". . . *fellow country-
men and revolutionaries, the twentieth century has been a time of terrific dynamism, but also of great fear. Yes, we are living in a world of fear. The life of
man is corroded and made bitter by fear—fear of the future, of the hydrogen*

bomb, of ideologies, of everything, but especially of the loss of man's safety and morality. Perhaps this fear is a greater danger than the danger itself, because it is fear that drives men to act foolishly, to act thoughtlessly. . . ."

"Just get to the point," Din muttered. A sharp chorus of shushing started and died down with equal swiftness, and once again the voice on the radio was the only sound to be heard.

". . . nowadays to hear people say, 'Colonialism is dead.' Let us not be soothed or deceived by this. I say to you, friends and fellow revolutionaries, that colonialism is NOT dead. How can it be, so long as vast areas of Asia and Africa are not yet free? I beg of you not to think of colonialism only in the classic form we in Indonesia have known—it is a skillful and determined enemy that warps, viruslike, into its modern form of economic and intellectual control. . . ."

Din sighed; it seemed very loud in the unnatural silence around them. "How many times have we heard this before?" he whispered in Adam's ear. Instinctively, Adam moved away from his hot, sour breath. In those few seconds he had missed what the voice had said, and he too began to wish that Din would keep quiet.

". . . the Indonesian Revolution has become a rocky mountain shooting fire amid the ocean of mankind's struggle to build a new world free of exploitation of man by man, free of exploitation of nation by nation. My fellow revolutionaries, there is a phrase in Italian, Vivere Pericoloso. *This means, To Live Dangerously. Yes, my brothers! You have understood me. For Indonesia and every other country that strives to be free, this is the Year of Living Dangerously. It is our duty as revolutionaries to do so."*

"At last we're getting somewhere," Din said. He was about to continue when Z lifted a finger to her lips, slowly, almost theatrically; Din's mouth lay half-open, his chin lifted in defiance, but he fell silent nonetheless. Adam looked at Z's curiously masculine index finger, poised lightly in front of—but not touching—her delicate lips. Her gaze lit briefly on Adam before returning to the radio, as if instructing him to resume listening to the speech.

"In the last few hours, brave Indonesian soldiers have begun to strike at the heart of this Malaysia that British Imperialists are so proud of. Here is proof of Living Dangerously. Our forces are now just a hundred miles from Kuala Lumpur, where the lackeys of Imperialism cower from us. They thought we were afraid. They thought we would not dare. They thought that the might of America would save them, but it will not. The British and Americans who seek to con-

trol the free world will be crushed in Southeast Asia. They will meet the same fate as the French in Vietnam. In the last few weeks a mighty fleet of British aircraft carriers and destroyers was forced to flee from us. Why? Because I will not allow the enemy's foot to step on the proud rampaging Indonesian Bull. It is no longer time to be conciliatory. Our revolution has foes everywhere. We have a duty to attack, to destroy every power, whether foreign or not, native or not, that endangers the security and the continuation of the revolution."

Z shifted in her seat. "I don't like the tone of this," she said. Her brow was only faintly troubled by a frown, but it was enough of a signal for the others to start a debate.

"The country is starving—let's fight expensive wars with the Americans!"

"What a convenient excuse to suppress anyone who dares to oppose him!"

"Revolution? What revolution? He has no ideology. Listen, listen . . ."

". . . I know a science that is efficacious, namely, Marxism. As you know, I am a friend of Communists because Communists are revolutionary people, and I am a friend of all revolutionary people, whatever their cause, be it religion or ideology. . . ."

Z spoke again, more firmly this time. "This man is unbelievable. He has no idea what Marxism is. It's just a word he's heard. He wants to keep everyone happy but he can't do so any longer. He shouldn't be allowed."

"As I wrote in my satirical epic poem in last month's *Z*," said the long-haired poet, "our dear president has supplanted the state in controlling the means of production in a classless society."

"It makes me so angry," someone else added, "because the economics and demographics of Indonesia would make it an ideal Communist state. That's what my thesis is all about."

There were more voices competing for attention now; the radio was forgotten. Din pushed his chair back quietly and tugged at Adam's elbow. "Let's go," he said. Adam did not want to leave. He wanted to hear the things being said. It surprised and excited him to have understood the things they were saying—not everything, of course, but the general sense of it. They were people his own age, people who were not too dissimilar from him, he thought; they were not unschooled kids from the Moluccas but people whose complexities he thought he could understand. He wanted to stay.

"Come on," Din said, continuing to pull at him. Adam did not resist; he did not want to make a scene.

Once they were out in the narrow alleys of the *kampung,* Din began to speak with his usual fervor. "It's always the same with those guys—all talk, no action. PhD this, modern Marxist theory that. What good does *Z* magazine do for Indonesia? It's just toilet paper. I wrote one article for them on the need for regime change. Good, very good, that Zubaidah girl says. Then I wrote another one, saying the only way to do this is by forceful means, and she says"—he mimicked her smooth voice and smart vowels—" 'We do not subscribe to such things.' What use is a Communist revolutionary magazine that doesn't subscribe to *action*? Twenty years of independence and look where we are. Come on, you're going to see what real revolutionaries look like."

From a distance Adam did not recognize the crowd as being made up of people. He saw a dark, amorphous band that seemed to hover just above where he thought the ground should be, erasing all detail of life and obscuring the buildings beyond it. The flags atop the presidential palace were just visible above this band of noncolor, but otherwise the city seemed to have disappeared. Perhaps it was the heat that induced this mirage, he thought, or maybe there was something wrong with him. He was very tired. He could not hear anything either, not even when they were quite close to the edge of the mass, this inhuman gathering of humans. The same silence he had experienced with Z surrounded him again, an absence of noise that acquired a weight of its own, like the soundlessness of being under water. When he dipped his head beneath the waves and kicked until his body skimmed the top of the reef, it was this that he felt: a noiseless void pressing against his temples.

They stepped into the hot swell of bodies: the sour smell of old clothes on unwashed bodies. Din forced his way through the crush, pushing people aside with one hand, holding on to Adam's wrist with the other, as if fighting through dense foliage. The bodies around them gave way with only minimal resistance; all eyes were fixed on some invisible point in the distance. As they waded deeper into this swamp Adam heard the same voice he had heard before: rhythmic, cajoling, powerful. It was impossible to tell where the speaker was—his voice seemed to be coming from all around them, becoming louder as they pushed farther forward. It was more urgent than before, quickening as the beautiful baritone dropped to little more than a whisper, each syllable compressed for emphasis, as insistent as a torrent of water forcing its way through a crack in a wall. It had been more than two hours since the speech had begun, but the voice did not seem to tire.

Adam could see the palace now, the brilliant white stone coming into view over the heads of the people in front of them; they were slowing down; the bodies were no longer giving way but standing firm: a wall of slick smooth shirtless torsos. "*. . . we approach the moment when each and every individual who cares for the future of humanity must fight. . . .*" Din continued to grip Adam's wrist even though they had ceased to move; Adam pulled away slightly, taking half a step back, but he was trapped by someone else pressing against him. Suddenly the space around him had disappeared; there was no air, just the stale, salty smell of skin and hair that forced its way into his nose and mouth and filled his lungs. There was a movement in the crowd, a tremor that Adam could feel working its way toward him, and then someone stepped on his foot, crushing his toes even as an elbow caught him in the rib cage; and yet he could not fall, for there were bodies around him, pressing tightly on all sides. "*. . . we must rise up, rise up and fight, fight, to live as free human beings as God intended. . . .*" There was a cry in the crowd, an indistinct roar of a thousand different words being shouted at once; and again, rising and then dying away sharply like a sudden squall out at sea, when the rains come from nowhere and bear down upon you, churning the waves into a froth before disappearing, leaving everything calm again. Adam found that he could not breathe. He knew that his mouth was open, that his chest rose and fell; but he knew, nonetheless, that he was not breathing. Maybe I am going to die, he thought; I am going to die alone, in this sea of skin. He looked for Din but glimpsed only part of his face, for someone was obscuring him. He could still feel Din's hand on his wrist, though, gripping tightly. Yet he could not locate his wrist—his arm was outstretched, pulled far from his body, and he could not see it. I am going to die, he thought. He felt calm about it. There was nothing he could do about it now. Another cry punctured the air and this time it did not fade away but grew louder: the sound of one million people cheering and shouting. Adam felt his bones vibrate with this noise; he felt quite unable to distinguish it from his own body.

And suddenly he was on the ground, his head falling onto the dry earth with a dull thud. He pulled his chin into his chest but even as he did so he felt a sharp blow on the back of his skull—a heel crashing into his head. And another one, this time against his ear, filling his head with a hollow ringing that blanked out everything else. He raised both arms to cover his head: Din had let go. He drew his knees up to his face and curled into a ball, and it was better. He felt the heavy tread of feet on his hips and thighs and calves, and the rough jerk of people tripping over him. An immense pressure pushed outward from within his skull, as if his head was about to split open. The ringing in his ears had turned into a dull rushing noise; he no longer knew where he was.

Come on. Run. It was Din, lifting Adam by his arm, pulling roughly, his fingernails digging into the soft flesh of Adam's armpit. Now it was he who stepped on prostrate bodies, tripping occasionally and landing heavily, elbows first, on someone's back. A space appeared around him, and he could see blood on faces and bruises on bare chests and open mouths with split lips. He saw the expressions on these bloody faces: not fear or anger, but a mixture of exhilaration and emptiness, as if the people who inhabited these bodies had fled long ago. The terrible noise he had heard earlier still hung heavily in the air, but it was fractured now, broken by distinct screams of individual men and women, which Adam could hear even through the blank ringing in his ear. There was another noise too, something he thought he had heard before, a series of short, sharp cracks, a pop-pop-pop that came in rapid bursts. Gunfire, he thought to himself, and wondered how he knew that. Later Din would tell him that it was the sound of shots being fired into the air in celebration of the victory of the revolution, to mark this Year of Living Dangerously, but Adam was not so sure.

Adam concentrated on running. He focused only on following Din, who turned to look at him every so often with a wild-eyed exhilaration. It was too much for him to think of anything else; he ran as fast as he could, trying to keep up with Din on the streets of this vast city, his chest heaving with the effort. He could breathe again, he thought; he could breathe.

15

_M_argaret thought: This time I am finished. Done for. A
goner. She could feel the car shaking violently, bouncing on its axle
even though it was stationary: There were people running over the car,
leaping onto the back of it, up over the roof and down onto the hood
before carrying on down the road. The noise was horrible. It was as if
the car had been caught in a rock slide and an avalanche of boulders
was crashing against it and threatening to carry it away. Margaret looked
up and saw the soles of bare feet and cheap rubber sneakers streaming
down in front of the windshield in a rain of dull colors that obscured
the light and turned the afternoon into twilight. _I'm a goner._ It was
funny how she remembered that one line from a novel she had read a
long time ago. It was about a girl who had fallen terribly in love with a
twenty-year-old Spanish boy, a matador, even (or was she just imagining that?)—and she was so crazy with love that she knew her entire
existence would be surrendered to the beautiful boy. Margaret remembered nothing of the rest of the story. She retained only a sense of
ridicule and mild contempt at the thought that someone could fall so
helplessly in love with a person she didn't know and allow herself to
become limp and silly like that. Falling in love is a matter of choice: If
you fall in love like that it must mean that you want to; it means you
want to lose your mind and self-control. You want to lose your sense of
independent existence, your_self._ The girl in the novel had been like
that. She had known that she was losing her self-respect; she was a
trembling wreck. I'm a goner, she had said. It was as if she was beyond
salvation; and all due to events beyond her control. It had so irritated
Margaret that she had rushed to the end of the book without paying
much attention to it. So it was funny that she should remember it now,
caught in this riot. Now it was she who was a "goner," but unlike the

girl in the novel she was really a goner, and it was due to events that really were beyond her control. And unlike the girl, she would die without knowing how it felt to be so in love that you could lose all sense of who you were.

Bill did not say anything. He sat with his hands on the steering wheel, staring straight ahead at the river of bodies flowing past and over them. Margaret could see patches of sweat seeping through his shirt, like the markings of deep water on maps of the ocean; he looked very calm, with only the slightest hint of a frown on his brow, as if they were merely caught in a traffic jam. The engine of the Buick was still running, and every so often it would rev up fiercely, a rasping growl that rose above the stampede of feet around them. Bill was doing it, of course, thought Margaret; he was scared too. It was very hot in the car. The windows were shut tightly and the doors were locked. Amid the torrent of bodies a face would occasionally appear: Someone would stop and press his nose to the window next to Margaret or throw himself across the windshield with a loud thud, his palms smacking against the glass as he hooted and screamed and jeered, his eyes staring and bloodshot, like some phantom from her sleep; and then he would disappear into the rushing stream once more, vanishing just like a nightmare. A young man stopped on Margaret's side of the car. She knew that he was no more than twenty or twenty-two, even though his face was wizened and scarred, his complexion mottled. She could not read the expression on his face—not aggression, not hatred, not lust, not anything in particular, just a blankness that could have been all those things, or none of them. It was an emptiness that frightened Margaret, for there was nothing in his face she could relate to. There were thin veins crisscrossing his yellowed eyes, and his teeth were dark little stumps. He opened his mouth and shouted a word that sounded like *BAAAAAAAAAAAAAAAA* that seemed to go on for a whole minute, maybe more, and even through the window Margaret could feel the coarseness of his voice, which was not just a sound but a physical thing that she felt brushing the hairs on the back of her neck.

"Don't look," Bill said, "don't look at him. Do not turn your head. Keep your eyes straight ahead."

She looked at the hailstorm of feet on the windshield, but she could not help herself, and she turned once more to look at the face by her side, at the red and white bandana and the furry pink tongue. The boy pulled open his shirt to reveal something on his chest. With a knife, he had cut an uneven X across his bony breastbone; it had not fully scabbed over and she could see patches of bright moist blood where the ends of the X reached for his collarbone. He brandished a machete, drawing it across his chest in a gesture that Margaret did not under-stand, and she thought—again—*I'm a goner.* But then, after another *BAAAA* (shorter, this time), he was carried off by the surging tide of bodies. Without knowing why, Margaret suddenly thought of Adam, a boy no younger than the ones rampaging through the streets in front of her. She thought of him asleep in her house, peaceful and innocent, and she was glad he could not see the things that were happening in this city on this day.

Bill reached over to the glove compartment and drew out a re-volver. It was just like a film, thought Margaret, a very stupid film in which she had the misfortune to have a minor role. She never knew that people actually kept guns in glove compartments. "What are you doing?" she said. "Is that legal?"

"Sure," Bill said. "Don't worry, we won't need it. It's just . . . policy." He held the gun firmly but quite calmly, and Margaret got the impres-sion it was not the first time he had held one. She felt reassured, and hated herself for feeling reassured: Did she actually enjoy being pro-tected by a man with a gun? It was his fault they were in this mess in the first place. No, no, no: It was hers. Today was just the latest episode in the bad comedy that was her life. She wondered if today would be the long overdue finale of this fine farce.

She had woken up very early that morning, with none of the dreadful lassitude of the previous days and weeks. The crick in her neck had disappeared; her shoulders were not stiff and her joints did not ache.

It had been a long time since she had appreciated twilight in Jakarta in this way: blue and mysterious, and full of murky promise. She re-membered how she had felt when she first came here after the long years of winter in the States and Europe: lithe and unencumbered by the weight of woolen clothing. On the crossing from Rotterdam she had given away her winter clothes, article by article, to whoever would have them: Her serge overcoat was the first to go, just after Aden, donated gleefully to a Lebanese mother of five; three sweaters disposed of on the Indian Ocean to Indonesian crew members. When she arrived in Jakarta her suitcase was virtually empty. She bought some blouses made from thin cotton, cut in the local style, which reminded her of the clothes she had worn as a child: cheap, functional, and not very elegant.

It was this feeling that she had woken up with: a feeling of newness, of change, even though she did not know what that change would involve: the sensation of purity and possibility that she thought she had forgotten. The predawn air was fresh and gave her arms goose bumps as she stood in the yard drinking strong, muddy black coffee. She had dressed nicely, putting on a skirt (something she was now regretting) and a vaguely matching blouse. She checked her appearance in the mirror and, for a moment, even considered putting on some makeup, but the lipstick she salvaged from the back of a drawer was so old and neglected it had become as cracked as mud beds after a long drought. Never mind, she thought, brushing her hair: She looked absolutely fine; her eyes had even lost their recent puffiness. Before leaving she checked on Adam and found him in deep sleep, one hand raised to his brow, palm outward as if shielding his eyes from bright light. His head was turned slightly to one side as if avoiding an invisible sun and his jaw twitched every so often, but otherwise he lay perfectly still. The thin sheet had become entangled under his body, and Margaret gently extricated it before drawing it up to his chest. She left a note on the table in the kitchen that said simply, "Stay and Wait."

On her way to meet Bill she had gone past groups of people performing their daily drills—star jumps, good-morning stretches, squats, thrusts, lunges, and arm blocks, feigning combat. A group of women marched briskly down the street, almost more quickly than the already heavy traffic. They were dressed in the standard uniform of volunteers— oversized khaki shirts, buttoned to the neck, and austere men's trousers— and their heads were held high, chins lifted in defiance of the unseen enemy that was everywhere. It was always like this on Independence Day. Every other vehicle on the road seemed to be a public bus, commandeered to transport students and people from the outlying villages to the center of town so that they could hear the president's address. Everyone else was left to negotiate the city on foot. There was a sudden explosion: mortar shells in the distance, and rifle shots and the piercing shrillness of whistles. A van nearby had broken down, its failing engine filling the air with thick smoke. Margaret lifted the collar of her shirt to cover her mouth and nose. Through the haze she saw figures making their way through the maze of cars. She knew she was not hallucinating: soldiers dressed in full army fatigue, crouching behind cars, their rifles trained on imaginary foes. One of them brushed past her *becak,* the twigs in his helmet rustling noisily, his radio crackling on and off as he stooped to avoid his mystery foe. She looked around her—people were watching with expressions of boredom; they knew these exercises would soon be over.

"What is it this time?" she shouted through the veil of her shirt.

Her driver laughed. "I think they're trying to recapture the telephone exchange. But you know, if we were actually invaded I think we should teach our enemies a real lesson and *give* them the telephone exchange."

Bill had just finished a meeting when Margaret arrived. He was standing in the shadow of a giant column in the shape of a crowbar crowned by a shaft of lightning.

"Come and have a look inside," Bill said, taking her by the hand. "You'll be amazed."

Each of the floors of the building celebrated the vision of modern, independent Indonesia, Bill explained; each story was seventeen meters high ("Independence Day—today—August 17, *geddit?*"), light and airy, made of polished concrete set in curves and angles. Everywhere Margaret looked she saw beautifully made models of highways, railways, waterways, hydroelectric dams, irrigation schemes, hospitals, factories, war planes, spaceships, nuclear plants, and luxurious hotels: entire worlds captured in glass cabinets. A modern port—quite unlike the rat-infested docks of Tanjong Priok—bustled with happy workers and angular, futuristic ships. In a Western-style living room, a smiling family sat on an orange sofa, pointing at a TV the size of a small cinema screen, their comfortable home filled with an array of electrical appliances Margaret could not identify. A bridge in the shape of a clover leaf—exactly the same as the one downtown—sat astride a network of streamlined highways, but the city around these roads was not the city Margaret knew. Here, in this other city that was Jakarta and yet not

Jakarta, the famous clover-leaf bridge was surrounded by buildings of uniform modernity, and the people were well dressed and clean and healthy, carrying smart briefcases as they went to work. The cars were shiny and the roads tree-lined and clean, and there were children playing next to the canal, which did not look black and slimy like the one she knew. There were no slums in this city.

"Officially we've stopped all aid to Indonesia, and relations between our countries are at meltdown, but on a personal level nothing's changed," Bill said. He was wearing a light blue shirt, open at the neck to reveal strawberry blond chest hairs unfurling toward the base of his throat. His sleeves were rolled up to the elbow and he did not look as if he had been in the office. "My friends in town still want to see me— there's still work to be done."

"I like the way you see friends as work," Margaret laughed. "Is there ever a moment when you let your guard down? I mean, do you ever *not* think of how everything fits into your master plan of world domination?"

Bill chuckled; she had forgotten how he looked when he laughed in this way, his cheeks shiny and blushed with red, almost cherubic and certainly unsophisticated. All of a sudden he was an Idaho farmer's son once more. She could imagine him growing up on a prairie, sitting on the back of a tractor amid bales of hay. "Don't tease me, Margaret Bates. You know I'm defenseless against your wit."

"Oh, not quite that defenseless, particularly when there's 'still work to be done.' Hmm, let me guess what kind of work that might be. Under-the-counter gifts of Rolex watches to your friends? A little Cartier necklace for the wife, perhaps? Or maybe just good old-fashioned cash . . ."

He put his hands in his pockets and chuckled his farm-boy laugh again. They were standing beside a model of an offshore oil rig. The sea was a clear crystal blue and the waves washed calmly onto a white sandy beach; beyond the beach there was a silvery petroleum-processing plant.

"I know what you're going to say," Margaret continued. " 'We're fighting a war out there! A war that will decide the future of the world! We cannot let Indonesia fall to communism'—right?" She dug him in the rib cage; she had intended merely to tickle him but misjudged her lunge and ended up catching him heavily between two ribs. He only flinched a little.

"It's kind of silly, the things we do in the name of ideology," he said, staring at the men in hard hats on the deck of the rig. Margaret saw the reflection of his face in the glass; his lips were parted as he smiled, but his eyes seemed to be narrowed in a frown.

"Seriously, Bill," she said, continuing to watch his reflection. "Do you actually have any friends?"

"Sure, I know lots of people here."

"No, I mean people who aren't of use to you in your work, people you like . . . you know, *real* friends."

"Look at that," he said, touching his index finger to the glass. A turtle floated in the water, a single leatherback drifting calmly in the ocean. "He looks kinda happy, don't you think?"

"Guess so. Lots of fish for him to eat—look." She pointed at a shoal of mackerel suspended in the glassy ocean.

Bill put his hand on hers. It sat awkwardly, covering her thumb and index finger, but otherwise it felt smooth and broad. Their hands obscured the oil field and cast a shadow on the sea, as if a rainstorm was imminent; she could no longer see the fish in the sea, and the fishermen casting nets from their boats seemed suddenly in danger.

She looked at the freckles on his wrist and his sturdy, waterproof Timex.

"We're not late for the speech, are we?" she said.

"Nope." He moved his hand slightly, angling the watch toward him to check the time. "I have my car outside."

A man walked briskly past them, heading for the stairs. "Hurry home, folks, the show's about to begin." He seemed barely old enough to have graduated from college—no older than thirty, in any case; his hair was Scandinavian blond, and his chinos were ironed with a sharp crease down the front.

"Thanks, Larry," Bill said. "Sure you don't want to come and listen to the speech with us? We have front-row seats."

Larry frowned, his pale features twisted in confusion. "You gotta be crazy, Bill. No way—I'm planning to stay home and enjoy the president's speech on the radio, like any sane human being. I'll leave the live show to you old pros. Nice meeting you, ma'am." He made a pinching motion in the space in front of his forehead, doffing an imaginary hat as he disappeared down the stairs.

"Who was that escapee from nursery school?" Margaret asked.

"Oh, Larry. He's a friend." Bill looked at Margaret and smiled. "I mean, he's a colleague. He works at the embassy."

"Enough said. I don't think I need to know more."

Bill put his hand lightly on her waist as they left the building. It was very hot and there did not seem to be any shade in the street.

As they approached the palace in his car it became more difficult to negotiate their way through the crowds. People were strolling in the middle of the roads, large groups of young men sauntering casually or skipping along with their arms over each other's shoulders as if they were on a day out, a picnic at the seaside. Their red and white bandannas and painted faces were meant to make them look frightening, but Margaret found it difficult to take them seriously. They looked like children on their way to a tea party where they would play musical chairs and pin the tail on the donkey (it was so easy to imagine the bandanna as a blindfold). It was precisely because they wanted to look like Dayak warriors, thought Margaret, that she found them so ridiculous. She could not help giggling whenever she saw their snarling faux-fierce faces on the street—they looked frail and pathetic in their flip-flops and nylon shorts and faded T-shirts that said COME ALIVE! YOU'RE IN THE PEPSI GENERATION. There were groups of young women too, soberly dressed in slacks and blouses, carrying banners that proclaimed them to be revolutionary women of God or young women striving for the goodness of mankind. You could always tell the university students too—they were just a little neater, in spite of the effort some of them made to appear scruffy, to blend in with their brothers on the streets. Margaret scanned the crowd for any of her former students. She could say that with some confidence: *former*. There had not been classes for some weeks now, and she doubted she would ever teach again. A group of women went past, singing the president's name in a childish monotone.

"What happened to your girlfriend, Bill?" Margaret said, looking out the window.

"What do you mean? I haven't got a girlfriend." The car had slowed to near-walking speed as Bill eased through the crowd.

"Come on, I mean that girl you were with a few days ago at the Hotel Java. Susie, or whatever her name was."

"Oh, that one. It never really got off the ground. I wasn't very serious—I never am with local girls. Hell, it's difficult." He cast a quick glance at Margaret, frowning slightly, then looked away again, concentrating on the thick soup of people ahead of them. "You must think I'm a real jerk, but it's not easy, you know, doing my job, being with the embassy. . . . It's hard just being in this city. Oh, shoot, you don't know what I'm trying to say, do you? I can see it on your face. You're okay here, you get along in this place. You adapt. I mean, really adapt. Me, I'm different, Margaret. I know what you think of me. I'm just this brute, this ugly Yankee who doesn't *get* life abroad, who's so American he'll never understand foreigners—"

"I don't think that."

"The funny thing is that I've always felt this way with you. Even all those years ago in college, the very first time I met you, I thought, I'm never going to be like this girl. Even if I graduate summa cum laude and know how to translate Turgenev, I'll still feel like a redneck next to her. I'll never have what she has. And in Jakarta I feel like that even more. Look at you—you have no idea what I mean."

The car came to a halt. The roads had been closed, and they were still some way from the palace. "I do know what you mean," said Margaret.

At the roadblock there were about twenty soldiers manning a barricade of rusty old drums and barbed wire. Two Soviet tanks stood nearby and an armored carrier against which more soldiers leaned, smoking their cigarettes and watching the crowds pass. Bill rolled down the window, but none of the soldiers seemed interested enough to approach the car.

"We need to get through," Bill called out. "We have an appointment at the palace. Let us pass immediately or else we will be late." When Bill spoke Indonesian he sounded stilted, magisterial; Margaret had always thought it was a language that suited him, but she was not so sure now.

The soldiers laughed; Margaret was not sure what they were laughing at.

"This barricade is barricading our progress," Bill continued in his efficient embassy voice. "We have the right to proceed immediately."

One of the soldiers walked toward the car. He cradled his machine gun in his arms with such ease that it seemed to be part of his body. "American," he said. Margaret could not tell if he was asking them or merely stating something he already knew.

"Yes, American. From embassy people," Bill said, tapping his watch. His Indonesian was faltering. "Must pass now, with quickness, appointment palace."

The soldier half-smiled, half-sneered. His eyes were invisible behind his sunglasses.

"Please, sir, could you let us through?" Margaret leaned over and smiled at the soldier. "We are guests at the palace and it would be very rude of us to be late for the president's speech. We've been looking forward to it for such a long time."

"Yes," Bill added sternly. "People no rude."

The soldier turned to look at his friends, momentarily uncertain of what to do.

Margaret said, "If you need to check with your superior, please do so. You can say that we are with the U.S. Embassy. We have papers, if you need to see them."

"Hurriedly, pressure, now."

"Shut up, Bill."

The soldier turned back to face them. "Who says you can go to the palace on the president's speech day?"

Bill smacked both hands on the steering wheel and let out a sharp sigh. "We have authority got. Minister important. Minister Hartono immediate. Call his office quick to confirmation."

The soldier laughed, his teeth flashing brilliantly in the sunshine. "Hartono. Hartono!" He called out to his friends, repeating the name several times. Margaret could hear their staccato laughs, punctuated by smokers' coughs. "The man of whom you speak, the man who is one of your dirty corrupt puppets, he is no longer a minister. He is no longer one of the people who work for you."

"Unbelieve. Call Minister Hartono now."

The soldier shrugged. "Your puppy dog Hartono has been . . . removed from office. We are not expecting him to return."

"This lies! Yesterday I telephone speak him."

"And this morning he is in prison. I'm asking you to leave now, sir, but I am not going to ask you politely again." There was a slight change in the way he held his gun; a minute shift, but enough for Margaret to notice it.

"Okay, okay, okay," Bill said. They reversed the car slowly into the gathering crowd, suddenly lost: There was nowhere to go. Everywhere they looked they saw only a shifting wall of people. No right turn, no left turn, no straight ahead. The city had disappeared in this growing swell of bodies. The car inched along. Every so often a passing kid would drum on the hood with his palms, and sometimes people would boo and jeer comically as they went past. Ameri-*ka,* piss off home. That kind of thing. Bill told her to roll the window up, and so she did. She was not afraid.

And now she found herself trapped in the car, wearing a skirt, sitting next to a man who was protecting them both with a single revolver. She could not remember when it was, or how it was, that her life had changed so much that she could be reassured by a man with a gun. She had lost track of how long they had been in the car before the riot began; she had forgotten when it was, precisely, that she first thought: *I'm a goner.* She used to be able to remember such details, the exact moments in time when important things happened to her. There had been a time in her life when she could recall entire conversations, the tone and inflection of someone's voice as they spoke, the way they pronounced a single word. The way they said, quietly, I shall never forget you.

She closed her eyes and tried to remember. She tried to shut out the hollow banging of feet on the roof of the car and replace the noise with the voices that she had known in the past. There, she could just about do it. She had to hang on to what remained of her memories, she told herself, for they would return. Surely they would return.

16

*T*he paintings were, at best, naive, Margaret thought as she tried to stifle a giggle, breaking instead into a choking cough.

"Shh." Karl raised a finger to his lips and frowned at her with an expression of theatrical severity. They were being shown around the home of a famous artist, a flamboyant German with a penchant for "parrots and boys," according to Margaret's mother.

"And this one, ah, this one, I am ashamed to say, is my humble attempt at capturing the spirit of Bali," the artist said, indicating a gouache of the inevitable rice terraces presided over by a kindly demon. "But sadly I don't know if I am ever successful in achieving what I hope to achieve." He spoke in a manner that suggested neither recognition of failure nor humility.

"Oh, Walter," Margaret said, "show Karl something more racy. Mother says you have the *naughtiest* paintings of men and women bathing in rivers."

Their host raised an eyebrow and smiled. "I have many pictures of great sensuality, it is true, but none of those are by me. I'd rather show you my own work—and besides, you're far too delicate and innocent to appreciate those images."

"I'm not delicate," Margaret protested.

"Yes, but your new friend is," Walter said, drawing his hand in a wristy, tender twirl in front of Karl's face before moving on. "This, my dear young friends, is one of my early works. Done when I was still living in Germany. You might like it, dear boy, coming as you do from a country full of rural traditions."

"Yes, it's very . . . arresting," Karl said, moving closer to the painting and feigning interest. Margaret coughed and looked away, beyond the veranda, across the valley to a ridge of palm trees. If she looked at Karl she would burst out laughing, she knew that.

"Margaret, really, look at this," Karl urged, taking her arm and guiding her toward a small, frameless oil painting of a darkened farmhouse, the fields around it lit by yellow moonlight. Misshapen, skinny black-and-white cows stood in the pastures, and over this surrealistic idyll there drifted a young bride and groom, suspended in the night sky.

Margaret giggled. "Oh, isn't it whimsical," she said, recovering quickly.

"This little tableau," said Walter, "is full of my conflicting emotions toward my homeland. Nostalgia, longing, but also fear and self-loathing and darkness—all those things are contained in this tiny piece. I did not realize this when I painted it many years ago. When one is young"—he raised his eyebrow and turned to look at Margaret—"one does not see such things. But now, in the long autumn of my life, I can appreciate all the happiness and indeed the despair that has colored my life." He waved his hand at the painting as if to prove his point.

As soon as they had left the compound Margaret dissolved into fits of hysterical laughter. Her body heaved with the sheer pleasure of laughing out loud, hot tears filling her eyes. Karl put his arm around her shoulders and she could feel the comforting warmth of his body as he shook uncontrollably with mirth too. "Regard this *petit tableau*," he said, mimicking Walter's languid vowels. Margaret opened her mouth to speak but was unable to stitch her words into a sentence. Wiping her eyes, she thought, This is what it means to be happy. Her entire life stretched out before her, an eternity waiting to be filled with the same delirious, light-headed joy. She felt as if the clouds had parted on a cool, overcast day and the sun shone down on a small patch of earth upon which she, and only she, existed. How had she survived the first fifteen years of her life without knowing such dizzy pleasure? she wondered.

They reached a spot on the ridge where a line of trees thinned out to offer them a view of the valley. "Could we stop for a moment?" Karl said, sitting down on the grass. It had not rained in a while and the grass was already looking dry, flecked with brown.

"You know, I've never sat on the grass in the Indies before," Margaret said as she sat down beside him, crossing her legs in a half lotus. "It feels weird—a very European thing to do."

"Never?" he said, running his palm over the grass lightly, as if enjoying the texture of a fine rug.

She shook her head. "It's not that surprising. I mean, there are bugs and snakes and *things* in Asian grass. It's not welcoming the way European grass is, you know—not that I know what European grass is like. I'd like Europe, I think—pleasant green meadows of delicate flowers and forests that aren't teeming with animals that eat you. And those lovely, clean cities with sewage systems—I mean, Paris sounds wonderful."

Karl looked across the valley, the smile still set on his face, but his eyes had gone blank. "I love sitting on the grass here. Or on the sand, the way locals do."

The land fell away sharply before them, a steep bank of velvet green shrubs that led to the river below. Margaret could see children bathing in its silver blue water; where it flowed into deep pools the water was still and dark, almost black, and reflected the wispy clouds on that day of brilliant weather.

"Sitting on this grass," Karl said, "I can almost remember being an infant in Buru. Almost. I pretend I can. But I can't really."

Margaret looked across at him and put her hand on his. He did not look at her, but continued staring down at the children splashing in the gentle current of the shallows. He did not blink, and there was a hollowness in his gaze that made Margaret feel that she ought to do something to fill that emptiness and make his eyes shine again.

"Can't you remember anything?" she said. "I can. I can remember things that happened to me when I was two." She laughed, but he did not respond.

"I can remember my *babu*," he said at last. "Not her face or eyes or nose or any details; I just remember her being there with me and then suddenly disappearing. I can remember my father shouting and my mother crying. A house that was very silent—apart from my father's tantrums and my mother's sobbing. But most of all, my *babu*. I remember her because I remember missing her when we went back to Holland. I remember asking for her, long after we had moved back to The Hague, asking when *Babu* was going to come back, but no one would ever answer. She was a proper *babu*, you know—she nursed me. My own mother couldn't express milk when I was born. When we were back in Holland, whenever I got ill—which was often—she would say, 'You're such a weak child because you were nursed by *that woman*.' "

"That's awful." Margaret noticed that Karl made no attempt to remove his hand from hers. "You weren't really ill that often, were you?"

"All the time. I hated The Hague. I hated that house. Now *that* I can remember. It had very low ceilings with beams that were painted black, and you could see the cobwebs forming on them, silky balls of fluff that I always wanted to touch. There was a small window in my room at the top of the house. Half the view was obscured by the sloping roof, and in the winter, when the snow settled on the tiles, all I could see was this blurred screen of white, and in the distance the gray of the sky. I would lie in bed with the sheets pulled up to my face, and the woolen blankets would tickle my nose. I never got used to wool. And I would feel the cold seeping into my chest, and I would know that I was falling ill. I think I had probably forgotten about Buru by then, but my body hadn't. It always craved warmth. When the other children put on their hats and gloves and went skating, I knew that I wasn't one of them, that I was from somewhere else. At school, during history lessons, whenever the teacher said, '*We* conquered' or '*We* civilized them,' it took me a while to understand who *we* and *they* were. Isn't it bizarre? On those cold days I used to imagine myself as a child in Buru, or somewhere else in the Indies—here, for example. I would re-create scenes. And in these scenes I was playing in the sun, swimming—oh yes, that's another thing I can remember from Buru, the sea. I would imagine myself playing with other local kids, imagine how the sand felt between my toes and my fingers. And that consoled me. Because I thought to myself, One day I will be there again. I didn't know when, but in the way that children do, I thought it could happen at any moment—and I would be a child in the Indies again. But then, of course, well . . ."

He smiled at Margaret—a smile that seemed as frail and ephemeral as a butterfly, so delicate that she feared she might crush it if she touched it. She reached out and touched his cheek, barely brushing his skin with the back of her hand, her fingers feeling the softness of his face. She wished her fingers were not so bony; she wished she did not have knobby knuckles, but the gracefully curved fingers of Balinese child dancers. He put his hand over hers, pressing her hand gently between his cheek and his palm, holding it like this for a few seconds; a minute; a lifetime. And then he leaned his head and rested it on her shoulder. She could no longer see his face but could smell his hair—a sweet milky aroma. She said, "But then what?"

"What?"

"You said, 'But then . . . ,' only you didn't finish your sentence." She began to stroke his hair, drawing her fingers lightly through the long, silken strands.

"I didn't know how to express what I was thinking."

"You were going to say, But then we grow up and we find we don't have our childhood anymore. Is that right?"

She felt the tiniest movement of his head, an imperceptible nod. "It's not so bad, being an adult," she continued. "I wish I were an adult. Officially, I mean."

"You are very grown up indeed, young madam."

"I can't say I ever had a childhood. I've been like this ever since I can remember. Grown up, that is."

He lifted his head and looked at her. The darkness in his eyes had lifted, she thought. "There's something else," he said, hesitating, waiting for her approval, it seemed, before he continued. His gaze dropped, and he began drawing his palm in little circles on the dry grass once again. Margaret did not say anything. His forehead was so close to her face that she could have leaned forward and planted a kiss on it, right on the thin crease in the middle of his brow. "There was something else I used to imagine. It was this: When I imagined being different from the other Dutch kids, it wasn't simply because I had lived somewhere else. I believed—I made myself believe—that it was because I *really* wasn't like them. That I wasn't Dutch. Shh. Don't say anything"—he reached out and put a finger to her lips; it was cool and very steady—"let me tell you, otherwise I'm never going to be able to share it with anyone ever again. I used to tell myself that I was only partly Dutch, that my *babu* was my real mother. Isn't that silly? It didn't seem silly when I was six or seven. It felt real, and it comforted me. One day my father was in a very good mood, I don't know why. We were eating pancakes and ap-ples. He said, 'When I was a young man in the Indies, pancakes were the food I missed most from home; none of the *babu* I had could learn how to make them properly.' And my mother said, 'Well the *last babu* learned *many things from you.*' Looking back, it probably meant nothing at all, absolutely nothing, but that day I took it as proof that my *babu* was my real mother. And as I grew older I would make this history more elaborate. I would imagine my father taking the boat from Buru to Batavia to search for a European wife and falling in love instead with a local girl and taking her back to Buru. He would go to Holland on home leave, and there he would meet my mother, but when they returned to Buru they would find the *babu* pregnant—with me. The funny thing is, the more I thought about it, the more I began to live it. Sometimes the boys at school used to accuse me of being an Indo—you know, a Eurasian. Look." He put his arm against hers so that their forearms touched from elbow to wrist. "See? You're pale. I'm much darker in comparison."

Margaret did not honestly see any difference, but she nodded anyway. He laughed and pinched her cheek. "I told you it was silly," he said. "I don't suppose you've ever had childish imaginings."

She shook her head. "No, can't think of any. I'm really pretty boring. I told you: Childhood just passed me by."

They stood up and began walking. The dappled shade of the trees cast intricate patterns over Karl's face as he talked. "I've never told anyone what I've told you," he said, "and I don't expect I shall ever repeat it to anyone. I don't think I shall ever need to."

Margaret shrugged and poked him in the ribs. "No one else would have the patience with you."

"That's just it. You . . . I don't know, you seem to understand me. We're similar, don't you think? I used to feel I was all alone in the world, but maybe I'm not."

"You've finally found someone as bizarre as you are, you mean?"

Karl laughed. "Do you think I should get married to a local woman and have lots of children? I want to have an Indonesian child. A boy. He'll be my alter ego, except better, and happier—all the things I could have been, but wasn't. We'll live in a house by the sea, just like the one in Buru that I remember as a child, only this time there'll be no unhappiness, just laughter and gifts."

"I think that is a really, really bad idea," Margaret said, laughing, as she linked her arm into his. The path began to descend, curving around to point them back in the direction of the village. There were clove trees on either side of the path; and in a field there was a plump cow that looked up at Margaret with big, bright eyes. The houses on the edge of the village began to come into view, perched on the far side of the ridge, half-hidden by vegetation. The sun was still high, its reflection flashing now and then in tiny starbursts on the surface of the river below.

Karl said, "I never believed I could be so happy."

Johan, wait. Don't let go of me.

They went into the bar. At the end of the narrow corridor, away from the noise of the street, there was another door, and on the door there was a poster of a young woman wearing a wet T-shirt. REACH FOR FLAVOR WINSTON OF AMERICA, she said. It was dark, the corridor lit only by a single fluorescent strip that glowed and flickered, and Johan could not make out if the girl was Chinese or Malay or Eurasian. Maybe she was just a Westerner pretending to be Asian. There was quite a lot of that nowadays.

It was not a big room, but there were many people there, and the air was heavy with cigarette smoke, a silvery veil that made it difficult to discern people's faces, and even when he blinked he could not tell who was who. He thought he recognized someone—a face here, a long sweep of hair there, a flash of shiny beads on a handbag that he thought he had seen before, but then again maybe not.

Johan, wait, don't go too fast, Farah whispered. She was holding his hand tightly and staying very close, so close he could feel the hesitant warmth of her body against his, her knee knocking into the back of his thigh as she said, Don't let go of me, please don't leave me alone.

Don't worry, I'm right here.

There was music now, something bright and brassy, a trumpet or a saxophone starting up, then some tin drums and castanets. Not this mambo rock shit again, said Bob as they eased into an alcove deep in the shadows where they could not be seen. A row of lights came on, one by one, and the chatter of the audience turned into a rowdy cheer. There was clapping and some men were whistling. There was no curtain, no elaborate introduction, just some girls onstage who appeared all of a sudden through the smoke, moving their hips from side to side, out of sync with the music, as if it was their first time and they were not sure what to do in this place. They were wearing only panties decorated with gold beads dangling from the end of thin filaments of thread, and when they shook their hips the beads shimmered through the hazy blue smoke in the room. Over the powdery whiteness of their bare torsos there seemed to be a thin slick of sweat, only more viscous, as if it would be cold and almost firm to the touch, Johan thought. Over their nipples the girls wore silver stars that shone in the harsh glare of the lights and appeared to Johan almost like real stars shining through clouds. He remembered the Christmas they had at the orphanage, just that once, in the year before he left. Some foreigners had come to the village and they had presents for all the children, old toy cars and clothes and bags of hard candy wrapped in colored cellophane. They gave Johan a globe filled with fake snow and a miniature Eiffel Tower. At the base of the tower there were tiny people playing in the snow, children, maybe, and when he turned the globe upside down the children did not fall but remained glued to their places. And when you returned them to their upright position it would be snowing on them, the flakes swirling around before settling at the feet of the motionless children. Adam spent hours looking at this miniature world, turning the globe on its head and then back again. He set it on the windowsill and watched the sunlight refracting through the glass, bathing the children in rainbow colors. Don't be stupid, Johan said, laughing, there can't be snow and sun at the same time, but Adam did not mind. Do you think we will ever see snow? he asked, and Johan said, No, probably not, because you don't like being cold.

Afterward, the foreigners who had given them the presents put on a play about the birth of the baby Jesus. They dressed up as shepherds and donkeys and they chose one of the orphaned babies to be Jesus and wrapped him up in cloth. Above them, a bright silver star they had made hung from the ceiling against patches of damp and mold, but if you stared at it long enough you could just about pretend you were looking at the night sky. Adam asked, What is going to happen to the baby? And one of the foreigners said, Well, he will die to save mankind from sin. To sin is to do something bad, something wrong, the foreigner explained. We are all sinners, you and I both. And Adam was so sad afterward that he did not speak. He sat staring out of the window, at the fields that were dry and barren that year, scarred by patches of ash where there had been fires. Johan gave him the snow globe to make him feel better. Adam said, We are sinners, aren't we? That is why we are orphans. That's why we are alone and no parents want us. No, said Johan, no, you've done nothing wrong. Don't worry, you're not alone. I'm right here.

Johan, *hey*, stop staring. Farah squeezed his hand sharply. Hey, why are
you staring? Hello? You're disgusting. This is so *horrible*. Can we go now?
Please. I don't want to stay.

But the main attraction hasn't even begun, Bob said. Oh wait, my god,
here she comes.

The music changed suddenly to a cha-cha and some men in the audience
stood up and whistled. The clapping was louder now and people were
smacking their hands on the tables. Johan could barely hear the music. The
girls hurried offstage, shoving each other as they disappeared into the wings,
and all the lights went out, except one, which was trained on a high, wooden
stool. A woman walked onto the stage, dressed as the girls were, but she had
her arms crossed across her chest, hands delicately touching her neck to form a
W that hid the top half of her torso. She turned her back to the crowd,
twisting her head to glance over her shoulder, smiling a coquette's coy smile.
Then she slowly spread her arms and held them outstretched. The flesh on her
arms drooped and her thighs were ample. Two men appeared from the wings
dressed in cheap dinner suits. They were holding a snake, a python whose skin
was patterned with black and gold diamonds. They draped the snake across
the woman's shoulders and across her chest, and she turned to face the
audience, the reptile curling itself languidly around her breasts, its tail flickering
downward, reaching for the space between her thighs until she halted it with
one hand. To catcalls and applause she threw back her head and closed her
eyes, feeling the smooth, cold touch of the snakeskin with her cheek, thrusting
her chest forward in fake ecstasy.

Farah said, This is sick. I'm leaving now, Johan. Don't care if you come or
not. Onstage the woman was struggling with the python, her face contorting
in an expression between pain and ecstasy as the snake's thick coils tightened
around her body. Johan did not know if she was pretending or if the pain was
real. He eased his way through the crowd, through the messy chorus of
whistles and clapping that accompanied every exaggerated motion onstage. He
did not look back.

He found Farah standing by the car. She turned her head quickly when she
saw him emerging out the door. She stared down the street, at the rows of
streetlamps that lit this nighttime city.

Don't be angry, he said, reaching out to hold her hand. It's just a bit of
fun. She had bunched her hand into a fist and he held the tightly knotted ball
until he felt her fingers relax and loosen.

I hope no one's seen us here, she said, still looking away. It would be so shameful if anyone did. Mummy and Daddy would die of shame.

Daddy's probably in there somewhere, we just didn't look hard enough.

She glared at him with narrowed eyes and he felt her hand tense once more, pulling away from him. What is the matter with you? You have such a good family and yet you are so angry all the time. Why? Just tell me: Why?

I don't know, I don't know. He tried to reach out to her but she shrank away from him again. I'm sorry, Farah, it just feels that there's nowhere for me to go. When I think of this life ahead of me I see so many empty years. Don't look at me as if I'm crazy. You know what I mean. There's nothing left for me, Farah. Sometimes I . . . sometimes I just want it all to end.

Nothing left for you? That makes me so angry. See how much Mummy loves you? She loves you more than she loves me and Bob put together, and yet you behave like some, some . . . I don't know what. Okay, so you're an orphan, so what? Think about what could have happened to you, what would have happened if you hadn't come to us. You might be an urchin, or you might be dead. . . . God knows what happened to all those other orphans.

It was he who turned away this time. The streetlamps that lit the broad avenue before them were too bright, he thought. Cars flashed by, their headlights adding to the glare, bleaching the darkness from the night. He wished the city were darker, without any light at all.

Farah leaned against the car, looking away. He thought she was going to touch him but she did not. I'm sorry, she said. I didn't mean to remind you of your brother.

He did not answer.

You know what Mummy says, Farah continued, we shouldn't talk about it. But I want to know, Johan. Tell me about your brother, I want to understand. Oh, *abang,* don't look so unhappy. What happened? Just tell me. You'll feel better. Don't cry. Don't cry.

Johan began to speak but all of a sudden he felt like he was choking. It wasn't my fault, he said. It wasn't my fault. I didn't know.

What wasn't your fault, Johan? Please tell me.

But he could no longer speak. The memories were too thick.

She held him with both arms and drew him close to her. He could smell the faint traces of coconut oil in her hair.

17

*A*dam awoke with the sensation of not having slept at all. His ribs hurt where he had been trodden on in the riot, and every breath was an effort, exacerbating the dull pain on the right side of his torso that only abated if he held his breath. His sleep had consequently been disturbed and dreamless, and once or twice he woke with a start, believing, in the midnight darkness, that he was actually back at home, in his narrow, soft bed, and he expected to hear Karl's footsteps in the other room, his bare feet padding on the linoleum, and then perhaps coming down the corridor to check that Adam was asleep. But the door did not open to let in that thin, comforting sliver of light; instead he found himself on the floor of Din's room, shifting awkwardly on the rattan mat that they had unfurled on the concrete floor for him to sleep on. Din had snored throughout the night, the adrenaline finally having drained from his body midway through the evening, whereupon he simply collapsed onto his mat, drawing one pillow under his head and another to his belly, folding his body into a tight fetal position in which he remained for the rest of the night. Just minutes before, he had been sitting in a cross-legged position, arms flailing as usual as he spoke in vehement criticism of the death of Sukarno's revolutionary ideals, riding the last waves of exhilaration from that afternoon's riot. "We supported him, but he betrayed us," he said, jabbing his finger at Adam as if the woes of Indonesia were his fault. "You heard his speech today—three hours of lies which we accept because we're too poor and uneducated to think otherwise. We had three hundred years of suffering under the Dutch and now we think anything will be better, even this"—he jabbed his finger at Adam again. "So I ask you, is it better to be oppressed by a foreigner or by someone of your own race? Oh my god, you're so stupid, you don't understand what I'm saying. Let me put it another way: Is it better to suffer because of someone you hate or someone you love?" But even as he pointed accusingly at Adam once more, Adam noticed his eyelids had become thick and dark, and he was blinking to try and keep himself awake. "Is it?" he repeated in a half slur, and then sank slowly from his upright position onto the mat. It was like watching a rare, night-blooming flower, something florid and extravagant, that suddenly curled up and withdrew from the world at the height of its display; and all at once Adam was alone with nothing but that insistent ache in his ribs to keep him company through the long night. In the morning the pain was still there, as was Din's final, niggling question, the answer to which Adam could not find: Is it better to suffer because of someone you hate or someone you love?

Adam drew himself into a sitting position, listening to the sounds of the unfamiliar neighborhood: crying babies, the hollow clanging of metal on metal, the sawing of wood, and, most of all, the curious absence of human voices. There was a sheet hanging over the window, screening the room from the fierce morning sun; the light fell on the floor in funny, swirly patterns—translucent sea creatures that wriggled, disappeared, and reappeared each time the sheet shifted. Adam listened for Din but could not hear him. He did not know what time Din had left; it must have been not long after dawn, just after Din had risen to observe Azan Suboh. Adam had stirred briefly from his sleep and seen Din rising and falling to his knees in seamless, graceful motions—weightless, like in a dream. He must have left soon afterward.

When he stood up, Adam was pleased to find that his ribs did not hurt quite as much. He ventured out into the corridor of the silent house. Din's landlady sat in a rattan chair, fast asleep with her head thrown back and her mouth open, a thin trail of dried spittle tracing its way from the side of her mouth to her chin. A box of buttons lay next to her, and in her lap there was a small tray containing spools of thread. In the palms of her upturned hands there were a few buttons attached loosely to a length of thread. Adam peered down the corridor in search of a toilet but there was only another bedroom and a minuscule open kitchen, beyond which lay the narrow empty street in this agglomeration of houses that was neither a suburb nor a slum but something in between, something that wanted to be decent and clean but appeared squalid and threatening. His need to relieve himself became instantly more pressing as he realized there was no toilet; he would have to urinate in the street, into a canal, or onto a pile of rubbish as he had seen others do since his arrival in Jakarta. Just a few days ago he had been shocked by this lack of shame, by the dirtiness of the people of this city, but now he was learning that it was not a question of modesty but one of need. There were no bushes in this neighborhood, nothing he could use to hide, and so he too would have to debase himself in public.

Out in the litter-strewn front yard he found Din and the girl called Zubaidah, or Z, who was holding a piece of paper up to Din's face, pinched between thumb and forefinger as if it were a dead animal. Her voice was terse and insistent, and she took no notice of Din's protests as she spoke. They stopped as soon as they noticed Adam.

"Don't worry," Din said immediately, "I've spoken to Margaret. She knows I'm looking after you."

"Hi, Adam," Z said. "I hear you had an interesting day yesterday. Shame you decided to leave us early. You might actually have learned something about the politics of this country."

"But I did want to stay," Adam said. "It wasn't my fault."

Din broke into cheery laughter. "This boy just cracks me up! You're only saying that because there's a pretty girl here, aren't you? Yesterday you told me you were tired and you wanted to leave. You said you didn't understand a word those university students were saying."

"But—" Adam protested.

"Then, as we were leaving, we accidentally got caught up in the riot, didn't we? It's not as if we went and joined some hard-core violent youth group. Isn't that right, Adam? Z thinks we've been mixed up with the wrong people and wants us to denounce all violent activity. But what violence have we been involved in? None, right?"

Adam shook his head. The pressure on his bladder was becoming intolerable.

Z looked at Adam with wide, expectant eyes, as if awaiting a more elaborate answer. He thought: She doesn't believe me.

"Just remember," she said, turning to Din once again, "that if you are involved with any violent factions, pro or anti Sukarno, you will lose all the support you enjoy now. You won't be able to write for *Z* magazine, and we will inform the university council of your unlawful activities, which will mean that you will lose your office, your stipend, and the use of university facilities. In addition, you won't be able to vote in any matters of student politics." Adam could not help but admire the fluency with which she spoke, the effortless articulation of each word. It was clear that she was angry, but she managed nonetheless to sound restrained, almost polite.

Din took half a step toward her but then turned sharply away, head bowed. The muscle at the top of his jaw twitched, and he said nothing for a few moments. When he spoke he was smiling again—a bright, cheery smile that Adam found frightening. "So this is what you educated Communists do, is it? Kick out anyone who disagrees with you."

"Don't play the victim. You know the rules," Z said calmly.

"You treat people with as much cruelty as your enemies do. In fact, I don't know who your enemies are—come to think of it, I'm not sure you do either. People to you are just stray dogs, nonsentient creatures who become pawns to your ideology. And you know what? Your whole life is just that—an ideology—no, an idea. There's nothing concrete about it."

Z folded the piece of paper she was holding and tucked it into Din's shirt pocket. "I don't think I need to get into a useless argument. Here's a list of the things you are accused of. You know we've always believed in nonviolent agitation. There's been too much bloodshed in the history of this country as it is."

"Nonviolent agitation," Din mocked as Z turned away from him. She moved toward her bicycle, which stood propped up against a tangle of old planks and rusty wire. "Adam," she said, as she began wheeling the bicycle onto the street, "please do not allow yourself to fall under the influence of someone with a misguided view of life, someone who's trying to avenge some imagined personal injustice. What's going on is not about one person, it's about a whole country. You're a clever person, anyone can see that. You've a bright future and you have a lot to offer. Only you can decide what's best for you. If you need me, you know where to find me—we meet in the same place virtually every day."

"Stupid bitch," Din said as she cycled away. "Don't listen to anything she says."

"I need to pee," said Adam.

"Miss High and Mighty—what a princess. Do you know what her father does? He's a director of Hati Mas, the international trading company. Bet you've never heard of it. Oh, you poor village idiot. It's the company that supplies things like screws and other hardware to big projects like the Senayan Stadium and the National Monument. It provides a 'professional liaison' between Indonesia and the Japanese and the French, or whichever neo-Imperialist is building our bridges or hospitals. What does that mean? Their offices are full of girls typing. Clickety clack clack all day long. Just typing. Where are the nuts and bolts and machinery? It's all just a front! And she, she dares to tell me what to do. It's all right for her—she can mess around with this idea of communism because if she loses her place at the university she just goes back to some huge palace in Menteng. People like us, you and me, where do we go?"

"Din, I need to pee."

"We have nowhere to go. This is all we have, Adam," Din continued, pointing vaguely with a quick flick of his hand to the area behind the house. Adam was not sure if he was indicating where the toilet lay or if he meant to say, This is where we belong. He might just as well have been swatting away an insect.

"You're like me, Adam—you understand what I mean. We have no real home to return to."

Adam followed the narrow lane beyond the house without knowing where it led. He just wanted to escape the sound of Din's voice. He winced every time Din said "you and I" or "we." At first Adam had thought that Din might have been referring to "we the Indonesian people," or "we who are not the government," or "we who are not them"; now it was clear that "we" meant all of those, but in particular the "we" that consisted of Adam and Din. He did not like the idea of belonging to a unit made up of himself and Din, which in turn belonged to some hazy group that seemed to include the million shirtless people who had been at the rally at the palace, but not, it would seem, Z or Margaret or Karl. Adam especially did not like it when Din said, "We have no home." He hated it because he knew it was true.

He reached a pontoon that jutted out over a stretch of stagnant, black water. A sharp smell of ammonia—of urine soaking into sun-baked, rotting timber—hung in the air; and underneath this odor was the rich stench of excrement. A young woman stood before a rusty water tank, dowsing herself with bowlfuls of water; through her wet sarong Adam could see that she was pregnant, and he averted his eyes. Flimsy panels of broken wood provided scant privacy on the jetty. With a sudden sense of horror Adam thought, I am meant to relieve myself there, in one of those half-open compartments, with a woman standing a few yards away from me. But he had no choice: He stepped onto the platform, wondering if it would give way, and stood facing the stretch of water. Patches of brown scum floated past him, held together by rafts of foam. Underneath the platform he could hear the sound of small creatures scrabbling along the muddy bank, their feet dipping occasionally into the water. Through the gaps in the timber he could see someone—a man—squatting in the compartment next to him; the sweet smoke from his *kretek* relieved the stink of the canal and Adam was glad for it. He thought maybe he too would take up smoking. Across the canal some children were kicking a *takraw* ball whose frayed edges spun messily every time it went up into the air, like the fireworks the Chinese kids set off during their lunar new year. There had not been many Chinese on Perdo, but the whole island seemed to celebrate their new year with them. Karl would take Adam into town, where rockets would light the night sky with brilliant sprays of flowers that seemed to remain suspended in the air, falling so slowly that Adam could hold his breath and count to four, five, six, before they began to dissolve into the inky blackness. There would be firecrackers and the clanging of cymbals and the smell of joss sticks and roasting meat, or even the unfamiliar perfume of tangerines imported at great expense from Java.

"What took you so long?" Din said when Adam returned. "Hurry up, I want to take you somewhere."

"Back to Margaret's house?"

"No, Margaret has gone out. She told me to look after you for a few days."

"But I need some clean clothes," Adam protested. "Why can't we just go back and wait there for her? I want to go home."

Din approached him and sniffed theatrically. "You smell okay," he said. "And did you say *home*? Margaret's house is not your home. Perdo is not your home, not as long as you share it with that white man. This is your home"—he waved his arms in the air, drawing a large semicircle above his head—"the revolutionary Republic of Indonesia. And you are going to be one of its new heroes, a true revolutionary, like me."

"You?" Adam said. "Me?" His ribs began to hurt again—a nasty twinge that ran down the side of his body every time he breathed. He felt tired, and he did not wish to be a revolutionary. All he wanted was to go home, wherever that was.

"Yes," Din replied, lowering his voice as if about to divulge a secret. His face, which had been set firmly in a scowl, softened into a smile. He put his arm around Adam's shoulders and guided him back to the house. "I will look after you, don't worry. I know you're confused, but trust me: Everything will turn out okay. I know it's difficult, but you must try and believe in me."

Adam wished the pain in his rib cage would go away. It made him feel weak and slightly teary, and his head was beginning to spin. He thought he heard the crackle of static, a fuzzy hum punctuated by low voices, a snatch of a soaring coloratura, the news, hail, hail, we progress, pride in our nation. He began to feel nauseous, his knees suddenly weak. The sounds hovered at the edge of his consciousness. He did not know what was happening to him. He leaned against Din's wiry, surprisingly solid frame as they made their way back to the house.

"Hey, hey," Din said, "you're looking pale. You need to sit down for a minute. It's very hot today. You're probably starving too. Let's go to Glodok and get some Chinese food—how about that, huh?"

Adam nodded weakly. The hum of the radio came back again, calmer and clearer now. This time Adam knew it came from his life with Karl. He remembered the songs on the radio, patriotic ones sung by children's choirs: *"The earth upon which my blood is spilt, that is where I stand."* He thought of the music playing in the sitting room and Karl's out-of-tune humming. Independence Day: He recalled the small feast they would have each year in the village, red and white flags hanging from the eaves of houses; and later, a present from Karl.

Yesterday was his birthday, Adam remembered, and he began to feel an emptiness in his chest. He was suffering, and it was because of someone he loved. Maybe if he hated Karl he would feel less bad. He considered telling Din about his birthday, but then, without knowing exactly why, decided not to.

"And then, when you're feeling better," Din continued, his voice still low, almost gentle, "I am going to show you how to be a true revolutionary."

18

*T*o be honest, I'm not even surprised. This is a perfect illustration of everything that is wrong with you—a classic Mick Matsoukis mess of the highest order." Margaret half-raised her hands in exasperation and then let them fall heavily on the arms of the rattan chair. It was shaped like a bowl, half a hollowed-out coconut shell set at an angle so that she was neither sitting nor reclining, her toes barely touching the floor. She tried not to think of Adam, for each time she did so she began to panic in a way that was completely foreign to her. She tried instead to remain perfectly still as she spoke, making no attempt to raise her voice or her body for emphasis; it was not worth the effort. She sounded tired, she thought, and she knew she looked dirty, inelegantly slumped in that awkward chair in Mick's office. She wanted to tell Mick about the riot, about how she and Bill had finally managed to escape just by staying still. She would have told him what her father had told her when he was teaching her to swim: Just let the waves wash over you, and you'll be fine. It had been like that in the riot. They had remained perfectly motionless and let the sea of people flow over them, and when the tide receded they were still there, like two pieces of debris stranded on the shore. Sure, Bill was so badly traumatized that he could only speak in monosyllables, but she knew he would recover his composure soon enough and be the same old appalling show-off. She wanted to say to Mick, You know what? We survived, and it really wasn't that bad at all. We can do this; we can find Karl and reunite him with Adam; we can face life and win.

But then she had arrived at Mick's and discovered this mess, and all the things she had wanted to say had rapidly dissipated into nothingness.

"It's not my fault," Mick said, stubbing out a cigarette that was only half-smoked and reaching into his shirt pocket for another. "You said you were going to ask Din to look after Adam."

"But I didn't, did I? I thought about it and it seemed like a bad idea—What if Bill's right, I thought, what if Din really is a criminal of some sort? I didn't want to risk it. If I had rung him, don't you think I would have told you?"

"I came by to look for you—out of my own initiative, I might add—and to check on Adam. How was I to know that he'd been kidnapped by your *colleague*?"

Margaret shook her head weakly. "This is precisely why you're in a back-street office in Jakarta, filing the odd report for second-rate newspapers instead of gracing the cover of *Time* magazine. No instinct. Life isn't an academic paper, Mick. It isn't theory. It's real. You have to *know* things." Next to her there was a bookshelf fashioned from planks of wood and blocks of concrete. She looked at the spines on the row level with her head: *Desire and Tragedy: French Painting in the Eighteenth Century; Romantic Failure: Jacques-Louis David and the Classical Spirit; Verlaine et Rimbaud: ou, La Fausse Evasion; Le Poète Qui s'Enfuit; La Vie Passionnée d'Arthur Rimbaud; The Peloponnesian War,* Vol II.

"But how? How could I *know* Din wasn't telling the truth? He said, 'Margaret told me to look after the boy,' and I believed him. It's called trust, Margaret. It's called not being cynical. It's called humanity. I haven't lost that. I don't want to lose it. Unlike," he paused and drank a mouthful of beer, sluicing it around in his mouth as if cleaning his teeth, his cheeks puffing out.

"Unlike me. That's right. Sad, cynical, dried-up Margaret. Look at her, all bitter and washed up. But at least I would have known that there was something fishy about Din's behavior. He comes out of my house with a bag of Adam's things and you don't think anything's amiss? My cynicism, as you call it, would have saved a poor boy from being abducted." This time she could not stop herself from imagining Adam being dragged around the city by Din. She saw him in some terrible slum, hungry and lonely and confused—and, worst of all, angry with her for having failed him. He had trusted her and she had promised to help, but in the end she had let him down.

"But do you or Bill Schneider actually *know* Din is up to no good?

This knowledge or instinct or whatever you keep talking about—what's it based on? You're being too suspicious. After all, you work with the guy and you've never had any reason to believe he's a criminal."

Margaret shrugged. The glow of the table lamp made Mick's face look broad and puffy, the deep lines in his skin accentuated by the shadows, his four-day-old beard fuzzy and indistinct. "It's based on intuition, Mick, on understanding how people behave. You can't just open some arcane textbook and find the answer. If you live in the real world, chances are you'll have this instinct. If, on the other hand, your life is rooted in the past, you almost certainly won't."

"It was a simple mistake. Nine out of ten people would have reacted as I did."

"Really?" Margaret reached for a piece of paper that lay on a messy pile on the floor beside her. "Listen to this. Your latest report—destined, I see, for the nether pages of the *South China Morning Post:* 'Jakarta, 15 August 1964. Indonesia is falling slowly into the grip of civil war. Sukarno's government is lumbering ominously toward its Aegospotami, and there are many who are ready to play Lysander to his Athenian fleet. . . .' I mean, honestly, Mick, who the hell is going to read this nonsense? We're living in 1964. We send men into space. We don't live in city-states drinking wine from urns and practicing boy love. Jesus! The only reason you get any work at all is because of your passport. With all the Brits and Americans kicked out there's only you Aussies and a couple of Frenchmen left—and still you can't make a name for yourself."

Mick did not answer; in the uneven light the contours of his face deepened, and Margaret could not be sure if he was grinning or grimacing. "Shouldn't we just concentrate on finding Adam, rather than discussing my shortcomings?"

Margaret nodded. "I'm sorry." Adam's face came to her again and she tried to picture how he would look when he finally returned—tired and slightly bemused at her concern. It was all a misunderstanding, he would say. I'm all right, I just went for a walk and got lost.

But no: However positive she tried to be, she knew that he had gone, and that she was responsible. This city was defeating her.

She looked around the sparsely furnished room. There was another bowl-shaped rattan chair and a small armchair, which Mick occupied, the stoutness of his frame making it seem like a piece of children's furniture. There was no table, no cabinet—nothing in which to store the various objects that lay scattered across the floor like the aftermath of an amateurish burglary: two pairs of sneakers, a badminton racket and three worn shuttlecocks, files, heaps of books, a broken radio, a postcard of Hobart's "beautiful waterfront" and a porcelain dish painted with the face of a very young Chairman Mao, which Mick had used as an ashtray. On the inelegant bookshelves, propped up against some paperback novels, there was a photo of Mick as a child, age four or five, dressed in a tweed jacket and striped tie, seated on a bicycle. His mother was bending over to hold on to the handlebars, her head tilted up toward the camera. Though she was a heavy woman, her features were fine, almost fragile, with an aquiline nose and narrow dark eyes that belonged to antique, Oriental lands—a kinder, gentler world, Margaret thought. Her wavy hair was brushed to one side and held with a small clip, and her dress was austere and black, the kind of thing she looked too young to wear.

"I think she was Ottoman Turk," Mick said. "My father was always saying she wasn't pure Greek. It was their little joke, something he always teased her about—though the whole Greek thing didn't ever mean much to me when I was growing up in the suburbs of Melbourne. My father wasn't a thin man either, so you see, I'm destined for obesity."

Margaret laughed. "There you go again, blaming everything on others."

"At least I'm predictable. Listen, you should get some rest. You've had one hell of a day. Adam will turn up tomorrow, I'm sure."

Margaret forced herself out of the chair. Her back felt very stiff all of a sudden. "I'm sure he's safe and sound with Din, doing whatever young men do in this city nowadays. I'm just, I don't know, overreacting, I suppose. This whole place is going crazy and I can't read what's happening. I've lost touch, Mick. I just don't have it anymore." She was glad the light was so dim; she knew she looked worn, and she did not want him to see her like this. She pulled at her skirt, trying to straighten it; she wished it were longer, that it reached all the way down to her ankles like a chaste Muslim robe.

"You know what? You should be doing my job and I should be doing yours—you're good at putting yourself in danger, and I'd be very good sitting in an office doing aimless research."

"Good night, Mick. See you tomorrow. Not too early. Let's give ourselves a break."

"Margaret," he called out abruptly. For a moment she thought that maybe he did not want her to leave, that he did not want to be alone. "I managed to find some news. On Karl. It wasn't easy. And I had to be inventive and think about how to get information that no one else could get—just as you told me to. You'd be proud of me—"

"Mick, just tell me."

"I'm afraid it's not good."

In the latter half of the eighteenth century the European population of Batavia began to move southward, away from the now cramped and unsanitary old fort on the coast, in search of better living conditions. They moved beyond the malarial swamps and the poorly drained stretch around Jacatraweg and eventually settled in an elegant suburb of sturdy white houses with colonnaded galleries, built along tree-lined avenues and pleasant open spaces. They called it Weltevreden: *to be contented*. The development of Weltevreden coincided with the sharp rise in Dutch military activity in the East Indian archipelago during the first decades of the nineteenth century, boosted by the arrival of Governor-General Daendels, whose nickname, the Iron Marshal (or the Thunder Lord, or any of the half dozen names by which he is known to Indonesian schoolchildren), gives some idea as to Dutch attitudes of the time. Under Daendels's rule, Weltevreden saw the construction of military barracks and houses with neoclassical facades for high-ranking army officers and civil servants. Enormous new administrative buildings were constructed using the stones from the dismantled fort, and lavish celebrations were held at the army club (called, one can only assume ironically, the Concordia). Each time a new island in the Indonesian archipelago was conquered, or whenever a Javanese prince submitted his lands to Dutch rule, appropriate celebrations would be held—an open-air concert, perhaps, where bands would play French operettas and finely dressed Europeans would drive up in their carriages and form a wide circle around the musicians, presaging the drive-in movie theaters that would one day exist in this part of central Jakarta. At the heart of Weltevreden lay a pure green space, one square kilometer: Koenigsplein; at various times a racecourse, a pleasure ground, and a military training ground. The whole of Utrecht would fit in it, the Dutch would say, laughing, as they passed the square on their way to drinks at the Harmonie Club or a play at the Schouwburg.

There were, of course, setbacks in this happy existence. Soldiers would return gravely wounded from the bloody guerrilla war in Aceh; they would be sent to recuperate in the great army hospital that stood on the edge of Koenigsplein, an ever-present reminder to the inhabitants of Weltevreden of the true nature of their lives in the East Indies. Some were foolhardy young men who were fond of saying that the greatest enemy in the Indies was boredom, but the truth was that there were many ways to die in the Indies; death lurked in the shadows, often well-disguised. If you were a white man there was only one thing to do: make as much money as you could and get back to Europe as quickly as possible. This is what older, wiser men said to themselves as they went past the hospital, whispering a silent prayer of thanks. Today the emptiness of Koenigsplein has been replaced by the emptiness of Merdeka Square; everything else has been swallowed up by the sprawl of Jakarta, but the hospital still stands.

"Please, we are family members," Margaret said to the nurse, who was finally beginning to relent; she reached for the key to the drawer and unlocked it, but seemed reluctant to pull it open. She stood behind the counter, staring at Margaret through thick black-rimmed glasses that made her eyes look bulbous and confused. She was about fifty, no taller than Margaret but strongly built. Her scratched, fuzzy badge announced her name and position: CANTIK HARTONO, SENIOR NURSE. Sensing that Cantik's resolve was weakening, Margaret subtly pressed home her advantage. "Ibu Cantik, please don't think of us as impolite," she said, bowing slightly, "we seek only your kindness and your help." A whole lifetime in Asia had taught her to back off in order to get what she wanted: If you insist too strongly you will cause embarrassment, and embarrassment leads to refusal, and refusal in Asia is irreversible, for about-turns involve loss of face, tantamount to humiliation. Therefore never be too (overtly) forceful; never insist, always suggest. Read body language. Smile. Bow. Do not overreact. Be humble. Acknowledge your foreignness. These were the simple rules by which Margaret had successfully lived in Asia, and they were proving effective once more. She turned to look at Mick, who was reaching into his shirt pocket, nervously feeling for his cigarettes. She shook her head slightly and frowned; his hand fell from his chest and hung limply by his side, fingerstips rubbing together lightly as if playing with grains of fine sand.

"We are not from the embassy, or from a newspaper," Margaret said, noticing that the nurse was eyeing Mick with a mixture of curiosity and suspicion. "The patient is someone very dear to us, and we—well, his whole family—have been suffering because we have had no news of him. He has a son—look." Margaret slid a photo of Adam across the smooth surface of the counter. It had been taken when he was much younger, and he looked timid and fragile, smiling nervously at the camera from underneath an enormous coolie hat. Margaret had chosen it specially from the scattered collection he had left at her house. "It's his adopted son. An orphan. His name is Adam. The poor boy has no one else in the world."

From the drawer, the nurse pulled out a thick buff-colored folder and began leafing through the papers inside. She paused several times and returned to documents she had already looked at, and then pulled out another folder and did the same thing. Margaret watched her trace her finger down each sheet of paper, noticing the rough, leathery skin on her hands; every time the finger hesitated, pausing at a name or a line of unreadable text, Margaret felt the urge to reach over the counter and grab the folder. Every time this nurse named Cantik sighed or tutted or shook her head, Margaret thought: Oh no. She hoped Cantik would say nothing, that her finger would continue down the page and then repeat the same journey down the next one, and the next, and the next.

"I'm so sorry," Cantik said at last. "I don't know what is going on. K. de Willigen—that's him, isn't it?—well, yes, he was here. Ward 5C. Intensive care. Discharged two days ago. Normally patients come out of intensive care and get moved into another ward, but he's no longer at the hospital. It happens nowadays. Not enough beds in Jakarta, especially with all the"—she looked around cautiously—"troubles going on in the country. Anyway, his medical record is missing. I don't know why. I can't even tell you what he was suffering from."

"But you're sure he's not dead?"

Cantik chewed on the end of a pencil as she flicked through the last pages of another folder. "I have no idea. I'm sorry. You know, in this place we often get people whose records are confidential. If your friend was someone important, well . . . a lowly person like me wouldn't know anything much. I just take my pay and go home."

"He wasn't really very important," said Margaret. Part of her felt an unusual relief at the lack of answers, for she knew that the answers were not likely to be comforting. She had become sentimental and cowardly, she thought, just like everyone else: afraid to confront pain, preferring to delay it instead. And yet another part of her felt cheated, frustrated. She hated this feeling of being thwarted, and so she stood at the counter, caught between these two conflicting sensations: Should she retreat into a cloud of uncertainty or push on with her quest?

"I know who can help you," Cantik said, looking at her notebook. "Dr. Hendro. He was on duty in the intensive care ward two nights ago. I can call him, if you want."

"No, really, Ibu Cantik," Margaret said, "that won't be necessary. We don't want to take up any more of your time."

"Oh, look, there he is!" She pointed behind them at a lanky youth hurrying down the corridor in a pigeon-footed shuffle. "Hey, Hendro!"

The man turned around but did not make any movement toward them. He did not look like a doctor: He wore nice brown trousers and a checked cowboy shirt, and his glasses were shaded, not quite dark enough to be sunglasses but not clear either. Margaret could barely make out the shape of his eyes.

"Yes?" he said. He had a rich voice that seemed too old and elegant for his long-limbed, gawky body.

"We're, um, we're looking for a patient you might have seen recently," Margaret explained. As she elaborated, the doctor shuffled toward them and went behind the counter as if taking up a defensive position. He flicked absently through Cantik's folders and shook his head before Margaret had finished.

"No longer here," he said, his voice becoming even more magisterial. "I remember him. Dysentery, dehydration. Suspected septicemia. Quite common among white people—as you know." He looked at Margaret and Mick with an expression of mild amusement (perhaps even contempt, thought Margaret, and she didn't believe she was wrong). "He asked me if he could be discharged. We don't keep patients here against their will, you know. We live in a *free* country now."

"You let him go, even though he was dying?" Margaret said, trying hard to remember her rules of engagement (Do Not Lose Temper, et cetera).

"If a patient no longer wishes to be treated, that is not our problem. There are five hundred people waiting for a bed in this hospital, so if someone is ungrateful for all the things Indonesia has done for them and wants to leave, we say, Please go."

"You obviously haven't heard of the Hippocratic oath here." Margaret felt Mick's hand on her elbow, exerting the faintest pressure. "How could you let a dying man out onto the streets? You say he had a blood infection—how could you stand by and do nothing?"

The young doctor smiled. "I want to ask you something. Have you ever seen a pregnant thirteen-year-old girl dying in childbirth because she is malnourished and doesn't have enough strength in her body to keep herself alive after giving life to her baby? What about boys of eight or nine who have arms chopped off in wars with their Christian neighbors, or grandmothers whose families try to poison them because they don't have enough money to feed them, only the poison doesn't work, or isn't strong enough, and they have to come to the hospital? I see these things every day here. Every day. So one white guy with a bad stomach isn't going to give me sleepless nights."

"A dying man is a dying man," Margaret said, and felt the tug of Mick's hand again, more insistent this time.

The doctor shrugged and made a cursory effort to flick through the papers again. "As I said, not my problem. Anyway, he was admitted under army rules. I don't get mixed up in all that. I just treat them while they are here. I think, however," he paused and smiled, "I think there are special rules for Dutch people. Maybe he has been repatriated. I honestly don't know what happened to him. I came in the day before yesterday and he was no longer in the ward."

It was very hot in the car. The old acacia tree under which they had parked had lost its leaves and offered little shade. "What a smug, self-satisfied, pompous bastard. I could have wrung his neck," said Margaret. "What has become of this country? Why can't we get anything done anymore? It's just so frustrating, Mick."

Mick shrugged as he reversed onto the cracked asphalt in front of the hospital. A hundred years ago they would have been in a carriage, Margaret thought; she would have been dressed in a fluffy, high-collared dress under the same unforgiving sun. She wondered which world she would have preferred living in: that lost world of the past in which she would have been powerful but despised by the locals, or this one, where she was completely powerless and only slightly less despised. She thought of the young doctor in his fashionable shirt and sunglasses, his cold, hard sneer. Maybe the past was a better place to live after all.

"For as long as I've been here, Indonesia has been like this," Mick said, navigating the car through the ranks of scooters and bicycles. The car kicked up a cloud of fine dust as it crawled along. "You know better than anyone how this place works."

"It hasn't always been like this. I remember a time when the people were . . . well, everything was just easier."

"But that was an eternity ago, before . . ."

"Before what?"

He shrugged again—a tic he had developed, Margaret noticed, a vague lifting of his shoulders that did not seem to mean anything. She was not sure if it signified stress or nervousness or anger or ignorance.

They were nearly out of the yard when they saw the nurse named Cantik running awkwardly toward them, tripping slightly on her flimsy sandals. She was clutching something in her hand—a white ball that turned out to be paper. She thrust it at Margaret through the open window, presenting it as if it were something rare and wonderful. "Sometimes patients leave things behind—when they die, for example, and no one comes and claims them. We put all these items in a box and most of the time we forget about them. Anyway, after you left I said to myself, Hey, why don't I look in the box, just in case? There was almost nothing in it. To be honest, the people who work in the hospital, they take things. They figure no one's going to come back for them, so why not? But at the bottom of the box I found this, and I remembered the photo you showed me of your friend's son. I remembered his name." She looked pleased with herself, even though she was squinting in the harsh white sunlight.

The cheap, almost translucent paper, so common in Jakarta, had been wadded into a tight ball that Cantik had only partially uncrumpled, and Margaret carefully teased the crushed sheets apart. They clung to each other with the brittleness of the autumn leaves she remembered from her years in America. The first few sheets she extracted were blank, marked only by deep, already yellowing creases. Only one sheet bore any words—elegant handwriting, the letters slanting forward and curling like the crests of waves. The first line read, "To my dear Adam . . ."

19

*D*aybreak. The sudden clearing of the skies, the fading of night into memory. The noise. The people. He recoiled from it all and wished he could retreat into slumber, where things were safer and, it seemed, more certain. In this daytime world everything was harsh and confusing and temporary. In this great city nothing remained the same for long. There was a time when he had been different and special, he thought, not so long ago in a place by the sea. But that place was far away and now he was just like everyone else.

"Here, have another one," Din said, handing him a sweet Chinese bun, its crumbly pastry shell topped with sesame seeds. Adam took it and pushed it into his mouth, cupping his palm under his chin to catch the falling crumbs. As the pain in his ribs faded slightly, a new irritation arose to trouble him: hunger. He could not remember ever having experienced this sensation in his life with Karl. It began as a twinge that seemed to expand into a hollow emptiness; it filled his insides so completely that he could think of nothing else. Din did not need to eat, it seemed to Adam. He scribbled furiously on scraps of paper and cut out articles from newspapers, deep in concentration. After he had returned from the rally, he had left Adam in the house to recuperate and reappeared sometime later with a small parcel of food wrapped in newspaper, which he presented to Adam with great ceremony, as if certain it would cement their new friendship. He also brought a satchel of Adam's clothes from Margaret's. Before they left the house that morning he had told Adam to put on some of these clothes—a nice clean shirt and smart trousers, as if they were going on an outing to somewhere special. "Where are we going?" Adam had asked, and Din had said, "Oh, somewhere special."

Adam searched the satchel for his notebook and photos, hoping that Din would have packed them too; but there was nothing but clothes. His life on Perdo with Karl—what he had always known as his Present Life—was slipping away from him. And it was being replaced by a newer Present that he did not like.

"Why don't you have the rest? I'm not really hungry. Didn't we have a lot of food this morning?" Adam knew that he was meant to say, Yes, it was a treat, thank you so much, Din. But he could not bring himself to enthuse about the curious assortment of stale snacks that Din had produced, for it had done little to alleviate the aching emptiness that filled Adam's belly. He did not want to recall his breakfasts on Perdo: copious quantities of rice and leftovers from dinner, and fruit and coffee. They had seemed restrained and sensible then, as had all his meals, but now he realized that each time he'd sat down at the table with Karl it had been a small feast. Still, Din was trying to do his best; and in any case those Perdo meals seemed to belong to some distant past. He was not going to find Karl—he had to accept that.

They were walking along a dirt road, beyond the limits of Kota, almost beyond the city itself. Tiny shards of grit and sand worked their way into Adam's shoes. Somewhere in a cluster of shacks by the road a radio was playing a pretty, lighthearted *keroncong* tune, the soprano voice tinkling in the air like splinters of glass. Adam thought he had heard it somewhere before, on Perdo, a long time ago. Din began whistling the tune as he walked; there was a spring in his step, and he seemed bright and full of energy, speaking without any of the previous day's vitriol.

"We're really not far from the coast now. Afterward, once we've done what we need to do, maybe we'll go and look at the ships at Sunda Kelapa. You know, those big colorful boats with the huge sails. Hey, I can smell the sea—can you?"

Adam nodded weakly. He could not, in fact, smell the sea; all he could discern was the faintest tinge of moisture in the arid breeze, but otherwise there was nothing but the sour, ever-present stench of rotting garbage and kerosene.

"Thing is," Din continued, "we forget that Malaysia is just over there. If we wanted to, we could almost swim there! It's really part of Indonesia—we could annex it so easily." He stretched out his arm and pointed at some unknown point in the distance, as if he could reach out and touch that country called Malaysia. "That's where your brother is," he said.

The road became gravelly, the tiny pebbles underfoot crunched loudly.

"You said you couldn't remember much about your brother," Din continued, his voice softening, becoming almost fatherly, the way it had when he met Adam that first day.

"I try all the time." Adam felt he could speak freely now; they were so far from Margaret or Karl or anyone else Adam knew that it did not seem to matter what he said. "But nothing comes back. Just the basics— he was older and bigger than me, and I have a vague memory that he was brave. And then he went away. I *know* that, but I can't *remember* it."

"You were very close, weren't you?"

Adam nodded. He did not know how he knew this—he just did. "I get so angry with myself when I can't remember anything. I try and think of him, but nothing comes back. I hate myself. I'm useless."

"No you're not," said Din, putting an arm around Adam's shoulders. "It's quite common, even normal. You must have suffered some sort of trauma that your brain has blocked out." He sounded authoritative and entirely certain, as if expounding a scientific theory.

"But I can't remember any trauma."

"That's the point. The brain is a very complex thing. When a human being suffers great emotional or physical pain, sometimes the only way to deal with it is to forget it altogether. You can't control this—the brain does it by itself, a kind of selective amnesia. You do know what amnesia is, I presume. Anyway, the brain creates a void in the memory. Other things associated with the pain might remain— noises or smells or visual recollections—but the pain itself is removed. The problem is that a lot of other valuable stuff is sometimes dragged into the void too."

Adam thought of the sounds and images that came to him from time to time. Din was right; everything made sense. It was as if all his life he had been standing in a room lit by electric lamps and suddenly someone had thrown open the windows and let in daylight. "I must be a freak," he said.

"Not at all. There are plenty of case studies that document the same thing. For example, I once went to a village in Sulawesi. I had a scholarship then and it was part of my so-called research—ha! Anyway, in this village there had been a bloody war between Muslims and Christians a generation before, but now the sons and daughters of the people who had butchered one another were living side by side again. The only way they could do this was by blocking out the pain. But wait, this is the weird part. There was hardly any noise in this village, no loud voices or arguments or laughter. Everyone walked about in a daze, as if they were daydreaming. It was as if their whole beings were devoted to suppressing their memories. Their brains had erased *too much*."

"I'm not that bad, am I?" Adam said, trying to laugh. "I'm not a zombie."

"No, of course not. We all suffer from it in one way or another. Erasing memories in this semiconscious way goes on everywhere, on a national scale, with culture—everything. We Asians are very good at it. If there's a drought that kills hundreds of thousands, or an earthquake, or the government fires on demonstrators—well, we just forget it and move on. It lingers in our psyche, but we never let it come to the surface. It just stays buried deep inside. When I lived in Europe I saw that Westerners remember everything—they commemorate bad things that happened to them. It was the only thing I liked about the West."

Adam thought about Karl, who never spoke about his past. He had always buried the things that had happened to him—good and bad alike. So it was not true that *all* Europeans commemorated everything; but at least they remembered them. Adam was sure even Karl remembered.

"What you're saying is that I need to find my brother," said Adam.

"What I'm saying is that you need to find your past, your real past. If that means finding your brother, then, yes, you must. Because to be ignorant of one's true history is to live in a void. It's as if you're floating aimlessly in the sea, being dragged every which way by currents and waves. You get pulled under water: There's nothing there. No people, no trees, no air to breathe. It's another world, a place your body occupies but where you don't really exist. So what's the problem? you ask. You're here, aren't you? As long as you're not dead, it's okay. Well, look around you, look at those babies sitting by the road, staring into space. Life has just begun for them and already it is empty. Is that really better than death? Do you think they're poor but happy? Those kids back there, begging, selling their bodies for a few *rupiah*—they don't know what their history is. Our history. We are not a country that was made for this. *This*"—Din raised his hand and brought it down in one violent chopping motion, as if cleaving an invisible foe in two—"is what we get when we don't know our past. We cannot claim our future. That is the problem. You can never go forward." They walked past two toddlers playing in a shallow puddle of muddy water, splashing each other's naked bodies with gray mud.

"You're right," said Adam.

Din began to whistle the *keroncong* tune again. He looked pensive, as if mulling over something that had just occurred to him. After a while he said, "Don't worry, I will help you find your brother. You must reclaim your past. I promise I will help you, Adam."

"And you," Adam said, "do you know what your past is?"

Din continued whistling, his hands tucked comfortably in his pockets. "Actually, I do." He seemed calm again, and smiled at Adam. "That is why I know where our future lies."

They reached a row of flimsy houses. Two old men sat on a wooden bench; on the dirt before them they had laid out a few things for sale: a carton of Winstons and a few bottles of honey-colored benzene. They nodded at Din, their sun-scarred faces livened for an instant by faint smiles. Din stopped in front of a sheet of zinc; pasted onto it were old advertisements for soft drinks and cigarettes, flaking away in the heat to reveal layers of even older posters. It was only when Din began to undo a heavy padlock that Adam realized that the collage of posters was a door to a shack so dilapidated it seemed to disappear into the shadows of the houses that flanked it. There was a flutter of tiny wings; nesting swifts, disturbed from their peaceful roosts, escaped from the deep gloom through the holes in the roof. Pools of light made nearly white circles on the dirt floor, but nonetheless it took Adam a few moments to make out what was in the shed: stacks of timber, damp and edged with crinkly mold; old worn tires piled up at the far end of the long, narrow space; a few bicycle frames hanging from the walls, stripped of their wheels, chains, and pedals, like skeletons of a strange creature. Din unfurled a length of tarpaulin and began to remove planks of wood; all the while he continued to whistle the same bright melody they had heard earlier, and it made Adam think of Perdo, of his house with its solid floors and solid roof that had no holes in it. He began to feel a sudden welling up of the bitter sickness that he had become all too familiar with in recent days.

"Come help me," Din said, tugging at a thick length of timber and sliding it toward Adam. It was rotting and splintered, and when Adam touched it he had to resist the urge to recoil from it. Together they moved all the wood until they had cleared a space, and it was then that Adam noticed an old tin chest that must once have been used to transport tea or spices from island to island. When Din opened it, Adam saw a tangle of wires and a few jars of pale yellow liquid, heaped together with some metal rods, an empty Bintang bottle (with part of its label scratched off), a child's doll with Western features, and other things that Adam did not recognize. It looked like a fisherman's net cast carelessly across a wash of flotsam.

Din delved into the contents of the chest and emerged with a canvas satchel that he slung immediately over his shoulders so that the strap sat across his chest, the small pouch resting safely against his hip. He put a hand on it, adjusting it minutely, as though reacquainting himself with something old and familiar and comforting. "Good," he said, and smiled; he was standing on the edge of a column of sunlight that flooded in through the patched roof; the light caught the side of his face, harshly illuminating half his smile while leaving the rest in the shadows. He held up the old bottle of Bintang. "A souvenir," he said. "The only time in my life I ever got drunk. I'd just arrived back from Holland. I was angry—I'd given up so many things to pursue a dream far away, and suddenly I was back home again with nothing. No 'Doctor' before my name, just plain old Din, no different from one hundred million people around me. All I had was the last of my guilders in my pocket. I went to a Chinese place in Glodok and drank five bottles of beer, one after another. I'd never touched alcohol before. I can remember the streets feeling very long and uncertain as I made my way home; in the *becak* I felt as if I were slipping downstream in a boat on a big, muddy river, like the Musi that I remembered from my childhood. I didn't feel happy, but I wasn't depressed either. It was just this feeling of in-betweenness, where it seems everything's possible yet you can't control anything. One day you might experience it, but I hope not. It was frustrating. Even when I fell asleep, I wasn't really asleep. I closed my eyes and I could still see the ceiling spinning. When I woke up I felt the worst I have ever felt, as if my body had been poisoned and rotted to the bone. I swore I would never drink alcohol again, and I never have. I keep the bottle to remind me of what I did." He was staring intently at the bottle as though he had been addressing it rather than Adam and was now waiting for it to respond.

"Oh well," he said at last. "It's only an empty bottle." And he threw it hard past Adam against a stack of timber at the back of the shed. It hit the wood with a dull thud and did not shatter but merely broke undramatically into three or four neat pieces that fell onto the dirt floor.

"Come on," Din said. "We have to get going."

THE ROADS WERE blocked off as they approached Monas, and their *becak* came to a complete halt in the tangle of traffic. They got out and proceeded on foot, skirting the edge of the square. Bicycles brushed past them as they walked on the grass-and-dirt shoulder of the great avenue, and sometimes, as they went past a stationary van, Adam would have to wait and let Din pass in front of him or else risk slipping into the ditch.

"Actually, it's better on foot," Din said cheerily. "You see lots of famous landmarks close up." He was still whistling the silly tune, never progressing beyond the same few notes of the chorus. Adam wished Din would stop, for it made him think of that place by the sea that was no longer his home.

At a crossroads they came upon barricades that held the traffic at a standstill. The perpendicular avenue was empty, a ghost town in the middle of the metropolis. Adam and Din stopped amid a throng of pedestrians at the barriers, straining to see the convoy streaming toward them: five or six magnificent black cars, some bearing a fluttering flag on their hood. Adam did not know that such cars existed in Indonesia; or, indeed, that they existed at all. They swept past the crowd in an instant, and a few moments later, when they were nearly out of sight, the soldiers removed the barricades, and the cars and scooters and bicycles recommenced their labored journey. As they went past the soldiers, Din put his arm around Adam's shoulders. "One day, you might be an important person—like those guys in the cars," he said. He drew Adam close to him, as an older brother might a younger brother, and Adam felt the satchel between them, bulky and hard and uncomfortable.

No trees lined the road. Adam could see no vegetation or foliage, just a forest of concrete structures built in fantastic shapes conceived in a dream. He was tired from the walking, he was tired of this city. It was not at all like the city he had once constructed in his imagination. He could barely remember that invisible world he had once known so intimately, a place full of love and possibility and promise. Walking along this interminable road, his ribs were beginning to hurt again, and the emptiness in his stomach reminded him once again that he was just like the millions of other people around him.

"It feels strange, knowing that I'm going to look for my brother after all these years. I never thought I could talk about it, or even think about it," said Adam. Contemplating this new future seemed the only way to alleviate the pain in his ribs and the sharp bite of blisters that were beginning to form on his heel and big toe. "In a way, I'm glad I can't remember anything about him. That way I won't be disappointed."

"Of course you won't be disappointed. You'll find your brother because that's your only choice in life—and I'll be there to help you, don't you worry." Din spoke with the same generosity as earlier, but he sounded brisker now, more distracted, as if he did not really wish to converse. Maybe he too was tired.

At last they approached a roundabout built around a perfectly circular pool of water; it was so wide that Adam could not make out the faces of the pedestrians on the far side. In the middle of the pool there was a fountain and a statue of a boy and girl holding hands on top of a giant plinth. In the streets there were clusters of soldiers everywhere, on foot and in trucks, chatting calmly among themselves, or smoking cigarettes. Adam and Din walked past a group of half a dozen of them manning a barbed-wire barricade in front of a badly burned building. One of them threw his head back in laughter as his colleague told a joke (Adam heard something about "a buffalo" and "wife" as he walked past) and in his black sunglasses Adam saw the reflection of ocher-colored clouds. These soldiers were older and more strongly built than the ones who had taken Karl away, thought Adam. They looked calm, even relaxed, but there was a tenseness in the way they held their guns, slung tautly from their necks, the butts cradled in their biceps.

"Are you admiring the Victory Monument?" Din asked, pointing at the statue of the blissfully innocent children above the fountain; frozen in full stride, they looked as if they were about to step off their platform and fall into the shallow water below. As they passed another group of soldiers, Din put his arm around Adam's shoulders once again. "Bet you don't have great monuments like this where you come from, out in the islands," he continued loudly. "Come on, you're impressed, aren't you? Don't try and act cool. This is a symbol of modern Indonesia!" He was still smiling, but as he continued Adam noticed the change in his voice, as if he were trying to conceal or suppress something. It took Adam a while to work out what this thing was: fear. He recognized it because it was something he had grown to know intimately over the last few days. He recognized it because, quite suddenly, he too felt a quick, inexplicable shiver of fear rush through him.

"But in fact we have just passed the truest face of revolutionary Indonesia," Din said as they made their way to the far side of the roundabout. "The burning of the British Embassy—that is what the revolution is really about."

"Look," Adam said as they approached a majestic, modern building, "there are the cars we saw earlier." A row of gleaming black cars stood waiting on the ramp leading to the building—many more than just the five or six they had seen before. "What is this place? It's amazing. Is it the president's palace?" he asked.

Din laughed—a cold, hard, sneering laugh. "That's the symbol of all that is wrong with our world today. It is the palace of corruption and hedonism and injustice and every other evil you can think of—so, yes, I suppose you could say it's the president's palace. That's very clever of you, my little orphan. You see, I was right all along: You are a revolutionary at heart."

They seemed to be walking past it, away from the great roundabout, into the dusty side streets where the buildings were lower and more modest. Adam looked back at the palace, admiring its perfect angular construction. He knew, of course, that it was not a real palace, but it comforted him to think of it as such. He liked the way it looked solid, permanent, and comfortable, unlike the tin-and-timber shacks where he had passed the last few nights. He also knew that it was a place where he would not be welcome. Not so long ago, with Karl to look after him, he might have felt perfectly at ease in a place like that. But that was his Past Life. In this, his Present Life, he belonged to the other side, the side of the nameless and hungry who walked the dusty streets looking up at the great buildings and shiny cars of this great city, trying to imagine what kind of people might inhabit that world.

They stopped in the shade of a concrete shelter surrounded by giant, rusty bins, emptied of their contents; the sweet stench of rubbish lingered in the air. Din reached into his satchel and took out a packet of 555s. "I didn't know you smoked," Adam said.

"I don't," Din replied, striking a match and lifting it hesitantly to the cigarette he had placed between his lips. His hand was trembling, Adam noticed, the flame refusing to settle on the stubby point of the cigarette. When he spoke, Adam could barely make out his narrowed eyes through the cloud of smoke. "Now this is the moment I need you to help me. Inside this palace of sin there are many people, many important people, many foreigners. These foreigners are intent on wrecking the great Indonesian revolution by paying corrupt officials to sacrifice the future of the Indonesian people—good, ordinary folk like you and me. A party is about to begin, a celebration of all the things that are wrong with our country. In an hour, even the president will be there."

"How can I help you?" Adam felt the quick chill of fear run through him again, more violently this time.

Din lifted the satchel from his shoulder and put it over Adam's— slowly, as if it were a garland. And now Adam felt the dead weight of it against his own hips, bulkier even than before. "Just take this into the building. Make your way to the men's toilet at the far end of the lobby, just beyond the place called the Batik Bar. The Batik Bar, got that? Go to the farthest stall and leave the satchel beside the toilet. Just leave it there. I have been there before, and it's simple. If you lose your way, just ask for directions. Be confident. You're not doing anything wrong, I assure you—you're just being a true, responsible Indonesian revolutionary. Remember the president's speech, when he said he loved revolutionaries? Well, you're just one of us, doing your duty. You're one of us now, my friend, one of us." He dropped his barely smoked cigarette before grasping Adam's shoulders with both hands and squeezing him gently. He wore an expression that spoke at once of tenderness and fervor and belief, and Adam thought, I really am his friend, I mean something to him. Adam nodded; Din's declaration of friendship made him feel less afraid. Din had helped him and was going to help him find his brother. Adam had to repay him.

"What will happen once I leave the satchel?" he asked.

"Nothing," Din said. "Once it's there, you just turn around and walk straight back out as if nothing's happened. Our revolutionary friends who work in the building will do the rest, and I will wait for you right here."

"What's in here?" Adam asked, feeling the straps of the satchel lightly with his fingers; part of him did not want to know the answer.

"That's not important," Din said with sudden alarm. "Do *not* open it. Just leave it in the restroom as I instructed you. Don't think too much about what you have to do—it'll be over in a few minutes."

"Can I ask you, Din," he began before hesitating. "Why me? Why do you trust me to help you?"

Din smiled and shrugged. "Because, well, let's just say it's the way you look. When you go up there, you will see. There will be people manning the doors, unfriendly people. They would never let someone like me in. But you—look at you, your nice shirt and trousers and hair. As soon as I saw you, I knew you were perfect for the job. You look like a decent boy from a nice family—even though you are one of us now." He looked at his watch quickly. "Okay, my little orphan, it's time to go."

"What is this place, really?" Adam said as he began to move away.

"It's a hotel. The Hotel Java."

As Adam turned and retraced his steps toward the front of the building, he heard Din striking a match that stubbornly refused to light; he was whistling the same tune he had been whistling all day long. "Remember," he called out to Adam, "just relax. Be yourself, little orphan boy. I know you will be fine. Come back quickly."

In the sunlight the hotel looked magnificent—a perfect oblong of smooth gray stone. Adam walked up the long, curving ramp that led to the lobby. He caught a glimpse of his reflection in the darkened windows of the big black cars that lined the driveway; he looked older, he thought, older and sadder. It was not just his face but the way he carried himself—the hunching of his shoulders, the tired, shuffling walk—that showed how his life had changed in such a small space of time. He ran his fingers through his hair, hoping it would make him look neater. He remembered Din's instructions and tried not to think about his simple task; he tried not to think about the satchel that chafed against his hip. Instead, he tried to focus on the future he would have with his brother; he tried to imagine the years of contentment that would stretch out before them: life waiting to be lived. But he could not conjure up this joy. That imagined future eluded him, wriggling away from his grasp, just as his past happiness had abandoned him.

Finally he saw the beautiful glass doors that led into the lobby; their smooth, clean surfaces reflecting images of the city: the tops of buildings, the ragged leaves of a palm tree, a bit of sky. The doors opened and closed slowly, like something in a dream.

•   •   •

Bloody bullshit. Our stupid badminton players can't win any more matches. Lazy bastards. Bad enough losing to those bloody Indonesians all the time, but now we're losing to Denmark, can you imagine? *Cis.* Country like ours shouldn't be losing to a country of paupers like Indonesia. Ya, well, I suppose they have plenty of starving kids desperate to make a name for themselves. That place is one big rotten egg, so many poor people there. No hope at all for them. Some more they want to invade us. What a bloody joke.

Johan picked up the newspaper his father had placed on the glass-topped table between them. The edge of the newspaper had touched a small pool of condensation at the foot of a long, cold glass; just for an instant, but it was enough to make it wet and soggy.

So. Here he is, the big fellah himself. Hardly see you nowadays, Johan. The moment you come back from school you just disappear into the wilderness. At least when you were at Kuala Kangsar we knew you were in the dorm every night. Now we have no bloody idea where you get to.

Johan did not answer. The paper had an article on the railways. It was always full of things that Johan did not understand. Modernization Scheme: 26 English Electric 1,500hp Diesel-Electric Locomotives Commence Service. Colombo Plan: Australia Donates 6 Railcars to Aid Boom in Malaysian Railways.

Johan, I said I hardly see you nowadays.

You'd see us more often if you spent more time at home. New Fares on Singapore Service. Weld Swimming Pool Complex: Photos.

There was a hearty roar of laughter at the bar where a group of men stood drinking heavy mugs of cold, yellow beer. Most of the men were local. There were very few Europeans now, compared to before. There were palm trees in pots and framed sepia photos of cricket and rugby teams on the walls. In the middle of the room an Indian bartender was mopping up a spilled drink on the black-and-white checked floor. There were no women in this place.

Put down the paper and talk to me like a man, Johan.

Okay. He could not fold the paper properly. He had turned it inside out and now the insides were showing on the outside. He had drunk a long drink and he felt sick. His father had ordered it for him, something called a Gunner. He felt sick and he needed to urinate.

You're a big boy now, Johan, a big, strong good-looking fellah, but you know what? You're still a mummy's boy. Nearly a man, yet you behave like a child with no responsibilities. A spoiled, ungrateful child. What do you say to that?

Nothing. Johan shrugged. Depends what you want me to say.

Don't be clever with me, young man. You better watch your mouth when you're with me or else there's going to be trouble. You got your poor mummy twisted around your little finger, but I'm smarter than that. You think you are one big-time genius, but one day you will learn.

Johan did not answer. They sat on a long, deep veranda, and beyond them there was an expanse of immaculate lawn. In the dark it looked blank, limitless. It could have been anything, anywhere. Like the sea, Johan thought, it was like the sea. He felt sick and he needed to go to the bathroom.

Here you are, you young people. You don't know how bloody lucky you are. Just merry-go-round all day having a gala time. When I was your age, I tell you, I was already working three jobs at once. No schooling, no Dickens and algebra like you buggers, and yet look at me now. Life gave me nothing and yet here I am. Self-made. Everything I have, I earned with my two bare hands. You drive around in my fancy car, think I don't know? Where do you think the money to buy that car came from? From Mars? Ya, you people don't know a thing about hard work.

We don't know a thing about corruption either.

What's that supposed to mean? I can't understand what you're saying, young man. Your mummy says you're so clever and so shy, that's why we can't understand you. You barely speak, and when you do, you just talk in riddles, and I ask myself, is it because you're clever and I'm stupid? Bullshit, of course not. It's because there's so much twisted rubbish going on in that handsome little head of yours. Maybe I spoiled the three of you too much. Ya, it's my fault. Mine and Mummy's. Nice toys, nice clothes, holidays here, there, everywhere. You guys have no idea of the value of money.

Yes we do. We know you have to earn it in proper ways, not abuse your position and take advantage of other people. Johan got out of his chair and went to the edge of the veranda. There was a low, wide balustrade and he placed his hands on it, leaning over the side to look down at the dark, empty space below. His eyes took a while to get used to the absence of light. And then he saw figures, shadows moving in the dark, silently, as though they were not connected to the ground. They would come together and drift apart again, here and there across the wide expanse of the playing fields. There was no wind in this city and he felt ill. He imagined himself in the car, driving fast with the windows open, and the thought of it made him feel better.

Don't listen to gossip, Johan.

I don't. I can make up my own mind. I know what you do. And I don't care. He continued to gaze at the shadowy figures drifting in the dark. He liked the dark. He wished he were there, in that black space. He had never been afraid of the dark at the orphanage. At night, in that long, bare room with the rows of cots, there had never been any light. Every evening, when day turned suddenly to night, the boys would stop moving because they were scared of what the night might bring. Some of them fell asleep immediately, but others would cry and talk and thrash around until they fell from their beds and hurt themselves. Johan never slept. When the Brothers blew out the candles and the kerosene lamps and the room became cold and empty and silent, Adam would come to Johan's bed and fall asleep in an instant, just as swiftly as day had succumbed to night. Once, when Adam was still very small, he had a fever and his skin was hot, and then it became cold and clammy. There was no medicine in the orphanage and Johan knew that it was malaria. He knew that children could die of malaria and he did not want Adam to die. The Brothers tried to take Adam away, but Johan clung to him, and in the end a Brother said, Leave them, there's nothing more we can do, they're a funny pair, those two. Throughout that night and the night after and the night after, Johan smoothed Adam's hair and blew on his brow to cool him when he was hot, and held him tightly against him when he was cold. Is this punishment? Adam asked, Is this punishment because I stole that fruit? Am I going to die because I am a bad boy? No, you are not going to die, Johan said. You are a good boy, the best boy in the world, and you are not going to die, you are a good boy. Adam drifted in and out of sleep; he could not control when and how sleep came to him. Late one night his body was so hot that Johan left the bed so that Adam would cool down. He was staring out the window at the blankness of the scrubby fields at night, and Adam called out to him. Johan, he said, are you there? And Johan said, Yes, don't worry, I won't leave you. Promise? Yes, I promise. Please don't ever leave me alone, Johan. I promise, Adam. And this was why Johan never slept, and why he was not afraid of the dark. He could not sleep because Adam slept, and he was not afraid because Adam was afraid.

Frankly, Johan, I'm worried about you. You just don't have any direction in life at all. No respect for anything. You're setting a damn bad example for Bob. And you're a bad influence on Farah. You're corrupting them both with that twisted stuff going on in your head. If you want to ruin yourself in spite of everything we've given you, then go ahead, but don't drag your brother and sister down with you. It's bad enough that you're upsetting your mummy.

There was a sound of breaking glass, something shattering on the cold, hard floor, followed by robust laughter.

Johan thought about his brother and sister. Bob and Farah. They were not his brother and sister; he could not think of them in this way.

He did not care about Bob. But Farah—he did not want to cause problems for her.

You make a lot of trouble for me, Johan. You drive around town at night going to all these bad places, smoking and drinking. What's more, I hear you're going around with a *girl*. A *prostitute* what's more. What kind of good Muslim boy does things like that? Don't forget I have an important position, you know. People see you, people talk: There goes Halim's son again with that *prostitute*. You bring shame on the family. I pray to god your mother doesn't hear these things.

I'm not the only one bringing shame. Anyway, don't listen to gossip, as you say.

Celaka. You are really too much. No respect at all. Enough nonsense, Johan, I have a proposal. That's why I wanted to have a drink with you tonight, a drink and a chat, man to man, father to son.

Yes, father to son.

Don't start that.

Okay, Daddy.

I think you need to be taught how to behave responsibly. You need to snap out of this stupid existence you have. You can't spend all your life being reckless and inconsiderate. Think about your poor mummy. So I have made plans for you. You're going to be enrolled at the RMC.

I can't. It's too late. You can't get into military college, you have to do stuff, tests and other things. I know people who've been trying for months.

Don't worry, it's all settled. Ya, I called my friend—you know, Uncle Zam. He's just been made a general. Brilliant fellah, went to Cambridge. No problem, he said, he can fix it. I told Uncle Zam, There's hope for my kid but we really need to be harsh on him, really beat him into shape. He's a wild kid, I said, but no one's beyond control. This kind of kid, all they need is a bit of discipline. So you're going to start in a few weeks, Johan.

Johan stood up. He felt the bitter aftertaste of the drink lingering at the back of his throat, and he felt sick again. This kind of kid? he said.

Aduh. His father sighed. What to do with you, Johan? Maybe it's my fault, after all. But Uncle Zam said, Don't worry, military college will straighten him out. Don't be hard on yourself, Halim, he told me, it's because of the boy's genes, no one can help him.

What?

Well, your, let's say, background. Being honest, it comes down to genes. Everyone knows Indonesians are a wild bunch. They're not really the same as us. We just have to acknowledge that.

Being honest, you've never loved me. You never wanted me in the first place, did you, *Daddy*?

How can you say that? Who told you that? Did Bob say that? Did he tell you that? I'll whack that fellah. Bloody big fat mouth.

No. I just know. Only Mummy wanted me. You didn't want some Indonesian orphan from the street, you wanted your own son, like Bob. I understand.

Why are you so ungrateful, Johan? I can't believe it, after all that we've done for you. Think about what might have happened to you if Mummy and I hadn't picked you out of that shitty place and brought you over here. You'd still be living in the *longkang* with the rest of the orphans, no clothes, no books, no home, no future, just like your—I mean, like the others.

Like my brother, you mean.

Johan, no. Stop. We told you a long time ago, as soon as you were old enough to understand. You have to face the truth. Your brother is dead. How many times have we told you that? Nothing can change that. Your life is here, in this place, you mustn't think of the orphanage. That is long gone. It is another world.

I wish you'd left me there, Johan wanted to say. I wish you had left me and taken my brother. He would have made a good son for you. He would have loved and respected you because he was full of love, and he needed to be loved. Johan had wanted to say this all his life, he had waited for the right moment to say it, but now that the moment had arrived, he could not find the breath to say it. He felt sick and he still needed a bathroom.

Okay, I have to go now. I have to go to dinner. Can't waste any more time with this. Just drop me off, then you can take the car. At least you won't have to steal it.

They walked the length of the veranda, past men dressed in nice batik shirts sitting down to their dinners of chicken and oxtail soup. There was still no breeze in the night but Johan felt less sick. In a moment he would be in the car, moving again.

You're right, Daddy, my place is here. This is my home. He tried to believe what he had just said, but he could not.

In the heavy shadows of the lane beyond the parking lot there were more shadows. Someone whistled at them from the dark, a high-pitched catcall.

Finally talking sense, young man. Where else do you want to go? Better stay put and make your mummy happy.

There's nowhere else for me to go.

That's right. Just swallow some pride once in a while. You'll enjoy RMC. It will be very good for you, you'll see.

They got into the Mercedes. The streets were brightly lit and there were many cars, for the evening was warm and still and young.

20

*T*here were not many things that Margaret did not understand about life. She understood quite well, for example, that love was not a constant thing, that it changed over time, drifting away from you and perhaps returning again when you had all but forgotten, that the inconstancies of love did not afflict one gender more than the other; women could be every bit as fickle and unpredictable as men.

And yet some things eluded her. She had not really been able to grasp the concept of children—why people felt the need to bring new life into the world, for it seemed to her something not just illogical but counterintuitive: Why sacrifice your life to something that is almost certainly going to turn out to be imperfect, something you will never be able to control? Why on earth had her parents decided to have her when they knew they would never be able to be good at parenting? Even now, at the age of forty-two, she had not yet figured it out. Yes, she had had a unique path through childhood and adolescence. Yes, it had brought (on balance) more good than harm and had prepared her for the harshness of life. But if she was honest, all she'd ever wanted was a normal childhood in a nice town, in Massachusetts, maybe, where the people had comfortable homes from which they never moved—someplace where people grew up, fell in love with the boy next door, and then raised happy families.

"Do you ever long to have kids, Mick?" she asked as they drove away from the hospital.

He smiled. "Of course. I'd love to have kids. I often dream of having a great big, noisy Greek family—you know, huge dinners with music and people arguing and laughing. Not like the miserable Christmases we used to have, just me and my parents, no one saying a word. Only problem is getting married. Don't like the idea of that."

Margaret smiled. In her hands she held five sheets of thin, crinkled paper, smoothing them with her fingers in the hope that the creases would disappear. She looked at the first sheet, at the lines of cursive handwriting that scrolled across the page; it was the kind of handwriting that seemed to emerge from a lost, earlier world, one in which typewriters and cheap newsprint did not exist. The letters were slightly spidery, the writer's hand shaky, unsure. Most of the lines had been crossed out, though not thoroughly enough to obscure the words that lay underneath. It was not as if the writer had wanted to hide what he had written, Margaret thought, but rather to rehearse what he wanted to say. She reread the lines that had been struck through:

A long time ago, I made myself a promise.
When you were six years old, I promised
Before I die
Ten years ago, when you were six When you were six I vowed promised vowed
Many years ago I promised vowed that on your sixteenth birthday
I would tell reveal

Only two lines survived intact in this jungle of barbed-wire deletions:

To my dear Adam

and

I always wanted a son like you.

The other four sheets of paper were blank, clinging to the first sheet with what Margaret considered a sort of desperation, as if they too wanted to be filled with deletions.

When the nurse named Cantik had given her those scrunched pieces of paper, she had allowed herself to think that this tangible link with Karl meant that he was still alive, still waiting for her to find him in this city. You can never predict what life is going to serve up. Always expect surprises. She tried to recall the times in her life when simply repeating phrases like these could cheer her up, when she could trick herself into believing that nothing was ever beyond salvation and once set on the right path she could make things happen by the sheer force of her will, turn a hopeless situation into at least something acceptable. It seemed such a recent thing, this blind confidence of youth, but now she had lost it—and she knew it was gone for good. What was worse, it had been replaced by an overdeveloped appreciation of reality, which now told her that she would never see Karl again.

"You're right, Mick," she said, "we just need to find Adam and take him back to his home, make sure he's all right. If Karl's not there, we'll find him somewhere else to live. Maybe," she paused, "maybe he could come and live with me."

"You seem to like him a lot. I've never seen you so *motherly.*"

"I loathe that word." She chuckled. "I mean, look at me. I couldn't be Mummy if I tried. But there's something about Adam that I under-stand—I don't know what it is, I just feel I know what's going through his head."

"Let's just see what happens. We might find his father, in which case it'll be happy families all around."

Margaret turned away from Mick. The highway in front of them dipped and curved slightly and offered a view of a shantytown, the tin roofs of the houses melding together to form a plain of rust and cor-roded metal. "I think we need to prepare ourselves for the worst, Mick. I have a feeling Karl's not coming back."

A group of students had gathered near the main gates of the cam-pus. Over the last few months there had been ragged bands of protes-tors almost every day, sometimes as few as five or six, sometimes as many as a hundred, often consisting of more nonstudents than students. Margaret was never clear what they were protesting against ("In In-donesia today there is much to protest against," Din had said not-so-casually one day). Sometimes they railed against the neodictators (meaning their teachers), sometimes against America and Britain, other times against the corrupt politicians, but mostly it was just the standard Ganyang Malaysia. *Crush crush crush Malaysia,* the chants would repeat tediously, and even the protestors themselves would seem bored. Today, however, the crowd was very large, two hundred or more, and relatively calm. This worried Margaret more than the usual rabble, who compensated for lack of serious intent by making as much noise as possible. Today's gathering was different: a young woman was standing on a podium, speaking animatedly through a loudspeaker—not an incomprehensible stream of vitriol but what seemed to Margaret to be a sustained lecture of some sort. There was a cohesion in the way the students raised their fists to cheer every crescendo in the speaker's voice, a sense of purpose that Margaret had seldom witnessed at these campus protests. Through the steady murmur of voices and the crackling static of the loudspeaker, Margaret discerned the words ". . . and so becomes dark, rotten, *evil to the very core.*" The woman's voice was dramatic and clear, the emphasis on each word perfectly judged, like the formal speech of a *lenong* play. Margaret strained to hear more, but the words were drowned in a chorus of cheers and whistles.

"Do you see Din?" Mick asked, slowing down as they skirted the fringes of the demonstration.

"No," Margaret said. "He might be in the crowd, of course, but he's not with those guys standing up by the podium. Those are the members of the student council. Let's drive around to the back. There's another entrance farther along where there won't be anyone and we can leave the car. I don't think it's a good idea to fling ourselves into the midst of this mob."

"Agreed. Students are the most dangerous ones nowadays."

Margaret looked back at the young woman who had been speaking. She was stepping down from the podium to raucous applause, shaking hands with a slim, long-haired boy. "She looks like a ringleader," Margaret said. "That's who we need to speak to."

They left the car and walked across the badminton courts; the smooth concrete surface was marked by cracks where tree roots were forcing their way slowly upward. Overhead the spreading acacias were shedding their leaves at the end of the long hot season, scattering their tawny confetti across the shady court. There were pieces of paper too, hundreds of leaflets urging hundreds of different things. Every day there were students handing out these flyers, but Margaret was never sure if anyone read them; they lay trodden into the dirt, bleached to a crust by the sun. Along some of the walkways outside the classrooms there was broken glass, and many of the panes from the louvred windows were missing. Not so long ago, from her office across the court,

Margaret had seen a boy remove one of these windowpanes and smash it over another boy's head. He had calmly walked up behind his enemy, raised the rectangular sheet of glass, and brought it down neatly on the boy's crown. The glass had broken very easily, as though made of thin, crumbly plaster. It had exploded into a million tiny shards that refracted the sunlight—balls of brilliant color that exploded into existence for a second, like those magical bursts of fireworks that light up for a moment before suddenly disappearing, leaving you staring at nothingness.

They could hear the scraping of chairs on hard, gritty floors; a distant voice on a microphone, harsh, exhorting; singing in the auditorium; a guitar; a sudden chorus of whistling—all the usual sounds of the campus, and yet there was an odd calm to the place. Margaret and Mick made their way up to Margaret's office, past a makeshift barricade of desks and chairs with a piece of paper pinned to it. *Revolutionaries only past this point,* it proclaimed in shaky handwriting; it reminded her of a child's den, a tree house that had fallen to the ground.

"That's weird," Margaret said when she got to the door. "I can't get it open. My key isn't working—the lock seems to be jammed."

Mick wiggled the key, teasing the handle at the same time. He leaned a shoulder against the door, pushing his weight against it. Margaret noticed how heavy he had become. He had always been sturdily built, even as a young man, but now he was heavyset. His hands, however, worked with a delicacy that was not in keeping with the bulkiness of his frame. "Someone's been tampering with the lock. Don't worry, it'll give, it's only a flimsy thing. And it's not really broken." He pulled the door toward him, and with a gentle twist eased it open.

Margaret's desk looked exactly as she had left it three days earlier. She sat in her chair and surveyed the mounds of paper and books: all in order. There were notes too, from various students, as well as political leaflets. Instinctively she reached for the bottom right-hand drawer, just below her knee; she found the key, hidden in the thin ledge on the underside of the desk, and when she unlocked the drawer she was comforted to see the same buff-colored folder that had been there for many years, on its cover the words: "Tchambuli: Kinship and Understanding in Northern Papua New Guinea." Her passport, too, lay nestled between the folder and the side of the drawer, its pages opening just enough to reveal the dollar bills folded inside. It had been a long time since she had seen either of those things; they seemed foreign, unreal— things that belonged to someone else. She considered taking them with her. But then she closed the drawer and locked it, returning the key to its hiding place. Somehow these two items—which amounted to a mere jumble of paper—seemed safer here, where they had always been. In spite of the riots outside, she trusted her office and the university more than she did her house.

Din's desk, however, had been stripped clean. The low shelves be- hind the desk were bare except for a thin trail of ants snaking their way into a tiny fissure in the wall. It reminded Margaret of her father's bed in the nursing home after he had died—ghostly, devoid of linen, of life; the room had been cleaned of all its contents, which had been placed in a few boxes. Din's desk had the same quiet emptiness: You could barely tell that someone had occupied this space up to a few days ago. Mick began looking through the drawers but found only bits of string and a few rubber bands.

"Nope, no clues whatsoever," he said, running his hand under the desk, "it's completely clean. Not even a porn mag taped to the inside. Is it normal for people to disappear like this?"

"Students often leave without giving notice. One day they're there, arguing with you about whether Brezhnev is a good guy, the next day they're gone. Sometimes they're killed in a riot or run over by a truck, sometimes they just give up. Mostly they run out of money and are too ashamed to be seen by their friends, so they disappear into thin air. But teachers, well, that's not so common. You normally have warning signs. And someone like Din . . . he's not the kind to surrender everything like that."

"Maybe there *were* warning signs and you just didn't see them."

"You don't understand, Mick: He's bright. And ambitious. What his ambitions involve, I'm less certain, but he wouldn't just throw it all away like that. He might not have been likable, but he was clever. He had a future. It's possible he's been fired, but then again, it wouldn't be so sudden—and I would definitely have known about it."

"Does anyone really have a future in this country?" Mick asked as they left the office and made their way down to the courtyard. Margaret could not tell if he was joking.

"We need to talk to the people who run the student council," she said. "They'll know where Din is—they're all basically Communists of one kind or another, even if they say they aren't. I lose track of all the factions, and I don't think they really know what's going on either. There are the most almighty fights on the council—mass brawls and chair throwing at meetings, death threats—that sort of healthy student debate. Recently a boy representing one of the Islamic groups found a dead cat hanging from the handlebars of his bicycle. He told me that someone threw a rock through his bedroom window at home—god, he was frightened, the poor boy. It seems the hard-line Commies on the council wanted him to vote with them on something, or march with them, and he didn't know if it was a good thing. Problem is, I don't know where Din stands on any of this. I think he's fairly neutral—or as neutral as one can be in this country."

They made their way toward the main gates, where the protestors were still gathered. They heard a steady chanting: a single word that sounded to Margaret like *rhi-no-ce-ros,* or perhaps someone's name. There was a time when she would have understood these not-so-clever in-jokes, these satirical references to things that happened in daily life, but she no longer grasped what was happening. She looked at Mick, who was walking quite calmly beside her, taking care not to edge ahead, as if waiting for her to lead the way.

"They're quite excitable, aren't they?" he said.

"They're only students," Margaret said, marginally reassured by her own voice. This was so stupid, she thought to herself. She was apprehensive about approaching a group of students with banners and silly bands of cloth around their foreheads. She even recognized some of them: There, that one waving the stick, she'd given him private lessons in English and taught him to say "Good day, how do you do?" He was harmless. They all were. And yet the memory of the previous day's riot was still vivid in her mind. The whiteness of her skin that stood out so completely in the sea of dark bodies, how she had been made to feel different—profoundly and utterly different—in this country for the first time in her life; her helplessness; her reliance on Bill, on other people, on chance—she could still feel all these things, and she was scared.

They paused in a narrow corridor behind a concrete stairwell that hid them from view.

"Won't this make good copy?" Mick said, laughing. "I'm finally a real foreign correspondent in the danger zone."

"Let's not get carried away. It's hardly the Bay of Pigs."

Mick was just feeling for his imaginary cigarettes when someone came around the corner, walking very quickly, brushing past him.

"Sorry." It was the girl they had seen earlier at the podium. She hurried along, not pausing to look back at them. Margaret recognized her as a member of the student council; she was certain she had seen Din talking to her on several occasions.

"Miss, hello, miss, excuse me," Margaret called out, starting after her. The girl did not stop; she did not even turn around.

Mick took off after the girl, catching up with her after a few (surprisingly swift) strides. "Excuse us," he said, catching her elbow. She drew away instinctively and looked up with a frown. Her eyes were dark, distracted, as if she did not understand where she was.

"Sorry," she said, blinking, "I didn't hear you. I'm rushing to get somewhere."

"Is the protest over, then?" Margaret said. "I thought it was just warming up."

The girl put her hand over one side of her brow to shield her eyes from the afternoon sun. The shadows that fell on her face accentuated her slim nose and shapely cheekbones. She blinked and rubbed her eye; she was very pretty, Margaret thought.

"Are you okay?" Mick asked.

"Yes, sorry," she said, "just a speck of dust."

"So you are abandoning the protest early."

"That?" the girl said, looking vaguely in the direction of the main gates. "I don't know how long that will last. I've done my speech, and now there's something else urgent I need to attend to. I'm sorry, but I'm very late already." Raising her eyebrows as if to excuse herself, she pointed over her shoulder, motioning to where the bicycles were kept, and Margaret noticed a stripe on her wrist, a band of light-colored skin that had been shielded from the sun by a wristwatch or a bracelet. Odd, thought Margaret, though she could not say exactly why she found this unusual.

"We were just wondering," Margaret said, trying to sound firm, "if you knew the whereabouts of Maluddin Saidi. You might simply call him Din, as I do. You know, my assistant. He's a research student. Do you know who I'm talking about? He serves on the student council, I think."

The girl nodded. "Of course I know him. I'm sorry to tell you that Maluddin has been reported for suspected membership in extremist groups that use violence to promote their political views—if you can call such views 'political.' Actually, I'm not sorry to tell you this. He deserves it. Those people are just idiots, if you ask me."

Margaret could usually tell where someone came from—their native region and level of society—but this girl was frustratingly elusive; she spoke fluently and without much of an accent. She reminded Margaret of those society girls one saw, the extravagantly dressed daughters of the burgeoning nouveau riche, educated in the States or Australia. At the same time, there was something of the shanties about her: the slight aggressiveness of her consonants, the confrontational way of speaking to someone in authority, the way she was nervously pulling at strands of her glossy black hair while trying to appear casual—all these things suggested to Margaret someone who belonged to the new-style socialist movement.

"You mean Din's been dismissed? Just like that?" The idea of him being locked out of his own office, kept away from his books and typewriter—all the things that were important to him, that held the key to his future—made her angry.

"No," said the girl, still squinting into the light and blinking with irritation (not because of the dust, Margaret thought, but because she was unhappy at being challenged). "For now he is merely suspended while the evidence against him is being considered. Of course we in the council will be pushing for his swift dismissal. The longer his type has any links to well-intentioned student activists, the worse it will be for everyone."

"The worse it will be for you, you mean?" said Margaret. "I suppose it was you who reported Din to the authorities?"

The girl lifted her chin slightly—a scant millimeter's change in the way she held her head; it would have been imperceptible to anyone but Margaret. "Of course," she said. "It was my duty. We can't take the risk of having someone violent in our midst. For Indonesia to progress, we need a pure, good-hearted revolution. I'm sure you agree."

"You're supposed to be his friend. I've seen you talking to him, laughing, having fun. I even wondered whether you were his girl-friend."

The girl laughed. It came out as a snort, an artificial chuckle. "I wonder why you are so concerned about him. Evidently you are suffi-ciently concerned about his private life that you have taken to spying on him. Yet you don't know him intimately, or else you would know about his violent ideals."

Oh my god, thought Margaret, this girl is *patronizing* me. Margaret could not remember the last time anyone had spoken to her in this way.

"Yes," the girl continued, "it's a good idea to defend this poor, clever boy from the *kampung.* All he wants is to finish his doctorate and help Indonesia achieve justice and fairness. By making bombs. By tak-ing men and women from their families in the middle of the night and making sure they never return."

Mick cleared his throat and laughed heartily. "That's not what Mar-garet meant, was it, Margaret?"

Margaret did not answer. She tried to hold the girl's gaze but was unnerved by the coldness of the nearly black pupils that stared back at her without flinching. The girl had stopped blinking but her eyes were still red and moist, irritated by that speck of dust; it was as though she wanted to prove how easily she could withstand something that both-ered her, how she could control her reflexes. It was something Asian women seemed to be able to do so easily, something Margaret had al-ways been able to imitate; but now she could no longer do so. She knew she was displaying signs of irritation. Do not get flustered, Mar-garet Bates, do not back down.

"What's your name?" Margaret asked, trying to sound calm.

"Zubaidah," the girl said. "Most people know me as Z. It's a nick-name my parents gave me." Her reply was even calmer than Margaret's question.

"Ah, yes, Z of the famous revolutionary pamphlet. Hello, Z. I didn't think you would be quite so innocent looking. I'd expected someone rougher."

"That's because you're full of prejudices. I'm sorry, but I really am very late," Z said, lifting her arm and turning her wrist in an instinctive motion; but there was no wristwatch there, and she looked up at Margaret again. "I don't have time to stand around discussing this."

"Z. Zubaidah," Margaret called out as the girl walked away. "We really need your help. Do you know where Din is right now?"

Z stopped and half-turned to face them again. She was still frowning but her face seemed to have softened and she looked puzzled.

She shook her head; her hair brushed against her jaw, making her look very young. "I don't know where he is. I would tell you if I did. I can tell he is very important to you."

"Don't you have any idea?" Mick said. "Please try and think. Did he mention anything to you about where he was going, what his immediate plans were?"

Z's frown deepened; she shook her head. "No, sorry. I really must go. I'm very late. Good-bye." She took a few quick steps and turned once more. "Just for the record," she added, "Din and I were never involved in *that way*. I don't have time for silly love affairs."

"You're young," Margaret said. "All young people have time for silly love affairs."

"Not me—I have more important things to do than chase after love," Z said, half-smiling. She turned to leave, walking fast; when she reached the end of the shaded walkway she broke into a run, kicking up dust in the hazy afternoon sunlight.

21

The studio was small but light and clean, built onto the side of a house overlooking the river valley. One wall had been more or less removed, exposing the room to the full view of the ravine that fell away steeply to the clean, dark waters below. In the distance, the hills formed an undulating ridge covered in bamboo. Against this backdrop Karl had built a platform; and it was on this flimsy wooden dais that his model now posed. She was a glum-looking girl of about eighteen or nineteen, sitting with her legs folded, idly drawing invisible circles on the floor with her index finger.

"What do you think? Do you like it?" Karl said to Margaret without looking at her. His eyes shifted languidly between canvas and model. He painted in short, jerky strokes, his wrist flicking rapidly in vertical movements or dabbing delicately at the canvas.

"Um, yes." Margaret hesitated. The painting was a mess, she thought: splotches of vivid color that bled into each other, violent green hills in the background and the head of a long-necked woman who bore little resemblance to the model.

"No, not the painting," said Karl, noticing the direction of Margaret's gaze, "my new studio. I couldn't have found it without your help."

Margaret shrugged. "I didn't do very much. I just pointed you in the right direction, that's all. There are lots of painters around Sayan, and I knew you'd feel at home."

"I feel more than just at home," he replied, pausing to turn to her, paintbrush poised featherlike in midair. She had never before seen a face so clear, so animated. "I feel this is where I was supposed to be all my life, my rightful place in the universe."

"I hope you're not going to say 'spiritual home.' That's what they all say."

"The light," he continued, as if she had not spoken, "is perfect. The vegetation, the temples—everywhere I look there is something my eye is not accustomed to. I feel like Gauguin must have felt when his ship first arrived in Tahiti."

Margaret peered over his shoulder and examined the painting. There was certainly a lot of Gauguin in it: the vivid patches of color; the doe-eyed girl whose bodiless head already bore the obligatory frangipani flower behind the ear; her demure, enigmatic regard, looking yet not looking at the beholder, inviting yet repelling the Westerner (no, Margaret thought: the Western *man*; she herself was neither drawn nor repulsed, merely bored). Margaret remembered her mother showing her picture books with color plates of Gauguin's paintings. She was twelve at the time, and her mother had embarked on a lengthy lecture on the "coming of age" of young girls in Tahiti. ("This is what some mothers might call the Birds and the Bees, or Facts of Life, or other nonsense," her mother had said. "*I* am going to tell you what happens to the clitorises of girls your age in places not too far from here—and I don't expect you to be shocked.") The long and short of it was that Margaret had thought Gauguin a terrible painter, amateurish and unhealthily drawn to sexual matters—not in a romantic or dashing way, but in a rather dull, predictable manner. Even at the age of twelve she didn't like what she saw. She did not find it the least bit surprising when her mother told her that Gauguin had died of syphilis.

"Look at her," Karl said, "isn't she perfect? So wonderful to paint. Her name is Nyoman. Isn't that the most wonderful name? Nyo-man. It sounds like something rare and delicate."

"It just means 'third child.' Every third Balinese you meet is called Nyoman, male or female. Where did you find her?"

"In the village. She was sitting by the road with a group of women—it was *just* like Gauguin—and they waved at me and wanted me to stop and chat. I was overwhelmed by their openness, the warmth they offered to a complete stranger—but also a bit sad, because I knew I would never be able to capture how I felt on canvas. I thought I should try, nonetheless, and therefore I asked Nyoman if she would come and pose for me. Fortunately, she agreed. I'm having trouble getting her skin tone the color it should be. Look. It should be clearer than that. But I think I have the form of her body just about right. It's quite unlike painting Occidentals."

Margaret looked at the outline of the body on the canvas, the flesh yet to be filled in; it was slinky and lithe. The girl herself was, thought Margaret, quite plump and already running to fat, as was quite often the case with girls in this area, where the harvests were dependable and the droughts rarely severe. Above her sarong her breasts were full and heavy, her arms stout, almost muscular. This Nyoman girl was only a few years older than her, but she was already a woman—a woman with an identifiably womanly body, ready to bear children. Margaret folded her arms across her chest; she felt like a flat-chested, malnourished urchin, a tiny young thing.

"Look at the grace with which she moves," Karl continued. "It's as if she will forever be a child, even though she's already a woman."

"She's only eighteen, you know," Margaret said, arms still folded tightly across her chest.

"I'd forgotten how effortless their movements are here in the Indies," said Karl, as if Margaret had not spoken. "We Occidentals lost this sense a long time ago—centuries, maybe even millennia. We lost touch with the primitive, unspoiled parts of ourselves, so we no longer know what it is to be innocent and childlike. Look at Nyoman, for example, look at her elegance."

Aware that she was being discussed (even an untuned Balinese ear could understand Karl's maceration of her name), Nyoman raised herself slightly and shifted her weight to adjust her sarong. She looked up at Margaret with bored, bloodshot eyes and broke into a rich, soupy cough; she turned her head and spat a thick glob of phlegm into the bushes beyond the platform, projecting it so cleanly and powerfully that it rustled the foliage.

"Elegant. That is the word, I think," Karl said, frowning in concentration as he stirred a pool of paint on his palette; it was the color of mud after a heavy rain. "Life in Europe is no longer elegant. It is no longer sensitive or welcoming or warm. No, we are no longer innocent. We have had our childhood snatched away from us and now we are old, argumentative men, decaying and ready to go to war at any moment."

"Why do you always paint women like that?"

"What do you mean?"

"With long necks and angular cheekbones. I mean, all of you do it. Walter, who really started this trend, I suppose, he paints them with thin, curving necks and seductive eyes—when he bothers to paint women at all, that is. Boys are really his thing, as you know. Rudolf is the same, though his women are a bit more interesting because they're sinewy and lean, just like men. Which, of course, they are—men with breasts and feminine lips; he's really quite repressed, Mother says, not at all like Walter. Jos Smit isn't a homosexual—well, at least I don't think he is—and yet he paints his women in the same way. And now you. You're not all copying one another, are you?"

Karl turned to look at Margaret. His sand-colored eyebrows were clenched tightly in a frown. "Do you think my work is . . . derivative?"

"I wouldn't say that, no," said Margaret quickly, though she was aware, even as she said it, that she sounded less than convincing. "I mean, you have a wonderful sense of color. Look," she waved a hand at the canvas, over the spot where patches of orange lay next to strips of absinthe green: the morning sun falling on the hills (or at least that was what she thought it was). "No one else in Bali does it this way. It's really, um, unique."

Karl returned to his canvas and began to dab some of the mud-colored paint into the outlines of the torso.

"So," said Margaret, "do you think you'll stay here in Sayan, then? For good, I mean. You know what? Your use of light is really very arresting. Wow."

"Yes, I'll stay," said Karl, not looking up from his painting. "I don't want to move anymore. This is my home now. I never want to move again."

"Great."

Karl set his brush down and turned to Nyoman, gesturing at her with upturned palms; the session was over for the day. "I like it here, I'm happy." (He did not sound happy, thought Margaret.) "The people here like me and I like them. I like them very much."

Nyoman rose from the platform and coughed some more. She came around to look at the painting and giggled, raising her hand to her mouth. "Poor thing," Karl said, stroking her brow gently. "I don't think she's feeling very well, even though she protests otherwise."

"Maybe she has tuberculosis," said Margaret.

Karl looked anxious; he laid his palm on Nyoman's forehead, checking for fever. "You think so? Just as well I've asked her to come and live here with me. I think it will be good for her—and for me. I need my muse near me."

"That will be a cozy arrangement for everyone."

He smiled weakly at Margaret. "I'm very optimistic about my new life here. I feel settled, after all these years. It's just an instinctive thing. You understand, don't you? I know you're still a child, but somehow I feel we're very similar."

"Actually, I'm not sure I do understand."

"Will you come and visit again? Soon?"

"Sure. Maybe. Yes, well, it's not the easiest place for me to get to. Anyway, *au revoir,* as they say."

"*Au revoir.*"

It was raining when Margaret arrived home. The journey had taken nearly two hours and the paths had become very muddy. She had slipped and fallen heavily on her shoulder and now her neck felt sore too. She was filled with a thick, insoluble despair, something so rich and dark that she thought it physiological: She felt nauseous, and there was a bitter taste in her mouth. Maybe she was catching a cold, she thought as she dried her hair and struggled out of her wet clothes. As she changed she noticed how small her clothes were—a child's clothes. She hated them.

She found her mother in her study, sitting amid piles of photographs, all of which appeared to be of the same people—Balinese dancers who looked dead.

"No, they're not dead," her mother said, busily sorting through the prints in no apparent order. "They're in a trance. Your father and I have been taking photographs of them. It's going to be a very comprehensive record. What's wrong with you? You look decidedly pale. I would ask your father to take your temperature, but he's off somewhere with one of those amusing homosexual painters, hunting for butterflies. At least, that's what he said. I hope it wasn't a euphemism for something pederastic. I've just lately had a faint suspicion that he might be doing slightly more adventurous fieldwork than he's admitted to, though of course that wouldn't bother me in the slightest."

"Mother, I'm not feeling very well."

"What is the matter with you? You hardly ever get sick. There was that one time in Tchambuli when you were bitten by a viper and had convulsions, of course, but you've never been sick since. Let's have a look at you. Why on earth are you crying? Oh god, it's that silly thing young Westerners call love, isn't it? Who is it? That delicate new Dutch boy? Listen, Margaret Bates, there's only one thing I can tell you in these matters: Never allow yourself to become too attached to a man—or a woman, for that matter, though men seem somehow worse. I've seen this boy; he's very engaging, but soon he'll be gone. I don't know if it'll be one month or five, one year or five, but they all move on. Man is a restless creature, nomadic at heart. We all seek new experiences, and that's the way it should be. Somehow it's easier for the male animal to do it than the female, but if you remain truthful to yourself you'll soon find that you are a nomad too. Don't settle down, darling; your home is where you are. You're in control. Not Karl de Willigen or anyone else. Falling in love is just a notion. You can control it like anything else. Now, do stop crying. Boil yourself some water and make a pot of tea. I have to press on with my trance dancers."

That night seemed very long. Margaret lay in bed without moving, blinking in the darkness, arms laid flat beside her. She tried to remove all thoughts of Karl from her consciousness, filling her head instead with a steady blankness. The emptiness brought relief but not sleep. Sometime after midnight she heard her parents arguing, their raised voices puncturing the fragile peace of her nonsleep, and suddenly she could see an image of Karl in her mind's eye; his slim hands and tawny hair, or his new house, perched precariously on the ridge. Or Nyoman. She could hear Karl's lilting voice too, and then she'd have to start again, this conscious process of deleting each image one by one, extinguishing them each time they resurfaced, like figures from a shadow play that refused to die. Pull yourself together, Margaret Bates, she repeated; you can do it. There, you see? Falling in love *is* a matter of choice. Gradually she began to feel better and, sometime toward dawn, as sleep finally came to her, she felt herself falling out of love with Karl.

・ 22 ・

*A*dam lifted his head and blinked. Light was falling onto the floor in a stream of constant color. He looked up: A crystal chandelier hung above him, its sharp nose pointing toward him like a huge icicle that he feared would crash down upon him at any moment. The dark, shiny floor reflected the light, and when Adam looked down he could make out the blurry outline of his face and body. At first he did not recognize himself; he looked different, as if lost in another world where all shapes, all things, all people were altered, only a fraction, but enough for him not to be sure where he was. Every time he moved the light would change completely and half his body would be shaded; and if he turned his head slightly, part of the ceiling would suddenly shift and make him seem taller.

He was surrounded by beautifully dressed people—the men in Western-style suits or military uniforms, the women in long dresses that swept around their ankles. They were wearing jewels too, these women—necklaces and brooches and earrings the likes of which Adam had never seen before. He tried not to look, to keep walking steadily; the problem was that he did not know where he was going. Young men in hotel uniforms paused before him. He could tell that they wanted to ask him what he was doing there, but he knew that as long as he kept moving he would be safe. He needed to keep calm and act as if he knew this place.

There were soldiers guarding the doors. None of them had even looked at Adam as he walked in. There had been a group of young men, not much older than himself, getting out of a van just as he arrived. They looked like athletes—soccer players, maybe. They were dressed simply but neatly, as Adam was, some of them clutching cameras. They were excited to be there, smoothing their hair with both hands and buttoning the top button of their shirts, wanting to look smart. Adam had slipped in with them, trying to blend in. He'd combed his fingers through his hair the way they did and made sure his collar was buttoned at the neck.

And now they were drifting away, shuffling uncertainly on the smooth floor of the lobby, and Adam was alone again. He tried to re-member Din's instructions: He looked around for the Batik Bar but could not see it. There were too many people here. Someone ap-proached him and he drew back instinctively. A young woman dressed in a *kebaya* was holding something out to him, a tray bearing purple and white orchids, each one wrapped in a glossy, green leaf, held together by a gold pin, and he understood that he was meant to take one of the orchids. At the far end of the lobby he saw a staircase, broad and curv-ing, lined with gold banisters, leading to a mezzanine level that over-looked the lobby; if he could just get there he would be able to go up to the gallery and get a clear view of everything. He made his way slowly toward the staircase, but he could walk no more than a few steps before finding his path obstructed. People stood chatting in large groups and Adam did not wish to announce his presence by saying "ex-cuse me," so each time he met an obstacle he had to stop and search for an alternative route. Each time he brushed past someone he felt the heavy bulk of his bag; it seemed to have become even bigger and more prominent since he had stepped into the hotel.

The stairs were not far now. A large party of foreigners—Japanese, he thought—blocked his way. Another waiter came by with a tray, this time bearing glasses of cold honey-colored drinks. He paused not far from Adam, hesitating; Adam could tell that he was not sure whether he should serve Adam. He looked like a boy from the islands, Adam thought, maybe even from Perdo. Maybe he recognized Adam from somewhere. He looked directly at Adam's face, then dropped his gaze to Adam's feet, scrutinizing every item of Adam's clothing before staring once more at his face. And then he turned away, offering his tray to a European man nearby.

Adam felt the strap of the satchel beginning to chafe on his collar-bone. Every time he moved, even if it was just to turn his head, it rubbed painfully against his skin. For a few moments he thought about opening the bag and taking some of its contents out in order to lighten the load. But he knew he could not do that. He knew he could not open the bag here in the lobby; he did not even want to think about it. All he needed to do was to find the restroom and leave the bag there. Then he could walk away and continue with Life, whatever Life was now. If he did what Din told him, Din would help him find his brother. They would go to Malaysia together and find Johan, and there would be a New Life, one which would not be burdened by empty memories.

He noticed a parting in the group of Japanese men: a small gap, just enough to squeeze through. It would not last long. Adam pushed his way through this narrow corridor, turning his body sideways so that he barely brushed past the men. Someone moved, knocking into him; he felt the softness of the man's jacket against his cheekbone and caught the whiff of fragrant aftershave; he heard the man say "sorry" but he did not turn back. He was at the foot of the stairs when he noticed a sign, a square board painted with a colorful motif of batik patterns. The gold letters and the arrow on it indicated where the bar was; Adam headed in that direction and soon saw another arrow pointing the way to the men's lavatories. Din was right, he thought, it was so easy. There was nothing to worry about.

The lavatories were cool and silent, sheltered from the bright chatter of voices in the lobby, lit only by wall sconces that cast a faint amber glow. The walls were of black marble, flawless and shiny even in the absence of bright light; and in one corner there was a large, white orchid plant whose leaves were beginning to turn leathery and brown at the edges. An old man in a white uniform was wiping around the sinks with a dirty cloth; he worked slowly, moving the rag in lazy, uneven circles, watching Adam in the mirror. A sudden hiss made Adam start: The urinals filled with water that gushed loudly, reverberating in the quiet space. Adam went quickly to the cubicle at the far end of the row of four; he locked the door and remained very still, listening for the old janitor as the flushing of the urinals subsided. At first he thought he could hear the limp flopping of wet cloth on hard marble, but then there was silence. The janitor's rubber-soled shoes squeaked on the floor but Adam could not tell where he was. Adam lowered the toilet seat, letting it fall with a clatter. He coughed. Still he could not tell if the janitor was there. He lifted the satchel from his shoulders and placed it very gently behind the toilet, deep in the corner. Even if someone came into the stall he would not see the bag unless he looked for it. Now that he had gotten rid of the bag he felt free and unencumbered once again. But if the janitor saw him emerge without it he would be in trouble; he had to wait until the old man had gone before he could leave.

He waited and listened: nothing. Was that someone moving? He held his breath and listened again. Was that the sound of running water, a pipe somewhere? In the lobby a band had begun to play, something bright and brassy, with wind instruments—a trumpet, Adam thought. It made it difficult for Adam to discern the different noises—which sound was being made by whom? He had to make a decision: If he stayed in the cubicle for much longer the janitor would begin to get suspicious. He coughed again, though he did not know what for—it sounded less unnatural than standing there in complete silence. He listened again: still nothing, as far as he could tell. He reached out and touched the door of the stall, feeling the smoothness of the varnished wood. He waited and wondered: How would this end?

Nothing in life is certain, he remembered Karl telling him; you just have to surrender to chance and let life take you where it wants to. If you do that, my son, you'll probably end up exactly where you dreamed you would be. They had been sitting on the steps in front of their house, early in the evening; the sun was disappearing theatrically below the horizon as it did on every clear evening in Perdo. They were trying to fix the radio, which had broken, and it was taking them a very long time. Tell me again about the war, *Pak,* Adam had said; so Karl told him about how he had left Bali by stealth, in the dead of night. Adam loved this story of danger and adventure. He loved hearing how Karl had traveled by boat for weeks until he finally reached Holland, thinking it was safer for him there, but then Holland was invaded anyway. Adam loved hearing Karl say, "I lay in bed every night praying that I wouldn't die because if I died I would not be able to get back to Indonesia; I used to dream about being somewhere else, in another world far far away." Why didn't you want to stay in Holland? Adam had asked. And Karl had said simply, "I don't know why. All I knew is that I had to come back here, to where I belonged. Life is like that, Son. Sometimes you don't know why you do something, you just do it. You just surrender yourself to chance and hope that it takes you to all the things you ever hoped for."

Adam reached for the door and opened it, walking quickly toward the exit. The old janitor was still there. No matter; he was free at last, able to move quickly and without fear. He had done what was needed of him, and now he would begin his New Life, and it would lead him eventually to Johan—to his past and his future. He walked briskly, past the Batik Bar and back out into the lobby. This time there was even less space among the people, but Adam was more insistent than he had been before, working his way through the tight maze of wool- and silk-clad bodies; he muttered quick excuse me's and ignored the sighs of annoyance that he received in reply. He fixed his sights on the great cubic chandelier that hung over the center of the lobby: If he could just make it to that point he would then be able to make a break for the doors beyond.

A military band on the mezzanine was playing silly, sugary tunes—folk songs that Adam thought he knew, though they had been altered to such a degree that he was not sure if they were the same songs. There was the one about the fisherman and the seagull. The fisherman was in love with the daughter of a rich farmer who wouldn't let her marry the fisherman because he was too poor. So every day the fisherman would pour his heart out to the seagull, and the seagull would give him advice; it would sing to him and say, Never lose hope for love, for love will come back to you, never lose hope for love, for love is true even if man is not. That was the chorus. Except Adam was not sure it was the same song; he couldn't tell because of the trumpets and the clanging of the drums. The song finished and they began "Bengawan Solo." He heard a murmur of approval, a sigh of nostalgia accompanied by a ripple of applause. But above the music Adam sensed something else. A few soldiers had come into the lobby, spreading out as if to look for someone; with them was the waiter who had looked at Adam earlier, the one who had not wanted to serve him drinks, who was now pointing in the general direction of the Batik Bar. The soldiers craned their necks to try and see into the crowd. Adam bowed his head; he knew they were looking for him.

A few more soldiers stood outside the doors, facing in. They had guns, cocked and ready. Some of the guests in the lobby noticed that soldiers had come into the building. Adam paused next to a middle-aged couple. "What's happening?" the woman asked. "Oh, nothing, darling, don't worry," replied the man, but he sounded worried. The music continued, but Adam could feel the unease in the crowd; some people had stopped talking and were watching the soldiers push their way toward the restrooms. Adam looked up briefly in the direction of the doors. He would make a run for it; he would wait until a new group of people arrived, and when the doors opened to let them in he would make a dash for it. Hadn't Din said that the president himself was due to arrive very soon? Surely no one would notice a boy slipping out just as the president's entourage arrived. He had to keep calm, be patient, then break for freedom. Chance, he thought, just surrender to chance.

But no one seemed to be arriving. Whereas previously there had been a constant stream of guests stepping out of limousines, now it was as if the hotel had been sealed off. Adam looked around him cautiously. The noise had died down; just a bit of nervous laughter, one or two men trying to sound jolly; all other sounds were drowned out by the music. The song was definitely "Bengawan Solo," even though the band played it as though it were a military march. Adam tried to remember how it really sounded; he imagined it playing on the radio as it always did; children would sing it at village celebrations and their parents would become teary and melancholic and talk about the war and the occupation. *"Bengawan Solo . . . Trapped by mountains/you journey forever and finally/escape to sea."* "But it's just about a river," Adam would say to Karl. And Karl would smile and say, "Not just that, Son; one day you will see." Adam thought about this now and he remembered how the song really sounded, away from this place.

He would make a break for it. At the count of three. A path had formed between him and the doors, a narrow alley that snaked its way through the static crowd. Adam began to step forward, feeling a sudden surge of strength in his legs. But at the end of his path he suddenly saw the waiter who had been looking for him, the waiter who was definitely from the islands and who knew that Adam did not belong in this place. The waiter raised his hand, beckoning to the soldiers. He was waving them over to Adam, pointing into the crowd to where Adam stood. His eyes were wide with fear, and Adam realized it was the first time in his life he had ever inspired fear in someone. He heard the clatter of boots on the marble floor across the foyer. He had to run, he knew he had to, but he couldn't.

"Adam?" someone said. A woman appeared before him, someone he had brushed past earlier. "Is that you? Oh my god, it *is* you. I wasn't sure if it was you. What are you doing here?" Her hair was pulled back from her face; her eyes were lined with black and shaded with a dark turquoise and her lips were pink and glossy. She wore a blue and red *kebaya* with red shoes; she looked like a film star, Adam thought. "It's me, Zubaidah," she said. "You know, Z. What a surprise to see you!" She reached out and took his hand, clasping it between hers as if greeting an old friend.

Two soldiers were now standing with the waiter. They were looking helplessly into the crowd, but not at Adam. Adam looked at the waiter and caught his eye, just for a second; but the waiter looked away swiftly. He stood with his shoulders hunched; he shrugged and shook his head before sloping away, leaving the soldiers to scan the room for the invisible enemy.

"So, are you best friends with the president too?" She laughed and raised her hand to brush away a wisp of hair from her face; on her wrist she wore a slim, silvery watch that glinted shyly.

Adam shrugged. He could not quite believe that this film-star woman was Z, but the voice was the same, the throaty giggle was the same. It *was* her.

"Isn't this awful?" she said, half-whispering. "All these terrible people. I'm here because of my father. He forced me to come. My mother's away and he needs to appear as if he has a nice, happy family. What could I do?" She spread her fingers, palms facing upward in a gesture of helplessness, and rolled her eyes. "In the end even revolutionaries have to do what their parents tell them. I like your shirt. It's nice."

"It belonged to my father," Adam replied.

They heard raised voices from the far corner of the lobby; a scuffle. A woman gasped loudly; people in the crowd stirred, trying to see what was going on.

"It's so stupid," Z said. "People panic so easily nowadays. Ever since that ridiculous assassination attempt on the president, things have been getting worse. All these rich people think that Communists are trying to bomb them to pieces at every turn. Look at them. Who would want to bomb this lot? The shrapnel from the jewelry would be terrible."

Adam noticed that there were even more guards outside now. Some of them ran into the lobby, heading for the corner where the restrooms were. The music stopped and everyone could hear the soldiers' harsh voices echoing in the lobby. There was a murmur in the crowd; a few people began to leave, shepherded by soldiers into their waiting limousines.

"Maybe it *is* serious," said Z. "Anyway, I think the party's over." The guests were being ushered out of the lobby by the soldiers and Adam could see that even the band had abandoned their instruments. "Come on, Adam, we should go."

"I thought you were with your father?"

"He has his own driver. He never comes home anyway—his poor mistress has the pleasure of his company most days."

As they left, they turned around to look at the commotion. Two soldiers had emerged from the men's room, marching briskly with the old janitor between them. His hands were cuffed, resting on top of his head, and he had a bruise on his face that Adam had not noticed earlier. A third soldier was holding the satchel by its long strap; he held it away from his body as though it were a dead animal.

"Come on, let's go," said Z. "Don't look. It's so pitiful. He's just an old man." They walked to a black Cadillac and the driver opened the door for them. When the door closed, Adam found himself cocooned from the city; he could barely hear the noise of the traffic. The car joined the line of limousines fleeing the hotel, inching its way down the curving ramp.

"So, what *were* you doing at the party, Adam?" Z asked. "I thought you didn't know anyone in Jakarta."

Adam's limbs suddenly felt lifeless, as if he could not control them. He wanted to lift his hand to wipe his brow but he did not have the strength; he could not even feel where his fingers were. His ribs were very painful again; he had forgotten about them, but now they were hurting. They were hurting badly and he wanted to throw up. He nodded. That was all he could do.

"Adam," Z said, lowering her voice. She cast a nervous look at the driver and leaned toward him. "You're in trouble, aren't you? What is it? You can tell me. Listen to me, Adam. Are you okay?"

He nodded again. He felt the sweat trickle down his temple, following the line of his jawbone before falling onto his neck. He was glad he was in the car and not out there, out in the city.

The Cadillac eased its way onto the road and joined the barely moving traffic. Through the tinted windows they saw more soldiers on the street. A group of them were surrounding a man on his knees; like the janitor, he had his hands on top of his head. A soldier reached into the man's shirt pocket and pulled out a pack of cigarettes. He tossed them toward his friends and smacked the man on the head, a heavy blow with an open palm which made the man tumble forward, his hands reaching out to break his fall. He picked himself up and returned obediently to his previous position, kneeling, hands on his head—like one of those children's toys that twists into a hundred different shapes but always folds back into the same position. And although the man had his head bowed, both Adam and Z could see that it was Din.

Z looked at Adam. Her eyes were calm and she did not say anything for a while.

"Are we heading home, Miss Zubaidah?" the driver asked.

Z nodded. "Quickly. Please." She did not stop looking at Adam. She said, "You're coming home with me."

· 23 ·

When she could no longer bear life in Ithaca, New York, Margaret left for Europe, as she'd always known she would. It was an unfussy departure, announced calmly and executed without drama or emotion. She had gone to the campus to tell her mother the news. It was early in the fall; a new crop of students, wide-eyed and gullible, were gathered in her mother's book-strewn office, listening enthralled as she held aloft a ritual circumcision stick from New Guinea. Margaret coughed to indicate her presence, and then simply told her mother that she had booked her passage to Europe—to Paris. Her mother did not reply for quite some time; she simply regarded Margaret with a look of confusion and annoyance, the long spearlike stick held aloft in her right hand like an oversized conductor's baton. Margaret felt quite proud of herself. It was just the kind of thing her mother would have done; she had out-mothered her mother.

"When are you going?"

"Next week," Margaret replied in a tone of voice that suggested mild irritation, as if it were obvious what the answer would be.

It took her mother a good few seconds to regain her composure. "Well," she said, finally, "that sounds like fun! Don't be too dissolute, will you—you *know* what those Parisians are like." She waved the stick as though cracking a whip or a riding crop; the students chuckled.

Outside, the trees had turned the landscape into a patchwork of gold and rust. The leaves were beginning to fall, spiraling gently to the ground like the first flakes of snow at the start of a heavy snowstorm, slowly, as if they would never reach the earth. Margaret went home and told her father she was leaving and that she did not know how long she would be away. He had been studying sheets of tiny photographs through a magnifying glass; he looked up and said, "Come back soon. Please." Then he went back to his photographs and did not look at her again.

The journey on the *Île de France* was quicker and duller than she had imagined. Her second-class cabin was simple, small but not at all cramped, shared with an aged woman who nodded pleasantly at Margaret but otherwise showed no desire to converse, which suited Margaret perfectly. It was here that Margaret remained for most of the crossing, staying away from the rich young Americans for whom she was already developing a distaste. They roamed the decks calling after each other in high-spirited voices, arranging rendezvous in the first-class dining room or tumbling noisily into their expensive cabins. The men were strong-boned and floppy-haired, the women sophisticated, almost world-weary, even at that age. Margaret thought she recognized two of them from Cornell; she could not remember their names but knew that she did not wish to speak to them. The farther she traveled from New York, the more justified she felt in disliking them; slipping away from the landmass of America, she no longer had reason to pretend to be one of them.

On the train from Le Havre to Paris she read the headlines on someone else's newspaper. LA CHINE DEVIENT COMMUNISTE, it shrieked in big bold letters: MAO PROCLAME LA RÉPUBLIQUE POPULAIRE DE CHINE. A much smaller picture caught her eye, and she tried to follow the pages as they turned—a fuzzy image of a man of darker complexion than a Chinese; Javanese, surely, or perhaps Malay. She waited for the reader to return to that page, but the picture was gone, and she could see only VIÊT MINH REFUSES TO RECOGNIZE PROCLAMATION OF INDEPENDENCE. There was a picture of the emperor Bao Dai, newly installed as head of state, but the Javanese man had disappeared. Maybe she had just imagined him.

When she reached Paris she felt she already knew the place. She remembered all the things that Karl had told her about the city, about himself. Every time she walked on a cobblestoned street she half-hoped to look up and see him walking toward her, collar turned up against the growing October chill, tripping occasionally on the uneven surface (he'd never learned to lift his feet). Or she would look in the window of a bookshop near the Sorbonne and imagine him hurrying away holding a new box of pencils. Sometimes she would pass someone and catch a whiff of cologne, and she would turn as though she knew him. It was the same scent she remembered on Karl: fresh, grassy, familiar.

She went to look at the place where he had lived, a narrow street of tall, white houses that did not seem to catch much sun. She found the address and stood outside the house for a while, wondering what she was doing there. Don't be silly, Margaret Bates, she said aloud to herself, he isn't here. She even smiled at her own stupidity and wondered if one day in the future she would look back and be embarrassed at how ridiculous she had been. And yet she remained standing there for a while, looking up at the windows, trying to remember which one of them Karl would have stood at. At the end of the street there was a pretty iron gate that led into the Luxembourg Gardens. She strolled along the gravel paths, under the drooping branches of lime trees that were shedding their leaves in the wind. She spent many afternoons walking in these gardens, not knowing what to do next.

She went to a grand brasserie in Montparnasse that Karl had once told her about. She loved the shiny brass railings and plush red furnishings, but she did not love the elegantly bored waiters and the immaculately dressed men who looked up at her with a mixture of surprise and suspicion. *"Vous êtes seule, madame?"* the man at the door asked. She hated the way he said "madame" with an almost imperceptible stress on the first syllable; the overformal politeness made her feel unwelcome, and old. She was only twenty-seven—still very much a *mademoiselle.* She held her menu upright so that it hid her from the stares of the respectable men around her. Her clothes felt shapeless and dull and slightly soiled, and under the table her shoes seemed clunky and enormous. She spent a long time looking at the menu because it comforted her to have it in front of her—a shield behind which she remained safely anonymous. She thought she would have something elegant, a sole meunière, maybe; but when the waiter came to take her order she suddenly thought: No, I am not going to have a delicate piece of fish, I am going to have something big and smelly and disgusting. She put down the menu and said, "Andouillette. I will take the Andouillette." She had never had it before but she knew it was pig's intestines, rolled up into a squat sausage, perfectly revolting. She smiled and sat with her coat on, her chin lifted to meet the gaze of anyone who stared at her. When her food arrived it was worse than she had imagined—a length of pungent meat covered in charred scabs. She cut off a big piece of it and tried to swallow it whole, like an oyster, but found herself gagging; she lifted her napkin to her mouth and coughed to hide her discomfort, starting to chew furiously until the moment of danger had passed. You are going to finish this, Margaret Bates, she thought to herself, you are going to finish every last bit of this. With each acrid mouthful she felt more resilient. She took a big gulp of red wine, which she didn't really like either, but it took away the taste of the intestines; before long she had finished a whole carafe and ordered another. It wasn't so difficult; she could do this. She looked at the other diners with a half smirk, challenging them to disapprove, but they looked away; only one man with a thick mustache smiled back, almost encouragingly. For dessert she had tarte tatin and two cups of coffee, which dulled the sharp taste that lingered in her mouth. She paid the bill and left a generous tip that she could not really afford. She enjoyed watching the waiter nod in grudging acknowledgment as he came to collect the silver tray, for somehow it made her feel strong and even a bit wicked, especially when she thanked him with a flourish. He inclined his head slightly and avoided her steady gaze, and that too made her want to smile.

Out on the street she felt light-headed and uncertain. It was a long way to her hotel, too far to walk. She had kept her coat on in the restaurant and only now, in the fading afternoon, did she realize that she had been sweating. She had been sweating in the restaurant and now she was cold. She was cold and she had drunk too much wine. Maybe she could make her way to the Luxembourg Gardens again, where she would watch the children running amid the piles of fallen leaves, laughing and calling out to their young mothers. She could sit on a bench, maybe, near the curving stone balustrade that Karl had liked when he was a young man, younger than she was now. She would like that, she thought. As she began to walk a man fell in step beside her. It was the man with the mustache who had smiled at her during lunch. He wore a gray herringbone coat and a felt hat. *"Bonjour,"* Margaret said. She realized how miserable she sounded, how miserable and cold and lonely. They walked for a while and chatted about things that Margaret cannot now remember. What she can recall is that after some time they reached a handsome building of pale stone. They paused at the heavy door. It was painted black and carved with foliage; next to it there were dark plaques with CABINET MÉDICAL and people's names written in gold letters. They went up to a room. In it there were two armchairs and a sofa covered in old, blue cloth embroidered with gold bees. There was a beautiful writing desk and a neat pile of cream-colored paper on it. He lit the fire, and when she felt warm again he led her into a smaller room, where there was a bed and nothing else. This is what you call a *garçonnière,* Margaret thought. The man's name was Georges, and he had broad, kind hands.

In the weeks that followed she saw her lover once or twice a week (she was someone's mistress, she thought, a real-life *maîtresse:* how exciting). She liked going to his pied-à-terre, which was warmer than her lodgings and not at all drafty. They went to the Louvre to look at paintings. He showed her a gallery full of portraits of heroic figures, Roman soldiers preparing for war, swords aloft, their women weeping in distress. There was another painting in the same style of a man lying dead in a bathtub. Margaret did not like these paintings, but she did not say so. She found them mannered and showy, and embarrassingly artificial; Karl would not have liked them, she thought. As she stood with Georges in front of a large canvas depicting a mass of beautiful classical warriors (Spartan, she thought, though she wasn't sure and didn't really care), she saw a young man making notes. He had made a sketch too, a crude one showing the principal figures as jellylike blobs with arrows showing their names. He looked up at her and winked, and then continued to scribble. He was writing in English, she noticed. The next day, when she returned on her own at the same hour, he was there again, in front of the same painting.

"Are you English?" she asked, although he was obviously Mediterranean, not at all Anglo-Saxon.

He shook his head. "Australian. You?"

"Guess."

He narrowed his eyes and shook his head, smiling. "French? Dutch? Don't know. Have I failed a really important test?"

Margaret laughed. She was pleased he did not say "American." She liked his dark eyes and timid smile.

They were both young and lonely in Paris, which is a terrible place to be young and lonely. And so they became friends.

Her days did not seem so long and empty now, and she no longer dreaded the winter nights that started midway through the afternoon. They went on long walks together, and Margaret was glad to have company, for it meant that she did not have to think about Karl and the places he had been. Their walks were sometimes guided by her new friend, sometimes haphazard; she no longer felt obliged to trace the invisible path of Karl's former life in this beautiful, cold city. She was also glad to be able to speak in English, a language she'd never thought she would miss. It was silly of her to be glad of this, she knew, but she was glad all the same. Even better than speaking English was listening to it, and on their walks she would often remain quiet for long stretches, just enjoying the sound of her companion's voice. He talked a lot; he knew many things about many things. He told her about Rimbaud, for example, who at twenty-two had joined the Dutch army as a mercenary to fight guerrillas in Aceh, but after a few brief weeks witnessing malaria, dysentery, snakebites, and amputations had fled the East Indies. Rimbaud believed that in life one will go where one does not want to go, do what one would rather not do, and live and die in not at all the way one ever had in mind. "Isn't that so true?" Mick exclaimed. "Look at us!"

Margaret also learned the following things: that her new companion was named Michael, that he was of Greek descent, and that there were many Greeks in Australia; that his ancestors were from Laconia but his parents had been uncommunicative rather than laconic; that, on leaving home on the eve of the battle from which he would never return, Leonidas, a great Laconian, advised his wife simply: "Marry a good man and bear good children."

Margaret could ask Michael anything and he would have the answer:

"Do you know a poem by Victor Hugo—something about a ladybug, and a boy who wants to kiss a girl?"

"Of course. 'La Coccinelle.' "

"What happens in it? A boy thinks a girl wants him to kiss her, but instead all she wants him to do is to get rid of a ladybug on her neck. Is that right?"

"Hmm. No. Let me think. No. The girl wants the boy to kiss her, but doesn't say so. She says, 'Something is tormenting me, look.' And she offers her face and neck to the boy. But the boy sees only the insect and not the kiss. It's about missed opportunities in life, about being too bashful and not taking your chance when it presents itself to you; about regretting things in old age—about not grabbing those fleeting moments of love, I suppose. Why do you ask?"

"Oh, no reason. It just came into my mind."

In truth it didn't really matter what she and her new Laconian friend spoke about. Margaret simply enjoyed the unfamiliar yet somehow comforting cadences of his voice, reminding her of another part of the world far, far away from Europe and even farther away from America. It reassured her to know that this other world was still there and that she had not forgotten it.

This is how Margaret remembers meeting Mick. She remembers everything he said very clearly, even now, in this sprawling Asian city where he has become middle-aged and less talkative—laconic, or maybe just downright uncommunicative. She remembers sitting with him in a cheap restaurant near the Panthéon, eating soup and ham and bits of stale baguette, and the excitement she felt when he folded the newspaper and handed it to her, showing her a picture of Queen Juliana of Holland greeting Mohammed Hatta in Amsterdam (with her near-photographic memory, she can still recall the caption: LA HOLLANDE ET L'INDONÉSIE PROCÈDENT AU TRANSFERT DE SOUVERAINTÉ, as well as the circular grease stain that had seeped through the picture).

Mick was with her when she arranged her passage to Java, on the *Willem Ruys,* sailing from Rotterdam to Tanjong Priok. He also came to see her off at the Gare du Nord. She told him to come and meet her in Asia, and that if he didn't, she would come looking for him and spank his bottom. They laughed. And Margaret remembered that she had said good-bye in this way to Karl; she remembered, also, that she believed she would never see either man again.

"Don't worry." Mick smiled. "You'll be lounging around in tropical splendor in some palace in Jakarta and I'll just turn up on your doorstep."

"And what if you don't?"

He turned up the collar of his coat and folded his arms against the chill. "Then marry a good man and bear good children."

*O*ww." Adam grimaced and flinched at Z's touch.

"Sorry," she said, withdrawing slightly. The rich smell of camphor mixed with other medicinal fragrances filled his nostrils. Z dipped her fingers into the jar of ointment and reached for Adam's rib cage again. "Think of something else—your home, or the sea. Something nice." She touched him lightly, resting her fingertips on his skin for a few moments to let him get used to her touch, waiting for him to calm down. When she felt the tenseness of his body ease and the rise and fall of his breathing return to a steady rhythm, she began to spread the ointment across his rib cage. At first it seemed she was barely touching him, her fingers skimming over the tautness of his skin. Adam held his breath; he held up his arm, bent at the elbow, his hand bunched into a fist, as if shielding himself from imminent danger. He tried to relax but the tickly, pleasurable sensation of Z's fingers running lightly over his skin made him want to giggle and gasp at the same time. He knew that if he laughed his ribs would tense up and hurt him again, so he remained caught in this funny in-between state: He wanted desperately to be soothed but could not allow himself to be.

"I think you've cracked a rib," said Z. "There's a bad bruise just here." She circled a forefinger softly on a patch of skin, and all of a sudden Adam recognized that she had alighted on the very epicenter of his pain, the precise root of the nausea that had filled his entire body. She continued to rub the ointment into his skin, more firmly now; a hot, comforting glow began to spread across his torso. He could still feel the pain in his ribs every time her hand passed over that spot, but it was duller, no longer sharp and surprising; it was isolated now, and he could anticipate how and when it would hurt him. Z's fingers worked steadily in long, gentle strokes or in widening circles, away from the tenderness of his ribs, moving on to his back and the sides of his chest. He closed his eyes.

"Something's definitely broken in there," she said, and laughed; and Adam could feel the warmth of her breath curling onto his skin, tingling, curious. "You're lucky not to have been seriously hurt. Did you know that nine people died in that riot? And that's just the number released by the police—the ones they couldn't deny because they had bullets in their backs. I don't know how many more kids were trampled underfoot and left lying on the streets. You see? You were very lucky. Why on earth did you agree to go?"

Adam said nothing. He remembered the promises Din had made, and how he did not really have a choice: What do you do when someone offers you something you had lost and never thought you would regain? He shrugged and began to explain that he had not understood that it would all turn out that way. He remembered how Din had looked, kneeling in the street, surrounded by soldiers: thin, defeated, frail, kicked into the dirt. And although he realized that Din had never cared for him, he could not shake this feeling of guilt. He had abandoned Din and left him to suffer on his own.

He looked around him. The furniture in the bedroom was edged with scrolling gold shaped like waves curling into themselves; the floor was of clear, cool marble, and the high ceilings made everything seem silent and airy. And this was the problem: He *liked* being here, and he was glad, so very glad not to be out on the streets or in some prison cell or on the floor of another shanty; but he felt guilty that he was here and Din was not. Before this moment, guilt had been a concept, something he thought he understood when people spoke about it. He had never actually known what it was to feel responsible for someone else's suffering.

"Keep still," Z tutted. "I knew Din was dangerous, but I said to myself, Don't worry, Z, that Adam is a clever guy, he isn't going to believe what Din tells him, he can look after himself. I was wrong."

"He was going to help me find my brother. All I had to do was help him with a worthy cause."

Z sighed. It seemed to Adam that she was frowning, concentrating hard on not saying anything, as if trying to restrain her impatience with his reasoning. He could not see the expression on her face; he could only feel her rhythmic massaging and the gentle pressure of her hand that did not change in the slightest. An ornate clock caught Adam's eye; it sat on a chest of drawers, a heap of molten gold cascading down the slopes of a mountain. The ticking of its pendulum seemed to fall in with the insistent kneading of Z's hands, like the metronome perched on Karl's broken piano. Adam had always thought it funny that the metronome should work when the piano itself was broken.

"Your problem," she said after a while, "your problem is that you don't know your own mind. You don't know what's in your head, you've never sat down and thought about what's important to you, so you're swayed by any passing notion. I don't know you very well, but that's how you seem to me: completely empty up here"— she lifted her finger momentarily and touched her temple, and then returned to massaging him. "Do you know what Din and his friends do? They put bombs in people's cars, people whose views they don't agree with. You heard about the assassination attempt on the president last year? We think it was Din's group that was responsible, though we can't be sure. They are trying to destabilize the country, which is already on the brink of complete collapse. The last thing we need is a full-scale civil war. But we will get it very soon. It's coming. How can it not, with people like Din around? You weren't stupid to have followed him—no, it was worse than that: You didn't even think about it."

This is strange, thought Adam: He was soothed by Z's scolding, by the steady, chiding tone of her voice. He did not want her to stop talking, even though her words embarrassed him. He felt drowsy, as if he was ready to fall into a rich, deep sleep, the first for a long time.

Z shifted her weight on the bed slightly so that she was now sitting behind him, rubbing ointment into his shoulders, and Adam felt the mattress give way ever so slightly. He had never seen a bed as wide or as soft as this one. He imagined himself stretched out on it diagonally; he didn't think his feet would hang over the edge. But then he found himself thinking of Din, crouching in a prison cell; and even worse, Karl, sitting with a dozen other people in a space no larger than Z's bed, while Adam himself enjoyed such luxury.

"And this whole business with your brother," Z continued. "Did you really think Din could have helped you? Let me tell you something, in case you haven't worked this out. You come from way out there"—she waved a hand casually in no particular direction—"so you won't understand. In this country, in this day and age, someone like Din is *no* one. I wish that were not the case, but it is. People like him can die in the thousands and no one would care. He has no power over anything, probably not even his own life. That is the harsh truth, Adam. You are the same now. From the moment you lost your adopted father you joined the masses—just like Din. Money is the only thing that counts. Money gives you power. This is the rule in our new republic. It's really very simple. This is what I want to change, but until then . . ."

Over her voice he could hear the ticking of the clock encouraging her hands on his shoulders. "Until then what?"

Z sighed again. "Until then, I suppose I just have to accept that I'm part of the system. Part of this." She lifted her hands from his shoulders, and although he could not see what she was indicating with them, Adam knew that she meant the beautiful, big house they were in. He was very drowsy now. He wanted her to keep talking.

"Yes, I'm a part of this whole disgusting system, a country divided neatly in two," Z said, her hands moving up to his neck. A heavy blankness was beginning to fill his head, an intense, pleasurable numbness that seemed to cloud his vision and impair his hearing so that he found it difficult to concentrate on what she was saying. It was a struggle to discern her words; her voice had become a low, steady lullaby, measured against the tick-tock of the pendulum and the kneading of her hands. "The rich—like me, yes, like me—do anything we please. Everyone else has no hope. They live and die completely by chance, with no control over anything. Sometimes some of them have dreams—like Din, I suppose. They have plans for their lives. But soon they discover that these dreams are worth nothing, and neither are their lives. We, on the other hand, never have plans. Life is simple for us, we just acquire, acquire, acquire. Every day is the same for people like me. We never, ever dream."

"Don't you?" Adam mumbled.

"No. A dream requires an ideal of some kind. Take my father, for example. He has no ideals. He just takes what he can, as much as possible, and will continue to do so for the rest of his life. He came from a very poor family and he has one simple goal and that is to distance himself from that poverty. All his friends are the same; they don't have ideals. You can't get rich and dream of creating a beautiful country at the same time. So you have to give one of them up. And if you choose wealth, then you give up your dreams. This is the reality of it. Someone like Din could not have helped you find your brother, but my father could do it tomorrow, if he wanted to. And it is precisely because he doesn't have dreams."

"And you? Do you have dreams?"

Adam felt a weakening in her hands. Something is wrong, he thought; and when he turned to face her he saw that her eyes were moist. She sat on the bed next to him, her arm pressing gently against his. "Din and his crazy lot, at least when they think about the future they have a vision of something wonderful. It's a stupid, misguided dream, but at least it comforts them. Me, I don't have that. Look at this place. It's not a home. Can you hear laughter, or music? No. There's just me. And you."

She stared at the clock, frowning as if trying to make out the time. Adam thought that she was perhaps waiting for him to say something, but he was afraid he would upset her by saying the wrong thing, so he kept quiet. He shifted so that he was facing her; he smiled, trying to catch her eye, but she continued to look at the clock. In a quiet voice she said, "That's the worst thing. People like me, we don't have dreams. I talk a lot about changing things, but deep down I know nothing will change. Not ever. That is why I don't dream, I don't think about the future. Because when I do, all I see is emptiness."

And this was when Adam realized that she was crying. She did not sob or sniff or weep hysterically or do any of the things Adam associated with crying. She did not move; her eyes simply filled with tears, and after a few moments she rubbed the back of her hand across her cheek, quite roughly, as if dislodging an irritation. When Adam reached out and put his hand on hers he found it damp and slightly sticky. His head still felt very heavy. He could smell the sour-sweet odor of her breath, and he could hear her breathing too, one exhalation to every five ticks of the pendulum. She raised her hand and brushed back the hair that fell across his forehead. You have lots of dreams, don't you? she said. Or that is what Adam thought she said. And then she leaned forward and let her head rest on his shoulder; he could not tell if she was crying. She pulled him gently until he was lying flat on the bed, and he could not stop himself from falling into what he knew would be a very long and very deep sleep. He felt her head on his chest, and the gentle reverberations of her voice in his rib cage, which did not hurt so much anymore. Go to sleep now, she said. Go to sleep.

· ● ·

Nightfall.

Sometimes the rain clouds that gathered in the afternoon refused to break and the skies stayed dark and cobalt colored, and the day turned into a long, purple dusk that hastened the arrival of darkness. Later, much later, once night had taken hold, the rain would at last fall and make the streets of the city slick and sometimes a little muddy, and the buildings would be quiet and empty, and out in the new suburbs the stretches of fields and scrubland that separated the clustered lights of the houses would be blank with darkness, and you could imagine that they were filled not with heaps of rubbish and broken bicycles but with trees and ponds. Sometimes you could imagine the sea. And this was when he felt happiest, for the night seemed longer and deeper and more silent.

They ran across the playing field, splashing through puddles of water. They stumbled and Farah laughed, a sharp, childlike cry that made Johan think that she had hurt herself, but when he turned to look at her he knew she was smiling. Even in the near-dark he could see that she was happy. There were goalposts at one end of the field, three wooden poles nailed together to make a spindly frame whose two feet stood in pools of water. Farah jumped and touched the top bar with her hand as she ran underneath it. Look, Johan, she cried.

They reached the shelter at the far end of the field that housed a wooden table and some benches. They tugged at the edges of their shirts and tried to wring the water from them, but it was useless, so they just sat on the table with their feet on a bench, out of breath from their dash through the rain, laughing.

I have mud in my shoes, Farah said, but she did not sound unhappy.

Me too. I suppose we just have to wait until the rain stops.

It was not a fierce storm but the rain was still heavy, drumming loudly on the flimsy roof overhead and falling in thin, steady streams where the grooves in the zinc sheeting sloped toward the ground. They stared out at the darkness but could not make out any shapes. The goalposts and the seesaw and swings in the children's playground had disappeared and they could see very little except the pale haze of the rain. Now and then the sky would be lit by a distant flash of lightning and suddenly they would see everything again, the young acacia saplings bending in the wind, the rows of thorny bushes, the merry-go-round. Everything would burst into life for a few seconds and then disappear into the darkness again, and there would only be the soothing rumble of thunder.

Daddy says you're going to military college.

Johan did not say anything for a while. He leaned forward and water ran from his hair onto his brow and began to tickle his eyes. He blinked. Yes, I suppose I am.

Farah imitated him and rested her elbows on her knees, cupping her chin with her hands. Are you upset?

He shook his head. He was thankful it was dark because he knew she could not see his face clearly.

Anyway, she said, Sungai Besi's not so far away. Daddy says you can come home from time to time.

Sure.

Don't be sad.

Who says I'm sad?

Me. Because I'm sad.

You mustn't be. Johan looked at her, but she was not facing him and there was not enough light to make out her face. He was glad he couldn't see.

Johan. He felt her hand search for his, her fingers stubbing clumsily into his thigh before finding his forearm, then his wrist. She let her hand rest gently on his. It felt very light. She said, Johan, please share with me. Your life, I mean.

We grew up together. You know my life.

No, I mean before that. Somehow I feel, oh, I don't know. I think sometimes that was your real life and when you came to us you stopped living, you just gave up. You shut us out. Even Mummy. Even me.

I'm still alive and kicking, aren't I? Johan laughed. And with his free hand he reached out and squeezed hers.

Johan, she said. She paused. Did something happen to you when you were small? At the orphanage, I mean. It's just, there's something I remember when I was very young, maybe eight. You must have been ten, a couple of years after you came to us. I had a nightmare one night and I went to Mummy and Daddy's room. I don't know why. I wanted a hug, I guess. They were arguing; not loudly, you know, just softly, keeping their voices down, and Mummy was talking in a really fierce voice, attacking Daddy the way she doesn't anymore. You remember how she used to be when she was younger. I couldn't hear the exact words, I just remember the tone. And then there was a silence, and Daddy said, So what if I know where the other one is, what do you want me to do, go back and get him? You made the decision, so don't feel guilty now.

Above the harsh clatter of the rain on the roof Johan could hear a gentler note, a hushing sound made by the rain falling on the soft earth, on the shallow pools of water that covered the land in front of them. It was a sound of trees disturbed by the wind, their leaves and branches flailing in the night storm. If Johan closed his eyes he could pretend he was by the sea, and the noise was that of rain falling on sand. He tried to concentrate on this noise, but it was difficult because of the rattling of the tin sheets overhead.

For a long time I thought I must have dreamed it, that it was late at night and I didn't know what was going on, Farah continued. She was talking very softly and it was not easy to hear her voice. You know what kind of imagination a kid has. Sometimes they dream things up and those things are so much more convincing than real life. That thing I heard Mummy and Daddy say, well, it was so real I thought I *must* have dreamed it. And anyway, even if it was true, so what? It doesn't mean anything, because we all know you had a brother, right?

You're right, it doesn't mean anything.

But . . . but if that's the case, why do I feel so guilty every time I think about it? Why do I feel so bad? Why did they sound so full of anguish? Especially Mummy. And even Daddy. It made me feel, I don't know, as though there was something I should have known about you but didn't. I felt as if you were all alone, you were all alone and suffering and I wasn't doing anything to help you.

Johan did not speak. The wind was blowing the rain into curious shapes, broad swirls or straight shafts that arrowed toward the ground. He remembered a picture he had seen a few years back, a kind of drawing or watercolor, he wasn't sure which. It was in an old book that had become wet sometime in its history and all its pages were brittle and stained. The picture was of a person so pitiful that Johan could not really even tell if it was a man or woman or boy or girl. And in the picture this person was doing nothing except gazing into the landscape with an expression so forlorn and lonely that it made Johan feel sick, for this pathetic person was all alone in the world, in a desolate place that looked like everywhere Johan had ever lived. He copied down the title of this picture, *Un Fou Dans Un Morne Paysage,* and when he looked up the meaning of this in a dictionary at school, he learned that the person was a madman. Johan had not thought of the poor creature as a madman. He was just someone who was alone in a barren place. But maybe that was what it meant to be a madman. Perhaps being really, truly alone in a desolate world meant that you were mad because you could not understand this world that belonged to others. Johan thought that maybe he himself was mad. And it was a relief of sorts to think that.

You're not crazy, Farah. Sometimes, he said, sometimes I have the same feeling. I think I must have imagined it all.

Imagined what?

Everything. The orphanage, my brother, coming to live with you. I *wish* I had imagined it all, but I know I didn't. You know how people say that things fade with time, that your memory becomes weaker? It doesn't. Everything becomes clearer. And you see it all the time All the time. You try and run away from it, but it just follows you every second of the day and night and you can't escape it.

What can you remember? Her fingers closed around his hand, pressing gently.

I can remember Mummy and Daddy coming to the orphanage. Mummy was wearing a dress made from batik, not really a *kebaya* but almost. She had a scarf over her head, not a *tudung* but something that hid her hair and neck. I remember thinking, What a beautiful woman. They were both wearing sunglasses, and they spoke in an accent that I couldn't really understand. We were brought into the Room. We called it the Room because it was the only proper room in the orphanage, you know, not a dorm or a partitioned space. A room. That was where, where . . .

Where what?

Where you were punished. If you were naughty, they took you there and closed the door, and they punished you. The Brothers, that is. They beat you with a *rotan*. On your bare skin where it hurt.

Johan.

This was where they brought us when Mummy and Daddy came. Both of us. Me and my brother. We stood up and the Brothers told Mummy and Daddy about us, and said all nice things, that we were good boys, always well behaved and quiet, never made noise, and Mummy said, They're not mute, are they? And the nurse said, No, no, of course not, and Mummy laughed. She made everyone laugh. Daddy kept looking at his watch, tracing its outline with his fingers. The same watch he has now, the Rolex. It must have been new. And the Brothers said, Don't worry, even though we are a Christian charity these are good Muslim boys, their mother was Muslim, from Sumatra, we think, we're not sure. I was so happy. I was happy because I knew Mummy wanted us. I knew we were leaving. I was holding my brother's hand and suddenly I could feel him trembling. He was looking out the window and not saying anything but I knew something was wrong. One of the Brothers came and put his hand on my brother's shoulder and his eyes went cloudy and he started to make a noise. Not sobbing, but a weird sighing, and he fell down on the floor as if his legs had no strength in them, and I tried to pick him up but his eyes had gone blank, black and blank, and it frightened me. And I called his name over and over again, but he wouldn't stop, and the more the other people tried to touch him, the worse he became. I put my arms around him and then he began to calm down. I thought he was dying. His breaths were quick, so quick, and hot. The Brothers were saying, So sorry, he's like this sometimes, it's not serious. Please, it's not serious. Later, we were in the dormitory, sitting on his bed, and he was okay, completely normal, playing with this thing, a globe with fake snow in it. He just sat there turning it upside down and then back again. Mummy and Daddy stood at the windows watching us, and I heard Daddy say, We can't stay long, we have a long drive, and then there's the ferry. You have to decide by tomorrow morning, but I have to say I don't like the small, sick one—oh, never mind. And Mummy said, But the poor thing, he is so weak. It was your stupid idea in the first place, Daddy said. I didn't know what this meant but I didn't care, it didn't seem important. After a long long while Mummy came to me and I could smell her perfume, like roses, so sweet, and she took off her sunglasses and said, Tomorrow we are taking you to our home, all right? And you can't imagine how happy I was. I felt as if my chest would burst because I knew we were escaping. They left us alone for a few minutes and I said to my brother, You don't have to worry anymore, *we're leaving*. There's nothing to fear, we're going away from this place, that lovely woman is going to take us away and we are going to live with her. He looked at me and smiled. He was happy, truly happy. I could not ever remember him looking happy. When the lights went out that night my brother came to my bed and said, Johan, are we really going away? And I said, Yes we are, but as I said it something changed in my head, and I felt scared, I felt scared because suddenly I thought maybe only one of us would go. Please god please god let them take my brother, I said over and over in my head, and after a while I thought, yes, they were going to take my brother because he was smaller than me and often he was sick and they could see that he needed help. He would be lonely without me at first but he would have a nice house to live in and nice parents to look after him and soon he would forget me, and that would be nice. But then I thought, What if they take me instead? He would not survive without me. He slept so soundly that night and hardly moved at all, and his breaths were long and deep and when I looked at him he seemed so peaceful I could have sworn he was smiling. I didn't want him to be on his own. We had talked so much about doing things together, climbing a mountain, swimming in the sea. You know, the sea was very close to where we were but we had never seen it, never. And suddenly I knew we would never do those things, I knew that Mummy and Daddy would take me and not Adam, so I thought maybe if I, if I . . .

If you what? Farah touched his arm lightly.

If I went away and did not tell anyone, it would be okay, they would have no choice, they would have to take Adam. I remember going to the window and listening for the sounds of the sea. It wasn't far away but we could never hear it, never. So I, I . . .

Breathe slowly, Johan, slow down. Farah stroked his hand. Please.

Okay. Sorry. Sorry. I waited for dawn, and when it came I began to feel better, and I thought maybe there was nothing to worry about, I was being crazy, getting worked up over nothing. When Mummy and Daddy came I felt good again because they were the nicest people I'd ever seen. It was early in the morning, and my brother was still asleep. Everyone was still asleep. Mummy came and took me by the hand and said, I want to talk to you, we're just going to have a quick word, okay? I said, We're both going, aren't we? She nodded, I swear she nodded, and I was happy again. She had her sunglasses on again and she said, Come along, hurry. Hurry. She walked very quickly. I thought she was going to show me something in the car, but when we got into the car and the doors closed I knew what was happening. The

Brothers and the nurse were waving to us, and the car started to move away. A kind of sickness welled up inside me, a terror. I couldn't move. I wanted to scream and shout for my brother and say, stop, stop, but my body would not move, and I could make no sound. I just knelt on the seat watching the orphanage recede into the distance. There was a cloud of dust that made everything seem yellow, the whole landscape, the trees, everything. And then . . .

Shh, Johan, oh Johan, please calm down. Farah touched his face, his wet skin.

And then I saw, I saw my brother. He was running after the car. He was a long way away, but through the dust I saw his plump little legs stumbling in the dirt, until finally he gave up and slowed to a walk, and I heard Daddy say, Don't look, don't look. He said it in a quiet voice. I didn't know if he was talking to Mummy or me. I hear this sometimes in my dreams, when I am all alone. *Don't look.* And that's when I wish I hadn't looked. It's when I wish I had dreamed it all.

You're shaking, Johan. You're hot.

The storm was not abating, but they both wished it would not end, that it would carry on through the night. He lowered his head and rested it on her collarbone, in that safe place between her chin and her shoulder where he could shelter and listen to the storm. Johan said, Sometimes when it comes back to me I get so angry because I think to myself, I should have run away that night. Mummy would have taken Adam instead of me and he would have this life, my life. But I didn't, Farah, I didn't have the courage.

She stroked his wet hair and felt his breaths, quick and hot against the chill of her skin.

You've never told me your brother's name until today, she said at last.

Adam. His name was Adam.

Adam and Johan. That's nice.

It's been so long since I heard anyone say his name. Johan laughed, and Farah felt his breath on her neck again. She was not so cold now.

I wish you weren't going away, she said. I don't want you to go away.

I have to go away. There's nothing else to do. I'm sorry. He shook his head, and she did not know what this meant.

Lightning. The water dripping from the roof turned into a trail of crystals, just for a moment, before becoming invisible once more in the darkness. And in the brief, pale violet light Johan could see Farah's face, and he could see that her eyes were red and glassy with tears, but he could also see that she was smiling.

We should go now, Johan, I'm sleepy.

Now? But it's still raining.

We're already wet, aren't we?

He sighed and stood up. Maybe you're the one who's really crazy.

*A*dam lifts his head and blinks. This is what he sees: light, falling in thin shafts onto the floor. There is a rug. The rug is red. The light makes funny shapes on the red rug, like spots of bright blood on a darkened floor. Why is the rest of the floor so dark? The room is gloomy. This is because the shutters have been drawn half-shut. Adam can see that now. There are people in the room, people he has never seen before. A man and a woman. The man has a big, shiny watch. Adam can hear it ticking, even though the people from the orphanage are talking; they are talking about Adam.

Yes, they are at the orphanage. Adam knows this place.

The woman says, Is he okay? Yes, he's fine, he's fine. The light makes him funny, don't open the shutters. Breathe, Adam. Slowly. You're okay.

There is one voice that Adam can hear over the others, quite clearly.

*O*ne of the most famous Indonesian paintings of all time might, at first glance, easily be mistaken for a fairly conventional nineteenth-century European work of art. It depicts a large group of people clustered around the steps of a colonnaded veranda; in the distance there is a volcanic mountain, suggestive of a tropical landscape. Most of the figures are dressed in Javanese costume; some are squatting on the ground, forlorn, others hold their heads in their hands, weeping, one presumes. But most of them are looking at a proud figure surrounded by Dutch army officers. This person is Prince Diponegoro, the Javanese aristocrat who led the resistance movement against the Dutch in the 1830s. Executed with great assurance and in a style that is unmistakably Western, it is easy to see this painting as yet another scene from the annals of European history: the conquest of a foreign land, the easy subjugation of the natives by the sophisticated, upright officers of a Western power. But look again. There is something unusual about these Westerners. Are their heads too big for their bodies? Almost certainly they are. And now that you've noticed this, don't they look gawky and ill at ease? This isn't due to a lack of painterly craft, because the Javanese people are beautifully rendered, full of humanity, grace, and pride. They do not confront the beholder as the big-headed Dutch characters do, but form part of the landscape; they are dressed not in rags but in sarongs and headdresses of batik. They may be defeated in this battle, but it is they, not the Dutch, who remain human.

The artist, Bill Schneider explained earnestly, was a Javanese nobleman named Raden Saleh, who traveled to Holland to study under Kruseman and Schelfhout, excelling early in his career at landscapes and portraiture, which brought great success and made him a favorite of Ernst I, Grand Duke of Saxe-Coburg-Gotha, in whose home he lived for five years, slipping quite easily, it seems, into aristocratic life in Dresden. All this time, however, Raden Saleh nursed a passion for painting wild animals, in particular, lions. He had once seen some at Henri Martin's circus in The Hague and was seized by the urge to depict their untamable instincts. He identified with their pride and fiery temperament, and began producing monumental works depicting these wild yet noble beasts attacking snakes, or horses, or Dutch army officers out hunting (never mind that there are no lions in Java). Now back in Yogyakarta, his work took on simple yet striking anti-Western overtones, culminating in the masterful *Capture of Prince Diponegoro,* which hangs in the royal palace in Amsterdam.

"I'm thinking," said Bill, "I'm thinking that it'll be a peace offering. A kind of sweetener to make the president more amenable to . . . well, to things in general. The idea is simple: We arrange for the return of this priceless, hugely symbolic nationalistic work of art to Indonesia, and in return he recognizes that we're good friends of his, not enemies. I've been working for weeks now, but I'm not making much headway. The Dutch are not in a giving mood. We've had endless negotiations— *endless*—but they won't give up these paintings easily."

They studied the slide under the magnifying glass, taking turns to peer at it.

"This is the one the Indonesian people would want to see back in the country," Bill said, tapping his finger in front of the *Capture of Prince Diponegoro.* "It would be very fitting in a grand, public space, maybe at the presidential palace. It's noble, dignified, bold in its statement, but still very classy. It's the subject of our official promptings, the negotiations that are, let's say, documented."

"Why do I always know that there's something dirty going on with you, Bill?" said Margaret as she leaned over to look at the slide. She thought Prince Diponegoro very handsome, but also somewhat fragile underneath his proud regard. She felt more than a twinge of revulsion for the Dutch figures in the painting; she thought them ridiculous and even disgusting. She was falling into the trap, she knew, but she didn't mind. She did not usually enjoy the sensation of being manipulated or of being slyly coerced into feeling or thinking something, but in this instance it felt entirely natural, as though she ought to side with the Javanese and that there was no other option.

"The question is," Bill continued, "how much is this painting worth to the president himself? I mean, personally?"

"You mean, is it worth giving us oil concessions in Sumatra? Or do you mean, is it worth turning his back on Russia?"

Bill smiled. "No, obviously no painting is going to be worth that much. What I meant was, does the president personally value this painting enough to make him feel favorable toward us again? It's a grand, public statement, but what does he himself feel for the painting?"

Mick reached for the magnifying glass, almost pushing Margaret out of the way. "Hmm, very good," he mumbled. "Very, very good. This guy knows exactly what he's doing. Brilliant composition." He bent over the magnifying glass, shifting it slightly now and then.

"Good, isn't it?" Bill said, opening a drawer. "But frankly I don't think it's quite the thing to push the president's buttons. It's too static, too quiet. It demands too much involvement from the viewer. If the president is going to make a grand gift to his nation, he'll want something more flamboyant. Something, oh, I don't know, aggressive, something that's more his style." He placed another slide on the desk and slid it toward them. "That's why I'm trying to get this painting too. Another Raden Saleh, not at all well known. I have a feeling that this is more likely to make the president sit up. It's totally the kind of thing he'd like to have in his private salon, or in his boudoir when he's seducing some wench. Or even on public display, as if to say, 'I'm still a powerful man.'"

Mick moved the magnifying glass over the new slide. "Wow. That is quite something. It's like Delacroix, *just* like Delacroix, in fact, only a bit rougher, more earthy. Fantastically romantic. Margaret, look!"

Margaret noticed Mick's quick breaths as she took the magnifying glass; his eyes were shining, like a child's—a child who had just woken up from a long sleep and found a present at the foot of his bed.

The picture was of two lions and a tiger mauling a chestnut horse that was rearing up in terror, its eyes wild with fear. Its rider—a white man—looked tiny and helpless and strangely calm, as if he had accepted his fate. Margaret felt sorry for him; he wasn't as beastly as his comrades in the first painting and didn't, therefore, deserve to be ripped to shreds by these beasts.

"It's called *Lions and Tiger Attack a Horseman,* dating from Raden

Saleh's time in Paris, not long before he moved back to Java. It's a monumental work, completely breathtaking in real life, ten by twelve." Bill stretched out his arms vertically, reaching for the ceiling, then sideways, as if doing exercises. "I heard of it from someone I had dinner with years ago and managed to track it down. It took ages, but I recently found it in a private collection in Geneva. We're arranging for its purchase—for quite a handsome amount of money, I must say. The owner isn't anxious to sell, says it's an heirloom or some nonsense, but everything has its price, even family history. Of course, the transaction is not being documented by any newspaper or auction house or dealer. Neither the buyer nor the seller wishes to be identified, I think the expression goes."

"I see what you mean," Margaret said. "It's right up the president's street." She was struck by Bill's unerring instinct for finding the way to appeal to someone's basest instincts, for knowing exactly what they would like to see or hear. And she realized why she had felt drawn to him all those years ago—not because she had fallen prey to his tricks, but because they were similar in this respect: They could both get what they wanted in order to survive.

"The only way to get him on our side again is to appeal to his human instincts, to touch a chord. It's gotten to the stage where no amount of official aid can make him see eye to eye with us. It's too late for that. His public rhetoric is way too anti-American for him to back down now. But behind the scenes we can still try and make sure that he finds us, well, of interest. We don't give a damn what he's obliged to say in his great speeches, as long as he feels that we can still help him." Bill watched Mick pore over the image. He raised one hand to his lips and began absentmindedly to nibble his thumbnail, his jawbone twitching. Margaret remembered this old habit of his, this tendency to switch off and become blank and introspective, as if no one else was in the room; he used to do it all the time in college, but she had not seen it since he became Bill Schneider, senior statesman. "The bastard's got to fall for it. He's *got* to. It's . . . magnificent."

"It's not like you to get emotionally involved in your job, Bill," said Margaret. "Aren't you the model professional, always detached and cold and analytical?"

He shrugged and laughed. "I don't know. Maybe I'm getting old.

But this painting is special. When I saw it, I was blown away. I just stood there, gaping. There was something about it that made everything else I've done in my work irrelevant and trivial. It was hanging there on the wall of this beautiful old apartment in Switzerland, so out of place. And I got that feeling I get when I go to a lousy zoo in a lousy town, and see some huge and powerful jungle animal in a cramped cage, and it's barely moving because it's so shell-shocked it doesn't know what to do anymore. Yeah, I guess I must be getting old."

"No you're not."

They stood watching Mick as he raised the image to the light, still holding the magnifying glass to his eye the way detectives did in movies. "I want to help you, Bill, honestly, I do," said Margaret, "but I've got to find the boy. He's out there, alone in a huge city he doesn't know."

Bill moved so that he was standing with his back to Mick, shielding Margaret from Mick's view. He dropped his voice. "Listen, please help me. I can't do this without you. No one in this whole building can do it. You're a neutral. The Indonesians don't really even consider you American. You're one of them, almost. I've fixed everything, all you have to do is talk us through the palace and get an audience with the president. We need to talk to the big guy himself. None of his acolytes will do. My name is mud over there, and besides, we have to be so careful now. We can't make a misstep—and you know what I'm like, I just can't judge these guys like you can."

Margaret shook her head. "No way. Absolutely not. I need to find Adam."

"We'll get him, don't worry. Uncle Sam may no longer be valuable to the president, but he still has enough influence at lowly police stations. My contacts have got your Maluddin guy well covered. As soon as they get him, they'll find the boy too. I'm sorry about Karl, but he just slipped away from that hospital, and I can't trace him. Zero. But the boy, I *know* we'll find him." He reached out and touched her, his fingers trying to encircle her wrist. "I promise, Margaret."

Margaret shook her head and pulled away slightly. "I told you, Bill, I don't know anyone anymore. When I was more, I don't know, in love with this country—yes, I knew how people thought, how they felt and spoke. Sometimes I used to think I knew how they dreamed. For the longest time my dreams were only in Indonesian and I thought, I'm one of them. But now I don't really have dreams, and when I do I see my mother, god help me. I'm of no use to you or the United States, Bill."

"It's not a question of use, Margaret, you're not an instrument of the state." He reached out and touched her arm again. "I'm asking you to help me as a friend. Yeah, sure, there's all that governmental bullshit at stake, but you know this painting is worth sticking your neck out for. It belongs here, in this country. I'm going to find that boy even if you don't help me. It's not a quid pro quo thing. This isn't an official request, it's a personal one. What I need is someone charming and sensitive to help me through this minefield. If I go in there myself—if they let me in—and I say something wrong, I'll be dead in three seconds."

"I've only met the president a couple of times."

"But he remembered you. He asked me about you once. 'What happened to that charming administrator with the Ford Foundation? She was so very nice, and she could speak Javanese too. Amazing.' That's what he said, I swear. If you appear at the palace, I guarantee he'll see us."

Mick looked up. He held the magnifying glass in the air as if it were a sign. "I think it's a great idea. Margaret can definitely do it. She's got everything it takes. I'll come as backup, if you need me. I can be your bodyguard or chauffeur, anything you please."

Margaret shook her head but she knew that all her nonverbal signs were communicating acquiescence. She thought of her early days in this city, when a problem such as this one would have seemed perfectly normal, barely even an adventure, merely something to talk about over dinner the next day. Oh, I smuggled a painting into the palace today; hey, you didn't tell me you were negotiating an arms deal; did you know so-and-so is actually screwing General Whatshisname? It seemed to be like that every day. She recalled how she had been, rampaging fearlessly through the city as if it were hers to conquer; she could not say at what point she had realized that it was the city that had conquered her, not the other way around.

"It won't work," she said.

There was unanimous dismay; Bill and Mick both protested.

"Your plan just isn't logical, Bill," she insisted. She was sure of this now. She was older, and more afraid, but age and fear also made her confident of certain things. "From what I understand, you're persona non grata at the palace. You have to keep out of it. Fix everything for me, make whatever phone calls you need to get me through the gates. I'll go on my own."

"No way," Mick said. "Absolutely no way. I'm going to come with you."

"You don't understand. They aren't going to hurt a single, unarmed woman. The moment a macho white guy appears it changes the dynamics completely. I'll unnerve them—which is the point of the exercise—but I won't threaten them. It's all to do with the way Asian men see white women, and the way men communicate with other men. Don't look so skeptical. Trust me. I'm sure of it."

THE FIRST TIME Margaret saw the palace she had been overwhelmed—by its imposing portico, by the white columns thicker than tree trunks, by the great glass-and-bronze lanterns that hung from the ceiling, and most of all by the smell of the place, the faintest aroma of soil and crushed vegetation intermingling with old cooking grease to produce a perfume that was perfectly Asian—powerful but not at all unpleasant. She had been overwhelmed too by the emotion of seeing the red and white flag everywhere she looked—in proud rows on the lawn, suspended between columns, draped across tables, as though staking a claim on the building. The red of the flag was deep and angry, like freshly spilled blood. She had been dismayed to have missed the formal ceremonies that marked the recognition of the new republic by the Western world; it irked her to think that she had been in Paris, pining after a lost love that had never even been articulated in the first place (really, how silly), when she could have been here, witnessing the official birth of the nation. It felt to her as though she had been left out of the creation of something that she was a part of, something that was a part of her. She would never be so foolish again. And so she made sure that she was there, milling among the crowds the following year during the first Independence Day celebrations. A few years passed before she was invited into the palace that first time (for an official reception of American educators and academics, though the pretext barely mattered to her), and she was overjoyed to find that this occasion too was over-whelming. She had remembered feeling perfectly at home there, en-joying the looks of envy and suspicion from her compatriots as she chattered merrily away in Indonesian with government officials, and even flirted with an air force general.

Now, passing through the metal and barbed-wire barricades and the heavy gates, the palace again seemed overwhelming, not because of its size or its smell, but because its foreignness was intimidating: She realized she had never really known it at all. It still seemed monumen-tal and noble, but now it also felt forbidding, as if there were a strict set of rules—STOP, do not proceed, SLOW, THIS WAY, remove crash hel-met and sunglasses, do not cross, do not speak, do not smile—that she had somehow managed to ignore during previous visits. It was no longer a huge playground full of adventure but a place where the ob-stacles were all too real. Her driver did not turn around to look at her, nor did he wish her good luck or even good-bye as she got out of the car; he simply stared straight ahead, hands on the steering wheel, and drove away as soon as Margaret swung the door shut, leaving her ma-rooned at the foot of the steps leading up to the immense porch.

A man in a dove gray suit came to meet her. The suit was too big for him and hung off his shoulders, making him look smaller than he was. He did not extend his hand for Margaret to shake but waved it gracefully to show Margaret the way. He kept half a step ahead of her, making sure there was always plenty of space between them. He wanted to remain aloof, she thought; his nonverbal communication was saying, "I really don't want you here. You are a pain in the neck and we're going to try to get this over and done with as quickly as possible."

"Thank you for receiving me on such short notice," she said. "I'll try to be as quick as possible. You must be very busy. I really am sorry to trouble you."

"Not at all," the man said, and smiled. "We are in no hurry. You're very welcome here."

That was the way Asians said, You're really getting on my nerves now. At least she knew that.

Everywhere she looked, Margaret saw soldiers manning doors or marching briskly along the edges of the lawns in pairs or tightly knit groups. Older men in military uniform walked along the hallways and disappeared silently into half-open doorways. Some of them looked briefly at Margaret but no one so much as nodded in acknowledgment. She found herself being led through a lavish reception room, her feet sinking into a plush carpet. There were a few armchairs covered in gold damask and a round table with a marble top and gilded, carved legs. On one wall hung a large mirror, also carved and gilded; everything in the room seemed to be carved and gilded; on another wall a row of photographs in (gilded) frames showed the president on Independence Day, leaner than he was now, and fresher looking, Margaret thought; back in those days he was still more of a revolutionary, less of a hardened statesman. She felt a sudden frisson of excitement, a quick, thrilling shudder as she recalled the atmosphere of those dreamlike days when the future of the country had seemed clear and full of possibility. She remembered the collective anger over New Guinea, the indignation she herself had felt when Holland refused to hand it back to Indonesia, viewing it as a personal slight, as if the Dutch had taken something from her own home and refused to give it back. When the president declared Indonesia's intention to take back Papua, she had seen it as the righting of a wrong.

"Please wait here," said the man in the too-large suit before disappearing into a door at the far end of the room.

She had been in this room before, she thought. The view from the windows was still the same: a giant suwar tree, its canopy dominating a stretch of lawn that ran down to the boundary railings; but the room had been much less opulent on her last visit, less gold, no carpet. Yes, she thought, it had been in this room that she had been chatting with some middle-ranking treasury people when, suddenly, the crowds parted and she had found herself face-to-face with the great man himself, dressed in his immaculate uniform, dark necktie, medals, and traditional black *topi*. He was smaller than she had expected, but this did not diminish the naked charm he exuded. He was forceful without being forced, convincing in every minute gesture, and his nonverbal language was simple, thought Margaret: He sought to conquer everything he encountered. When he shook Margaret's hand she felt the roughness of the skin on his palms and saw the pockmarks on his face when he smiled. His first words as he took her hand in his were, "And what is your name?" as if they had been chatting for some time and had presumed some degree of familiarity. He spoke in English, and she, of course, replied in Indonesian: "Margaret Bates, honored to meet you." Actually, she had responded not merely in standard Indonesian but in what scant Javanese she knew. It was said that Sukarno was never caught off guard, but her brief cameo was enough to cause him to raise an eyebrow and incline his head ever so slightly. She enjoyed that. And before he had had a chance to speak, she continued in Indonesian, knowing that she spoke with none of the hesitation that nonnative speakers usually did. It was a little hot, wasn't it, and the rains were late that year, but, well, one mustn't complain, for at least one wasn't a rice farmer, poor things. "Hmm, what an exceptional woman," he said. "And I was told you were an American!"

"Well, hardly. I was born in Irian, you see. The first years of my life were in the farthest reaches of Indonesia."

"If you believe what the Western world says, you were born not in Indonesia but in the farthest reaches of Dutch New Guinea."

"But anyone in their right mind—anyone with a sense of justice— knows that Papua has always belonged to us. I mean, to Indonesia."

He smiled. "The problem is that it is ours but it does not belong to us, at least not officially."

"Not yet. I'm very heartened to hear of the president's intention to confront the Dutch."

"You are not afraid of battle, I see."

"It depends on the purpose of battle. Why do we fight? Who are we fighting? We must always ask ourselves this."

His eyes were very dark and direct. "How wise. We fight to bring nobleness to our souls. Nobleness brings order. Order brings peace. But sometimes the struggle itself becomes, how shall I say, essential. And sometimes," he paused and smiled, "this fighting makes you feel *alive*."

"Life is a battle." She shrugged. "Without battle there is no life."

He laughed, the lines on his face creasing deeply. "What a fascinating American you are." He continued to look her in the eye as he moved away, and she lifted her chin to meet his gaze. Afterward she had felt flushed and giddy with something she could not articulate; it was a feeling that lasted days, if not weeks.

Virtually everything had changed in this room, even the smell. Before, there had been that pleasant aroma of food and wood, slightly musty but entirely welcoming, but now Margaret could smell nothing except the faint whiff of wool carpets. She was certain that there had been a Toraja carving mounted on the wall where the mirror hung; and she could not remember the Venetian chandelier (there had been plain glass lanterns, surely). She sat patiently and drew her fingers idly across the envelope she was carrying, feeling the outlines of the two slides contained inside.

Someone appeared in the doorway at the far end of the room. It was not her guide with the ill-fitting suit, but a much younger man in a smart, vaguely military-looking suit, not quite a uniform but not really civilian dress either, the buttoned epaulets and breast pockets giving him the air of an adventurer. There was a colored emblem stuck to his lapel that looked like a military decoration, but Margaret could not be sure; she was never very sure about these things. He walked briskly, with the upright bearing of a soldier, quickening his stride as he approached her.

"So sorry to have kept you waiting," he said. "I'm one of the president's aides-de-camp. Hello, pleased to meet you. Unfortunately, there's been a slight problem. There was an incident yesterday." He smiled and frowned at the same time, managing to look at once unruffled and concerned. "The president's schedule has therefore been rearranged."

"Goodness, that sounds serious. Where was it?"

The smile-frown played across his face once more. "Don't be alarmed, it was nothing serious. A security threat at an official occasion the president was attending—not far from here, actually, right in the center of town. At the Hotel Java. It shows that such things can happen anywhere. Sadly there is much unrest on the streets of Jakarta these days. We have to treat everything seriously, no matter how minor."

"So where is the president? Does this mean I won't get to see him today?"

He smiled, without the frown this time. "I'm sorry, but he is—detained elsewhere."

She imitated his half smile, half frown and stood up slowly. "That is a shame because I've brought something of great value to the president, something that would interest him very much. A gift from the people of America."

"The president is not interested in gifts from the United States of America." He held his smile firmly.

"I understand. But I said that this is a gift of the *people* of America, the good ordinary people who are his friends. I didn't say it was a gift from the president of the United States."

He hesitated, his smile beginning to weaken. "I fail to understand the difference."

"Here," she said. "See what you think." She reached into the envelope and took out both slides, handing him one. "I'm sure you'll be able to recognize its worth."

He held it up to the light, turning it from side to side, like a child regarding an unfamiliar new toy. He doesn't have a clue what it is, thought Margaret. She said, "It is something very rare and very valuable."

He did not answer but glanced at her with a look of self-conscious disdain, which Margaret knew was a giveaway signal as to his lack of understanding of the situation. "It is something important to the Indonesian people."

"Please do not tell us what the Indonesian people value. I think I would recognize something that was truly valuable to us." He lowered the slide and held it out to her, turning his shoulder slightly as if preparing to leave.

"It is, above all," Margaret said quickly, "something dear to the president himself. Something he treasures. Its beauty and value may not be obvious; maybe you and I cannot see it, but the president can. Only he can judge for himself. I wouldn't dare presume to do so on his behalf. Would you?" She did not reach to reclaim the slide; it remained almost motionless, tiny and lightweight.

"I don't think this is an important thing," he said, and looked at the translucent square resting gently between his thumb and index finger.

Margaret shrugged and made a bowing motion with her head, as if deferring to his decision. She took half a step backward to show that she too was ready to leave. "Very well. That decision is yours to make, I understand. But please do remember that what might be valuable to you might not be so to someone else. Beauty and nobility and all the unquantifiable things that the Javanese value are, unfortunately, overlooked by us, the people of the West. There's so much beauty in this painting. I thought perhaps you—you are Javanese, aren't you? Yes, I thought so—well, I thought you might see that. But I have done my duty and you have done yours. It is time to bid each other good-bye, I think."

The aide-de-camp blinked at Margaret for a moment or two. He shook his arm, flicking his wrist to look at his watch. "Follow me," he said. "I'll give you three minutes, that's all."

They left the room and walked quickly along a narrow corridor that seemed dark in spite of the windows that lined it. Outside there was a row of newly planted saplings that had not quite taken: Their leaves were beginning to turn crinkled and dry, falling on the bare earth. It was hot and musty in the corridor; the windows had not been opened in a while. Margaret hurried after the young man, struggling to keep up. They passed through an office manned by men and women dressed in pale khaki uniforms that gave the impression they were about to leave on an expedition somewhere remote; they did not look at Margaret as she went by but carried on bending over filing cabinets and typewriters and maps. Half-empty bottles of Fanta stood on desks along with overflowing ashtrays that permeated the air with the scent of *kretek,* which comforted Margaret. On one wall hung a crude oil painting of a volcano shrouded in cloud, and the national flag had been pinned loosely to a wooden board, where it fluttered at the edges as it caught the weak draft of the ceiling fan. They went through a sort of anteroom filled with mail bags and suitcases, and then finally emerged into another room whose windows opened once more onto the expanse of lawn, with the fountain in the distance. Three men in smart gray military uniform sat around a table, chuckling at something that had just been said; they looked up when Margaret entered. One of them had many medals pinned to his lapel. He said, "Who's this?"

Margaret recognized the president immediately. He had not aged well; his face was jowly, despite the lips set tightly in permanent defiance of the world. His cheeks seemed even more pockmarked than before, and he looked much heavier. When he spoke, Margaret felt none of the dazzling power of youth he had once had; and the frown on his brow made him seem confused, not angry.

"It's, uh, this is the American visitor I mentioned earlier," said the aide-de-camp.

"I told you, I'm not in any mood to receive visitors," the president replied, lifting a fine china cup slowly to his mouth. His lips reached for the rim of the cup as if uncertain of where it was, and he sipped hesitantly, noisily; he did not look at Margaret.

"I promise I will only be a few minutes, Abang Karno." She spoke in Javanese, as clearly and calmly as she could, and when she heard her own voice she felt as if the voice belonged not to her but to another person, someone she had long forgotten. "It is an honor to meet you again."

All three men at the table were studying her now. The president looked her squarely in the eye and his mouth began to draw into a faint smile. "Age is a terrible thing, for it destroys the memory. I have always had an excellent memory, but I cannot place you. I find this extraordinary." His voice was still clear and strong, perhaps a touch deeper than before; but it did not excite Margaret as it once had.

"You have many things to think about, many people to remember. I wouldn't want you to waste time on just one person like me."

"Every person is worth remembering."

"I have brought something for you," said Margaret, pointing at the envelope the aide-de-camp was still holding. "It is something my, um, people would like to present to you as a gesture of goodwill and friendship."

"And who are your people? You speak as if you come from the foothills of Merapi, but clearly you do not mean the central Javanese." The men at the table laughed, and Margaret allowed herself a smile.

"Sadly not. I mean the good, honest people of America. Not so long ago you said that if America gave you a billion dollars and Russia offered you a loaf of bread, you would take the loaf of bread, because it would be given with love. Many of us understood why you said that. But we were hurt too because there are those of us who love this country very much."

The president smiled broadly and Margaret felt a chill of excitement. "But this country is your enemy. I am your enemy, I am dangerous to your country. Isn't that true?"

"I don't know. That is something for politicians to decide, not ordinary people like me. But even if it is true, are we not meant to love our enemies?"

"This woman speaks like an Indonesian, not a Westerner," the president said, turning to his companions. "Does she not?" They nodded and smiled. He said, "I think I do remember you now." He took the envelope and shook it gently so that its contents fell onto the table. His fingers reached for the first slide with a certainty that suggested he already knew what it was. He held it level with his eyes for a second or two and lowered it without comment. "I see," he said, sliding it neatly into the envelope. "A gift of something that is ours. Tell me, how does one make a gift of something that already belongs to the other person?"

"One can't do that. It is impossible."

His smile was charming yet severe. "So there is no gift."

"The gift is not of the painting, of the object itself. It is the restoration of ownership, the reversing of an injustice. Some might say that this is not a gift, that it is simply the course of natural justice, but you and I know that in today's world it takes courage and no small measure of generosity to provide the gift of fairness."

The president looked at his colleagues and at the aide-de-camp. He nodded. "What are we to make of this?" They smiled nervously, unsure of the required response.

"I take it you have seen the *Capture of Prince Diponegoro*," Margaret continued. "Please have a look at the other one. It is something chosen for you."

Holding Margaret's gaze, the president felt for the slide that remained on the table; even when he had brought it to eye level he continued looking at Margaret, not the slide. She felt a quickening of her pulse, a heavy tapping in her chest, and a tingle in her temple; she smiled. His eyes moved slowly to the dark square framed between thumb and forefinger, staring at it with no discernible change in expression. Without moving, he raised his eyes to look at Margaret for a split second before returning to the slide. He remained motionless, unblinking.

It is said that Sukarno had such great powers of concentration that he was able to read Dutch backward, or, rather, in reverse. It was a skill he was reputed to have honed as a teenager in Surabaya, where he would sneak into the projection room at the picture house and watch the films from behind the screen, hidden from the good seats occupied by Dutch people. Margaret had never known if this was a true story or one of the thousands of myths about him. In this country you had to surrender to myths, to the uncertainty of stories, to the failure of logic— that was something she had learned as a child, and she had rediscovered the aptitude quite easily on her return to Jakarta in adulthood. In this case she thought the story was probably true. She liked the idea of a young Sukarno sitting behind the picture screen, for it must have reminded him of the shadow plays so beloved of the Javanese, and given him the impression of being in control. He was not the poor-but-smart young boy the myth made him out to be, but someone already quite powerful. He could see the foreigners and understand what they were watching, but they could not see him. And although those eyes were older and smaller now in the gathering fleshiness of his face, Margaret could still see the intensity of the teenager's gaze.

The president cleared his throat but did not move. Behind him, on a sideboard, stood a framed photograph of him with President Kennedy. They were riding in the backseat of a convertible with the top down, both smiling broadly. In the fuzzy background, across what might have been a parade ground, a row of cadets were standing at attention, their white gloves and belts dazzling against their dark uniforms.

"This," he began softly, still staring at the slide, "I do not think I have seen this before." He cleared his throat again. "I cannot remember." He blinked at the slide—once, twice. A thin frown crept over his brow and his eyes appeared glassy, as if suddenly troubled by a speck of dust.

Margaret wanted to fill the silence but she could not find the right words, either in Indonesian or in English. She looked again at the photograph of the two presidents. A slight wind made Kennedy's hair wispy and his eyes squint; Margaret could not see Sukarno's eyes, for they were hidden behind his very modern sunglasses, which matched the perfect blackness of his *topi*. They looked like a schoolboy and his fashionable-but-stern uncle on an outing, each trying to appear happy, even though they had little to say to each other. It was the kind of cheerfulness put on when nothing one said would make sense to the other person, and to avoid the awkwardness of a ruined afternoon together, both parties make every effort to be happy, yet this pretense of great happiness leaves them feeling empty and lost, for each thinks: I should know what it is like to be this happy, but I do not.

The president blinked at the image a few more times and then lowered it, sliding it neatly back into the envelope. He said, "I think the time for gifts has passed." Margaret began to reply but he continued to speak. "There was a time when this—how shall we say?—this relationship between us, between our two countries, might have worked. We might even have loved each other. For a time, maybe we even thought we did. We gave each other many gifts. We were both much younger then, and much more foolish. And now, I am afraid that time has passed."

"Perhaps," Margaret began; she breathed deeply, trying to sound calm, "perhaps it was not foolishness but hopefulness."

The president looked at her, his expression changing minutely, becoming less benign, Margaret thought, the edge of his mouth lifting as if to mock her. But when he spoke his voice was very calm. "Hope. Americans always talk of hope. What you hope for now is that I will do something for you," he said at last. "Is this correct?"

Margaret did not answer.

"When Western people offer gifts they expect something in return. When Asian people receive gifts, on the other hand, they think immediately of how to return this kindness. So in fact, the two work very well—though not always fairly. This is why I cannot accept your gift, for I have nothing to give your country in return. Now I must get back to my work as leader of this country. It was pleasant to meet you." He pushed the envelope to the edge of the table and the young aide-de-camp retrieved it swiftly, handing it back to Margaret as he put his hand lightly on her elbow to lead her out of the room.

"Please," Margaret said, turning back to the president, "you do not want to give anything to my country, I understand that. But would you give *me* something—the gift of kindness? I have nothing to offer you, I can only ask—plead—for your help."

The president raised his eyebrows.

"I am asking for your help, as one humble human being to another."

He nodded. "Go on."

"There is someone I need to find. He is lost in this city. Maybe he is with the army, maybe not. No one seems to know. He is Dutch by birth but Indonesian by nationality, and now I am afraid he has been taken away."

"Ah, *een Nederlander,*" the president said, laughing his slow, rich laugh. He had taken a cigarette from a silver box sitting on the table. "I understand from your voice that this is someone you love."

Margaret felt light-headed and very hot. She nodded. "Some might say that."

He studied her for some time, and then he looked at his colleagues; the cigarette was very slim between his thick fingers. He shook his head and smiled. "As I said, the time for gifts has passed."

*J*n an earlier time, in a place far from this city, gifts had seemed plentiful in Margaret's life. This period had not lasted very long—a year, perhaps—but it seemed to fill the entire canvas of Margaret's adolescence so that whenever she thought of her childhood now, all she could remember was that there had been so much to give and receive. Maybe this was what happened as one grew older: The tiny incidents of youth acquired a magnitude they did not really possess. "Never, ever trust your memory," her mother used to tell her, "it never gives you what you want. When you go back to it, hoping for solace, all you get is misery. And when you need to use it as a library, purely for information, it's always blank. Just leave it all behind and concentrate on the present."

This was what Margaret tried to tell herself over the years, whenever her forays into her memory provided her with nothing but an emptiness in her chest, as if her heart had stopped beating for about five or six seconds. But the problem was that she knew her memories were all true, every last detail. She remembered how this period of gifts and gift-giving had ended, the very moment her life passed from the clarity of childhood into the murky depths of adulthood. Her memory of it had never warped, never blurred; it always retained the sharp edge of truth.

"I'm leaving," Karl said. It was one of those nights when the Balinese moon was so full and clear and the air so still and warm that there did not seem to be any need for day; one of those dry evenings that come in the middle of the rains and make you forget the days of mist and mud. They stood in the yard at the center of Karl's compound, surrounded by the silvery outlines of the houses.

"I know. I heard about what happened." Margaret could see his face clearly—more clearly, she thought, than if it had been day. When he blinked she could see the bright moistness of his eyes. He did not answer. "Lots of people are leaving," she continued, filling in the silence. "It hasn't been the same these last few months with all the news we've been getting."

Six months ago, Margaret had never heard of Sudetenland, or of Moravia or Silesia. She knew about the independent state of Czechoslovakia, but she thought that Bohemia was a place inhabited by penniless writers and artists, or people such as her mother, who was often called "Bohemian." For a while she had believed that to be Bohemian was to have no fixed home, so she herself might have been Bohemian. Now she knew all too well where these places were.

"There's going to be a war, isn't there?" Margaret said.

Karl nodded. "We can't pretend anymore, we have to accept it. Ever since Anschluss I've feared this day would come. Everyone was saying, Oh, but no, the Germans didn't invade Austria, they didn't fire a single shot. But we knew, *we knew*. And now this." For a moment he sounded almost angry and Margaret realized she had never known him to be angry. She reached out for his hand and tried to picture these invaded countries, their hills covered with pine forests tinged with patches of melting snow, the tanks rolling slowly through the river valleys while small children watched fearfully from the windows of their mountain houses, muttering silent prayers. She wanted to share in the distress and helplessness that he was feeling, but she could not. All this was happening so far away, in places remote and beautiful, places that had nothing to do with her. You could only feel pity for somewhere if you belonged there, she thought. Karl belonged to Europe, but she did not.

"Sorry," he said, "I have to sit down."

"Sure, oh god, of course." They crossed over to a bench at the edge of the yard. "How is your leg?"

"Not too bad. Some days it's worse than others. Today it seems to be all right. The doctor tells me I'm always going to have a funny walk. But I think he's wrong." He laughed; a clear, bright laugh that made Margaret feel better.

"What happened, exactly? I've only heard sketchy details."

Karl sighed and bowed his head, nodding weakly. "It's terrible. I can't understand how we can do such things to other people." He paused for a moment, looking at his leg. "I was at Walter's for dinner. We had just sat down at the table when we heard the police arrive. They simply marched into the house and took him away. There was nothing I could do. I spoke to them in Dutch, I shouted at them. It was barbaric and unjustified, I said, 'You have no authority to arrest him, I will attest to his good character.' And that policeman—that brutish Friesian who's just arrived from Jakarta to lead this witch hunt—do you know what he said to me? He said that if I continued to defend a German national he would assume I was a Nazi sympathizer and a traitor. But that wasn't the worst of it." He did not raise his voice but Margaret saw his fine hands curl into fists. "There were two other Dutch people there, Jos Smit and Rudi Kunst. They remained silent the whole time. They never once tried to intervene. Rudi looked down at his food and Jos coughed and looked out the window, and when the police had taken Walter away he started humming along to the music on the gramophone, as if the party was still going on. I stood up and said, 'We have to do something. Walter is our *friend*. Nationality isn't important, he's one of us here in Bali. *This is our home.* We have to defend ourselves.' And these people, these people I've called friends, all they could say was that I shouldn't antagonize the police, that we have to remember that we are Dutch and there was nothing we could do for Walter anymore. We were in his house, eating his food, and that was all they could say. The host was no longer there, but they wanted the party to continue. I don't know what came over me. I can't remember very clearly what happened, but next thing I know I was clinging to the policeman's back like a barnacle on a huge turtle." He laughed again, but this time it did not make Margaret feel better. "He shook me off and then all I could see was this hulk standing over me, and when he kicked my leg it was as if he wasn't even making an effort to hurt me. It was just this gesture to say, You're nothing to me. At first I thought nothing was wrong, I didn't feel any pain at all. But when I tried to get up I found my foot was completely useless. I felt so weak and helpless, Margaret. And Jos turned to me and said, 'Here, have some cognac.' It was unbelievable. He behaved as if nothing had happened. At that moment I hated him." He sighed. "I hate this *pretense*."

"I can sort of understand it, though," Margaret said. "I mean, look at us. We're a million miles from the troubles in Europe. People like Jos and Rudi, they think they belong here."

"But that's just it," Karl said, turning to face her once more. He took both her hands and grasped them firmly in his. "It's all a charade. They don't belong here. They're merely trying to run away. I know this because that's what I was trying to do when I came here—running away from a country I didn't like, from responsibilities, from family, from everything that was mine. But when something like this happens, you realize that you can't flee. You have a duty to confront the things that frighten you. You can't just stand by and watch."

"But what can you do?" She felt his hands tighten around hers; they felt warm and comforting, and she tried to savor the feeling of his skin against hers. She wanted to capture the sensation so that in years to come she would be able to summon it whenever she wanted, in times when she needed comforting or reassurance, for she knew that she might never feel those hands on her again.

"I don't know. But there must be something. Do you know why they are rounding up every single German now, even a completely harmless artist like Walter? Three weeks ago a terrible thing happened in Germany. You *must* have heard about it. In one night, thousands of Jewish shops and synagogues were destroyed and Jews were beaten, killed. Many disappeared in the night. There was glass everywhere on the streets. Ordinary people were turning against their neighbors, those who had been their friends for years but who'd suddenly been declared evil and dangerous. What madness is responsible for this? That, for me, was the sign. It was when I knew I had to leave. My family is still in Holland. Who knows what might happen to them? Hang on, I need to move my leg, it's getting a bit stiff."

He led her across the yard toward the studio. There were no more canvases or pots of paint and Margaret could only make out the silhouettes of a few easels framing the view of the valley at night. They sat on the steps at the back of the house, where the land fell away steeply. It was very late; the moon bathed the valley in a white light and at that precise moment it was hard to believe that even daylight was capable of such brilliance.

"Look at this," Karl said softly. "I don't think I can bear to leave this place, but I have to." A night bird started to sing, a two-note call that re-peated without the slightest variation.

"Why?" said Margaret, calmly. "If you want to, that's one thing, but I don't understand why you *have* to." She was lying, she thought, or at best half-lying, because she *could* understand. Yet a germ of a thought had lodged somewhere in her head, and this invisible, unrea-sonable thought said: Don't go, I don't understand why you are leaving without me.

"Staying here makes me feel helpless. I can't remain in this paradise while such things are happening in Europe. Everyone on this island pretends that the war has nothing to do with them, but it does. We can't hide here forever. Look at poor Walter." The night bird was still singing; the noise it made seemed too sharp and loud for the perfect stillness of the evening.

"We're probably going to leave too," Margaret said. "Not immedi-ately, maybe in a few months. My parents are finishing up their work anyway, so it's time to move on. Nothing ever lasts very long in my life. But this time I think we might at least be moving somewhere with running water and electricity."

"Where will you go?"

She shrugged. "I'm not sure. I heard whisperings about America. You?"

"Holland. Then, who knows—probably Paris. I liked Paris. But who knows if it will ever be the same again. Things change so quickly, and once they've changed they never change back. It's not true that people leave things or places behind—it's the things and places that leave us behind."

The bird that was singing seemed to have changed its tune; now it sounded like an owl, calling in single, ghostly bursts.

"That's silly," said Margaret, "I don't agree. Look at you. Bali is stay-ing put, you're the one who is leaving. You have a choice, Bali doesn't."

"But it is changing, Margaret—you can see that, can't you? And someday soon it will change so much that you'll find yourself ma-rooned in a place you no longer know."

"Not if you change with it."

"The place I knew a year ago would not have allowed Walter to be taken away so easily."

"Maybe you didn't know this place as well as you thought."

Across the valley, just below the shoulder of the broad hill, Margaret could see a row of lights—a string of pearly globes that glowed like white fireflies. The lights bobbed up and down slightly, as if they were lamps carried on the end of sticks; but the slope of the hill was very steep and Margaret had never noticed any paths there. There was a tightening in her chest and she began to feel a little pale and light-headed, as if she were about to faint. Sometimes in Bali she had nights like this; she would wake up from a troubled sleep, her lungs and wind-pipe constricted, making it difficult to breathe. No matter how hard she coughed to try to clear this congestion it would not go away, and she would have to stay awake, listening to her parents' whispered arguments in the other room, waiting for daybreak, which was the only thing that could bring relief. These were the nights when the malevolent spirits roamed the valleys, the people in the village said; there was dark magic in the air, and that was what caused Margaret's malaise. "Nonsense," her mother would say, "it's just a touch of asthma." But Margaret had never experienced this discomfort in any other place she had lived. Maybe these Balinese demons were responsible after all; they had taken away the vigorous health of her childhood. And on these nights, if she got out of bed and went to the window, she would often see tiny balls of glowing light drifting across the valley.

"Do you know Hugo's poem about the ladybug?" said Karl after a while. "It's odd, but I woke up thinking of it the other day. It's about a boy who wants to kiss a girl but he isn't sure whether to do it—I read it when I was a boy myself. I don't know why it has come back to me all of a sudden."

"Why doesn't he just go ahead and do it? It's not one of those silly poetic things, is it?"

"He's not sure. She offers him her neck and he thinks she loves him. But when he comes close he realizes that all she wants is for him to get rid of the ladybug on her neck. She didn't really love him after all."

"Poor boy. He has my deepest sympathy."

"No, you mustn't feel sorry for him, because at the end he sees that it is a good thing. The truth may be painful, but it's better than an illu-sion. At least that's what I remember. And I can see now that my love for Bali has been like that. This island—she hasn't really loved me, has she? The longing is all one-sided. It's because of you that I can see this."

"I don't understand."

"Whenever I'm with you I see the Indies through your eyes, and it's wonderful. It's as if you're truly a part of this place. It belongs to you and you to it. You don't have to make any effort, yet you understand it completely. You view it all as a whole, not in parts as the rest of us do. You belong here. When I see that, I realize how I don't."

"No, I don't. The only thing I really understand is that the color of your skin is the only thing that matters." In the moonlight, her arm almost touching his, she saw that they were almost exactly the same shade of sandy gray.

"I wish I were like you," Karl said, "but I can't be. I'll never have that ability. In the past few months I've thought about fleeing to some remote outer island where there are no other Europeans. I'd be like some character from one of those novels—you know, about seafaring Dutchmen who wash up on some shore and father children with a local woman. But I know I wouldn't belong there either. And this is why I must return to Holland, even though I hate it. I must go and fight."

"Then I'll come with you," said Margaret. "I'll follow you to Europe."

"That's ridiculous," he said in his calm, quiet manner. "You're too young—what would you do? Where would you live?"

"With you." Margaret tried to imagine the house he had described, a tall, narrow, dark house. "Or somewhere else. I'd just be close to you."

He sighed. "You have the rest of your childhood to live, Margaret, the rest of your life. You know you can't come. It's impossible."

The bird had changed its tune again, singing sweetly but very loudly, drowning out all other sounds in the night.

"Maybe someday we'll wash up on the same shore," said Margaret.

He laughed. "Maybe."

She waited for him to say something else, but there was nothing but birdsong. They remained sitting on the steps for some time, looking at the dancing lights across the valley and listening to the solitary bird. Margaret could feel the warmth of his arm—almost, but not quite, touching hers, the fine hairs on his forearm tickling her skin; but she could feel him slipping away from her, easing himself out of her life. She felt the constrictions in her chest once more and tried to suppress the urge to cough. I am not in love with this man, she said to herself, I am not in love with him. She hoped that she would feel herself fall out of love with him, just as he was falling out of her world, but that sensation would not come to her.

After what seemed a very long time, Karl put his hand on hers. He said, "I shall never forget you, you know." The bird was still singing. Margaret wished it would shut up and leave her alone in this moment with Karl, so that she could commit every detail to memory, where it would remain pure and untroubled for the rest of her life. The outline of his jaw in the moonlight. The damp coolness of his skin. The hesitation, maybe even a slight tremble in his voice.

But the bird did not stop. So nowadays, whenever Margaret recalls this moment of being thrust from the safety of childhood into the murkiness of adulthood, all she can hear is the bird's insistent call, repeating endlessly.

The orphanage was not far from the sea, and though you could sometimes hear the waves and smell the dry salty air, you could never see the water. Even if you climbed up on the small hill behind the orphanage—which you were not supposed to do—the ocean remained out of view. Therefore, for the first five years of his life, Adam never knew what color the sea was. Sometimes he thought it was turquoise, other times green, even a dull red. There was a sea called the Red Sea somewhere in the world, near where the Prophet once lived, so why couldn't Adam's sea be red too? The other boys laughed at him when he said this, so he kept quiet and did not speak about it. But now he remembers the first time he saw its true color, something between gray and brown: a mouse-colored sea. He remembers now that he saw it once. Only once.

*W*hen Adam woke up, Z was no longer there. Even as he reached out in half slumber to where she had been, he knew that he would not find her. He lay on the immense bed, blinking himself into awakeness, and found that he was stretched out diagonally, his toes touching the place where he had been sitting the night before. The patient ticking of the gold clock was the only noise he could hear; he could not quite make out the time, but he knew it was late, even though the room was dark, for the thinnest sliver of light was forcing its way over the top of the curtain rod.

He remembered that there was a room in the orphanage that had shutters on the windows, and when the shutters were closed the light would frame the window in thin strips, just as it was doing now. Adam had been taken to this room when he was ill—when he fainted or suffered those shivering fits. "That boy has gone funny again," he remembered people saying, and he would feel sickly and ashamed, a freak.

Adam did not know why he could remember this detail of the orphanage, or how other images had returned to him, gently folding themselves into the spaces of his memory as if reclaiming some rightful, long-forgotten spot. And although there were many other things that remained beyond his reach—for now, at least—he felt calmer. When memories come back to you there is always the expectation that they will make you happy. Adam had always thought that regaining his past would be unequivocally joyous. Now, blinking in the daylight darkness of this room in a city hundreds of miles from his home, he could see that this was not the case. Sad memories remain longer than others. But sometimes the sadness makes things clearer, and with clarity comes a certain calm. This is what Adam felt.

The previous night, when images of his past life had begun to return to him, he had fallen into a heavy slumber as the pain in his torso dulled to an almost comforting numbness. He remembered Z kissing his forehead, remembered the cool touch of her lips on his brow when he had woken in the middle of the night. Shh, don't worry, nothing's going to hurt you, she had whispered. You're all right, it's just a bad dream. You're okay, you're okay. It had taken him a few moments to realize where he was, for when he opened his eyes there had been only darkness, and it was Zubaidah's voice that helped him to locate himself in this absence of light.

My brother, he said. I remember.

Shh. Calm down. What do you remember?

Things. Not much. But I remember him now. How he walked, the sound of his voice. Johan. He was named Johan.

Wait; she got up and pulled the curtains apart, throwing the windows open as wide as she could. There was a thin breath of air in the room now, and Adam could hear the distant barking of dogs. That's better, she said, it was so airless before.

She eased her head onto the pillow next to his so that her mouth brushed against his chin. And when she kissed him he surprised himself by knowing how to respond, moving his torso slightly to press against hers. Her body had surprised him because it felt so foreign, unlike anything he had ever imagined, but also familiar, like his. Her belly was flat but fleshy, not at all like his own; her thighs were very lean and when he squeezed them with his fingers, he could feel the long sinews running down to her knee. He had been fully awake for those few minutes during which they had clung to each other tightly, urgently, like sea swimmers to a raft. When she moved on top of him he could feel every part of his body with a clarity he had never experienced before, as if each muscle was an articulated word or thought.

Afterward, when they lay side by side in the darkness, she asked him about his brother, and he told her the few things he knew.

His brother was older and stronger than he; his brother had left the orphanage first, leaving Adam alone. And those moments of aloneness were filled with a blankness that seemed to expand all the time, until he found he was not terrified by it but reassured by its constant presence.

He told her about the long, low shack where everyone slept, about the leaky roof and the rats that ran along the foot of the walls and the sound of boys crying in their sleep. He was very calm. He wanted to talk, he wanted to tell Zubaidah what he knew. He could remember, now, how it felt to be alone, just as he could recall the warmth of Johan's body against his when he woke up in the middle of the night. He had been afraid all the time, afraid of everything, and the only thing that made him less afraid was being near Johan, who was not afraid of anything. But once Johan told him, If we ever get separated I will not be able to live. And that had surprised Adam because Johan could deal with everything. It was he who would not survive without Johan, he thought.

What did he look like? she asked in the darkness. Did he look like you? Adam did not answer. The precise features of Johan's face still eluded him, but he remembered someone who did not look at all like him, someone who was taller and fairer and stronger. An almond-shaped face cast in permanent half shadow. For the moment, this was the best he could remember.

Sorry, said Zubaidah, it must be painful to remember these things.

No, he said. If someone stays with you often it is painful when they go away. But that is all it is. Pain. When someone is there next to you every second of the day and night their sudden absence does not cause pain, it creates a vacuum, an emptiness with which you have to live every day thereafter. So it is not painful; it is worse than pain.

She put her hand between his legs and left it there, even though he was not hard. She asked if he missed his brother and he said no, he didn't. It was the truth. You can't miss something you can barely re-member. He tried to feel a longing for Johan, but all that came to him was a calm that was slowly replacing the yawning emptiness that had been there before.

We can find him, Zubaidah said, we can find him if you want to. Nothing is impossible. But Adam said no, he did not want to. Why? she asked, but he was unable to answer. There is a time for everything, he thought, and the time for finding Johan had passed, or maybe it had never been the right time. Maybe that time would come in the future, or maybe it never would. He was no longer sure if he wanted to find

Johan. My father used to say that you can't control your future, you just have to let fate run its course. I'm not going to find my brother. It wasn't meant to happen. Why should it? He doesn't even know I exist.

Rubbish, Zubaidah said. If you want to do something, if you want to find someone, you can. He could feel her fingers in his pubic hair. He did not argue with her; it was no use.

So what do you want to do? You can't stay in Jakarta. He said, I want to find my father. Okay, she said in the dark. We will find him. Not long afterward, as they were talking, he felt himself harden in her hand, and he propped himself up with one arm so that he could kiss her. It was, he thought, the first time he had ever done anything with such clarity of purpose.

He rose from the bed and pulled the curtains open; Z must have drawn them before she left to protect him from the harsh light of the morning. He squinted into the sudden sunlight, looking around the room. There were things he hadn't noticed in his exhausted state last night: a picture of Che Guevara pinned to a corkboard, next to a photo of a Western film star Adam did not recognize. He could not tell if this was Z's bedroom.

He dressed and made his way slowly downstairs, pausing momentarily at the top of the staircase that curved elegantly in a horseshoe of gold and marble. The floor was cool and smooth underfoot, and in the kitchen he found a box of European pastries—pretty squares and triangles with colorful cream toppings. He was not sure if they were meant for him, but his hunger was greater than his caution, and he ate one, then two, until he had eaten half the box. They were very sweet and tasted of cinnamon. There was a large mustard-colored refrigerator of the kind he'd only seen in magazines, but when Adam opened it he found it to be empty except for a few bottles of beer and the remains of a celebratory cake, the icing hardened into a crust by the cold.

"Good morning, sir." A man dressed in a bush jacket and pressed trousers came into the kitchen. Adam recognized him as the driver who had brought them home yesterday. "Miss Zubaidah has asked me to take you wherever you want to go today. If you'd like to stay here, you're most welcome, she said, and we should go and buy you some clothes and food or whatever you need. However, she said she had the feeling you might want to go home immediately."

Adam paused and looked at the birthday cake. He could make out scrolling pink letters that read . . . *ppy birth* . . . *love from* . . . "I haven't made up my mind," he said. "I need to think about it for a while."

. ● .

They were a long way from the city now, in a place where there were no lights and the dirt roads were hard to see, for they snaked through the jungle where the foliage was thick and did not let the moonlight through to the ground. Sometimes the trees would give way to a palm oil estate or a rubber plantation and there would be a little more light, maybe even a single kerosene lamp hanging from the low branches of a tree, and in the pool of light Johan and Farah would be able to discern the outlines of branches, or the fragile roof of a rubber tapper's hut. Warm wind came through the open windows, eddying and swirling and blowing wisps of hair across their faces.

Farah said, I'm glad you can't drive like a maniac out here.

The moment the clouds part I'm going to put my foot down, you wait and see, said Johan. Country road or no country road, I'm going to drive fast.

No you won't. She laughed. You can't.

The Merc jolted over the potholes and sharp gullies where the rain had swept away the surface of the road, and sometimes it seemed to Johan that they were on a little boat on a choppy sea where you never got the sense of moving forward and you could no longer discern where you had come from or where you were going. It had been like that on the ferry to this country, to his new home. The boat had rocked on the waves and did not advance, and all the while Johan's new mummy kept saying, Don't worry, not long to go, we aren't far away. But when he looked over the side of the boat he could not see the land they had left or the land they were traveling to, and beyond the misty haze of rain there was only sea and sky and a boat that was going nowhere. And he had thought, maybe they would spend all that time traveling and end up where they had begun, back in Indonesia, back near Adam.

You still haven't told me where you are taking me, Johan.

If I told you, it wouldn't be a surprise, would it?

But I can't stand not knowing. Don't torture me. *Jahat sekali.* She smacked him on his shoulder.

Wait, just wait. It's not far now.

The road was getting rougher and the axle of the Merc was squeaking as the car stumbled along.

It's like being at the playground. Farah laughed. God, I hope you don't wreck the car, Daddy will be furious. You'll be grounded for life.

Johan laughed too. I'm going to be long gone, so what do I care? I won't be grounded because I won't be around. He'll just have to take it out on you and Bob.

What time are you leaving tomorrow?

Lunchtime. Daddy's driving me himself.

They could hear the squelching of mud as the car went through a shallow puddle, and ahead of them the headlights lit up swarms of insects that floated dreamily in a river of light that seemed almost opaque.

If you wreck the car, maybe you won't be able to go.

Maybe.

They stopped in a clearing and Johan got out. He walked around to Farah's side of the car and opened the door.

It's all right, it's not muddy here.

Ahead of them they could see a stretch of water, a wide bend in a river that did not flow very fast. It was black and still and quiet. On the riverbank the trees grew out over the water, low and squat, as if they were floating on the surface. Farah looked up at the sky and said, I can't see the moon.

I know. It's cloudy. That's why I chose tonight.

Why? What does that mean?

You'll see. Come on.

They walked along a path that followed the curve of the riverbank and disappeared now and then into long grass. Sometimes the sharp edge of the grass caught their hands and Johan yelped with pretend pain. He wanted to make Farah laugh, but she didn't. He stopped and turned around to take her hand, leading her down the path that had disappeared once more. They walked through a thicket of trees and for a few moments there was no light at all, and when they emerged the path curved sharply and brought them around to an old pontoon.

Johan. Farah spoke in a whisper. *Johan.*

That's what I wanted to show you.

Johan. She stepped onto the pontoon with him. My god.

Before them there hung a huge mass of fluorescent green light, like the beginnings of a raincloud on a hot, windy day, billowing slowly, expanding here, contracting there. It stretched out languidly as if pawing at an invisible fly, and then pulled back again, illuminating a stretch of black water and then casting it into darkness once more.

Fireflies, said Johan. I really wanted you to see them.

There were clusters of the same glowing light on the trees, shimmering. Johan took Farah's hand and walked along the path, and all along the riverbank there were clusters of this gold green light in the trees, even on the very highest branches where they colored the night sky.

It's like Christmas, Farah said. Christmas in some Scandinavian country.

How would you know? It's not as if you've ever been to Lapland.

I don't know. She laughed. I just imagined it this way.

Johan thought of the Christmas tree they'd had at the orphanage, which never had any lights on it and wasn't even a nice Christmas tree, just a half-dead sapling with its branches cut to make it less messy. Sometimes there would be a few trinkets hanging on it, palm leaves woven into balls, or some fruit on short lengths of string, but it didn't matter, because none of the children knew what Christmas was. There were presents, like an old pair of socks or box of biscuits or a toy that some rich city kid did not want anymore but you did not know better, and when you do not know better you are happy for what you have.

Later, when Johan was with his new family, he had learned all about Christmas and he knew what it was really like. He saw the kinds of presents that people gave each other, the nice things that parents put in boxes and wrapped up, like the tricycle that Bob once got. Mummy would always say, Oh, we can celebrate too, even though we're not Christian. Christmas belongs to everyone! Daddy would come back from the club in a good mood, singing "I'm Dreaming of a White Christmas," trying to make his voice sound like Bing Crosby's, and Mummy would laugh and say, Eh-ey, darling, I hope you haven't been drinking. And Johan would know what it meant for people to be happy, even though he was not. He realized too that his Christmases at the orphanage had not really been happy, because when you don't know the truth you can't be happy, not truly. And he would think of Adam, who had never known what

Christmas was. He wished that Adam had never known that fake Christmas with its fake tree and fake presents, like that snow globe that he loved so much. He wished that Adam had never known all that. They stopped to look at a cloud of fireflies that clung to a branch over the river, dipping toward the surface of the water.

I shouldn't feel bad, but I do, said Farah. It's so stupid of me.

Yup, it is stupid. Johan squeezed her hand.

You're not going to come back, are you?

The mass of fireflies curled slowly toward the water, and Johan wondered what would happen if it touched the river, whether all the lights would suddenly switch off and they would find themselves plunged into darkness, or maybe night would switch suddenly to day.

And because he did not answer, she said, Are you going to find out what happened to your brother?

No, he said firmly. He's gone and I don't want to know any more.

Good. Promise me you'll come back safely.

He felt her fingers wiggle in his hand. You're crazy.

She turned to look at him and there was enough light in the moonless night for him to see that her eyes were clear and wide. Thank you, she said. Thank you for bringing me here.

He could smell the richness of her breath, a slight saltiness, and her hand began to feel hot and slightly sticky in his.

He leaned toward her and when he kissed her he found her lips were cooler than he had imagined, and firmer too. She did not press against him but she did not draw away either, and Johan wondered whether for these few seconds he was happy. He wondered if feeling her lips on his, and smelling her and touching her waist, whether all this meant that he might be happy.

No, she said at last. He could feel her breath against his neck. It's wrong, Johan.

Why?

You know why. She did not move away from him but let her head rest against his collarbone.

I'm not your brother, he said.

Don't say that, Johan.

When they looked at the trees on the bank opposite they saw a mass of fireflies, rising and curling like a wave reaching out for some invisible, unattainable shore, a wave in some dream where everything was black and silent.

It's beautiful, Farah said.

He nodded, but it was dark and he did not know if she could see him. He said, I'm going to take you home, Farah. Then I'm going out for a drive by myself.

· 30 ·

The ride home from the palace took longer than usual. Road-blocks and demonstrations choked every other street, it seemed, and the car would crawl along for a while then pause for twenty minutes without moving. Everyone turned their engines off, starting up only when there were signs of movement. It was a nice car, a Buick, and the driver whom Bill had sent spoke English with an American accent. He had been an engineer, he said, in Malang, and had followed his wife to the States when she won a scholarship, but she had left him for an American man because she wanted to stay there, so now he was back home, working as a driver for the embassy, but it was okay, he spoke English, he had a good job. Not like everyone else out there, he gestured.

Margaret listened without paying too much attention, fanning herself with the envelope containing the two slides. There was a radio or a walkie-talkie or something in the front that crackled and hissed with static as the car inched along. She felt as if she were on a boat on a big, silted-up river, carried along by an imperceptible current, occasionally running into a mud bank, then flowing along again. Normally she would be fretting and in a rush to get somewhere, but today she was not at all anxious. There was nowhere for her to go, nothing more she could do. She had done her best with the president, she had given it everything she had, and still she had come up short. She had never ex-perienced this feeling of utter defeat before and she did not know how she should feel. Angry? Frustrated? Frightened? Humiliated? No, not any of those, and yet all of them at once. She felt helpless—yes, help-less, that was it—but this state of helplessness was not terrifying as she'd always feared it would be. It brought with it something worse than ter-ror (which could, after all, be overcome): an eerie unease, a feeling that the worst was yet to come. When she thought of the future now (*the future*: what did that even mean?), she could see nothing, feel nothing. She did not know what she would do, either for herself or for Adam or anyone else, today or tomorrow or anytime thereafter. There was no vague sense of possibility, of things simply sorting themselves out by a combination of fate and manipulation. There was just a dreadful emptiness waiting to be filled with the unknown.

She had always thought that even if she learned of Karl's passing away, or if she had known, definitively, that he was never to come into her life again, she would experience a certain calm—a relief or a profound liberation. Finally that niggling grain of hope embedded in her would go away and she would no longer fall asleep remembering his slim hands and uneven walk. But she did not feel calm now, nor relieved nor liberated. She had lost Karl, she was sure, but she still—irrationally, stupidly—hoped that he was out there. The years ahead of her were filled not with calm, but with a horrible uncertainty. And it was all her fault.

Her fault.

She thought about Adam. She looked out the open windows at the dusty shantytowns, the mass of people on the streets, jostling for space in the city. She hated the idea of Adam wandering alone here, and she hated the idea that she had abandoned him to this fate. That was something she would have to live with for the rest of her life, she thought. But she would manage. There are some things that cause you pain, that lodge themselves in your consciousness the way a splinter or piece of shrapnel might embed itself in your flesh; but the human body had a way of dealing with it that could dull the pain so that you didn't feel it after a while. Your life would continue as usual, and only you would know of this thing that you carried in your body.

The car finally broke free of the worst of the traffic and the hot air began to sweep through the open windows. The driver told her that there had been riots earlier in the day and all major roads had been closed off. He apologized for this; Indonesia has become so messy, he said, not like before. It must be terrible for you foreigners.

"Yes," she said, "sometimes it's difficult." She imagined the scene she would have to face in a few moments, returning to announce her failure to Mick and Bill. She would arrive at the house and find Mick sitting in a chair, gesticulating, Bill pacing around the living room, looking down at the floor; they would watch her as she walked across the yard and through the door. She would feel as children must feel when they have done something wrong or failed an exam, and the moment of confession arrives, only their parents already know what happened. Her own childhood had been free of such moments of anxiety, but she wished it hadn't. God she wished it hadn't. She wished that when she was a child she'd known how it felt to fail and to have someone say, It's okay, next time it won't be so bad, you can try again, it doesn't matter. But she was not a child, she had never really been a child; and there would be no next time. Mick and Bill would, she thought, try their best to comfort her, which would only make things worse. They would shrug and smile, as if they had prepared themselves for her failure, and she would know that they had agreed on their response. Mick would say, Hey, it's fine, it's okay. But no one would say very much because they knew that it was not, in fact, okay.

She did not think she could face them. She wished the traffic would close in again, ensnarling her in this city forever. But for once they seemed to travel fluidly, cutting their way with relative ease through the tangle of darting scooters and bicycles and trucks, everyone rushing headlong toward nowhere.

Eventually the car eased into the lane that led to Margaret's house, slowing to dodge the dogs that lay spread out under the meager shade of the papaya trees. As it came to a halt, Margaret could see through the windows that it was just as she'd imagined: Mick sitting, Bill pacing anxiously. But Bill was not pacing anxiously, as she'd expected; he was standing quite patiently, as if studying someone—a third person. Margaret swung open the low metal gate, its hollow bars clanging loudly against the cement columns. There was a third person. Thank god, there was a third person.

31

*Y*ou should have seen it," said Mick, sipping a bottle of beer, "a black Cadillac so huge it could barely squeeze down the lane. Even Bill didn't have a clue what was going on—for a moment he thought that Sukarno had personally escorted you home! We certainly didn't expect young Adam to hop out."

Margaret squeezed Adam's hand. She had barely let go of him since stepping into the house. When she first realized he had come back, she'd felt like crying. For the first time since adolescence—maybe even infancy—she'd felt an uncontrollable urge to weep. She hugged him and put her head on his collarbone, letting her tears wet his shirt. She looked ridiculous, she knew, but she didn't care. He had been eating when she came in; there were half-eaten packets of *nasi Padang* on the table; fat flies sat motionless like sultanas on the turmeric-stained rice. "Don't ever leave me like that again," she scolded, sniffing loudly.

"I'm sorry," he said. When she looked at him she saw that his eyes were moist and slightly teary too. He lifted his hand to wipe his eyes; there were grains of rice sticking to his fingers. He smiled but she could see that he was preoccupied with something. His eyes seemed pinched, older now than they'd been a few days ago. He wiped his hands on a dishcloth that was lying on the table; the cloth was printed with the words *Good Morning,* which skipped up and down as he cleaned his fingers. He reached for her and put his arms around her slowly, embracing her for a few deliberate moments. "I'm really glad to be back," he said.

"Where's Din?" Margaret asked, thinking she already knew the answer.

"He's in jail—where he should be." Bill told her everything he knew—*honestly,* he said: There had been a plot to assassinate the president, which Bill and his people had known about, and Bill had thought that if they could prevent it and find evidence against the culprits, he would be able to present it to the president as proof of American good-will. No, he was *not* intending to find and fund these terrorists so that they would kill a president who was no longer favorable to the States— god forbid such cynicism. Why would the United States of America want to destabilize this country? It was unstable enough as it was. Call it currying favor or bargaining or whatever you want—the ultimate aim was to help Indonesia in some way or another. Din was one of the ringleaders they had heard about, and Bill had been anxious to keep track of him, that's all. And Adam, well, Adam had come this close—*this close*—to being implicated in a major conspiracy. Thank god for that girl.

"What girl?"

"The one we met," said Mick, handing Bill another bottle of beer. They moved and talked slowly, as if they had been doing something physically strenuous. It was the relief, thought Margaret; they were ex-hausted by the relief of finding Adam.

"Her name is Zubaidah," said Adam. "I guess she saved me."

"Turns out she isn't a red-blooded Commie, after all," Mick said.

"I knew there was something weird about that girl. I just couldn't figure her out. I didn't like her. I thought she was duplicitous and insin-cere," said Margaret. "But it does at least prove that it takes a woman to straighten things out."

Mick said, "Margaret didn't like being out-Margareted by the young lassie."

"No," said Adam. "She was not insincere. She helped me see things clearly. Without her, I would have ended up doing things I didn't want to. This time it was Din, but it could have been anyone. I was just al-lowing anyone to take advantage of me. But Zubaidah didn't. She didn't push me, she just . . . I don't know. She helped me, that's all I'm saying."

Margaret watched him as he spoke; he looked down at the table, raising his eyes to meet hers only now and then, as if afraid of challeng-ing her. She put her hand on his forearm. "I'm sorry," she said. "I was just worried about you, that's all."

"Don't worry," said Adam. "It's not your fault things turned out the way they did."

Margaret wanted to believe that this was true, that she was not in some way to blame for the fact that Adam was now truly an orphan and that Karl was missing forever, most probably dead. She could not shake the feeling that the current state of affairs was due, in some major way, to her shortcomings, her misjudgment, despite Adam's trusting, almost grateful smile, which made her feel even more guilty. He had trusted her too readily, she thought, too unquestioningly. And his utter faith in her had, in turn, made her believe that she was capable of achieving anything. She remembered something she had seen when she was a child on Irian: a small, dull buff-colored bird attacking a snake, falling on its thick coils in swift, stabbing dives until the reptile was forced to retreat. A villager told her that the bird was a mother protecting her nest from predators, to which Margaret had said, Oh, I understand, the bird loves its children so much that it becomes brave enough to attack a much bigger animal. And the villager said, No, it is not love that makes the bird do what it is doing. It is foolishness. This bird actually believes it is stronger than the snake, it actually believes that no harm can come to it. It is a very silly bird.

Margaret understood, now, that it was not love that made her want to help Adam but a vain and unthinking sense of heroism. It had flattered her to think she could change his life, and hers.

"Adam," she said, trying to sound as calm as possible. "I don't know if Bill and Mick have spoken to you. We have had no news about Karl. We have tried everything, but I think you should know that the signs are not encouraging. I think," she paused, wanting to sound firm but supportive, "I think you should prepare yourself for the fact that we might not be able to find your father."

Adam stared at his still-greasy fingers; he let them hover rigidly over the table, watching them as if entranced by their stillness. "He might still come back somehow. Nothing is impossible. I know you think so too."

Margaret nodded. "That's right, I do. I guess some stupid part of my brain will always be wired to think like that. But we all have to face the facts sometime—even me."

"What are we going to do?"

"I don't know. I really don't know."

A few drops of rain had begun to fall, playing a tinny percussion on the zinc roof over the yard. In the distance a patch of cobalt blue cloud was marooned in the otherwise colorless Jakarta sky. Sometimes, at the end of the dry season, there would be times like this, when everyone would think the first of the rains had arrived. You would feel one or two heavy raindrops on your arms and the skies would darken, and you would think that the drought was over, but then the clouds would dissolve and the air would lose the smell of moisture and the aridity would return. You could never really tell when the monsoon would arrive.

IT WAS MICK who decided they should leave.

"You mean, leave *Indonesia*?" Margaret had protested.

"Got a better idea, sweetheart?" said Mick, lowering his voice as they stood in the yard. "This country is falling apart—not just at the edges but at its core. I'm staying because it's my job. Why are you staying? Because it's your home? Wake up, darling. You need to leave, for a while at least. Maybe one day you can come back. Or maybe you'll never come back. Who knows? You can decide all that later, once you're far away from this madness. Go somewhere: Singapore, Bangkok, the States, Paris—wherever. Somewhere you can sit down in a nice clean café, drink coffee, and take stock of things, think about the future in an objective way. Take the boy with you. You *do* have a future, it's not too late for you. Don't end up like, well, me, just bumbling through life. It suits me. It doesn't suit you." He produced a pack of cigarettes from his pocket.

"Where did you get those? I thought you'd quit."

Mick smiled as he sucked on the just-lit Marlboro, his lips contorting into a funny shape. "I've started again."

It was a good idea, Bill agreed—at least for now. He would arrange a visa for Adam; they could go to Singapore, wait for a while to see if there was any definitive news of Karl, before moving on. Or perhaps it would be better just to go to the States. Bill would fix everything; he could at least do that for them. But they had to act now, quickly. There was no time to lose.

Sitting calmly in the Buick, Margaret looked at Adam. He held his canvas bag in his lap, cradling it with both arms the way a heavily pregnant woman might hold her belly. He said, "I didn't have time to say good-bye to Z. I waited for ages, but she didn't come back."

"You liked her, didn't you?"

"Yes, I did."

There were not many cars on the road this evening but every so often they would see convoys of army trucks carrying troops or armored vehicles posted outside buildings. Evening brought with it a sense of anxiety. Margaret did not think that she had ever associated darkness with fear; no, that was wrong: She had done so when she was a child.

"I'm sorry I was negative about her," said Margaret. "It's just that my judgment has been so shaken by everything that happened with Din. I couldn't trust anyone with you."

He nodded.

"Because Din was not a bad person," she continued. "I shared an office with him, for god's sake, I couldn't have been that wrong about him. Very, very misguided, perhaps, but not fundamentally evil. But from the moment he involved you in whatever he was up to, well, that's when I stopped having any sympathy for him."

"I think we should wait awhile," Adam said. "Just a while. You never know what might happen. Z might be able to find my father. We just need to get in touch with her. I still have this feeling he's not far away. I know there's still hope."

Margaret looked at Adam's face, so much older now than it had been a few days ago, but still that of a boy. It was this ridiculous thing called hope that kept it that way, she thought, but she could see it changing, the hope ebbing slowly away. Soon he would be a man, and quickly, inexorably, old. It was what happened when hope slipped out of your clutches. In certain isolated near–Stone Age tribes in Irian, Margaret had seen how the aging process was far less defined. People did not blossom in adolescence then fade painfully into old age; they were born elderly, mature beyond their years—child-adults—but then they seemed to remain this way, their faces permanently etched with the quizzical smile of an infant even as their hair became flecked with gray. It was because they were not programmed to hope, to look forward to some magical potential, and so did not degenerate as the boundaries of their lives shrank with age.

"We can't stay any longer," Margaret said. "We haven't got much time. We need to get out while the embassy can still help us. God knows how much longer the U.S. is going to maintain diplomatic relations with Indonesia. We aren't the most popular people here at the moment."

Adam looked out the window. The early evening air was still warm and unsoothing. "When I was small I used to dream about going abroad. I used to read stories about children living in Europe and imagine what it would be like to live among them. My father used to say, Son, you have no idea, it's better here. I always thought it could not be better here. Now I'm not so sure. I don't know what it's like in Europe or America, or even Malaysia, but I don't want to go. I've heard your explanations and I agree with you, but I still don't want to leave. There's no logic, I know. I'm stupid. I guess my father was right—you can't control the future. You just have to take what comes."

Margaret could find no argument to counter this. There was no reason for her to take him away from Indonesia, yet she had no choice. The campus was dark and silent, except for the rhythmic banging of a tin door at the far end of the badminton courts. In the distance, at that undefined place where the range of solid university buildings gave way to the flimsy shacks of the semi-slums, they could see a few kerosene lamps, their lonely dim lights revealing a few figures moving in the shadows. There was a Western song playing: "Smoke Gets in Your Eyes," Margaret thought, though she could not be sure. Thin clouds of insects had gathered above the drains, anticipating the showers that would become more frequent from now on; but Margaret would not be in this city for the coming rainy season, she thought, nor, perhaps, for any other.

They went up the flight of stairs to her office. The barricade of piled-up desks had been removed, leaving nothing but splinters and iron bars on the floor. The door to Margaret's office was ajar, and when Margaret tried to switch on the light she found that there was no electricity. In the last remnants of the evening light she could discern the clear, pale space where Din's desk had stood on the far side of the room. The piles of paper on her desk had been shifted around, and several sheets had fallen to the floor, where some of her books and files lay scattered haphazardly. The only thing missing seemed to be the blue and white jar that had held her pens and pencils. She went around the desk and sat in the chair, reaching down for the lowest drawer. Even in the dark, she had no trouble finding the crevice that sheltered the key; she unlocked the bottom drawer, her fingers feeling the ample mound of paper that was her thesis. She wondered why she had kept it for so long; at this point, it seemed a ridiculous object, a dead thing, a hindrance. She pushed it aside and felt around for her passport. On the way here, she had, just briefly, wondered what she would do if the passport was missing. She had given it so little thought, been so casual in her treatment of it, but now she'd found herself praying that it would be there; thank god, it was.

It took a while for them to find their way back to the car. Stripped of all light and movement, the campus buildings did not seem to be where they usually were. The embassy driver was standing by the Buick; they could see the pinprick glow of his cigarette. He had left the engine running, and when he saw them approaching he got into the car and put his hands on the steering wheel. "I got a call on the radio. Mr. Schneider says don't come to the embassy. I am to take you to this address." He passed them a piece of paper as the car reversed sharply before taking off again. Margaret could not make out the handwriting. "Mr. Schneider says come quick, no time to lose."

32

*O*nce, when Adam was still very young, he'd gone for a walk on his own, along the rocky shoreline near the house. He must have been playing truant, for it was in the middle of the day, the sun slicing through the scant canopy of the scrubby seaside forest. And it had to have been a good few years after he'd arrived at Karl's house, for he'd walked without hesitation or fear, scrambling over the patches of slippery rock that had become familiar to him. He recalls this now, his ease with his surroundings, his feeling of intimacy with the trees and the water and the sand. He had walked for some distance when he saw Karl about twenty yards from the shoreline, sitting on a fallen tree trunk, half-hidden by the shade of some shrubs. He was bent over slightly, concentrating on a book, or a sheet of paper, looking up occasionally to squint at the sea.

Adam slowed down immediately, trying to tread as lightly as possible, but the crunch of dead leaves and coarse sand underfoot seemed to reverberate every time he put a foot down. He considered turning back and running away—the risk of being discovered was too great. But there was something in Karl's actions, the intensity with which he looked at those papers, that made Adam curious. He skirted around in a wide arc, moving farther inland so that Karl would not see him, but the noise he made as he pushed his way slowly through the undergrowth was considerable: Karl must have heard. And yet Karl did not once look inland, in the direction of the rustling foliage, focusing instead on the sheet of paper in his lap. From a slightly elevated position, Adam saw that Karl was drawing, his hand moving fluently across the page, sometimes in long smooth strokes, other times in tiny precise flicks. He had never seen Karl do this before and was amazed at the delicacy of his father's hands, which he had only ever seen wielding a machete or an ax or a broom. He could not, from where he was hiding, make out the shapes in the drawing, so he began to inch closer, until he was certain that Karl would turn around and confront him. He had thrown all caution to the wind: He just wanted to know what Karl was drawing. At last he could see, over Karl's shoulder, a low ridge of penciled hills, a house perched precariously on a slope. He came closer still. There was one person in the drawing, a young person, though Adam could not quite make out if it was a boy or a girl. Its features were exaggerated but clearly Western. It was a girl, Adam decided.

"Who's that, *Pak*?" Adam said. It no longer mattered to him that he would be found out.

When Karl turned it was clear that he'd had no idea of Adam's presence. He frowned and blushed and smiled, all at once. "I thought you were at school," he said. There was a look on his face that Adam recognized because it was something he was all too familiar with: shame.

"Who's that?" Adam said, pointing at the sheet of paper.

Karl looked at the drawing for a few moments and then he laughed loudly, folding it in half with one neat movement. "Oh, that's nothing, I was just, um, bored . . . playing around. Look—see what your father can do with this simple sheet of paper!" And with a few deft folds he turned the drawing into a paper boat. "Come on!" he said, and ran down to the beach. He waded into the shallows, his thin trousers getting wet up to the knee. He set the boat gently on the calm afternoon waves. The little vessel rocked back and forth for a few seconds before being overcome by the swell.

As he walked home with Karl, Adam did not think about the drawing, or about Karl's embarrassment at having been discovered. He was merely thankful to have avoided a reprimanding for having skipped school. But now he recalls experiencing a quite distinct feeling, something more powerful than relief: that of being forgiven.

He does not know why he felt like this, because he had, in retrospect, committed no great crime. He only knows that life with Karl amounted to one long act of forgiveness. It was as if he was being excused for all the nameless things he had done wrong, all the things he could not remember.

As the Buick swept through the neighborhood, past the high walls that surrounded the mansions, Adam began to recognize the style of the buildings: Western, massive, a touch bizarre. A motorbike lying by the side of the road, its wheels twisted and crushed. He had seen this place before and he knew they were going to Zubaidah's house.

They drove through ornate wrought-iron gates painted with touches of gold paint; they drew up alongside a sports car that Adam did not recognize. The house seemed even bigger than he remembered. The front doors were made of heavy, dark timber, their veneer reflecting the light cast by the car's headlights.

"Margaret, thank god you made it," Bill said, running to meet her. He reached out to her and held her elbow as if to reassure himself that she was really there. "There was a demonstration outside the embassy that's carried on into the night. Those guys were lighting fires—it was getting very tense out there, so I thought you should come here. It isn't safe around the embassy. The paperwork's done. You can be in Singapore by lunchtime tomorrow."

"This is Zubaidah's place, isn't it?"

"Her father's, yes. How's the boy doing?"

"Okay, I think."

"We got him, Margaret," Bill said, his voice dropping almost to a whisper. *"We got him."*

Margaret felt a sudden tensing in her chest, a rush of blood to her temples.

"Well, actually, the girl found him," said Bill, carrying Adam's bag into the house. "Come on, we need to hurry."

Adam ran up the steps ahead of Margaret and Bill. He rushed into the hallway and paused briefly at the foot of the great, sweeping staircase. Z emerged from her bedroom; she was wearing pajamas and her hair was down. She looked more childlike than Adam remembered. He started toward her but she was pointing at a spot behind him. He stopped and turned around. At the threshold of a door off the hallway, Karl was standing looking up at Adam. He held on to both sides of the door frame, supporting himself as he tried to smile. He coughed— a heavy, dry spasm.

Margaret said, "Good god."

"Bapak," Adam cried. But his voice seemed to choke even as he called out to Karl and he could say no more. He ran down the stairs and

eased Karl's arm over his shoulder so that he could support him. He helped him back into the room and laid him down on the sofa. He had never realized how small and light his father was; perhaps they were both small and light in this enormous house in this enormous city. Adam covered Karl with a blanket that Z had given him.

"Margaret," Bill whispered, "I know he's ill and weak, but if you want to get out of this place I'd advise you do it *now*. I've got papers for him too. All of you."

"Out of the question, Bill. Look at him."

They made Karl drink as much water as he could. Margaret boiled some rice porridge and made sure he ate two bowls of it. She remembered how, when she was a child in Bali—just before she had met Karl—she had fallen ill with malaria and her mother had fed her rice porridge. It was something all Asians ate when they were ill, her mother had said; the body can't deal with anything more when it is in distress. Margaret did not know why she remembered exactly how her mother had done this, and why she now had no hesitation in preparing this food for Karl. It was as though she had been doing it her whole life.

Adam stayed with Karl, holding his hand until he drifted off to sleep. Margaret and Bill left the room and Adam could hear them arguing outside. They were trying to keep their voices down, and although Adam could not quite hear what they were saying, he understood the gist of their conversation. It did not matter to him now whether he left this country or not. All that mattered was that he was not separated from his father.

"Quite against my principles," explained Z later, "I went to see my dad. Adam told me about the search for his foster father and it's no secret that my dad has—oh, I hate saying this word—*connections*. I don't even like thinking about it; it makes me ashamed. But I had no choice. It's the only way to get things done quickly. In this country you could say it's the only way to get things done."

"Yes," said Bill, "I know about your father. He's very friendly with the president."

"I don't know how far their friendship extends, but they help each other out in one way or another—mostly financially. They were schoolmates in Surabaya, you see. So he put in a call to the president—a personal instruction from the president carries much weight, as you can imagine. They found Mr. de Willigen at once. It seems he was to have been repatriated—mistakenly, they claim—but then he fell ill and had to be moved from one hospital to another. Police bureaucracy isn't very efficient."

"It was a very brave and generous thing for you to do," said Margaret, "and I hope your father didn't mind too much."

Z shrugged. "He didn't seem too concerned. He was quite preoccupied with something else—a painting, I think, something the president has asked him to finance. My dad was being quite grumpy about it, says he's been paying for too many of the president's personal luxuries recently. I think the president is getting more and more extravagant. Apparently this painting is huge and has lions and tigers in it, and Dad can't really afford it, but what can he do? He still needs the president to help him with his business—or whatever they do together. I never ask too many questions; I don't want to know about all that sordid business."

Margaret smiled. "I bet it's some painting," she said. "Thank you nonetheless. I know it must have been difficult for you."

Z paused awhile, gazing absently at the ceiling. She smiled weakly. "It's funny. I always swore I would never ask for his help, that I would be independent and do whatever I pleased. But now that I've done it, well, it doesn't seem *so* bad. It feels quite, I don't know, *normal*. I guess I'll just have to live with it."

"Terrible, isn't it, how that happens." Margaret laughed. "The way things suddenly become acceptable."

Z nibbled at her fingernails, frowning. "Problem is, it feels more than acceptable, it feels almost nice." She looked at Adam and put her free hand out to him. He clasped it with both hands but did not say anything.

*W*here are you going, Johan?" Adam called out. "Wait for me."

Johan was some ways ahead and Adam struggled to keep up, for Johan was stronger and taller than he was. They were a long way from the orphanage now, in the low, rocky hills that lay between the orphanage and the sea, sheltered by trees that would never grow very tall because of the brine and the poor, sandy soil. In the dark Adam could not see Johan's face clearly, not even when he finally caught up with him.

"Go back, Adam, you shouldn't have followed me."

"But what are you doing? We aren't allowed here. We should be asleep."

"I know. That's why you should have stayed in bed."

"I couldn't sleep. I'm excited about tomorrow."

Johan did not reply. All Adam could hear was the sea breeze that had picked up a little; it carried the sound of the water beyond, and suddenly the sea seemed close by, attainable. Johan sighed. "Idiot," he said, but he did not sound angry. "Come on, it's not far."

They stumbled over rough ground, their ankles scraping against rocks. Ahead of them they could hear the foamy rush of the retreating tide, the froth and pull of the waves on the shore; and underfoot they could feel the thorny grass giving way to sandier ground. But still the sea remained out of sight, beyond a screen of scrubby bushes and a thick barrier of rocks. There was light in the night sky, enough to make out the thin tidal rivulets that snaked toward the sea; but when Adam and Johan looked up at the sky they saw it was shrouded in cloud and they could not tell where the moon was. They reached the foot of a mound of sharp volcanic rock that was silvery with brine. Johan went first, picking his way nimbly amid boulders that were powdery to the touch. Sometimes loose shards fell away beneath his feet, but he was quick and sure and did not slow down. From time to time he would stop and wait for Adam, reaching out to guide him and make sure he did not fall. He did not like it when Adam fell. But the sea was close by now, and Johan and Adam could smell the freshness of the breeze and hear the rumble of the waves that grew louder as they scrambled up the slope; even when they slipped they did not feel the sharpness of the rocks underfoot.

"There, Adam," Johan said when they reached the top of the rocks. "There it is."

Adam sat on the low, flat boulder beside him. He was out of breath from the climb, and his eyes took time to adjust to what lay before him: an immensity of darkness, flecked now and then with glimmers of light on the crests of waves. He had not expected the color of the sea, either, an inky blackness that matched the color of the night sky. He could not make out the horizon.

Johan put his arm around Adam's shoulders. "We've done it. We always said we would see the sea one day. Together."

Adam nodded. He pulled at Johan's arm and Johan felt how small his hand was. "On the other side of the sea," Adam whispered, "is that our new home?"

Johan did not answer.

"Our new home is far away, I guess," said Adam, "all the way over there."

"Yes," said Johan at last. "Somewhere over there."

"Really?" Johan felt the tug of Adam's hand again, his quick shallow breaths that always came when he was excited, or scared. "We won't be able to see the orphanage from over there, will we?"

"I don't suppose so. The sea is very wide."

"I don't think I like it. The sea, I mean. It frightens me."

Johan continued to stare into the distance. "It's time to go now, Adam. You have to go to sleep and be up early tomorrow. Be a good boy. It's a big day for you."

"Okay."

"You can find your way home. Don't look back, just keep going until you're at the orphanage, okay? I'll be along soon, don't worry."

"Why don't you come back too?"

"I just want to stay here for a while, look at the sea. I like it. Anyway, I'm older than you, remember?" He laughed and Adam felt better. "Go home and sleep. I'll be back soon."

Adam got up and began to pick his way between the rocks. He did not like being on his own, but he had always done what Johan told him to do, and Johan had never been wrong. He began to think that maybe he was silly to have been frightened by the sea. Johan was not frightened by the sea; Johan was not frightened of anything. Adam paused at the foot of the rocks. He had been silly to tell Johan that he was afraid of the sea; perhaps he would go back and sit with Johan and show that he was not so afraid after all. He would climb the rocks again, and they would sit together for a while, and then they would walk back to the orphanage and in the morning they would travel to their new home; there was nothing to be afraid of.

Johan was not there when Adam traced his way back to where they had been sitting. He looked down along the line of boulders, but there was no movement. Out to sea: Halfway along the wide, flat beach Johan was walking slowly toward the dark water, to the area where the sand was not light-colored but gray and wet from the outgoing tide. The shallows were scattered with rocks that protruded from the water like sea creatures emerging from the depths. Adam did not want to venture into the water; he was seized by the urge to call out to Johan. Don't go there, Johan, don't go there, he wanted to shout. But Johan was already too far away and the wind had picked up again and Adam knew Johan would not hear him.

Adam ran toward the sea. Suddenly he knew that Johan should not go into the water. *"Johan!"* he cried. He ran across the sand; tiny sharp things pricked his feet but he did not stop running. It was difficult to run in the thick sand. He slipped and fell. It did not hurt when he fell. At some point it turned damp and muddy and sticky underfoot and there were rocks everywhere. Still he did not stop running. Johan was far away now, wading in the shallows, the water up to his calves. Adam slipped on a rock. He felt it slice through the side of his foot like a sharp, thin blade but it did not hurt. The sand turned to mud, and he could not run quickly. *Johan.* He looked ahead but Johan did not turn around. The mud was cold and there were things in it, cold, hard things that Adam could feel on his feet and he did not like it. Shells, maybe they were shells. He felt water between his toes, then up to his ankles. The water was warm and made the mud feel less cold and Johan was standing still now, looking out at the emptiness of the sea before him. The water came up to his knees but sometimes it would swell and rise to his waist before falling away again. Adam waded deeper into the water. He could see Johan's back, the white shirt streaked with dirt. The people at the orphanage had made them put on shirts that morning, him and Adam, because they were to be presented to those nice foreigners who were going to take them away. The shirts had been fresh and clean, but now they were dirty.

"Don't go there," Adam cried as loudly as he could. "Don't leave me, Johan."

Johan turned around slowly. It was dark and Adam could not see his face properly. The waves washed around his knees and made him feel unsteady.

"Go back, Adam. I told you, you shouldn't have followed me." He spoke calmly, but Adam knew he was not calm. Adam waded toward him; the sharp pebbles and the mud did not bother him anymore.

"Adam, don't."

"But why? What are you doing?"

Johan turned away from him, looking out to sea as if searching for some invisible object. Adam could feel the water rising to his rib cage.

"Johan, what's wrong? Come back. I can't see your face. I can't see your face." And it was this faceless Johan that terrified Adam more than the sea and the dangerous things that lurked in the mud.

Johan did not move. "Don't look at me, Adam. Go back. Please."

Adam did not want to cry, he did not want to upset Johan even more, but his eyes were already cloudy with tears. He stopped trying to reach Johan. He would never be able to get to him. He knew that now. His brother wanted to go away from him, and there was nothing he could do. He said, "You said you would never leave me, Johan." The waves washed gently around his waist and made his shirt damp and cold. He rubbed his eyes and they smarted from the saltwater on his hands. He was right to have been afraid of the sea. He did not want to be here. He wanted to forget this place, this time, forever. This world, he thought, was not a good place, for in this world you could find yourself alone in an instant. You turned away and all was lost, washed out to sea. He wished he were in some other world, someplace other than this.

"Don't cry, you idiot," Johan said. He was alongside Adam now; he smacked Adam on the back of the head and pulled his ear. "Silly boy," he said, "I only wanted to go for a swim, see what it's like. I've never been swimming. You don't like the sea. That's why I said you shouldn't have come."

"I was frightened. The sea. I was afraid."

Adam could not stop crying. It was stupid, but he could not stop: Johan was with him now, and everything would be all right. Everything would be all right.

"You idiot," Johan said, putting his arm around Adam. "Just forget about it. Just pretend it didn't happen."

They reached the shore where the sand was dry and not muddy. They climbed the rocks again and found that it was not so difficult this time. They walked home in the murky darkness, and when they reached the orphanage they found it just as it had always been. They took off their wet clothes and slept in Johan's bed. Adam felt safe again; he felt the unchanging warmth of Johan's body and he was no longer afraid. Tomorrow their lives would change, but he was not afraid.

Johan said, "Go to sleep now, Adam. Forget it all. You're a good boy. Don't worry, I won't leave you. Go to sleep."

The Great Post Road stretches a thousand kilometers across the north coast of Java, from Anyer in the west to Panarukan in the east. It is surprisingly smooth, especially given the terrain through which it runs: It cuts determinedly across the mosquito-filled marshland on the coastline of the Java Sea and does not flinch when it begins its ascent into the hills around Sumedang. It is all the more remarkable when you consider that it was built in less than a year, in 1808. What is less surprising is that thousands died during its construction—of malaria, sunstroke, famine, and simple exhaustion. Even with modern cars it is a long journey. The road is sun-baked and the air that comes in through the open windows is warm and dry and does little to alleviate the discomfort of the traveler. There is plenty of time to think about the things that may have taken place on this route in days past; all the things that may have happened in your life.

The road ends in the far east of Java. Farther along there are ferry ports to the islands, like Ketapang, just a short hop away from Bali, and then on to the outlying islands that few ever visit. In these ports that lead to nowhere it sometimes feels as though you are at the very edge of the world, at the end of all things familiar. Small boats sail toward a barren horizon, toward emptiness it seems. The places that lie beyond will, you think, always remain invisible.

ADAM SAT BETWEEN Margaret and Karl in the back of the Buick. They had both fallen asleep; the hot, dusty air swept in through the open windows and made Adam's eyes itchy and teary. In the front passenger seat Z was asleep too, her head lolling sideways. From time to time Mick would look in the rearview mirror to make sure that Adam was all right. Adam would nod an acknowledgment before returning his gaze to the long, constant road ahead of him.

Adam had plenty of time to think about his conversation with Karl the previous night when, exhausted but lucid, Karl had wanted to tell him things.

"I promised myself that when you turned sixteen I would take you to find your brother in Malaysia," Karl had said.

"You always said you didn't know where he was."

"I . . . I wanted you to be happy with me. I thought that if you re-built your life with me you would be able to make a choice later, when you were old enough to make those decisions yourself. Please, don't say anything, hear me out. It was selfish of me, I know that. But you were so happy when you came to me, and I didn't want to spoil that happi-ness. I wanted you to have a life, to know what it was like to be safe in your own country and not spend your childhood thinking you be-longed somewhere else. Does that make any sense to you?"

"Yes."

"I hated keeping the truth from you. I hated lying. But you were happy. Weren't you?"

Adam nodded. "So where was Johan all along?"

Karl reached for his trousers, which were folded neatly at the foot of the bed. He took out a piece of paper from one of the pockets and gave it to Adam. There was a name written on it. "That is the name of the family who adopted your brother. They are Malaysian. That is all I know."

Adam took the piece of paper and looked at the words on it—someone's name followed by Kuala Lumpur. He stared at the name for a long time but he did not feel anything. He folded the scrap of paper into a neat square and put it in his pocket.

Karl sighed. "I was going to take you on a holiday to Malaysia for your sixteenth birthday. I imagined it all: We would go for a nice din-ner and I would tell you everything when we got there and let you make the decision. But then all this happened."

They both managed to laugh.

"I guess it's true what you've always said," Adam said. "You can't control life. You just have to let it take you where it takes you."

Karl nodded and sank back to a reclining position. He closed his eyes and looked as if he had slipped into deep sleep. "I know you want to find him. I know you want to do it without me."

Adam did not reply. He shook his head, but Karl could not see this.

"You must, Adam. Go without me. I hate feeling that I'm holding you back." His voice began to trail off into slumber.

"Don't talk anymore. Rest now," said Adam as he left the room.

"I forgot, Son," Karl said as Adam paused at the door. "Happy birthday. I'm sorry I missed it."

AT THE JETTY where the ferries depart for the islands there were not many people, it seemed. Margaret stood with Karl, watching the small boats loaded with logs arrive at the flimsy pier. He said, "Are you sure?"

"Oh, quite certain," she replied. "I want to follow you. If the idea doesn't repulse you, that is. At least for a short time, while you recover and find your feet."

"Are you sure you won't be bored? I mean, what will you do? You're a person who needs challenges and variety. I'm sure that hasn't changed."

"You forget that I grew up in the sticks, so I'd just be going back to my roots. Island life isn't exactly foreign to me, you know. I thought maybe I could just spend time with you and Adam, helping around the house. I don't know. I wouldn't be *entirely* domestic, of course—I don't think that is ever going to come naturally to me. There's also the matter of an unfinished thesis. I could pretend to do some fieldwork, write up my notes, produce articles that no one will ever read. Who knows? I'd just be close to you, that's all."

When she looked at him she saw how much older and calmer he was now. It was not merely a question of years, but something else she could not quite define. She knew this because she too was older and calmer. He said, "I have the feeling that we've had this conversation before, haven't we? A long time ago, not so very far from here."

"I didn't think you remembered that sort of trivial thing."

"I do, Margaret, I do."

Zubaidah was already sitting in the car, sunglasses shading her eyes. She hated good-byes, she said; she had no time for them. She had held hands with Adam for a long time before saying, "No, you need to go home with your father. I'm not going to argue with you—remember, I'm cleverer than you, and older too, so I'll win any argument! You can't make decisions like that overnight. What would you do if you came back to Jakarta now? Where would you live? If in a few years' time you still want to come, then I'll be there. I think."

"Come on, kiddos," Mick called. "I need to hit the road again. Bill will go nuts if I don't bring this car back on time. Even he can't hide the fact that he's pilfered an embassy car for personal reasons."

"Thank Bill again for me, won't you?" said Margaret, giving Mick a hug. She held him close and rubbed his back. "And thank you, Mick."

"Will you be okay?" he asked.

"Yup, don't worry. I'm just going to take a little time off, I don't know—*travel,* as young Americans keep saying nowadays. It sounds so vague, doesn't it? Finding myself, and all that nonsense. I might as well do it now, before I'm too old. Besides, I have a lot of catching up to do." She looked over at Karl and Adam.

"You're not going to come back to Jakarta, are you?"

"Oh, I might, one day."

"And if you don't?"

She had begun to walk toward Karl and Adam; she turned around and said, "I'll just marry a good man and bear good children."

    •   ●   •

He drove through the silent city at speed, neon lights staining the night with color. At darkened intersections he ran the lights without looking. He never looked out for other cars, he never looked out for anything. In this fast, young city he did not want to stop, he did not want to sleep. Rain was falling. It made the streets slick and muddy, and the buildings were quiet and empty. Out in the new suburbs the stretches of scrubland that separated the clusters of houses were blank with darkness and he could imagine they were not filled with heaps of rubbish but with trees and ponds. Sometimes he could imagine the sea. And this was when he felt the happiest, but also the saddest, for the night seemed long and deep and silent. He wished that this place had no past. He wished that last night were just a dream, that last month had never existed. He had to keep moving. As long as he did not stay still he would be okay. Rain was falling. Sometimes he could imagine the sea. He drove through the silent city at speed.

Acknowledgments

I am greatly indebted to Nicholas Pearson, as sensitive and wise an editor as any writer could hope for; his hand-holding helped me weather numerous storms. Thanks, also, to everyone at Fourth Estate and Harper-Collins worldwide, especially Michelle Kane.

My thanks and gratitude to my agent, David Godwin, for his vision and matchless enthusiasm; and to Kerry Glencorse, Heather Godwin, Sophie Hoult, and Charlotte Knight at DGA, for their tireless support.

Beatrice Monti von Rezzori provided me with a room with a view and six weeks of calm at Santa Maddalena, which helped revive this novel—thank you.

Cindy Spiegel in New York, Lara Hinchberger in Toronto, and Anne O'Brien in London all made valuable editorial comments on the manuscript, for which I am extremely grateful.

The conversations I had with Judith Sihombing on her life in Jakarta in the 1960s helped to bring me closer to the novel. I owe Margaret's character (and much else) to Judith.

Kadek Krishnan Adidharma and Nukila Amal—brilliant poets and translators—performed wonders with *Hartini*. My admiration and gratitude know no bounds.

Thanks to Adam Thirlwell, Clare Allan, and Diana Evans for chats and coffee breaks; to James Arnold and Alistair Griffin, for dinners and occasional lodging; to Francis Hétroy for *la douceur de vivre*; to Philip Goff for commenting.

And finally, thanks to my parents, for their support and understanding.

About the Author

TASH AW's debut novel, *The Harmony Silk Factory,* was the winner of the Whitbread First Novel Award and the Commonwealth Writers' Prize for Best First Novel and was long-listed for the Man Booker Prize. He is Malaysian by birth but now lives in London.

About the Type

This book was set in Bembo, a typeface based on an old-style Roman face that was used for Cardinal Bembo's tract *De Aetna* in 1495. Bembo was cut by Francisco Griffo in the early sixteenth century. The Lanston Monotype Company of Philadelphia brought the well-proportioned letterforms of Bembo to the United States in the 1930s.